An Unwinnable Fight

Still ignoring the Alexdrians, the dragon took another leap, landing with an earthshaking thump not far from Alain. Alain looked up at it, knowing what the dragon represented. It was told to seek me. My Guild wants me to die. There can be no doubt. *But he stood his ground, knowing that trying to run would be futile, putting everything he had left into the most destructive fireball he could manage, the heat of the spell almost burning his palms as he added to it until it held all of his remaining strength. He aimed at where the weakest point in a dragon's armor was supposed to be, under one of the forearms. In an instant of time his fireball went from between to his palms to* there. *The dragon howled with pain as the scales under the arm were scorched and darkened, and that arm flopped into uselessness. But the dragon did not appear otherwise affected, its remaining forearm flexing claws as long as Alain's arm.*

The huge, glinting eyes glared at Alain as he fell to his knees, totally used up and not able to run now that his last effort had failed. The dragon's hind legs tensed to bring it the short distance closer so it could smash Alain. The Mage watched the dragon, knowing that nothing he could do could change things now, his mind filled not with fear but with regret that he would never see Mari again...

PRAISE FOR THE
PILLARS OF REALITY SERIES

"Campbell has created an interesting world... [he] has created his characters in such a meticulous way, I could not help but develop my own feelings for both of them. I have already gotten the second book and will be listening with anticipation."

–Audio Book Reviewer

"I loved *The Hidden Masters of Marandur*...The intense battle and action scenes are one of the places where Campbell's writing really shines. There are a lot of urban and epic fantasy novels that make me cringe when I read their battles, but Campbell's years of military experience help him write realistic battles."

–All Things Urban Fantasy

"I highly recommend this to fantasy lovers, especially if you enjoy reading about young protagonists coming into their own and fighting against a stronger force than themselves. The world building has been strengthened even further giving the reader more history. Along with the characters flight from their pursuers and search for knowledge allowing us to see more of the continent the pace is constant and had me finding excuses to continue the book."

–Not Yet Read

"*The Dragons of Dorcastle*... is the perfect mix of steampunk and fantasy... it has set the bar to high."

–The Arched Doorway

PRAISE FOR THE LOST FLEET SERIES

"It's the thrilling saga of a nearly-crushed force battling its way home from deep within enemy territory, laced with deadpan satire about modern warfare and neoliberal economics. Like Xenophon's Anabasis – with spaceships."

–The Guardian (UK)

"Black Jack is an excellent character, and this series is the best military SF I've read in some time."

–Wired Magazine

"If you're a fan of character, action, and conflict in a Military SF setting, you would probably be more than pleased by Campbell's offering."

–Tor.com

". . . a fun, quick read, full of action, compelling characters, and deeper issues. Exactly the type of story which attracts readers to military SF in the first place."

–SF Signal

"Rousing military-SF action... it should please many fans of old-fashioned hard SF. And it may be a good starting point for media SF fans looking to expand their SF reading beyond tie-in novels."

–SciFi.com

"Fascinating stuff ... this is military SF where the military and SF parts are both done right."

–SFX Magazine

PRAISE FOR THE LOST FLEET: BEYOND THE FRONTIER SERIES

"Combines the best parts of military sf and grand space opera to launch a new adventure series ... sets the fleet up for plenty of exciting discoveries and escapades."

—Publishers Weekly

"Absorbing...neither series addicts nor newcomers will be disappointed."

—Kirkus Reviews

"Epic space battles, this time with aliens. Fans who enjoyed the earlier books in the Lost Fleet series will be pleased."

—Fantasy Literature

"I loved every minute of it. I've been with these characters through six novels and it felt like returning to an old group of friends."

—Walker of Worlds

"A fast-paced page turner ... the search for answers will keep readers entertained for years to come."

—SF Revu

"Another excellent addition to one of the best military science fiction series on the market. This delivers everything fans expect from Black Jack Geary and more."

—Monsters & Critics

PRAISE FOR THE LOST STARS SERIES

"Campbell maintains the military, political and even sexual tension with sure-handed proficiency...Campbell focuses on the human element: two strong, well-developed characters locked in mutual dependence, fumbling their way toward a different and hopefully brighter future. What emerges is a fascinating and vividly rendered character study, fully and expertly contextualized."

−Kirkus Reviews

"..if there is at this present time a better writer of pure popcorn explosive-BOOM military space opera working in the field, I haven't found them."

−Tor.com

"I truly enjoy Jack Campbell's writing and pacing...One of the most interesting aspects of the story is the internal fighting that has become part and parcel with advancement in their system of government. The rampant abuse of power and casual disregard for underlings is so pervasive that no one can imagine a way that it could be different."

−SF Revu

"The military battle sequences are very well done with the land-based action adding a new dimension...Fans of the 'Lost Fleet' series will almost certainly buy and enjoy this book."

−SF Crowsnest

ALSO BY JACK CAMPBELL

THE LOST FLEET
Dauntless
Fearless
Courageous
Valiant
Relentless
Victorious

THE LOST FLEET: BEYOND THE FRONTIER
Dreadnaught
Invincible
Guardian
Steadfast
Leviathan

THE LOST STARS
Tarnished Knight
Perilous Shield
Imperfect Sword
Shattered Spear (forthcoming)

THE PAUL SINCLAIR SERIES
A Just Determination
Burden of Proof
Rule of Evidence
Against All Enemies

THE ETHAN STARK SERIES
Stark's War
Stark's Command
Stark's Crusade

THE PILLARS OF REALITY
The Dragons of Dorcastle*
The Hidden Masters of Marandur*
Books 3-6 forthcoming

STAND ALONE NOVELS
The Last Full Measure

SHORT STORY COLLECTIONS
Ad Astra*
Borrowed Time*
Swords and Saddles*

* available as a Jabberwocky ebook

THE HIDDEN MASTERS OF MARANDUR

THE PILLARS OF REALITY: BOOK 2

BY

JACK CAMPBELL

Published by
Jabberwocky Literary Agency, Inc.

This print-on-demand edition published in 2015 by Jabberwocky Literary Agency, Inc.

Cover art by Dominick Saponaro.

Map by Isaac Stewart.

ISBN 978-1-625671-33-2

To
my daughter Carolyn

For S, as always

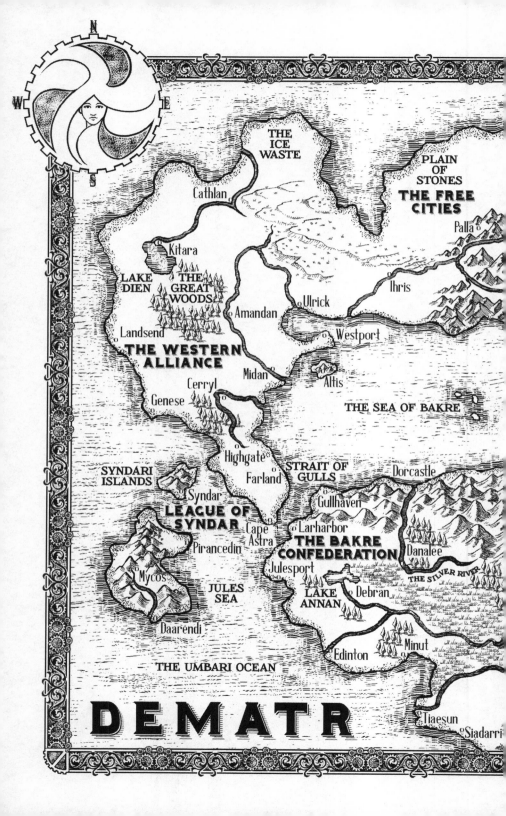

THE
ICE
WASTE

PLAIN
OF
STONES

THE FREE
CITIES

Cathlan

Palla

Kitara

LAKE
DIEN

THE
GREAT
WOODS

Ihris

Amandan

Ulrick

Landsend

Westport

THE WESTERN
ALLIANCE

Cerryl

Midan

Altis

Genese

THE SEA OF BAKRE

Highgate

SYNDARI
ISLANDS

Farland

STRAIT OF
GULLS

Dorcastle

Syndar

Gullhaven

LEAGUE OF
SYNDAR

Cape
Astra

Larharbor

Pirancedin

THE BAKRE
CONFEDERATION

Danalee

Julesport

THE SILVER RIVER

Mycos

JULES
SEA

LAKE
ANNAN

Debran

Daarendi

Minut

Edinton

THE UMBARI OCEAN

DEMATR

Tiaesun

Siadarri

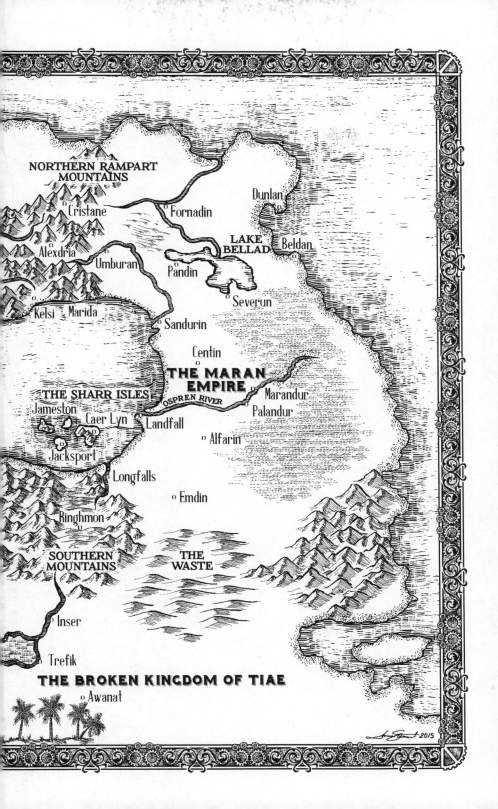

NORTHERN RAMPART
MOUNTAINS

Cristane

Fornadin

Dunlan

LAKE
BELLAD

Beldan

Alexdria

Umburan

Pandin

Kelsi

Marida

Sandurin

Severun

Centin

THE MARAN
EMPIRE

THE SHARR ISLES

OSPREN RIVER

Marandur

Palandur

Jameston

Caer Lyn

Landfall

Alfarin

Jacksport

Longfalls

Emdin

Ringhmon

SOUTHERN
MOUNTAINS

THE
WASTE

Inser

Trefik

THE BROKEN KINGDOM OF TIAE

Awanat

2015

Acknowledgments

I am indebted to my agent, Joshua Bilmes, and to Steve Mancino and Eddie Schneider, for their relentless championing of this series and their ever-inspired suggestions and assistance, and to the rest of Jabberwocky (notably Lisa Rodgers and Krystyna Lopez) for their tireless labors, and to editor Betsy Mitchell for her enthusiasm and editing. Thanks also to Catherine Asaro, Robert Chase, Carolyn Ives Gilman, J.G. (Huck) Huckenpohler, Simcha Kuritzky, Michael LaViolette, Aly Parsons, Bud Sparhawk and Constance A. Warner for their suggestions, comments and recommendations as Dragons took the long path from draft to reality.

CHAPTER ONE

Her pursuers had not shown their faces today. Instead, shadows stalked Master Mechanic Mari of Caer Lyn through the streets of Edinton. "I didn't see any Mages on the walk here," Mari said.

Her companion furrowed his brow in thought. Mechanic Abad of Highgate was a stolid, unimaginative sort. He had doubtless never questioned his own loyalty to the Mechanics Guild, and he had been assigned repeatedly to go out on contracts with her. Some might call him Mari's coworker, some might call him Mari's safeguard, but she knew that Abad was also a spy for the Senior Mechanics here at Edinton. Every Mechanic submitted a routine report after completing a job, but Mari knew that Abad was also providing her superiors in the Mechanics Guild with updates on everything she said and did.

Fortunately for Mari, loyalty to the Mechanics Guild also meant that Abad was even more suspicious of Mages than he might be of her. "There's always a Mage," he muttered, looking around carefully. "There's always one watching when we go out, following us." His eyes went to Mari. "Watching you. They don't hang around when I go out with other Mechanics."

Mari nodded. She couldn't very well explain all of the reasons for that. Not to Abad, and not to any other Mechanic. "Then you know I'm not exaggerating," Mari said. "Ever since I had a run-in with the Mage Guild back at Dorcastle they've been watching me."

"The Senior Mechanics don't believe you," Mechanic Abad said. "Even though I told them in my, uh, contract reports that the Mages were always hanging around when you were out. But I don't see any today. Do you think they've given up?"

"Mages? Who knows how they think?" She kept her words properly disdainful. Even though she was only eighteen years old, the youngest Master Mechanic in the history of the Guild, Mari probably knew more about how Mages thought than any other Mechanic did. She knew enough not to be truly scornful of Mages. The Senior Mechanics suspected that, which was one reason why Abad was watching her, and one reason why she had been sent to the place nicknamed "End-of-the-World Edinton."

Mari knew enough to be worried about Mages she couldn't see.

Abad snorted in derision. "Mages? Think? Let's get this done and get back to the Guild Hall."

Together they walked up the broad steps leading into the city hall, the dark Mechanics jackets they wore standing out amid the brighter clothes of the common folk entering and leaving the building, common folk who hastily made way for the two Mechanics. The commons bowed respectfully to the Mechanics' faces, but Mari knew that if she turned fast enough to look behind her she would see expressions that held hostility rather than respect. The Mechanics Guild and the Mage Guild hated each other, but they were masters of the world of Dematr, and therefore the commons hated both of the Great Guilds equally.

The stone steps, grooved from centuries of foot traffic, had been here for a very long time. Mari kept her eyes on those worn steps as she climbed them, thinking about her Guild, which worked so hard to keep anything from changing in the world it controlled. And about the chaos to the south of here, in the land once known as Tiae, where all order had collapsed over a decade ago despite the efforts of the Mechanics Guild. Here, in the southernmost city of the Bakre Confederation, fear of similar anarchy helped keep the commons of Edinton in line.

At the entrance to the city hall two guards stood, wearing armor and weaponry that were, at least for common folk, state-of-the-art. Their freshly polished chain-mail armor gleamed in the sun, short-swords hung by their sides ready for use, and crossbows nestled in the guards' arms.

Mari kept her gaze impassive as she met their eyes, but one of her hands strayed under her jacket, closing about the semi-automatic pistol holstered under her arm. She hadn't met any commons in the Confederation who posed the kind of threat those in Ringhmon had, but the memories of her kidnapping and imprisonment there still jumped to the fore whenever she encountered armed commons. Few could afford the expensive and rare Mechanic weapons like Mari's pistol, but either a sword or a crossbow bolt could be just as deadly as a bullet if it struck home.

"Contract," Abad said to the guards, his tone arrogant in the normal way of Mechanic to common. "Calculating and Analysis Device."

The guards saluted, their faces almost as expressionless as those of Mages, then the female guard gestured to her companion. "Escort the honored Mechanics to the city leaders," she said.

Mari could almost hear the resentment buried beneath her outwardly deferential tone of voice. Alain would have heard it clearly, she thought, then winced inwardly. *Don't think about him. Never think about him. That's the only way to protect him.*

The city leaders presented smiling greetings, the polished skills of politicians enabling them to seem perfectly sincere in their welcome as they led Mari and Abad to the room holding the Calculating and Analysis Device. Most of the city hall was lit by oil lamps whose wavering light provided adequate illumination, but in the room holding the CAD two electric light fixtures provided a steady glow. Mari gave the lights a glance, thinking of the other electric light fixtures they had passed in this building, all old and non-operative. The electrical current provided by the Mechanics Guild was as expensive as everything else the Mechanics sold, as were the individually handcrafted light bulbs. At some point in the past, Edinton had been forced to cut expenses.

But even a city strapped for cash had need of the number-crunching and data storage a CAD could provide. Nothing smaller than a city could afford one, though. There were only two CADs in the city of Edinton, this one leased by the city and the other within the Mechanics Guild Hall itself. "What's the exact problem?" Mari asked.

"It will not function," one of the city leaders said.

Abad smirked as Mari fought to avoid rolling her eyes at the vague description. Even the smartest common was banned by the Mechanics Guild from learning anything about Guild technology, so she really shouldn't blame the man for his ignorance. Going to the control panel, she typed in the commands to run a simple functionality test. Instead of lights blinking in response and a punched tape emitting with the results, nothing happened. "Yeah. It's not functioning," Mari agreed.

Abad watched her, frowning again, this time in concentration. "Can you fix a dead CAD?"

"If I can't fix this, no one else in the Confederation can," Mari replied.

It wasn't a boast, just a statement of fact. Abad, who had been watching her work long enough to know that, nodded and waited for instructions. He was a good general-purpose Mechanic, but not one of the few trained in CAD work. With so few of those devices made by the Guild, not many Mechanics needed those skills, valuable though they were.

She paused, thinking through possible causes for the CAD to be totally nonfunctioning. Most of the possibilities involved major problems and a lot of work. Where to begin? Just finding the problem might take most of the day.

Then she recalled a test that Professor S'san had put them through at the Academy, one that had baffled every student before S'san pointed out the simple cause of the problem. *It can't hurt to check that first.*

Mari knelt by the back of the machine, where the power wire ran into a metal fitting over the wall junction with the single electrical power line within the city hall. That power line originated at the

Mechanics Guild Hall, fed by the hydroelectric generators there. As far as commons were concerned, it might as well all be magic.

She unscrewed the cover and peered at the connection. Her brief sense of satisfaction faded rapidly as Mari studied what had been hidden. "Abad, take a look at this."

He went to one knee beside her, eyes intent. "One of the wires is completely loose. How did that happen?"

Mari pointed to the screw which should have held the wire securely. "It's been unscrewed."

Abad's breath caught. "Unscrewed? Who could have done that?"

She didn't answer, even though Mari had a suspicion. Commons weren't supposed to have such tools, weren't supposed to know how to use Mechanic tools, weren't supposed to know how to do anything with Mechanic devices, but she had encountered some who did, the ones she called Dark Mechanics. The ones she had been ordered by her Guild superiors never to mention. "We'll have to report this," Mari said as she quickly reconnected the power and set the screw firmly in place. Maybe *now* the Guild would finally listen to her instead of trying to muzzle her.

On the heels of that thought came another realization. Someone had sabotaged the CAD in a very simple way that might have tied her up for hours. That someone must have known that Mari would be the one sent to investigate a problem with a CAD.

Someone had wanted her here. Which meant she had better leave here as fast as possible.

But as she straightened to see the lights on the CAD blinking through its startup routine, Abad turned to the city leaders. "We need to ask some questions. Close the door," he ordered.

Exchanging worried looks, the city leaders gestured to one of their assistants, who turned to the door and began swinging it closed. Even though nothing could be seen in the doorway, the door abruptly stuck on something when only halfway closed, then as the baffled assistant tried again it swung closed without a problem.

Mari's hand went to her pistol again, closing tightly about the grip this time, her heart pounding in her ears. The group of commons was between her and the door. Mari rammed forward into a couple of them, shoving the two city leaders toward the door, but both staggered against something unseen, going down in a heap that abruptly included not only the two commons but also a Mage.

Everyone froze for an instant. Then the female Mage on the floor raised her eyes and met Mari's gaze. She was short, strands of stringy dark hair escaping from the cowl of her hood. Her face held no expression at all as she looked at Mari, even her eyes betraying no emotion, but in one hand she held a long knife ready for use.

Mari didn't remember having drawn her weapon, but she suddenly realized that she had the pistol out and pointed directly at the Mage's face.

Abad glared down at the Mage as the wide-eyed commons in the room cautiously moved away from both Mage and Mechanics. "Kill her," Abad suggested.

"No," Mari said. "Guild policy," she added, to avoid admitting that she didn't want to harm anyone unless absolutely necessary to save herself or someone else. "Unless they're actually attacking us, we're supposed to ignore Mages. This one might have been after one of the commons." She didn't believe that. This Mage was looking right at her, not at any of the city leaders. "There might be more around. Let's go."

Mechanic Abad hesitated a moment, but obedience was drilled into Mechanics from the time they first became apprentices, and Mari did have Master Mechanic rank. Abad nodded and followed as Mari walked sideways to the door, keeping her eyes on the Mage and her weapon aimed straight between the Mage's eyes. Abad yanked the door open, followed Mari out, then slammed the door shut behind them as he and Mari quickly headed out of the building.

She didn't slow down until they were again on the steps leading out of the city hall, her eyes scanning the plaza in front of the building for any sign of other Mages.

"How did you know?" Abad asked. "I didn't see her until—until those commons tripped over her."

"There's a Mage trick, a trap," Mari explained, choosing her words with care. The unwritten but firm rule of the Guild was that no Mechanic ever saw a Mage do anything that the Mechanics Guild couldn't explain. "You can tell they're setting it if the door to a room sticks when there's nothing visible blocking it. I found out about it in Dorcastle." It wasn't a lie, just a partial truth. The trick had been Mage work all right, but the door had actually hung up on that Mage bending light around herself to be effectively invisible. Alain had told Mari that a Mage needed to maintain concentration to keep something like that working, so Mari had shoved the commons at the Mage in hopes of not just knocking the Mage off-balance but also breaking her focus.

"A trap?" Abad nodded slowly, his expression uncertain. Just like Mari, he had seen that Mage appear from out of nowhere. But to admit that would mean admitting that Mages could do things Mechanics thought impossible, and no Mechanic was allowed to do that. "Yeah. Someone deliberately unfastened that power connection to get us in there, and she must have hiding, waiting for us. Maybe she didn't actually unscrew that wire, but just pulled on it and somehow pulled the screw out that way."

"It would be awfully hard to do it that way," Mari said. Abad must know he was trying to rationalize what had happened, but he couldn't admit the truth without admitting that the Mechanics Guild was lying about Mages and maybe other things as well. *Somebody used a screwdriver to loosen that screw. Only Dark Mechanics could have done it…or could my own Guild have set me up? But how could Mages have also been involved? Alain told me, and I saw in Dorcastle, that Dark Mechanics get along with Mages no better than regular Mechanics do. How could they be working together here? Or was the apparently joint move mere coincidence?*

She hated lying to Abad, and wished she could have discussed her thoughts with him, but the truth about Dark Mechanics, as with Mages, would have imperiled Abad with their own Guild even if he had believed it. As far as the Mechanics Guild was concerned, people who could do the work of Mechanics but were not Mechanics did not exist. She had been told that, ordered to believe it, and warned never to tell anyone else that any other truth might exist. Even though Mari had no intention of abiding by those commands forever, she had no evidence with which to convince any other Mechanics. The hard evidence she had given her Guild superiors in the past had simply disappeared once in their custody. But perhaps this incident would help break the logjam of denial. "We need to get back to the Guild Hall and report this as soon as possible," Mari said.

Abad nodded quickly and firmly this time. When he had first been paired with her for contract work, Abad had eyed Mari will ill-concealed suspicion and subtly questioned her every move, but that had been fading as they worked together. Now, after this latest incident, Abad no longer hesitated to follow her lead.

They had kept moving across the plaza, turning onto the street leading back to the Mechanics Guild Hall. The crowds of commons were separating before them, leaving a clear path and an open area around the two Mechanics, not out of real respect but because the Guild insisted on such preferential treatment in all things. Abad looked back, momentarily falling a step behind Mari. She paused in mid-step to allow Abad to catch up.

She heard the sound of the gunshot at almost the same moment as she felt the wind of the bullet's passage as it nearly grazed her forehead, followed by the harsh crack of the bullet striking the stone building beside her. Tiny chips of stone blasted from the wall by the impact struck Mari's neck, but she had already begun diving forward before the sound of a second shot was followed by another bullet slamming into the building exactly where she had been standing an instant earlier. Pulling out her pistol, she rolled down and came back up crouched with her back against the building. Mari held her weapon in both hands, her heart hammering, as she stared past the suddenly panicked commons running along the street in all directions.

Mechanic Abad dashed up beside her, urging Mari to her feet. "Whoever it was can't get a good shot with the commons getting in the way," he said as he grabbed her arm. "Run!"

They ran toward the Mechanics Guild Hall, Mari next to the buildings they passed and Abad keeping himself between her and the street as a living shield. No more shots sounded behind them, but Mari could hear the sound of city watch members calling out alarms as they converged on the site of the attack.

"Could that have been another Mage?" Abad asked as they finally slowed to a brisk pace.

"No. Mages don't use Mechanic equipment," Mari said, trying to calm her still-racing heart. "They can't use it. Not even a Mechanic weapon."

"They can't?" Abad watched her. "Neither of those shots was aimed at me. If you'd frozen in place instead of diving right away the second one would have blown your brains out."

"I...react fast," Mari explained, unable to stop a shudder. "In emergencies."

"That's a good talent to have. Were you hurt? Your neck is bleeding."

"It's not serious. I'll see the healer at the Guild Hall," Mari said, hoping that she hadn't betrayed knowing too much about Mages.

"The Senior Mechanics say you're not really in danger. They told me that. They're wrong."

Frustration and lingering fear made her answer honestly. "Do you think they'll believe you now when they've refused to believe me?"

"Why won't they believe you?"

"I don't know." And she truly didn't. She had some ideas, some ideas very dangerous to the see-nothing-wrong philosophy that ruled the Guild. But why the Senior Mechanics—why the Mechanics Guild they ran, which controlled all technology—would ignore such things made no sense to Mari. "I've been doing everything the Senior Mechanics ask. I've been doing my job. And they treat me like someone they can't trust."

Abad finally asked the question she knew he had been holding inside since first meeting her. "Are you loyal to the Guild?"

"I have been. I swear that I have been." Was she still loyal, though? *I don't know. What a scary thought. I've been taught to depend on the Guild, to be part of the Guild, since I was a little girl. Now...what can I depend on?*

An answer came: the face of a man slightly younger than she, toughened by hardship, strangely emotionless except for eyes that lit when they rested on Mari. *Alain. But you're far away. And I don't know when we will meet again.*

Barely an hour later, the Guild Hall still buzzing with the news that someone had fired shots at a Mechanic on the streets of the city, Mari found herself standing before the desk of the Guild Hall Supervisor. Senior Mechanic Vilma offered a small, meaningless smile as she greeted Mari. Most of the Mechanics in Edinton detested Vilma because her insistence on perfection never yielded to reality in any form. "Mechanic Mari, how fortunate that your accident did not result in injury."

"Master Mechanic Mari," she corrected. Ever since Mari had earned the status of Master Mechanic at such a young age, Senior Mechanics had shown a habit of forgetting to use her proper title. Mari raised one hand to the bandage on her neck. "There was some injury, and it wasn't an accident."

Vilma's insincere smile came and went again. "An official investigation will determine what actually occurred," she said.

"I've already reported what happened at the job site and what happened afterwards. Mechanic Abad can confirm—"

"You won't be working with Mechanic Abad anymore," Vilma interrupted.

That brought Mari up short. "Why not?"

"Because I and the other Senior Mechanics here underestimated how quickly you could negatively influence even a Mechanic of Abad's reliability."

"What?" Mari felt her face warming with anger. "Since arriving in Edinton I have done nothing—"

"I'm not interested in debating the issue with you," Vilma broke in again. "Not when there's an important assignment that only you can carry out properly." She gave Mari a packet of papers.

Mari stared at Vilma, then down at the papers. "A mission? Who else—?"

"Just you. You're a Master Mechanic. There's a CAD that needs to be recovered, and you are by far the most qualified to undertake the task of evaluating its current status and, if appropriate, its transportation back here to Edinton."

Back here to Edinton? Leaving town might not be a bad idea at all if people were actively trying to harm her. Maybe, despite Vilma's hostile attitude, the Senior Mechanics were taking the threat to her seriously at last, even if they wouldn't admit it. Mari read quickly through her orders, dawning hope vanishing as a single word jumped out at her. "Minut?" The word made no sense. She knew what it meant, what it was, but how could it be there in her orders?

"Yes. Minut." Senior Mechanic Vilma made it sound like no big deal. "When the Guild pulled out of Tiae, the CAD was left at Minut. You are to go there, see if it is worth recovery, and then bring it back."

"Minut?" Mari repeated, disbelieving. "There's no government there. No police, no authority, nothing. It's anarchy. All of Tiae beyond the border with the Confederation is total anarchy."

"You'll have a strong escort," Vilma promised. "You'll meet them at that town."

Mari checked the orders again. "Yinville? That's also in Tiae."

"Not very far inside Tiae. The escort should be there when you arrive."

Mari looked at the Senior Mechanic, trying to understand these orders. "This is suicide."

"Nonsense. Capable Mechanics have done similar tasks in the past for their Guild," Vilma said, her tones hardening. "Are you refusing the orders? These are of the highest priority and steps are being taken to ensure you can carry them out safely and successfully. If you refuse the orders despite that, I will have to order a competency hearing and a loyalty evaluation."

"You're serious? A single Mechanic inside Tiae?"

"There is a strong escort awaiting you at Yinville," Senior Mechanic Vilma repeated. "This is a necessary task which poses no unreasonable risk. You are to leave today, as soon as possible."

"Alone?" She could take care of herself. Mari had prided herself on that. But young, female, and alone in such a place?

"Are you incapable of traveling by yourself? Even apprentices don't need someone holding their hands on the road!"

Mari looked down at her orders again, not really seeing the words, trying to think. *Ever since Dorcastle, I've done everything they wanted. I've kept quiet. I've obeyed orders. I wanted to make sure that Alain wasn't endangered, and I wanted to establish my loyalty and my skills beyond any doubt before I asked any more questions about things that aren't supposed to exist. And still they're sending me to Tiae.*

A strong escort awaiting me at Yinville. Once, six months ago, I would have believed that. Words in the orders swam into focus. *"If the escort is not at Yinville when you arrive, they will be very close and you are to wait the short time until they join you."* Perfectly reasonable orders, if that hadn't meant waiting alone in an area overrun with petty warlords, bandit gangs and desperate men and women of all kinds.

Why send me to Tiae? Why send anyone to Tiae? To get rid of them. Death is one of the nicer things that could happen to me there. I am to be condemned for what I might know, for what I might do. Mari knew what was really happening. So did Vilma. But for the first time since arriving at Edinton, Mari refused to just play the game, refused to pretend that nothing out of the ordinary was taking place. "Senior Mechanic Vilma, can I ask why? Why is this being done?" she said bluntly.

Vilma gave her a bland look in return that provided no clue that anything other than a routine meeting was taking place. "For the good of the Guild. That is why we do everything. Now, for obvious reasons, for your own safety, we want this kept low profile. You are to mention your mission and where it is to take place to no one."

Low profile. If Mari didn't return, she would eventually be declared lost, far too late for anyone else to do anything about it or object to her assignment. Mari would be a Mechanic who had died trying to carry out her orders, a good example for all other Mechanics. An arrest, on the other hand, couldn't be kept low profile now. Too many people knew Mari, too many rumors were going around about Ringhmon and Dorcastle. An arrest might feed dissent, might cause others to ask questions.

But she didn't doubt what the outcome would be if she refused these orders. The competency hearing to strip Mari of her Master Mechanic rank and a loyalty evaluation to decide whether she should be sent to a cell at Longfalls, the results of both predetermined before either "assessment" even began.

It left her only one option.

Mari gazed at Senior Mechanic Vilma. "I'll be gone before nightfall."

Less than two hours later, Mari strode toward the main entry of the Guild Hall, a pack on her back holding her tools and her small collection of personal possessions, as well as a far-talker that had been signed out to her for the trip. The far-talker, as big as her lower arm, was heavy and had only a short range, a symbol of the deterioration of Mechanic technology over the decades and centuries. Still, it provided a capability that no means of communication available to commons could match.

Despite Vilma's instructions to tell no one that she was leaving, Mari knew that word had spread that she had been seen packing, that she had picked up some journey food from the Guild Hall kitchen, and now she was heading for the exit bearing a large travel pack on her back. Her "low profile" departure was probably already known to everyone in the Guild Hall.

Mechanics and apprentices watched her go, some of them openly upset, others pretending not to see her. Three of the Mechanics hastened to intercept her. "Mari, what the blazes—" one of them began.

"I can't talk about it," Mari broke in.

"Are you going to be all right?" another asked.

"I don't know."

The three Mechanics exchanged looks. "Listen, Mari," Mechanic Ayame insisted. Middle-aged, shrewd, and frustrated by Senior Mechanic rules, she should have been the leader of discontent here. But burdened by long years of bitter experience with the cost of dissent, Ayame had been sullenly submissive to the Senior Mechanics when Mari had arrived at Edinton. Since then, Ayame had increasingly sought out Mari and grown more bold. Was that the sort of thing Senior Mechanic Vilma had meant when she complained about Mari's "negative influence" on others? "We're willing to take a stand on this," Ayame declared. "Just say the word." The two other Mechanics nodded in agreement.

Mari stopped walking, speaking low and fast, aware that Senior Mechanics were watching. "No. It wouldn't do me any good and you'd all end up in serious trouble. This isn't the end of this. I'm going to get some answers. I don't want anyone else getting burned until I have those answers and decide what to do. Please let it go, look after yourselves, and I'll deal with this."

The three exchanged looks, then Ayame nodded. "All right, Mari. Most people here are either unwilling to buck the Senior Mechanics or else afraid to go against Guild policy. But not everyone. Not any more. We'll wait to hear from you. When you need us, call us. Got it?" Without waiting for an answer from her, the three stepped away to let Mari continue on her way.

One more confrontation awaited her, though. Mechanic Abad waited by the main entry, his expression stubborn. "They said I shouldn't talk to you, but I wanted you to know. I never told them you'd done anything wrong, Master Mechanic. I told them you did good work, I told them you never said anything against the Guild, and I told them the truth about what happened when you got shot at. I don't understand why you're being sent off like this."

"Me, neither. Thanks for being a good Mechanic and a good working partner," Mari said, not having to feign sincerity.

"They kept asking me what you promised me, or what you told me, like the Senior Mechanics thought you'd messed with my head or something. I'm sorry, Master Mechanic. I must have done something wrong."

"No, you didn't," Mari said. "You did your job and you did it right. But as I've been finding out, you don't have to do anything wrong to get in trouble, or to get sent to Minut."

"They're sending you...to Minut? Minut?"

"Yeah. That's what my orders say." Let the Senior Mechanics answer the questions that would generate after Mari had gone. "Goodbye, Mechanic."

Mari left the Guild Hall, crossed the wide plaza surrounding it, then walked steadily toward a nearby stable, wondering if Dark Mechanics seeking revenge for what she had done at Dorcastle would take another shot at her. Little wonder the Senior Mechanics still showed no concern on those grounds. A Dark Mechanic bullet would solve the Guild's problem with Mari and leave the hands of the Senior Mechanics clean. She noticed a Mage following her at a distance, but making no attempt to get closer. Perhaps her sudden reappearance on the streets so soon after the two failed plots to get her had thrown off her stalkers.

Mari's orders called for her to rent a horse and take it south across the border, as no regular transport still operated between the Confederation and what used to be Tiae. "Have you heard of any strong force going south recently?" she asked the owner of the stable.

"South?" he questioned. "To the border, Lady Mechanic?"

"South of there. Into Tiae."

Clearly startled, the common shook his head. "No one goes across the border, Lady."

Mari looked at the stable owner, remembering the commons she had met in Dorcastle and how differently they had acted when she had hidden her identity as a Mechanic, how much more they had told her. "It's very important that I know," Mari said, speaking in the same tones she would have used with another Mechanic. "Can you tell me anything?"

The owner looked back at Mari, uncertain, then relaxed a bit and shook his head. "I'm sorry, Lady, but no. A single rider might be missed, but...you say a strong force? Many riders? Everyone would be talking about that. My cousin is in the border troops, with the cavalry. I saw him just yesterday when he brought a few of their mounts in for new shoes from our blacksmith. He would have said something."

Mari nodded, trying her best to look calm as her worst suspicions were confirmed. "What about a lot of riders, or foot soldiers, getting ready to head south? Have you heard anything about that? It might have been kept secret."

"Hah! Secret they can say, but it would be well known, Lady." The stable owner spoke more freely as Mari listened attentively to his words. "There's been nothing like that."

"Ships? Do any of those go south?"

The stable owner pursed his lips in thought. "Not many. Not anymore. I remember when Tiae was whole, and commerce with them made a lot of people wealthy. Now only a very few ships poke around the southern coasts in search of some quick trade while they try to avoid pirates. There would be a great deal of gossip about any ship or ships heading south with a lot of soldiers. Everyone would have heard. No, Lady, no one in their right mind goes into Tiae, not unless they have an army with them."

Mari nodded slowly. "Thank you."

"Lady?" The stable owner stared at her, startled by the small and simple courtesy from a Mechanic. He hesitated as a restive mount was led out toward them by a stable-hand who was trying to hide a smile. "Hold on, there, Gazi. This Lady might prefer a steadier horse."

Gazi the stablehand looked puzzled. "But we always give Mechanics—"

"Not this one. If you can wait but a little longer, Lady, I can get you a steadier mount."

A short time later Mari settled into the saddle, grateful that the stable owner had provided a more sedate mount for her. Some people were natural riders. Mari wasn't one of those people. She loved horses, but she had never been that good at riding them.

She headed out through the city streets toward the southern parts of Edinton, but as the crowds thickened Mari dismounted to lead her horse and make herself harder to spot amid the multitude, weaving on a crooked path that bore more west than south, bending gradually north. If there were Mages watching, then even invisible Mages would have trouble getting through the crowded streets Mari chose. Dark Mechanics should be equally hindered, as well as anyone sent by the Senior Mechanics of her own Guild to ensure that Mari went toward Minut. Glancing back quickly at irregular intervals, she didn't spot anyone nearby trying to keep up with her.

Finally reaching the city wall, Mari paused at the entrance to an alley to remove her Mechanics jacket and stuff it into her pack, replacing it with a coat like those the commons wore. Then she remounted and rode out the nearest gate, heading northwest.

In the last several months, since her adventures in Dorcastle, she had learned a lot of things about surviving that weren't taught at the Mechanics Guild Academy in Palandur. Mari had thought for a while that the way to survival followed a path of doing exactly as she was told, but that route hadn't satisfied the Senior Mechanics, who seemed to view her every move as an act of possible rebellion. Now, continuing on that path of obedience would lead her to Tiae and near-certain death. *I no longer have any choice. I'm not taking the Guild's way any more, not until I find out what the blazes is going on. No. This is my way, and it doesn't lead to Tiae.*

She didn't spot anyone obviously trailing her along the road, though the number of other travelers still provided plenty of cover for someone like that. Stopping before sunset at a tavern alongside the road, Mari led her horse to the watering troughs set out to attract travelers. As her horse drank, Mari listened to the commons talking around her. Anonymous without her Mechanics jacket, she heard the commons saying things they never would have spoken around a Mechanic.

"You've come lately from Julesport? Have they relaxed the curfew there yet?" one trader asked another.

The stout woman shrugged in response. "No. Officially, the curfew is still in effect. Ask me if the city is enforcing it, though."

"But do you need to bribe the city watch to move around?" the questioner pressed.

"No," the woman repeated. "It's not being enforced, except around the Mechanics Guild Hall in Julesport. The city leaders have kept the curfew on the books, but only because the demon-spawn Mechanics have insisted on it."

The traders and several other commons spat to one side at the mention of Mari's Guild. Mari stayed silent and kept her face turned toward her horse to hide her reactions.

"Dematr would be a better place if every Mechanic died tomorrow," someone growled.

But that caused the woman to shake her head. "We need what they have, blast them all. Imagine a world where every Mechanic device broke and could never be used again. And if the Mechanics were gone, who would be able to counteract the Mages? Who wants the Mages as undisputed rulers of Dematr?"

"Better both vanished then."

"And how will that happen?" another traveler taunted.

"The daughter." Tense silence fell as the one who had said that looked around cautiously. "Have you heard about Dorcastle?"

"I've heard rumors," the woman trader admitted.

"Rumors? She was there. The Mechanics and Mages were fighting among themselves, grinding Dorcastle and the city's people between them, and the daughter showed up and stopped them both." He paused to bask in the attention his words gathered. "I heard from one who was at Dorcastle. He saw it. An entire warehouse reduced to ruin, a dead Mage dragon and a bunch of broken Mechanic devices inside, and a young woman seen leaving just as people came to see what had happened. The Mechanics showed up quickly enough to get rid of the evidence, but everyone in Dorcastle knows of it."

"I've heard something the same," another traveler admitted. "But that doesn't prove the daughter did it, that she's finally come."

"Who else could have done such a thing? Defeated Mechanics *and* Mages? That's the prophecy, isn't it? The daughter of Jules will appear someday, and she will overthrow both of the Great Guilds and free us all. That young woman seen in Dorcastle *slew a dragon*. You ever seen a dragon?"

"Only at a great distance, and that still too close," someone else said. "But I've heard of what happened at Dorcastle, and it's the same as you said. A dead dragon and a whole mess of Mechanic devices shattered, and the Mechanics sealing off the place as soon as more of them got there. There was for certain something they didn't want us knowing."

Quiet fell for a moment, broken only by the wet noise of horses drinking at the troughs and the sounds of travelers passing on the nearby road.

"I won't believe it," the woman trader finally said in a low voice. "It would hurt too much to believe and then learn it was a false hope. But if she truly came at last to free us all, if my children could grow up without Mechanics and Mages lording it over them, that would be the greatest day ever seen."

"Bless her wherever she is, and may she come soon," another said, and the other commons murmured in agreement.

"It has to be soon," one of the travelers muttered, her voice despairing. "The madness in Tiae is spreading."

"Not into the Confederation—"

"No? There have been riots in Julesport and Debran."

"And there was some kind of civil disturbance in Emdin that a legion had to be called in to suppress," a man said. "Citizens of the Empire acting up! They haven't done anything like that since the great revolt that destroyed Marandur over a century ago."

"Some people went crazy in Larharbor last month," a man said.

"I heard that, too. I heard that they killed a Mage before they died," one of the other men said. "What would make people just snap like that?"

The woman traveler snorted. "Keep an animal in a small cage long enough, beat it every time it complains, and it will snap, sure enough. Isn't that us? If the daughter doesn't get here soon, she's likely to find nothing to free but the ruins of the world."

The commons fell silent. Some of them urged their horses away from the troughs and back to the road.

Mari stood, eyes on the neck of her horse, waiting a few moments before moving on and thinking that the commons had some good sources of information. The incident in Larharbor had scared her Guild's Senior Mechanics, because anyone crazy enough to attack a Mage would have been crazy enough to attack a Mechanic. She had hoped it would finally move the Senior Mechanics to admit to growing problems, but instead the event had been blamed on the Mage who had been killed.

Of course, the commons who had killed the Mage had themselves all been killed, too, so no one could ask them why they had done it.

But for the moment, Mari was more concerned that the commons had heard something about Dorcastle despite the Guild's efforts to hide everything. And, unlike the Mechanics Guild, the commons were willing to talk about the dragon found amid the wreckage. *They think the daughter of Jules did that? Alain and I barely survived it. I thought we hadn't been seen getting away, but someone must have spotted us. Spotted me, anyway.*

The Senior Mechanics must know that the commons are talking this freely about the incident in Dorcastle. Is that why they chose to send me on a one-way mission? Because they still suspect I didn't tell the full truth about what happened at Dorcastle? I would have told them, if they would have listened, if they hadn't threatened me and told me to say nothing.

Instead, the commons are thinking the mythical daughter of Jules did it. What if they had known it was me? What would they have said when they learned I was a Mechanic?

She thought of the woman trader, wistfully and sorrowfully dreaming of freedom for her children. Freedom from Mari's Guild, as well as from the Mage Guild. In her many years confined within Mechanics Guild Halls, isolated from the commons, Mari had come to accept the beliefs the Guild had drilled into her: that Mechanics were inherently superior, that commons couldn't rule themselves. But like so many other things she had been taught, those beliefs had been badly battered by what Mari had seen and experienced in the last few months.

She led her horse back to the road, looking intently in both directions in search of anyone lingering to keep watch on her, but seeing no one like that Mari mounted her horse and headed on toward the north.

Mari kept moving slowly along the road until night fell, the number of other travelers dwindling rapidly as darkness came on. Finally she halted, sitting silently in the gloom. Almost everyone else using the road had stopped for the night, either finding shelter at an inn, tavern or hostel, or simply camping on the road's edge in groups for safety. From here, Mari could see and hear no one else.

Sighing, she finally dismounted and settled her pack on her back. "Thanks for the ride," she whispered to the horse, then started to turn the animal loose. At the last moment she noticed the dangling reins and remembered that she had to do something about them. Mari tied the reins back across the saddle so they wouldn't catch on anything. The horse would surely find her own way back to Edinton. The saddle and other tack had the name of the stable on it, and if those were lost the horse had the brand of the stable burned into one haunch. Nonetheless, Mari felt guilty as she watched the tired horse wander slowly back down the road, worried about abandoning the animal even though she had no alternative.

Already weary, her legs and thighs stiff from riding, Mari turned off the road, walking to the east through rough country. Even if she hadn't been forced to abandon her horse in order to avoid revealing where she might have gone from there, the lack of visibility and the poor terrain would have made it too dangerous to ride through here at night. Mari picked her away along through the dark until she literally stumbled onto the impossible-to-miss tracks of the single train line connecting Edinton with cities farther north. Hoping she was heading in the right direction, Mari walked north alongside the tracks until with relief she reached a place the Mechanics in Edinton often complained about, a spot where the track curved while it also climbed a short, steep grade, forcing trains to slow to a crawl.

It would have been easy enough to fix that section, to excavate a portion of the rising terrain and straighten the track, but that was how the original line had been built centuries ago. Fixing it would mean changing it, and the Senior Mechanics didn't approve changes except on those rare occasions when no other alternative existed. Since this section of track was still passable, it would be repaired when necessary, but otherwise remain as it had always been.

Thoroughly worn out, Mari sat down to wait. Only two trains ran north from Edinton each week, using a schedule which hadn't varied for decades. One of those trains should come by here tonight.

Despite her efforts to stay alert, she was drowsing when the sound of the approaching train brought Mari to full wakefulness. Lying on her stomach in the darkness to be as inconspicuous as possible, she waited tensely as the ancient steam locomotive chugged past, straining at the burden of hauling its train of freight and passenger cars up the slope. She could see the engineer in the cab of the locomotive—probably some Mechanic she knew—along with a couple of apprentices, visible in the dim orange glow from the grate on the locomotive firebox.

Mari watched freight cars rolling past, then jumped up and ran toward the train as the first passenger car loomed into view. Leaping up, she caught at the platform at the end of the car, shaking with effort and anxiety as the gravel roadbed swept by below.

Her hands gripped the railing on the platform so tightly they hurt as Mari swung over the railing and found secure footing on the platform itself. Sighing with relief, she turned and peered into the darkened interior of the passenger car. She knew that only the last car, the one reserved for Mechanics, would have any electric lights. The candles or oil lamps commons would have used were banned for fear of fire in the wooden cars.

Unable to see much of the inside of the car, Mari eased the door open and slid through as quickly as she could. Inside, vague shapes were all that could be seen of passengers trying to sleep through the night journey. Fortunately, the Mechanics Guild kept the price of train tickets high enough that some seats were empty, so by moving cautiously Mari was able to find one and sit down.

The train began speeding up again as it crested the slope and the track straightened. Mari sat among the sleeping commons, staring ahead through the darkness. The port of Edinton and a ship north had been a tempting alternative, but she had thought the passenger piers too open and too easily watched. Hopefully by this roundabout overland route she had thrown off her path any Mages and Dark Mechanics as well as the Mechanics Guild itself. There was a small terminal just south of Debran where she could leave the train with little chance of being spotted and take back roads the rest of the way to Danalee.

But all that did was buy time. She needed to talk to someone else, someone she knew would listen and judge whether Mari had totally lost it or if she really was marked for death. If there was anyone else in the Guild like that, someone she could still trust to tell almost everything that Mari had learned, that person was now at the Guild's weapons workshops in Danalee. *Alli, I hope you are still the best friend I knew back in Caer Lyn.*

And beyond that, Mari's thoughts went to someone else much farther north. *The Mages have decided to stop watching me and instead are trying to kill me. What if they are also after Alain?*

What if his Guild suspects or learns the truth about him, and like my Guild decides to send him on a mission of no return?

I've been so afraid that my Guild would learn my biggest secret. If it had, the Senior Mechanics wouldn't have played around with schemes to get rid of me. They were afraid I knew more than I was supposed to about Mages and Dark Mechanics, they thought I was a negative influence on other Mechanics, and they completely rejected what I once said about where the Mechanics Guild's own policies are leading. But all they would have had to do to destroy me was to find out that Mari of Caer Lyn was in love with a Mage.

CHAPTER TWO

Mage Alain of Ihris went to war.

The elders who had informed him of his new contract had of course betrayed no emotions. He had managed to keep his own expression unrevealing as one of the elders spoke in the cold monotone of a Mage. "You will accompany a military force from the Free Cities during an attack on Imperial territory east of the mountains. Provide whatever services you deem appropriate."

"Who will be the other Mage assigned to this contract?" Alain had asked, his own voice just as unfeeling as those of the elders.

"There will be no other Mage." The elders had watched him, as if expecting to see some betraying emotion, but Alain had not given them that satisfaction.

"This one has questions," Alain said.

Instead of giving the formal reply of "This one listens," one of the elders simply shook his head. "The Free Cities cannot afford more than one Mage on this expedition of theirs. You will do this task alone. Perhaps you will succeed this time."

Had Alain's face or eyes revealed emotion then? The elder's brutally emotionless reference to the caravan which Alain alone had been contracted to defend, a caravan almost wiped out by overwhelming force, seemed to have been intended to provoke Alain into showing some feeling.

But elders had been using similar tricks ever since Alain had been taken from his family to become an acolyte, and the punishments for any visible trace of feeling had been severe. The scars he bore testified to that. After years of such training, Alain felt sure his voice, his face, and even his eyes revealed nothing as he answered. "This one understands."

Alain had accepted the contract. He had no choice but to accept it.

Now, a week later, he rode among the soldiers of the Free Cities.

He turned in his saddle, gazing back at the mountains named the Northern Ramparts. They rose majestically skyward, seeming to leap up from the flat lands that lapped at their feet. It was as if nature itself had raised the Ramparts as a barrier to block the Empire's reach. The column of soldiers had left the foot of a pass at the base of those mountains earlier today. Settling back into his saddle, Alain looked forward again, where the rolling, fertile plains of the northern reaches of the Empire stretched away toward the horizon.

The Free Cities sat nestled within the rugged reaches of the Northern Ramparts, while the Empire had dominated the part of the continent to the east of those mountains for almost as long as history recorded. This attack would not change that, would not change anything, because nothing in the world of Dematr was allowed to change. Some of the shadows who rode and marched around Alain—those the Mechanics called common folk—would die, along with some Imperial soldiers. But in the end the border between the Free Cities and the Empire would remain as it had always been. The Mage Guild wanted nothing to change, unless that change involved something harmful to those who called themselves Mechanics.

The teachings of the Mage Guild were that none of these others was real, no one else and nothing anywhere was real, that everything around him was merely a shadow born of Alain's own illusions. He had accepted that wisdom—until he met Mari. In a world where nothing was allowed to change, Alain had been changed.

He could let himself feel emotions again. He had learned what it meant to help someone else. He had learned what a friend was.

He had forgotten what love was. Until he had fallen in love.

He had learned that this unchanging world was threatened by catastrophic change, a storm of death and destruction that only one person could prevent—by overthrowing the power of the Mage Guild and the Mechanics Guild.

The elders suspected something was wrong with him. If they ever learned the depth of his failure, he would die. If they ever learned about Mari, that she was the one long ago foretold to overthrow the Great Guilds...

She would die.

Master Mechanic Mari of Caer Lyn. Even the thought of her name gave him a feeling of forbidden pleasure. No matter how hard he resolved, no matter how he tried to concentrate on the danger that he and these soldiers might encounter, Alain could not stop thinking of her, wondering where she was, wondering whether she was safe. Such thoughts could lead to Mari's death, even if the Mage Guild elders never learned of the vision Alain's foresight had given him.

Every thought could betray him—and. worse, betray her. She was somewhere far south of here, on the other side of the Sea of Bakre, far from him and the danger his presence would bring Mari. And...it could well be that her thoughts of him had changed. She had said that she cared for him, but they had been separated since then, and Mari had been among her fellow Mechanics. Did Mari still think of him as a friend? As more than a friend? Or had she already regretted and cast aside feelings which could only add to the dangers she faced?

But even if she forgot him, he could not forget her, no matter how hard Alain tried to wall away all feelings, all thoughts of Mari.

He rode alone, about two lance-lengths separating him and the horse he rode from those ahead and behind. Commons kept their distance from Mages, more out of fear and revulsion than respect, but that did not matter to Mages. Nothing mattered to Mages, because nothing was real.

In front of and in the wake of Alain, the soldiers of the Free City of Alexdria marched, following the track they were on eastward and deeper into the Empire. Farthest forward rode a long column of cavalry, their harnesses jingling with a merry sound that clashed strangely with the sharp, businesslike points of the cavalry's lances. Behind came a long file of foot soldiers, tramping along steadily, every one of them carrying a few empty bags which they expected to fill with loot by morning. Last of all came wagons, pulled by mules and similarly empty, clattering along over the dirt road.

"Do you require anything, Sir Mage?" The question came in a voice that trembled. Alain had a special escort, a young man in new cavalry gear. There had been a time when Alain would not have cared about how the young soldier felt, about the dread Mages inspired in common folk. Alain would not even have deigned to take notice of him, the young soldier and every other person being mere shadows cast on the illusion which was the world.

But Mari would have noticed that young soldier, would have cared about him. She had even noticed and cared about the fate of a young Mage. *"I don't leave anyone behind."* A simple thing. And yet with it she had saved his life and then, unwittingly, began to undo much that long years of very harsh training as an acolyte of the Mage Guild had drilled into Alain.

I will be eighteen years old tomorrow. Master Mechanic Mari is eighteen as well. Will I see her again, as my vision on the wall of Dorcastle foretold? Is she safe, for I know she feared her Guild's reaction if it learned we had come to know each other? And my own Guild had resolved to kill her if she were to be seen near me again. That is why I knew we had to separate, to ensure that Mari did not die because of me. But what if my own Guild learned of my vision, which foretold Mari would bring a new day to Dematr? If my elders learn of this, they will seek to have Mari killed no matter where she is, for they want change no more than do the leaders of the Mechanics Guild.

Alain became aware that the nervous young soldier was still awaiting his reply. "I require nothing," Alain answered in the properly emotionless tones of a Mage.

Could even a common soldier sense feelings in him now? Alain had been increasingly certain that other Mages and Elders had noticed the changes in him. Some of them resented Alain for having been declared a Mage at such a young age, and watched for any sign of unfitness. Others had heard that Alain had, unimaginably, actually spoken to a Mechanic in the desert waste east of Ringhmon, and watched for signs of corruption in him. And surely the signs were there, in the feelings he could no longer suppress.

And now the memory of Mari and those feelings caused Alain to look over at the young soldier, to take notice of him. "What do I call you?"

"P'tel, Sir Mage," the soldier said quickly, wide-eyed with nervousness at being addressed by a Mage. "P'tel of Alexdria."

"You have ridden against the Empire before?" Alain asked.

The young Alexdrian hesitated. "N-no, Sir Mage." Then Alain saw defiant pride rise in P'tel, something Alain understood all too well. "I am a soldier of Alexdria. I turned eighteen three weeks ago and was given my shield."

"You are a soldier of Alexdria," Alain repeated without feeling, knowing how it felt to be singled out for seeming to be too young. Then he put on his Mage aspect again, trying to ignore all of the commons around him as a Mage should, only vaguely aware of the passage of time.

"Sir Mage?" General Flyn, middle-aged, full-bearded and in command of the Alexdrian force, had brought his horse up to ride near Alain. Unlike the new armor which P'tel wore, Flyn's cuirass and helm were worn and battered with age and use. "Is there a problem, Sir Mage?"

"Why would there be a problem?" Alain asked in his most emotionless voice.

"Your escort says that you spoke with him. If something is amiss, Sir Mage, I ask that you tell me so that I may deal with it. If you are... not satisfied with your escort, I will assign someone else."

Alain rode silently for a moment, trying to decide how to reply. "I am satisfied," he finally said.

General Flyn kept his own expression controlled, but the attempts by commons to hide emotions were child's play for Mages to see through. He was worried by Alain. That had been obvious from their first meeting. "If—" Flyn began.

"General." Alain's voice held neither feeling nor force, but somehow that gave it the power to override other sounds. "Why could your city afford to hire only a single Mage for this expedition?"

Flyn shook his head, looking steadily at Alain. "I must tell you two things, Sir Mage. First, Alexdria is not my city. I am hired by those who seek a capable commander, and Alexdria is the latest such employer. Secondly, the city attempted to hire more than one Mage, but was told by your Guild that only you were available."

He was not lying. Alain, like all Mages, could easily spot a lie in a common's voice, eyes and expression.

But Mage elders could say anything and reveal nothing. Lies did not exist for those who did not believe in any truth.

"Sir Mage?"

Alain realized that he had been riding without speaking for a while, considering the implications of what he had just learned. The column of soldiers had reached a stout wooden bridge spanning a gash in the plains, Alain's horse clattering over it now with a hollow sound of hooves on planks. The channel below the bridge was not a terribly deep gully, not much deeper than a lance-length, but the sides were steep. A fair-sized, shallow stream ran along the bottom of the gully, surrounded by thick brush growing amid the mud of the floodplain. Small as the gully was, crossing it without a bridge would be slow and tedious work.

On the other side of the bridge, the Empire truly began. Instead of wild fields used for grazing herds in the spring and summer, cultivated farmland now spread away on either side of the road.

Alain turned his eyes on the general. Unlike most commons, Flyn met that gaze without flinching. "You go to raid the Empire," Alain said.

"Yes, Sir Mage."

Should he say it? A Mage would not. "I know of one whose parents were killed by those who raided."

Flyn stared at Alain, stunned to hear such a thing from a Mage.

"Do you go to kill those who cannot defend themselves?" Alain asked. His voice carried no feeling. A remarkable thing, given the pain tearing at him at the memory of his own mother and father, who had died while he was confined within a Mage Guild Hall as an acolyte. And now he was supposed to assist those who would do the same?

"No, Sir Mage," Flyn said, his face darkening with emotion. "Ask any man or woman in this force. I have issued firm orders, the same I give every time. No one shall be harmed unless they attack us. We come to take property, Sir Mage, not to take life. Am I permitted to ask a question?"

His training told Alain to say no. But his elders had sent him out alone and denied that they had done so. "Ask."

"Why does this matter to a Mage?"

"Nothing matters." Leave it at that.

"If any soldier under my command commits an atrocity," Flyn said, each word clearly spoken, "they will be left behind when we depart. They will be left behind hanging from their necks. I have told them so and they believe me, for my reputation tells them I mean it."

Once again, the general did not lie. Alain felt a weight leaving him. "I will fulfill my contract."

"Of course, Sir Mage." Flyn eyed him, clearly wanting to ask more questions, but then caution born of experience with Mages won over, and the general remained silent.

The general rode off to check on other portions of his force as the column kept moving down the road. Alain watched as farmhouses appeared alongside the road, the Alexdrians sending out small groups of cavalry to seize horses. As the raiders rode away, they did not leave the silence of death in their wake. Instead, Alain could see and hear the farmers and their families lamenting their property losses. So far, at least, the general had spoken truly.

The afternoon wore on, the sun sinking toward the wall of mountains behind them. Alain had stood silently by while the general outlined his plan before the expedition began. A march through the night, a strike before dawn overwhelming surprised defenders, a quick looting of the large town, and then an equally quick withdrawal before any elements of the Imperial legion responsible for protecting this area could catch the invaders. Simple enough. If something went amiss, if some part of the Imperial legion was encountered despite all precautions, then Alain was to use his skills to discourage the Imperials.

General Flyn returned as the sun finally began to set behind them, casting their shadows far ahead. "Is all well, Sir Mage?"

Alain turned a Mage's unfeeling gaze on Flyn. "Why do you ask?"

"I don't rightly know," Flyn confessed. "There's no sign of trouble ahead, no sign that the Imperials know that we're coming, but I feel uneasy. Do you have the Mage gift to see that which may be, Sir Mage?"

"I do." Alain looked ahead and shook his head. "I see nothing."

"Thank you, Sir Mage."

"You are wel—" Alain bit off the response, the one which Mari had taught him, the one no Mage should know, let alone speak, but he didn't succeed in stopping himself quickly enough.

Flyn had been in the act of riding off again, but now simply stared at Alain.

What is the matter with me? Alain wondered. It was not just memories of Mari. There was something else. His eyes came to rest on a weapon carried by one of the Alexdrian soldiers, and Alain suddenly knew the answer for his own disquiet. It was a weapon like a crossbow, but without any bow. A weapon Mari had called a rifle. One made by Mechanics.

He remembered dust and death and the sound of many rifles as the caravan he had been tasked to protect had been destroyed. That was it. Memory of fear and failure.

"General," Alain said, "do the Imperials have many weapons such as that?"

Flyn's eyes followed Alain's gesture. "Mechanic weapons, Sir Mage?" The general's voice was cautious again, worried. Every common knew how Mages felt about Mechanics and their works. "We have a few rifles. Three, to be exact. Like any military force that can afford them."

"How many do the Imperials have?"

"A full legion will typically have five or ten at the most," Flyn replied, not trying to hide his bafflement that a Mage was acknowledging the existence of Mechanic-made weaponry.

"Only ten?" Alain felt a sense of reassurance. "I have faced more than twenty." Why had he told this older man that?

Flyn's astonishment grew. "Twenty? And you survived? That is most remarkable, Sir Mage."

Alain had expected the general to show some skepticism, some disbelief in what Alain had said. No Mage elder had ever accepted that Alain had faced such peril and survived it. But Alain felt a need to disabuse Flyn of any exaggerated expectations about him, he who had failed to save many others in the caravan. "Only myself and one other survived. All the others died."

"Others." Flyn let the word hang for a moment. "Your pardon, Sir Mage, but it is unusual for a Mage to speak of...others."

"As it is unusual for a Mage to speak of Mechanic weapons?" Alain asked. He was being reckless. Amazingly reckless to confide in even so small a way with a common. But with Mari he had learned what companionship could be, and since parting from her had missed more and more the ability to speak of things large and small with another who might understand or simply listen. Something in this general, his steadiness and his openness, made Alain want to unburden himself a little. "I have seen what such weapons can do. I have seen what my own weapons can do."

Flyn nodded, his eyes intent on Alain. "It is an ugly thing."

"Does it hurt you to kill others, General?"

The question so startled Flyn that he stared wordlessly for a while before he could reply. Then Alain saw understanding dawn on the common's face as he looked at Alain. "It is a hard thing, Sir Mage, for any man or woman with a conscience. I do what I must, and in the heat of battle the excitement fills me, but afterwards I feel the pain of it." He paused. "The first time is the hardest. I've never forgotten the face of the first man I killed. I was...eighteen at the time."

Alain nodded. "I was seventeen."

"When you were facing more than twenty rifles? It is a hard thing, Sir Mage," Flyn repeated. "A hard thing to remember, a hard thing to face afterwards, for anyone who thinks life has value." Flyn rode a little closer to Alain, lowering his voice. "I have never met, nor heard of, a Mage who had such concerns. If I did, I would tell that Mage what I tell my young soldiers. They do not believe me, but perhaps a Mage would. I would say that what we do is an ugly business but a necessary one. We keep the Empire off balance, we keep the soldiers of the Free Cities experienced and sharp, and so perhaps we prevent worse things. Preventing something worse, defending something worth defending, helping those who need and deserve such assistance are the only justifications for what we do."

Flyn jerked his head toward where the young soldier P'tel rode, far away enough that he could not hear their words. "I know that. He doesn't. He still thinks of glory and excitement, proud of his shiny armor and his new lance and the shield his mother gave him before he rode off with us. The young ones look forward to battle and hope to encounter a legion so they can come home to celebrations, covered in what they see as glory. Not me. If we meet a legion, it means some soldiers like P'tel will die, never to come home to mothers and fathers who sent them off with pride and tears. My job is to get those soldiers home, and I hope you will do your utmost to assist me in that if necessary."

"You do not wish to fight?" Alain asked.

"No, Sir Mage. My job is to get our mission accomplished while losing as few soldiers as possible. That's why I do this. Because I'm pretty good at it, good enough that I can usually get the job done while losing as few of my own men and women as can be."

"Two are more than one," Alain said, remembering what he and Mari had been able to do together. "I will do all I can to assist you in your work."

Flyn nodded, no longer distant, but almost reassuring in his attitude. "You'll do fine. Twenty rifles! Where was that, if I may ask?"

"Far south of here. In the Waste east of Ringhmon."

"Ringhmon!" Flyn spoke in a disgusted tone. "They wanted to hire me once, but I told their emissaries that from what I knew of Ringhmon no sum of money would be enough." He paused. "Some interesting events occurred in Ringhmon not too long since. Do you know of them, Sir Mage?"

Alain felt that thing Mari called humor, though he did not let it show. "I was involved."

"Were you, Sir Mage?" Flyn grinned. "Your Guild slapped Ringhmon with some sanctions, and that on top of—"

"Of?"

"Your pardon, Sir Mage. There were actions taken by others."

Alain turned a direct look on the general again. "The Mechanics Guild?"

"Yes, if you wish to speak so directly of them. An interdict. Ringhmon can receive no services from that Guild and must pay a large fine when it can raise the money."

So Mari's Guild had finally done something. But Alain did not believe that the action was in revenge for what had been done to her by the leaders of Ringhmon. "And the Empire?"

Flyn's eyes evaluated Alain shrewdly. "They've made noises about snapping up Ringhmon while it is in a weakened state, but rumor has it that your Guild, and another Guild, have told the emperor it will not be permitted."

Alain gazed along the gently rolling fields at the horizon. "The Empire will never be allowed to take Ringhmon, or the Free Cities."

"Not as long as the Great Guilds rule, no," the general agreed.

"Nothing must change," Alain said, his voice flat.

But he wondered if something in his voice or face had betrayed his feelings. Flyn gazed wordlessly back at him before finally nodding once.

Flyn returned to his duties elsewhere, and Alain rode onward with the column as night came on, thinking about the shadows among which he rode. The commons. Mari had said the common people—all those who were not Mages or Mechanics—were like Alain and Mari even though they lacked the skills of members of the Great Guilds. Alain did not want to kill any more commons, but when his Guild elders insisted that Alain take this contract, he could not refuse it. Not simply because no Mage would accept Alain's reluctance to strike at shadows, which would be an unmistakable sign of just how far he had strayed from wisdom. But also because Alain had been asking for contract work as the weeks wore on, wishing to prove himself and knowing that the elders distrusted his skills and perhaps him.

In the darkness of full night, he imagined Mari riding beside him.

He had sought out some female Mages when he arrived in the region of the Free Cities, seeking distraction from thoughts of and feelings for Master Mechanic Mari. But the female Mages, with the expressionless faces and lifeless voices which were proper in Mages, had no interest in conversation. Nor could he feel any physical desire for them, not when Mari entered his thoughts the moment he touched any other woman.

Midnight passed, the soldiers marching steadily, any talk in the ranks silenced as the weary Alexdrians concentrated on walking or riding.

Occasionally Alain would see pairs of cavalry riding past on scouting duty, or the figure of General Flyn accompanied by several other riders.

The quiet and the motion of his horse made Alain so drowsy that he dozed off in the saddle a few times, jerking himself awake when he started to slip. Then he came fully awake, staring at the vision of a burning tower that had appeared beside the road. Though the flames leapt high from the tower, they cast no light upon the road or the fields.

Then it was gone.

Alain twisted in his saddle, seeing his soldier escort P'tel drowsing in the saddle nearby. "Get the general here. Immediately."

P'tel jerked with surprise and alarm at Alain's order, then saluted and rode off as fast as he could spur his horse.

A very short time later, two horses came racing down the line of the column, P'tel pulling up well short of the Mage but General Flyn riding up right next to Alain. "Is something amiss, Sir Mage?"

"Is there a tower ahead?" Alain asked. "To the left. A few lances off the road. Square. Wooden. Perhaps the height of four men."

Flyn nodded, frowning. "There is such a tower. Not far ahead at all. An abandoned Imperial watch tower. It hasn't been occupied for a decade, and my scouts just reported it still empty."

"I saw it burning," Alain said. "My foresight warned of something to come. How far ahead is it?"

"The head of the column should be almost reaching it," Flyn said. "Sir Mage, I have three pairs of scouts out, all experienced soldiers. None have reported danger."

Alain started to reply, then he felt something. Several somethings. The unmistakable sense that Mages were not too far distant and working spells. Alain pointed ahead and to the sides, surprised that he could keep his voice steady. "Do your scouts ride there, and there, and there?"

Flyn stared. "Yes, Sir Mage."

"Then at this moment they are probably dying at the hands of the Mages I sense."

The general did not hesitate for another moment. He rose in the saddle to roar out orders in a voice that carried easily through the night. "Ambush! Everyone off the road! To arms! Move or die!"

Alain looked ahead as shocked soldiers roused themselves from the stupor of march and flung themselves toward cover. He could now see the dim outline of the watch tower visible in the night. The world illusion seemed to have slowed down, everything happening with terrible sluggishness, General Flyn's words coming out oh so slowly, Alexdrian soldiers running and reaching for weapons with the agonizing snail's pace of those caught in a nightmare, Alain trying to gather power to himself yet not knowing which spell he needed to use.

Lightning flared, not from the sky but from the ground, racing across the surface to strike the watch tower and cause it to erupt into flames that illuminated the Alexdrian soldiers as they scrambled off the road.

The sudden blare of the brass trumpets used to pass signals among Imperial forces came from the left side of the road, and time shot back into motion as a storm of crossbow bolts came hurtling out of the darkness. Deeper thrums marked Imperial siege machines called ballistae hurling their projectiles toward the Alexdrians. Much louder than all the rest came the thunder of Mechanic weapons from the Imperial position, the fire of several rifles adding to the havoc among the Alexdrian soldiers.

Alain's horse reared, screaming in pain, then twisted and fell. Alain barely managed to jump free of the saddle before his horse crashed to the ground. Toughened by his Mage training and partially cushioned by the robes he wore, Alain landed hard but unhurt. Jumping up, he looked down at the horse he had ridden, seeing the crossbow bolt protruding from its chest and the bloody foam on the horse's muzzle as it twitched out the last vestiges of life. Alain turned away, his eyes coming to rest on the Alexdrian soldier named P'tel. The boy had fallen on his back, a crossbow bolt protruding from his neck. Blood pooled beneath the new armor which had not been able to protect him. P'tel's sightless eyes stared up at the stars, his expression forever frozen in surprise.

Alain went to one knee beside the body, momentarily oblivious to the battle around him. *He is nothing. Just a shadow. No. My training cannot be right in that. For the loss of a shadow would not pain me so.* Eighteen years of age, only a few days older than Alain, and P'tel would never see another sunrise. *You journey to another dream, soldier of Alexdria. May your next dream end better than this one.*

Standing up again, Alain stared around, feeling a curious calm mixing with the anger and fear that he kept suppressed. He could find few targets for his spells in the uncertain light cast by the burning tower. Dead Alexdrian soldiers littered the road and its verges, while the Imperial crossbows and other weapons continued to flay the other Alexdrians who had sought cover.

Focusing on one of the dimly seen ballistae, Alain concentrated on changing the world illusion. The air above his palm was hot, much hotter than the surrounding air. Very, very hot. His own strength went into the spell, aided by the power held by the land around him.

The illusion of heat was above his palm. Alain looked toward the ballistae, and imagined the heat *there* instead of *here*. In an instant, the heat had gone from *here* to *there*, and the wooden ballistae turned into another torch as it caught fire, the distant figures of its crew hurling themselves away from the inferno.

In the light cast by the burning tower and siege machine, Alain could see that General Flyn had rallied his cavalry, leading it in a charge against the flank of the Imperials entrenched on the left side of the road. The Imperial troops had not expected their targets to be warned and able to recover so swiftly from the shock of ambush. In the darkness and the confusion, the legionaries did not notice the Alexdrian charge coming until it was too late. The Alexdrian cavalry hit the Imperial forces and rode over them, breaking that end of the Imperial line. Overrunning one of the Imperial war machines, some of the cavalry turned it and fired its huge bolt down the ranks of the Imperial trenches, causing chaos. Flyn wheeled his forces, preparing them to charge down the length of the disrupted Imperial line.

Alain was watching, waiting for good targets, when lightning came again from the ground among the shadowed areas behind the Imperial line. The forks of lightning shot out, smashing into the Alexdrian cavalry, sending horses and soldiers flying. Those horses unhurt or singed by the attacks panicked, stampeding away riderless or with riders vainly trying to regain control. The lightning struck once more, and then a third time, weakening with each bolt, but disrupting the attempts by some groups of Alexdrian cavalry to hold their ground.

The Imperials have a lightning Mage, and a very strong one to cast so much lightning so fast. But he could do nothing about it. Even though Alain could sense the position of the lightning Mage, the Mage Guild did not permit Mages to attack each other when the forces they were contracted to clashed in battle. The Mages could only strike at commons. Alain stood, helpless, as the Imperials rallied and the fleeing Alexdrians streamed past him.

Imperial trumpets sounded again. Alain could see lines of mounted soldiers coming toward him. Imperial cavalry this time, moving at a steady pace, preparing to charge down the road and sweep away the shattered Alexdrian force.

Leave them to their fates, Alain's Mage training told him.

Run, save yourself, Alain's fears cried.

I don't leave anyone behind, Mari's voice said, so clearly he wondered for a moment if she truly stood beside him. That insubstantial thread he had once sensed tying them together was present again, and he felt strength and resolve fill him simply because he was conscious of that thread.

Alain braced himself, facing the ranks of Imperial cavalry. *These Alexdrians depended on me. I am their defense against disaster. I cannot fail them. Not as I once failed the caravan on its way to Ringhmon. I will save these people, because Mari would want me to do this, because it is the hard thing but also the right thing.*

He gathered the power in the area to himself, feeling where it had been already drained by the Mage who hurled lightening. But enough remained. As much remained as he could use.

Heat flared above his hand as he created it there. Alain stared at the ranks of Imperial cavalry, trying not to think about what he was going to do to them. Then he willed the heat to a spot in the stones of the road just ahead of the front rank of the cavalry.

The area exploded, hurling fragments among the Imperial soldiers. Alain had already created another fireball and willed it to strike a little distance from the first. Then another, then another, his strength draining away as Alain sent fireballs as rapidly as he could. The ranks of the Imperial cavalry disappeared in a succession of explosions that hurled men and horses in all directions. As the last fire left his hand to create a weak burst of heat among the Imperials, Alain fell to the road, his vision hazed by exhaustion so great that he could make no attempt to cushion his fall. Dimly aware that he must not lie here to die, Alain struggled to move as cries of panic and shock sounded from the Imperial troops.

Lightning flared above him, tearing through the space which Alain had occupied moments before. Then it came again, flaying the body of a horse lying between Alain and the Mage sending the lightning. Even through the haze of fatigue clouding his mind, Alain wondered why the lightning had been directed so close to him. Could not the lightning Mage have sensed where Alain was?

He had to have. Then had the lightning been aimed at Alain on purpose?

Alain tried to move again, his limbs shaking with effort, but could not manage to rise even to his elbows. Several horses came to a halt near him. *The Imperials. Will they dare to slay me in revenge for what I did to their comrades?*

But the boots that came into Alain's field of vision were those of Alexdrians. The voice of General Flyn sounded above him. "Forgive us, Sir Mage, the familiarity of laying hands upon you, but we feel obligated to save the life of the one who just saved ours!" Hands grasped Alain, raising him and tossing him into an empty saddle, then a mounted Alexdrian soldier was on each side of him, holding him upright, and the group was heading away from the site of the ambush. The brass trumpets of the Imperials blared in their wake, sounding victorious but also frustrated at the escape of so many Alexdrians.

Alain tried to regain enough strength to keep in his saddle on his own, dimly aware of General Flyn organizing the survivors of his cavalry to drive the remaining Alexdrian foot soldiers ahead of them in a race to safety. Detachments of the remaining Alexdrian cavalry fell back occasionally to hamper the Imperial pursuit. General Flyn seemed to be everywhere at once, tireless as he drove his soldiers onward.

The general stopped by Alain briefly at one point. "Sir Mage, your warning saved us from suffering much worse losses in the first onset, and your stand against the Imperial cavalry saved us from being wiped out. I will admit I doubted the abilities of a young Mage, but I was wrong, Sir Mage, very wrong. I have never heard of any Mage who stood their ground so to defend common folk. If any one of us lives to reach the Northern Ramparts again, it will be because of you."

Alain, still swaying in the saddle and holding on to his horse with great difficulty, could only nod. The general saluted him and rode off, urging another group of his soldiers to greater effort.

The rest of the ride seemed like a nightmare brought to life. The unchanging plains made it seem as if they were making no progress as they rode on, the enemy always behind. Alain slowly regained some strength, but was grateful for the escorts on either side of him, who remained alert for any sign the Mage was going to fall. *It is odd. I should have died back there, struck by the lightning Mage who violated Guild rules by attacking me directly, or impaled on the lances of Imperial cavalry. But I still live, because these common soldiers, these shadows who my training says do not even exist, risk themselves to save me.*

They clattered back across the wooden bridge as a faint glow to the east announced that dawn was not far off. General Flyn sat, watching his soldiers stream past, his face grim. From their conversation the day before, Alain knew that the general was thinking of how many soldiers had not lived to reach that bridge. The escort accompanying Alain brought their horses near the general and stopped, their mounts trembling with weariness.

"What can you see, Vasi?" Flyn asked one of the other Alexdrians. "Have you still got your Mechanic far-seers?"

That soldier put something like two tubes joined together to his eyes. "They're coming, sir. Four or five bowshots off, I'd guess."

A small group of foot soldiers came staggering across the bridge, herded by two more Alexdrian cavalry on exhausted horses. Flyn stopped one of the mounted soldiers. "Who's behind you?"

The woman stared at him for a moment, too tired to think, then sat straighter in the saddle. She had lost her helmet in the battle or the retreat but had kept her sword and now raised it in a salute. "None but the Imperials and the dead as far as I know, General."

"Then keep going. Well done." Flyn ran his eyes across the group. "Akiko, you've got the freshest horse. Gallop a bowshot from the bridge and see if you can spot any more of ours coming, then get back here."

The Alexdrian officer named Akiko turned a fearful but determined face forward and urged her horse across the bridge, its hooves thundering clearly in the stillness that marks dawn. Alain, finally able to sit in the saddle by himself again, watched the figure of the Alexdrian recede into the still, dark landscape. They waited, the only sounds the deep breathing of their blown horses and the rattle of equipment on the road where the fleeing Alexdrian force sought the refuge of the Ramparts.

Hooves sounded again, no longer galloping. General Flyn and his escort stiffened, tightening their grips on their weapons. Then Akiko reappeared, urging her horse on in a shambling trot. As she reached the far side of the bridge Akiko called out her message. "I couldn't see anyone but some bodies lying in the road, sir, and the Imperials coming on strong behind."

Flyn nodded grimly. "Sir Mage, had I a hundred soldiers still in fighting shape I would make a stand here and hold off the Imperials for a while. But the force I have here is too small and too tired. It would be a great service to us if this bridge were destroyed before the Imperials got here, because that is all that might delay them. Everything we had that could start a big fire fast is gone, lost in the retreat. Can you destroy this bridge, Sir Mage?"

Alain sat straighter, eyeing the wooden structure. Like anything else built by the Empire, it was stout enough to stand for centuries. Fortunately, this far out in the hinterlands, it was not made of stone but of wood. Still, it would take a good sized fire to make it unusable before the pursuit arrived, and he had very little strength. "Get your soldiers back from the bridge. I will do what I can."

The Alexdrians fell back, eyeing him nervously. If Alain had not been so tired and so frightened, he would have been pleased to see that the soldiers who had seemed so skeptical of him now feared his abilities. His dismount wasn't quite a fall from the saddle, as Alain managed to keep his feet. He stood unsteadily gazing at the bridge, then concentrated, seeing his hand trembling, finally using his other hand to grasp his forearm to steady it. There was plenty of power here to use, but his strength was so low. *I cannot do this. I need my own strength, and it is gone.*

CHAPTER THREE

Alain took a deep breath, looking around and seeing the Alexdrians watching him, hope and fear mingled in their expressions. *If Mari were here, I could do this. If I die here, I will not ever make it back to the walls of Dorcastle, and I will never see Mari again.*

It happened, as it had before in Ringhmon and in Dorcastle. The thread he sensed connecting them had faded once more, but as Alain thought of Mari he was more aware of it. His feelings for Mari had shown him how to find a place inside where strength could be found even when all strength seemed to be gone. From somewhere, Alain felt that extra strength. Not much, but enough. He used it to draw on the power here, building the heat, making it larger than usual, less focused so it would set more of the bridge afire, feeling himself about to collapse again from the effort, then gazed at the center of the bridge and sent the fire there.

Fire bloomed as the entire central section of the bridge erupted into flame. Alain barely noticed as darkness filled his eyes and his body went limp, dropping to hit the ground hard for at least the third time this night. Though miraculously untouched by Imperial weapons or Mage-sent lightning, he had surely picked up more bruises than he had suffered since his early days as an acolyte.

But once again hands came to him, pulling him up and hoisting him into his saddle and steadied on either side. Alain wavered at the edge of consciousness as the fire roared ever stronger behind them and the faint sound of angry cries came from the Imperial forces. "It'll take them a long time to get foot soldiers through that gully, and the cavalry will have to ride north a long ways before they can cross," Flyn told Alain. "We can't relax, but I believe we will make it, Sir Mage."

Alain could not even nod in reply.

By the time the sun rose behind them to cover the peaks of the Northern Ramparts before them in a blaze of red-tinged glory, Alain had completely passed out, sagging in the saddle between his two escorts.

It was fully light when he blinked back into awareness. Most of the horses were being walked now, no longer capable of being ridden. A few in slightly better shape were carrying soldiers too badly wounded to walk themselves. All around, soldiers were tramping wearily onward, their eyes on the entrance to the pass into the Northern Ramparts, which lay not far ahead now.

General Flyn came walking back along the column, as apparently inexhaustible as ever. "We'll leave all the horses at the entrance to the pass," he called out to his soldiers. "None of them can make the climb after last night."

One of Alain's escorts looked stricken. "Will they be slain, sir?"

"Not by us," Flyn growled. "Let the Imperials have them. I'll not kill good beasts who've ridden their hearts out for us."

Alain looked up the pass, remembering the trip down it. When had that been? It seemed months, yet it could only have been a day or two ago. The first stage of the pass was fairly steep, normally a tough but manageable climb. But the horses of the fleeing Alexdrians were too worn out to make that journey. They stood, legs splayed, their heaving sides coated with foam, wherever soldiers dropped their reins. Alain wondered how many of the horses would die anyway from the stress of the retreat.

A few of the wagons had made it out of the ambush. Now the wounded within them were being hoisted out and carried by their fellow soldiers as the wagons were overturned and left lying at the foot of the pass.

Flyn got his exhausted soldiers moving up the pass, cursing and cajoling while Alain sat and watched. Finally the general came to Alain and bowed. "Sir Mage, there are times to lead from the front and times to lead from the rear. This is a time for the latter. I need to keep my soldiers moving and I need to command any rear-guard required to hold off Imperial pursuers who get too close." He gestured to the east, where rising dust warned of the legionaries who were still after the Alexdrians. "You have earned the right to a place of safety in the middle of the column," Flyn continued, "but you have proven yourself a stout ally. Will you accompany me to help guard the rear of the column, Sir Mage?"

Alain looked over at the common man, who was not supposed to matter at all, not even supposed to exist at all, feeling a warm glow inside from the respect this general obviously now felt for him. "Yes. I will accompany you." He managed to get up on his own, suppressing any visible winces as some of his new bruises protested, then walked stiff-legged beside the general, hoping his muscles would loosen up as he traveled.

There was a sense of relief as the soldiers entered the pass, high walls of living rock rising around them as if the mountains themselves were prepared to defend the Alexdrians, but Alain knew the perception was false. If the Imperials had gotten past the ravine quickly enough to catch the escaping Alexdrians, the surviving soldiers would be in dire straits once again. As the retreat continued, climbing higher along the steep slope here, the Alexdrians could look back and see the Imperial forces still heading for the pass. The legionaries had been slowed, but not stopped, and that sight lent a little more strength to the weary limbs of the fugitives.

Flyn allowed the retreating soldiers to stop for brief rests occasionally, then bulled them into motion again. By noon the surface of the pass had leveled out considerably, still climbing but without the leg-burning slope of the earlier stretch. The Alexdrians had reached a point where the twists and turns of the pass no longer allowed them to see back into Imperial territory. Instead of reassurance, this created more fear, since they could no longer see how close their pursuers might be getting.

Alain had become numb by this time. The burning pain in his legs had filled him, then as if too great to endure had faded into a great dull ache. He put one foot before the next, grateful for the tough training of an acolyte. If ever there was a time when the ability to ignore physical stress was needed, it was now.

By mid-afternoon the fleeing force reached a place Alain recalled. Large rocks had long ago fallen from above, blocking one side of the pass but also providing good cover. General Flyn got as far as the rocks, then stopped walking, staring downward with a bleak expression. Alain stopped beside him to see four Alexdrian soldiers, three men and a woman, lying in the shelter of the rocks. The exhausted Mage barely managed to avoid showing a reaction as he saw the terrible wounds the four soldiers had suffered. "What is this?" Flyn asked in a quiet voice.

One of the Alexdrians, who still had two good arms even though his legs had been ruined, pointed at himself and his companions. His face was very pale and drawn, so that to Alain the dying soldier appeared to be half ghostly already. "We won't live to see another dawn, General, sir," the soldier rasped in a weak voice. "We know that."

"I won't leave wounded behind," Flyn stated, his voice now rough.

"We're not abandoned, begging your pardon, General," the woman mumbled through a bandage covering most of her face. "We're the rear guard. All volunteers."

Flyn made as if to speak again.

"Please, sir," the first soldier said, his voice faltering from weakness. "We'll be dead by nightfall anyway. I can see my death waiting for me. Let us do something worthwhile with our last hours. We can hold up the Imperial pursuit for a little while. They won't know how many of us there are, or how bad hurt." Apparently having used all of his strength to make the speech, the soldier sagged back against the rock.

Flyn looked from soldier to soldier, then over at Alain. "There must be times, Sir Mage, when it is a great comfort not to be able to feel."

Alain met the general's gaze, then looked back at the four soldiers, feeling sorrow fill him. "I lost that comfort long before this day," he whispered.

"Can you give them the means to stay with us, Sir Mage? The means to live through this day?"

"No." His weariness and the stress of recent events caused Alain to say more, to say things no Mage should tell a common. "It is not a matter of strength or skill. No Mage could save these soldiers. I...wish I could."

The general shook his head as if in denial, his face worn, then straightened to attention as he addressed the four badly wounded soldiers. "Very well. I can't deny you a final wish, though my wish is that I could bring you with us." He gestured to another soldier standing near. "You've got a Mechanic rifle. Bring it here."

The man brought the thing over. It bore a resemblance to the Mechanic weapons that Alain had seen before, but beyond that he could not tell anything. It might have been identical to what Mari had called a "lever-action repeating rifle," but to Alain it was just another incomprehensible Mechanic device.

"I only have two bullets left for it, General," the soldier reported.

Flyn took the weapon, holding out a hand for the bullets, then handed the rifle and ammunition to the four soldiers behind the rocks. "This is all I can leave you. That and my prayers and my thanks for your sacrifice."

The woman among the wounded started to protest. "It's too much... the cost...keep the rifle."

"No." Flyn's voice was unyielding. "You'll take this. Fire a shot when you see them coming. Facing a Mechanic weapon will make them pause and fear a strong position. Fire the last shot when no hope remains. That way we'll know you've met them and how long you held them." He swallowed before speaking again, this time to one of the officers who had stayed by Flyn's side through the retreat. "Akiko, make sure we have all four names for the wall of heroes. These names are not to be forgotten." General Flyn saluted stiffly and walked away, not looking back.

Alain followed, though he occasionally glanced behind to see the four. To his surprise, they seemed relieved and fairly relaxed. *Why? Where is the fear of death which commons feel? Perhaps it is because they have chosen their fate and know when their suffering will end. It is the best they can do for themselves now. Did seeing so many comrades die aid them in accepting their fate?*

Accepting their fate. The phrase echoed in Alain's mind as he thought about the ambush and the retreat. *What was my fate meant to be? How many Mages did the Imperials have to silence the scouts, without the scouts being able to give warning? Six. One for each scout so that all died at once. And the lightning Mage, judging from the position from which he struck, was not one of them. So, seven. Against this the Alexdrians had only me. Against this, the Alexdrians were told only I was available.*

And the lightning was aimed at me. Would the Mage have done that without orders from the elders?

Can it be that my Guild intended my death on that field? Have I revealed the changes inside me to such an extent that I was marked for death without even being warned of the need to regain wisdom as the Mage Guild sees it?

Unaware of Alain's thoughts, Flyn marched along silently for a while, then gave Alain a searching look. "You said no Mage could help those soldiers?"

"No Mage spell can heal. No means has ever been found to do that."

"But if Mages can alter a person in other ways—"

Alain's look caused Flyn to stop in mid-sentence. "Have you ever seen such a thing, or have you but heard of it?"

Flyn stared back at Alain. "I've only heard of it."

"If Mages had such a skill, do you not think you would have seen it with your own eyes?" Why was he telling the general that? The Guild elders would be outraged, accusing Alain of treason and folly for betraying the secret that no Mage could directly change another shadow. But bitterness filled Alain as he thought of the many deaths on the field of the ambush, as he considered the treachery which had nearly claimed him on that same field.

The general did not reply for a long moment. "That is surely something that your Guild does not wish known. It encourages commons to believe otherwise. Why are you telling me this, Sir Mage?"

"Because I wanted to help them and I could not." Alain knew that stress and weariness was bringing emotion into his voice, regret and sorrow, but could not prevent that. "I want you to know that I would have saved them if I could."

"Help? A Mage knows that word?"

"This Mage does."

"Why should my opinion of you matter, Sir Mage?" The general's voice was quiet, questioning, but also full of wonder.

"I do not know. I wish I could ask—" Alain pressed his lips together, trying to control his feelings and failing.

Flyn nodded, not pursuing that broken-off thought. "How old are you, Sir Mage?"

The question did not sting, not coming from this man. "Eighteen, in a few more days."

"I had a son who would be about your age," Flyn commented, his eyes distant. "He died of an illness many years ago. I never thought to say this to a Mage, but had he lived I wish he could have grown to be such as you. Do not blame yourself. If there is any fault here, it is mine. Ensuring we did not get surprised was my job."

"There were many Mages against us," Alain said. "I cannot be certain how many. Seven, I think."

"Seven." The general let the word hang for a moment. "We must have offended the Mage Guild mightily, or the Imperials must have spent more than I ever imagined they would to set us up for that ambush." His eyes went to Alain.

Alain knew the question that Flyn wanted to ask. "I did not know. I was not told." Alain prepared himself for the disbelief in Flyn's eyes, because all commons knew that all Mages lied without the slightest remorse and that the word of a Mage meant nothing, but instead Flyn slowly nodded.

"I do not doubt you, Sir Mage. Not after the risks you ran for us. May I ask, Sir Mage, why you are so different from every other Mage I have encountered or heard of?"

The question should have been shocking coming from a common, but in a brief span of time Alain had shared and survived many things with this man. And Alain was tired, and still overwhelmed by all that happened in the last day. So he gave the simple truth. "I have a friend."

"A friend?" Flyn paused, then smiled wearily. "That is a powerful thing, Sir Mage. A most unusual thing in a Mage, as well, though you know that better than I do. I hope you survive this day to see him once more."

Alain could have left it at that, but something moved him to correct the general. "Her."

"Her?" The general appeared very surprised again, but this time his smile was stronger. "That does explain much, Sir Mage. How does your Guild feel about that?"

"I believe I know, but I am not yet certain." Through his weariness, Alain imagined that he could feel the thread to Mari again, the insubstantial tie which he had thought long ago broken by distance. He clung to the fantasy for a moment, then let it go, knowing that Mari must still be far, far distant from him, somewhere far to the south where Imperial legions and hostile Mages did not threaten her.

Not much longer after that the retreating Alexdrians came around a bend in the pass, gazing up along a lengthy stretch leading onward, widening a bit into what was almost a valley framed by tall, steep canyon walls. An Alexdrian officer came scrambling back to speak to the general in a voice breathless with fatigue. "Sir, we've spotted a rider coming toward us from the far side of the valley."

Flyn raised his head and squinted as if trying to see from here across the distance to the other side of the valley. "Only one rider, Vasi? You're certain it's but one?"

"Yes, General, though the person is too far off to make out any details. We lost sight of the rider when he or she rode into a section of trail screened by rock falls, but whoever it is won't meet up with us for a little while."

"Maybe one of our own," Flyn speculated. "Could it be another Mage?" he asked Alain.

Alain shook his head. "I do not sense another Mage near, though my tiredness makes it harder for me to do so. But Mages would not travel alone through land such as this."

"Maybe it's someone coming out from Alexdria to meet us. Doesn't seem possible that they could be an enemy, not that far ahead of us. Was this rider hurrying?"

Vasi nodded. "As fast as seemed prudent to me across that terrain. Maybe a little faster."

"Unlikely to be an enemy then. They could just wait for us instead of rushing to contact." Flyn barked a harsh, bitter laugh. "Let's hope it's not a messenger telling us to beware of Imperial ambush. Well, we will meet up soon enough and find out. Even if the rider brings bad news, it's not likely to be worse than what we're carrying."

The retreating column walked on through the mountain valley, the path wending between occasional piles of stones or large boulders which had fallen from the walls of the gorge. Trudging up the slope, they reached a point where the road crested before dipping down for a ways and then rising again. As they paused there, a single shot from a Mechanic rifle rang out from farther down in the pass. After a brief pause, a second shot sounded. Then silence.

Flyn stared back down the pass. "They were supposed to hold off the second shot until they were about to be overwhelmed. How could the Imperials have gotten to them so fast and then overwhelmed them so quickly? If they're moving that fast they'll be on us in no time at all." He shook himself, then jumped into action. "All troops! Form a line here! Behind this crest, where we'll be sheltered from the projectiles of crossbows and Mechanic weapons!" the general roared. "I don't care if there's a full legion coming up that pass, we've got the numbers and the guts to hold this line against them and pay them back for what they've done to our friends and comrades!"

The Alexdrian soldiers began scrambling into line below the crest. Their few remaining pennants seemed forlorn against the sky, but the Alexdrians faced the oncoming enemy with the determination of despair.

Flyn came up to the Mage again. "Sir Mage, where will you stand?"

Alain gazed around, then pointed to where the road rose again, a long bowshot behind the line being formed by the Alexdrians. "If I stand among your ranks behind that crest, I will not see the approaching enemy in time to prepare spells. If I stand there, I will be able to see the Imperials approaching and strike at them."

The general shook his head. "They will also be able to shoot at you, Sir Mage, and with no direct sight of my own soldiers at that point you will be their target of choice."

Alain nodded, feeling a fatalism born of his fatigue from the disastrous night and the long retreat through the pass. "Then that alone may aid your soldiers, even if my spells fail. I am far from being at my best strength. But I will do as much as I am able to manage."

Flyn bared his teeth. "You are a man, Sir Mage. My soldiers will do all they can as well. Those troops won't run again, Sir Mage. They're good, and they've got something to prove."

"Then we will win or die," Alain said, feeling no bravado, but rather a tired sense that only those options remained. He turned and began walking to the high point. When he was far enough along that he could see over the heads of the Alexdrian line to the place where the pass took a sharp curve, Alain stopped, resting against a nearby rock. Black mist flickered across his vision as he stared down the pass, not the result of tiredness but of foresight trying again to warn of imminent danger. But this time the warning was only a vague one, providing no clear vision.

Alain felt a trembling in the rock beneath his feet, like that he would feel if a large wagon or a column of cavalry were passing close by. But what could have the weight to create such a sensation from such a distance? It was as if a huge creature were approaching...

An emptiness filled him as Alain realized what must be coming, and knew that it was something far deadlier than a mere legion of Imperial soldiers.

A roar echoed and reechoed from the cliffs around them. Alain, barely aware of the great void which had grown where his insides had been, stared down the canyon. He had heard the howl of an enraged dragon before. *Eight Mages, then, at least. There is one more test that will tell me for certain why I was sent to face such odds unknowing, but I have little doubt now of what that test will reveal.*

General Flyn had obviously heard the roar of a dragon before, too. He was barking commands, steadying his troops, as he gazed back at Alain with an expression which even at this distance was easy to guess. He knew only the Mage could possibly save him and his remaining soldiers. Alain, meeting that pleading gaze, felt his strength and the power around him, and knew that the odds of him succeeding were very small indeed.

Moments later the face of his death appeared at the head of the canyon. Not only a dragon, but a large one, as large as the biggest Alain had ever heard described, at least ten times the height of a tall man. The beast stood upright on two mighty hind legs, its two smaller forearms armed with wicked claws as large as scimitars. Behind it, the dragon's massive tail helped balance the creature as it ran forward, covering ground rapidly. Its great armored head turned this way and that, the huge eyes seeking prey, as a few strides brought the monster to a point where it could look down upon the frail Alexdrian defensive line. Instead of attacking immediately, though, the dragon swept its head from side to side as if searching, ignoring the Alexdrians who were firing their crossbows at it, sparks winking impotently from the thick, armored scales of the dragon as the projectiles ricocheted off without doing any damage.

The dragon, not having found what it sought, raised its gaze to search the area behind the Alexdrian line, the dark, glittering eyes finally coming to rest on the figure of Alain in his Mage robes.

The creature roared again. Far too big to fly even if it had wings, it used its massive hind legs to propel it forward in a leap that took it over the Alexdrian defensive line, crossbow bolts bouncing off of the dragon's scales as if they had been sticks thrown by children.

Still ignoring the Alexdrians, the dragon took another leap, landing with an earthshaking thump not far from Alain. Alain looked up at it, knowing what the dragon represented. *It was told to seek me. My Guild wants me to die. There can be no doubt.* But he stood his ground, knowing that trying to run would be futile, putting everything he had left into the most destructive fireball he could manage, the heat of the spell almost burning his palms as he added to it until it held all of his remaining strength. He aimed at where the weakest point in a dragon's armor was supposed to be, under one of the forearms. In an instant of time his fireball went from between to his palms to *there.* The dragon howled with pain as the scales under the arm were scorched and darkened, and that arm flopped into uselessness. But the dragon did not appear otherwise affected, its remaining forearm flexing claws as long as Alain's arm.

The huge, glinting eyes glared at Alain as he fell to his knees, totally used up and not able to run now that his last effort had failed. The dragon's hind legs tensed to bring it the short distance closer so it could smash Alain. The Mage watched the dragon, knowing that nothing he could do could change things now, his mind filled not with fear but with regret that he would never see Mari again.

CHAPTER FOUR

A different kind of sound came from behind Alain, farther up the canyon, like the boom of the Mechanic weapons but louder and followed by a sustained rumble which grew rapidly in volume. A streak of smoke flew past over Alain's head, soaring straight into the center of the dragon's chest where its armor was strongest, ending in a flash of fire, a bigger gout of smoke and another crash of thunder.

Time seemed to pause then, Alain and the Alexdrian soldiers gawking at the smoke trail, the dragon staring down at its chest, the echoes of the explosion fading down the canyon. The smoke blew to reveal a crater in the dragon's chest, not so much wide as deep, as if a huge, invisible lance had driven through the armored scales and well into the flesh inside.

The dragon raised its head slowly, glaring at Alain. Its remaining good arm began to rise, then the enormous spell beast started to lean forward. It kept leaning until suddenly it was falling, its whole length going limp. The body hit so hard the ground shook again, dislodging rocks which clattered down from the canyon walls. The massive head landed less than a lance length from Alain. The gleaming eyes were still fixed on him, filled with the need to kill him, but as Alain watched, the light in the eyes faded and went dark.

Alain just stayed there, still on his knees, trying to comprehend what had happened. Slowly he became aware that the Alexdrians were cheering. Racing up the canyon, streaming past the dead body of the dragon, they gathered around him to shout his praises as a hero until the canyon rang with them.

General Flyn was beside him, offering a respectful hand as Alain struggled to his feet. "Sir Mage, I would not have believed it if I had not seen it. We've never cheered a Mage before, but any other Mage would have run and left us to our fates and no other could have done what you did here. You're twice the man I am, and I'll flatten anyone who says otherwise!"

Alain shook his head, still bewildered. "I did not do it."

"What? What's that?"

"I did not kill it." Alain pointed at the huge body sprawled almost literally at his feet. "I do not know what did." He stared at the commander.

The Alexdrian cheers began faltering up-canyon, and Alain heard the sound of iron-shod hooves clattering their way. He stared as the ranks of the Alexdrians parted, making way for a single rider. The one they had seen earlier coming their way. A rider in the dark jacket of a member of the Mechanics Guild. A rider whose raven-black hair was cut short at her shoulders. Alain's heart leaped. *It cannot be.*

But he felt the thread once again, the thing which had been hovering on the edge of his awareness as he faced the dragon. Insubstantial but now intense, it led straight to the Mechanic.

Mari rode up to Alain and dismounted a bit clumsily, her horse standing with the lowered head and sweat-soaked sides of a mount which has been ridden hard. Mari wore her usual clothing, a light shirt under the dark Mechanics jacket and a pair of trousers of tough material tucked into leather boots. She carried a large tube of some sort, almost as long as she was tall and with an opening in the end so big that Alain could easily have put his fist inside. A mist of smoke still drifted from that opening. A second tube was strapped to the saddle of her horse.

She walked a few more steps, the soldiers giving way before her. Finally stopping directly in front of Alain, Mari dropped the tube on the ground where it clattered like an empty container. Mari took a deep breath, then nodded to him. "Mage Alain."

Still dazed, Alain nodded in return. "Master Mechanic Mari."

Mari glanced at the Alexdrian soldiers standing around with wide eyes, all of them shocked at seeing a Mechanic and a Mage speak to each other. "A little room," she asked, and even though her tone wasn't that of an order, the soldiers hastily backed away several lance-lengths.

Looking at Alain again, Mari smiled and toed the empty tube. "After what happened in Dorcastle, I thought we might run into another dragon. I figured I ought to be ready for one this time."

"It is fortunate for me that you were."

"Are you hurt?" A rush of feeling came through in those words, even though Mari kept her expression controlled.

Alain spread his arms. "I am somewhat battered and bruised, as well as exhausted, but I avoided other injury."

"You promised me that you'd stay safe," she accused him. "Typical Mage. Your word isn't worth much."

Alain had to pause a moment to think of a reply, realizing that Mari was using what she called her sarcasm. "I told you that I could not control where my Guild sent me, or what my contracts might be."

She waved away his words. "Excuses." Then she took another deep breath. "I'm so glad I got here in time. Blazes, it's good to see you again. We need to talk."

"We are talking."

Mari shook her head in exasperation. "Alone, you literal Mage. We need to talk alone, just you and me." She gestured to the crowd of Alexdrian soldiers still staring at them.

General Flyn, though apparently as stunned as his troops, had now recovered and stepped forward, his face determined. "Lady Mechanic, you are here alone?"

In response, Mari turned and looked back the way she had come. "Looks like it. Are you expecting anyone else?"

The general frowned, puzzled by her attitude. "No, Lady, but we were not expecting you, either. Mechanics do not normally travel alone."

Mari shrugged. "These are not normal circumstances. Not for me, anyway. I came here after this Mage and would appreciate being left alone with him."

Flyn stood his ground. "Lady Mechanic, this Mage is attached to my command. He has given his all to defend us and cannot protect himself now, but I will not allow someone hostile to his interests to make a prisoner of him or harm him. Not even a member of your Guild can order me to do that, not when a Mage is involved."

Mari quirked an eyebrow at the Alexdrian commander. "A common is willing to fight to protect a Mage from a Mechanic?"

Flyn's frown grew deeper. "I agree that is unusual, Lady Mechanic. But this is an unusual Mage."

"I figured that out long before you did," Mari replied. "You do realize that if I was hostile to this Mage's interests, instead of killing that dragon I could've just let it turn him into a bloody smear on the rocks. You don't have to defend him from me."

"I hope that is true, but with all due respect, Lady Mechanic, the hostility between your Guilds is longstanding. We know this Mage, but we don't know you. We owe this Mage our respect, for he has saved us by his efforts."

"And I haven't?" Mari asked. "How many dragons does a girl have to slay to get some respect around here?"

Flyn considered that, but he still sounded a bit reluctant when he answered Mari. "I apologize for appearing to disparage your actions, Lady. Killing a dragon is a feat which few ever achieve, especially a monster such as that one."

Alain hoped his voice stayed properly emotionless despite his tiredness and elation. "That is the second dragon this Mechanic has slain, General."

"You've slain two?" Flyn eyed Mari, visibly impressed now, but also clearly baffled. "I hope not to meet you on the field of battle at any future time, Lady Mechanic, unless we are fighting on the same side."

"The first dragon was smaller," Mari said, mollified.

"If I may say so, Lady, it is strange to hear a member of your Guild speaking of dragons. Whether or not the first was smaller, I've never met any dragon I wished to encounter again." Flyn waved toward the carcass. "You have my thanks for the slaying of this, your *second* dragon." He looked at Alain and stepped closer, speaking quietly. "Nonetheless, Sir Mage, we owe you much for your service to us, and I must be certain that you willingly choose to be with this Mechanic, strange though that seems to me."

Alain nodded to Flyn and spoke equally quietly. "I am safe in the company of this Mechanic. This Mechanic is my friend."

The general stared back at Alain in disbelief, then at Mari, then back at Alain. "This is your friend? The one you spoke of?"

"Yes."

"A Mechanic?"

"Yes."

"I never thought to see the day. I had wondered how to describe these events to others, but now I see no need for it. No one will believe a word." Flyn stepped back again, trying to regain his composure. "Then I will no longer attempt to defend you from her, Sir Mage. But, Lady Mechanic, there is one thing I yet need to know. You have done a great deed here, and done us a great service. Now I would know what that deed will cost us."

"Cost you?" Mari lowered her head, sighing loud enough for Alain to hear. "Of course, because I am a Mechanic, and Mechanics never do a deed for free, instead charging the maximum that they can get."

"You said this, Lady, not me."

"Then here is my price, General." Mari looked up again, meeting his eyes. "You and your soldiers are to forget they ever saw me, no matter who asks."

Flyn regarded her for a long moment. "No matter who? Including members of your own Guild, Lady?"

"Especially including members of my own Guild."

Another long pause, then Flyn nodded. "That part of the price we can pay. And?"

"Oh, you want to pay more?" Mari asked. "My horse. The poor beast has been ridden hard for a few days and needs proper treatment. I'm neither experienced nor good at handling horses, so if someone else would take care of her now it would be to the horse's benefit and mine."

Flyn nodded again. "And?"

Mari gestured. "And a private campsite, fire and food for myself and the Mage."

"The Mage has already earned that for himself, Lady. We can do that for you as well, but I must tell you that after our reversal and retreat our provisions are neither extensive nor of great quality."

Alain saw Mari run her eyes across the beat-up soldiers. Alain wondered if the commons could see the sympathy in those eyes. "As long as I get the equivalent of what your own soldiers receive I'll be content, general."

"Lady? Perhaps I was not clear as to how limited our means are at the moment—"

"I will not eat better than men and women who have been through what these soldiers obviously have recently," Mari snapped. "I will have the same as them, General, nothing more."

Flyn regarded Mari once more with outright astonishment. "Very well. And?"

Mari narrowed her eyes at Flynn. "*And*, General, you will immediately cease to ask me 'and?'. If you say that word one more time, my price will go up dramatically."

The general gazed at her, then nodded. "Very well, Lady Mechanic. I accept your price, ridiculously small though it is. I do have one other question."

"Which is?" Mari asked.

"Am I allowed to use that prohibited word in other contexts?"

Mari kept her hard look for a moment longer, then grinned at him. "Certainly, General. Use the word 'and' in as many other contexts as you desire. It appears to be your favorite word and I'd hate to deny you the use of it."

Flyn barked out laughter. "A most unusual Mechanic and a most unusual Mage, and both are here with me this day. Sir Mage, if you, and the Lady Mechanic can but wait a short time, we will attend to your camp as soon as possible."

Mari shook her head. "Ensure that your injured are looked to first, General. There are some medical supplies in my saddlebags. Not a lot, but all I could carry. Since this Mage has no need of them, you may take what you require."

"Medical supplies?" Flyn paused, looking at her.

"Don't say it," Mari added before he could speak. "There's no charge."

Flyn watched her again before replying. "Lady Mechanic, you have my thanks, and I say that this time not because I must but because you have truly earned it." General Flyn looked east, toward the Empire. "I sent some scouts back down the pass a little ways, but they haven't signaled any warnings. No Imperial forces are following close upon that monster."

Alain nodded. "The dragon could too easily have turned upon them. Any Imperials continuing their pursuit into these mountains would be far behind to ensure their own safety. More likely the Imperials left the destruction of the rest of this force to the dragon."

"A good estimate, Sir Mage, and a reasonable assumption by the Imperials if not for the arrival of a Lady Mechanic whose name I shall honor." He bowed toward Mari. "I'll post sentries down the pass and we'll camp here." His gaze went to his battered force, and Flyn's smile vanished. "We paid a high price and have little to show for it but our lives. I need to send someone back to check on that forlorn hope we left behind as well, in case the dragon passed them by and left some alive. The medical supplies we have been so graciously given might serve to save even those hurt as badly as they are. By your leave, Sir Mage and Lady Mechanic, I must see to my soldiers." This time Flyn saluted them, then walked off, calling out orders.

As the general and his surviving officers directed their remaining soldiers in setting up a camp, everyone moving away from Mari and Alain, she turned to Alain and smiled broadly. "I've missed you so much. Did you miss me?"

"Every moment we were apart," Alain replied. "But how did you come to be here? It is not that I am not very...very..."

"Happy?"

"Is that the right word for what I feel?"

"I hope it is," Mari said.

"Then that is what I feel," Alain assured her. "But I thought we were agreed that it was not safe for us to be together. You are in danger when you are with me."

"I was in danger when we were apart, Alain." She looked at the nearby, immense carcass of the dragon. "And you were supposed to stay away from me to keep yourself safe, and that obviously didn't work either. I'll explain it all later. You're obviously very tired, and I don't want to talk when some passing common might overhear." She bit her lip, gazing at him. "I really want to hug you, but that'll have to wait, too. Seeing a Mage and a Mechanic embrace might be too much for these soldiers to handle."

After everything else, after having her appear, her last words were almost too much. Feelings nearly overwhelmed Alain. "You wish to embrace? You still feel as you did in Dorcastle?"

"I never stopped feeling it, not for instant, my dear Mage." Mari grinned. "I'll whisper it so no common will hear. I love you."

He stared at her, trying not to smile here where the commons could see. "You said it again. I had feared you had changed your mind, that you must have changed your mind."

"I don't say 'I love you' lightly, Sir Mage," Mari said, looking severe for a moment but then smiling again. "I meant it then and I mean it now. I'm hoping you still feel the same way." Even though Mari was trying to appear casual, Alain could see her gaze on him turn anxious.

Alain started to attempt to control his voice, but then decided not to try. "Yes. I have carried that feeling with me since we parted."

"You even sound a bit like you mean it. Have you been practicing?"

"I have. In private. It is hard to show emotion when I spent so many years trying to avoid that, but I think I am learning how to do it again. But, Mari, the danger—"

"*Later*, Alain." Her smile faded, and he saw on her the stress of weeks of worry. "There's a lot to cover." She beckoned toward the dead dragon. "Things may be even worse than I thought, though." She bent to pick up the empty tube, then hurled it off to one side, where it clattered down among the rocks. "Single-shot. That one's useless now. I can handle one more dragon if it shows up."

"I do not sense another dragon near." Alain could not stop watching Mari, the way her hair rippled in the breeze, her eyes, her lips—

"Hello?" Mari said. "Alain? Are you sure you're all right?"

"Seeing you, I am better than I ever thought I could be," Alain told her, and for some reason those words brought another smile from Master Mechanic Mari. "You are well?"

She shrugged. "Mostly. My thighs and my butt are killing me thanks to the last few days riding hard to try to catch up with you. I am not looking forward to sitting down again. But other than that, I'm still in one piece so far." Mari gave him a fond look. "You are so tired. Sit down. Relax. I'll keep an eye on things for a while."

"I will not sit while you stand," Alain objected.

"A Mage who's a gentleman! I told you that I'm not interested in sitting at the moment. It may be days before I want to sit down again. Now relax, my Mage."

My Mage. Alain liked the sound of that from her. He sat down reluctantly, feeling the weariness of the retreat and the fighting and the spells overcoming him. Alain leaned his back against a boulder as Mari stood close by like a sentry, watching him, watching the Alexdrian soldiers at work, and occasionally gazing eastward. He saw her draw the Mechanic weapon she called a pistol from under her jacket, checking it in clear view of the soldiers about, then returning it to hiding, but keeping her jacket loosely open so the weapon was easily reachable.

At some point Alain fell asleep from tiredness, waking when it was nearing sunset, Mari still stood nearby on guard, arms crossed, looking down as she heard him move. "The camp is almost ready. I think we'll have a fire and something to eat before long."

Alain tried to struggle to his feet, finding it unexpectedly hard. Her hand reached out and he took it without thinking, accepting her help and feeling a great sense of comfort in her touch. When he had first met her, Alain had not even remembered what "help" meant, had forgotten the very idea of offering aid to another. She had countered his long and bitter years as an acolyte, countless harsh lessons. He still could not understand how Mari had done it. "All is well?" he asked her.

"Yep." She gave him a smile, as if sensing his feelings. "Though my feet are starting to hurt now," Mari added, "and my butt still hurts, too, so it looks like I can't win. We've gotten quite a few looks from commons." Mari seemed amused by that. "What do you suppose they're thinking right now?"

"I cannot imagine." Alain let out a sigh of his own before he could block it. "I was taught the thoughts of others did not matter, so I am not accustomed to considering what their thoughts might be."

"That doesn't mean you can't change, Alain."

"I have already changed a great deal." Alain tried another smile.

She reached out both hands, using her forefingers to push the corners of Alain's lips upward. "Like that. And I disagree, Sir Mage. You were always like this inside. You're just letting it show now."

Mari blew out a long breath, looking upward at the peaks around the pass, her expression pensive. "No. You haven't changed. But other things have to change."

"You will make that happen. You will stop the storm."

Mari gave him a questioning frown. "That's the same sort of thing you said before we parted in Dorcastle. What . . . We'll talk about it later. Here comes your General."

Flyn strode up and bowed. "We have a site prepared for you, Lady Mechanic, in that direction, and one for you, Sir Mage, over there."

Mari's frown deepened. "Two locations? I asked for one."

The general just watched her for a long moment. "One camp. For the two of you?"

"Is that so hard to understand?" Mari demanded.

"Yes, Lady, it is. I am sorry I misunderstood, but surely you realize why I assumed that you and the Mage wished to sleep apart rather than together." A moment later the general flushed as he realized the other possible meaning to what he had said.

Mari's face darkened as well, but she kept her voice level. "We're not exactly sleeping together, General, not that it would be anyone's business but ours if we were."

"My pardon, Lady Mechanic, I did not mean to imply otherwise."

Mari eyed him for a long moment. "Do you respect me, General?"

Flyn nodded. "Yes, Lady. Anyone who has slain two dragons has earned my respect, even apart from the other services you have rendered us. I truly did not mean to imply anything. But I admit that I don't know how to handle you."

"I tend to do that to people."

"If your question is, do I still respect you because you don't act like every other Mechanic that I've encountered, then the answer is still yes. Indeed, I respect you the more because you treat me with courtesy."

"Thank you, General." Mari frowned toward the main camp. "Do you have any broken Mechanic equipment?"

The general took a moment to think. "We have a couple of Mechanic rifles which no longer work. They are all that remain to us."

"Bring them to me once we're settled. I'll see if I can fix them with what I have."

Flyn nodded again, studying her. "Am I still prohibited from asking that question?"

Mari smiled. "Yes. But I'll answer it anyway. No charge. This Mage's life is worth a great deal to me, and it seems I owe that life to you."

Instead of replying, Flyn smiled, shook his head, and left.

"I believe that you have rendered the general speechless," Alain observed.

"I'm sure it's just temporary," Mari said. "I can use the distraction of working, Alain, and it's been awhile since I've been able to fix something. Do you get a little restless if you haven't worked spells for a while?"

Alain thought about that. "I do not know. If so, I have always tried to repress it, like every other feeling."

Mari looked at him, her face somber, then away. "I never know what to say when you say things like that."

"You have said the things which showed me that another road existed, a road that I could follow," Alain said.

One corner of her mouth rose in a lopsided smile. "I guess we're even. You certainly helped put me on a road *I* never expected to follow."

A short time later Flyn returned to escort them both to a small depression sheltered by boulders on two sides, a fire already blazing in the center. Two soldiers with him tentatively offered Mari the Mechanic weapons they were holding, but she took them without comment, pursing her lips as she examined each quickly. "This one has a broken lever action. I can't do anything about that. You need a replacement part. But the other one just has a jam in the spent cartridge ejector. That's easy to fix."

Alain watched as Mari knelt, placing the Mechanic weapon on the ground and pulling out some of the metal devices she called tools. Within moments she had removed pieces from the apparently solid weapon and was prying at something, eventually giving a sigh of satisfaction and holding up a bright object. By the time soldiers returned with some food, Mari had the weapon back in one piece. "I'll trade you," she suggested dryly as one soldier offered her a tin cup filled with thin stew.

"Thank you, Lady Mechanic. Is there anything else?" The soldier took the weapon, once again uncertain.

"No," she assured him. "Thanks for the food."

The soldier stared in amazement at receiving courtesy from a Mechanic, then bowed toward her. He left with an occasional glance back at Mari, who was drinking the hot stew slowly.

"Mari," Alain said, "is it wise to act in such a way with commons?"

"I want to see how they react, Alain." Mari looked at him over her cup. "One of the things my Guild taught was that the commons had to fear Mechanics in order to respect us. I'm trying to see what happens if I treat commons differently."

"I know you must add commons to your allies, but such behavior may cause them to suspect who you are."

She lowered her brow at him. "And just who am I?"

"You said you did not wish to speak of it," Alain reminded her.

"Our relationship is no one's business but our own, Alain. People are going to gossip regardless, but I don't think any commons will guess what is really going on between us." She settled into a sitting position, wincing. "Oh, my poor rear end. I hope you appreciate what I went through to get here."

Alain watched her anxiously. "You have hurt your…"

"My butt. Yeah." She returned his gaze, puzzled. "I'll survive. Why are you blushing?"

"Blushing?" His face felt warm. What did that mean?

"Yes." Mari laughed. "Does talking about my butt embarrass you? I'm sorry. It's nothing special."

"I…" His face felt even warmer. "I think it is."

"You do, huh? Where have you been all my life?"

This time he gave her a mystified look. "I spent almost all of it inside a Mage Guild Hall. The one in Ihris. You know this."

Mari laughed again. He had forgotten how good it felt to hear her laughter. "That's called a rhetorical question, Alain. That means you're not really expected to offer a literal answer."

"Is it like your sarcasm?"

"It can be." She leaned back against the nearest rock. "Where were we before we started talking about my butt? Oh, yeah. I've spent a lot of time recently among commons while hiding from my Guild. They're not stupid. Well, most of them aren't stupid. It made me realize that just about everything I know about commons is stuff I was told by my Guild superiors. How much of it is true? I want to find out for myself. Especially considering the things we speculated about in Dorcastle, that the world is headed fast for a big smash. I wanted a better grasp of what commons were thinking."

She gave him a sidelong look. "It's like learning about Mages. Some of what I was taught is true. I wouldn't trust another Mage than you. But a lot of what I was taught was false, so I'm experimenting and gathering more information. I suppose studying something that way doesn't make any sense to you, though, because of your Mage training."

Alain tried his own stew as he thought about her words. After being trained to pay no attention to the food he ate, Alain had begun trying to taste it again, one more effect of having spent time with Mari. In this case, though, the best that could be said of the meager rations were that they would stave off hunger. "It does make some sense, because it is acceptable for a Mage to learn about aspects of the world illusion. To manipulate the illusion, a Mage must be able to see it. That is how I justified my own time studying history and the world: to be better able to grasp what I had to ignore."

"I've been around a Mage too long. That actually sounded reasonable."

Alain gazed at her. "Your idea is an interesting one. You help me see things I never see on my own."

Her smile shone white in the growing dark. "I love it when you say things like that, because I know you really mean them. You never learned the silly games most men learn growing up." Dusk was falling rapidly as the sun sank farther behind the mountains. Mari sat looking at him, light and shadow rippling across her face as the fire flickered to one side of them. "Alain," she asked in a suddenly tense voice, "can anybody see us right now?"

He looked about carefully, seeing his view blocked by the boulders around them. "I do not think so, as long as we are sitting."

"Good. Put down your cup. Over there a bit."

Alain did so, wondering why he had to put down the cup and why it had to be a little distance from him.

Mari sat down her own cup a long arm's reach distance from herself, then lunged forward, wrapping her arms about him as her lips sought his.

Alain had never imagined anything like this. No wonder the elders warned both male and female acolytes against kissing. All wisdom would crumble in the face of such a feeling.

Her hands ran down his back, her body pressed against him, and as the kiss went on and on he heard Mari gasp and then sigh softly. His own hands caressed her, touching lightly, then pulling her hard to him.

But then Mari finally broke the kiss, pushing backward to separate them, breathing heavily. "I've been wanting to do that so bad. But that's enough. We have to stop."

"But—"

"No more, Alain."

He would have argued further, but then looked into her eyes, startled by what he saw there. Passion, he guessed, but also something he easily recognized. "You fear me?"

Perhaps his dismay could be heard in his voice, because Mari quickly shook her head. "No! I'm not afraid of you."

"I could see it," Alain said, his voice low. "Fear was in your eyes. I do not want to ever cause you to feel fear. But I am a Mage, and I know how others fear Mages."

Mari cringed, then reached out to grasp his hand. "No! That's not it. I don't look at you and see a Mage. Not that way, anyway. What you saw wasn't fear of you. I swear it. I was afraid of...myself."

"Yourself?"

"Yes." She sat back, running her free hand through hair tousled by their encounter. "I've really missed you, and...well, there's been some physical longing there, too. Wanting to hold you and...all that. But when I finally had you in my arms and we were kissing and touching and...let's not go there again right now. Anyway, it surprised me how much I wanted you. That's all."

Alain could see some deception in her, but did not want to accuse Mari of lying. "I did not see surprise," he finally said.

She flinched again, looking away. "All right. It scared me. It scared me how badly I wanted you. It was so hard to stop myself, and it would have been so easy to just surrender to it. To surrender myself to you. I've never felt that before. There have been plenty of men who have tried to pressure me or charm me into bed, but I never had any trouble resisting that kind of thing. Not until just now, when all my defenses and my smarts dissolved into a hot flame. And it scared me, even though I still want you. But we can't, Alain. We're not promised yet. And...and I can't afford to take any risk of getting pregnant."

His mind fixed on one word. "Pregnant?"

"Yes. Not...not when I'm running for my life."

There was something else. He could tell that Mari was not saying everything. There was at least one other reason left unspoken. But even if Alain had been inclined to press her, he could not because of the strange paralysis that seemed to have gripped him.

"Alain?" Mari peered at him, worried. "What's the matter?"

His voice began to work again, but only haltingly. "You... children...me..."

"I don't—" She looked away, then back at him. "Maybe. I don't know. If there was anyone, it would be— Look, I'm not ready to talk about a family. All right?"

"A...family?" Where for long years a narrow, solitary path had loomed before him, now a wide plain seemed to stretch, uncounted possibilities awaiting depending on the steps he chose. Alain blinked at Mari, amazed by the change her words had wrought. "It does not happen to Mages. We do not have family. Only the Guild. But now... could this happen? With...with you?"

Mari blinked too, then wiped away tears. "Maybe. I really can't talk about it now. We shouldn't even be thinking about it. I mean, how long have we known each other? And we're in danger of our lives and fighting dragons and stuff and...have you known any other girls, Alain?"

He nodded, trying to keep up with Mari as she jumped from topic to topic. "Acolytes."

"I don't mean, did you know them," Mari said, sounding awkward. "I mean, have you *known* them."

"I do not understand."

"Never mind. I don't want to know. I don't want to know how many or anything else. Understand? You say things that other people wouldn't say. Don't tell me that."

Alain stared at her. "Do not tell you what?"

"Forget it." Mari ran both of her hands through her hair this time. "Can we talk about something else now?"

He felt confused again. "But you—"

"Something else, Alain. Get your mind off my body."

"My mind was not there before," he objected.

She laughed. "Oh, sure. I saw how you were looking at me. I know a look of male lust when I see one aimed in my direction, even though yours is the first look like that I've welcomed."

"Perhaps you are right," Alain admitted.

Mari grinned this time, her mood shift startling him. "I always wanted a boyfriend who would tell me that I was right as often as you do."

Alain tried to think straight again. "What is it we must speak of?"

Her smile went away. Mari settled back against the boulder behind her again, looking outward. "I wasn't sure I'd find you and be able to tell you again that I loved you before they caught me. It's weird, but I spent more time worrying about not ever being able to say 'I love you' to you again than I did worrying about dying."

"Dying?"

"Yeah. My Guild must know. They're trying to kill me."

CHAPTER FIVE

Alain's heart seemed to pause in its beating. "Who is trying to kill you? Your Guild?"

"At least my Guild. Maybe others," Mari said. "Dark Mechanics, Senior Mechanics, Mages, maybe Dark Mages, too. I can't tell the difference between regular Mages and Dark Mages like you can. As far as I know, none of the commons are after me, but that's probably just a matter of time." Her tone seemed light on the surface, but he could sense the tension under it, the worry.

"You believe that your Guild has learned about you?" Alain asked, wondering how the Mechanics Guild could have discovered that Mari was the daughter of the prophecy, fated to overthrow the Great Guilds if she lived.

"Well, they haven't sent a dragon to kill me, but they've tried a lot of other things," Mari said.

That reminded Alain of something else. "What did you kill the dragon with? I have never heard of a dragon being slain by a single blow."

She grinned. "A shoulder-fired, fin-stabilized rocket with a shaped-charge warhead. There are only two in the world, and I have them. Or had them. There's one left now. You have Alli to thank for those weapons. Lady Mechanic Alli, that is. She was a friend of mine when we were apprentices. Alli has always been interested in how to make better weapons and bigger explosions."

"This Mechanic Alli must be highly regarded within your Guild if she alone can make such weapons."

Mari laughed sharply. "No. She's in trouble with my Guild, even though Alli was careful. She found authorized texts describing each component of her weapon—the propulsion, the stabilizing fins, the warhead—and then she combined them into those two prototypes. After which she told the Guild, assuming in her youthful innocence that the Guild would be thrilled to have a weapon for sale that could punch holes in walls and anything with thick armor. Instead, the Guild decreed it to be a *new* weapon, and since independent innovation is strictly prohibited, the Guild reprimanded her most severely, told her never to build another one and to dispose of those two."

Alain looked toward where the dragon's carcass still lay. "But she did not do as your Guild ordered?"

Mari looked guilty. "I talked her into giving them to me. I said, 'Alli, the Guild said to dispose of them. Dispose means for you to get rid of them. If you give them to me, you've disposed of them.' Alli wasn't too sure that was a good idea, but she was angry enough at her Guild superiors that she decided to follow the letter of her orders." Mari shrugged in an unsuccessful attempt to make her words seem casual. "Hopefully my Guild won't find out what I did with one of the weapons, but how can they complain? According to them, dragons aren't real."

"Dragons are not real," Alain said. "Nothing is real."

"I thought we'd agreed for you not to say that anymore."

"You told me not to say it," Alain pointed out. "Is that how Mechanics define agreement?"

Mari looked at him, then laughed. "I'm acting like a Senior Mechanic myself. Please, Sir Mage, do not keep reminding me that nothing is real." The humor went away again, replaced by worry. "Alain, when we parted at Dorcastle I thought we needed to separate partly because I was afraid that the Senior Mechanics who run my Guild would try to kill you if they saw us together."

He nodded. "You told me that you had to go away from me to protect me from your Guild, just as I felt the need to leave you for a time in order to prevent my Guild from killing you."

"Yeah. You think we would have gotten a little credit for being willing to leave each other." She took a deep breath, staring into the flames. "Not that I could tell anyone that I'd fallen in love with a Mage. And I do love you. Even though it's completely crazy and impossible, and even though everyone else in my Guild would totally freak out if they knew. How could you fall in love with a Mage? they'd ask. That's sick and disgusting and perverted, and Mages are awful."

Alain nodded, trying to smile at her once more. The gesture still felt unfamiliar, and his muscles had been trained to avoid showing emotion, so he never knew how well it came off. "It is strange that my own Guild would say similar words about my feeling the same about a Mechanic."

Mari perked up, her eyes shining in the firelight. "You really do love me?"

"Yes. I...I...." Alain fought to say the simple words, but they stuck in his throat, blocked by too many years of unforgiving training as an acolyte, too many years of conditioning to reject any emotions or feelings for others. He swallowed, then tried again. "I..."

"It's all right, Alain," Mari said, her voice gentle. "I can tell how hard you're fighting to say it. Someday you'll be able to say it easily, and it will mean a lot to me when you do. But you've already shown me how you feel. Months ago, when you risked your life to come rescue me in that dungeon in Ringhmon, and later in Dorcastle when you stood beside me while a dragon charged at us." Another sigh, then Mari slumped back again. "If only every threat was as easy to dispose of as a dragon."

"Easy?" Alain asked, wondering how much incredulity had sounded in his voice.

"Relatively easy," Mari corrected herself. "Maybe simpler is a better word. If you see a dragon, you know it's a threat, you know it wants to kill you just because it saw you, and you know you have to kill it. Simple. Not like having to figure out who is after you and why they want to kill you and what the right thing is to do."

Alain nodded. "You seek to see through the illusion."

"Pretty much, yeah. Where was I? We separated at Dorcastle, but I didn't tell you that I was also worried that my own Guild was also a threat to me." She gave him a guilty glance. "I thought you might insist on staying with me if you knew that. Besides, it still seemed crazy then, to worry that my Guild would try to hurt me. Would a Mage be a danger to me? Sure. Present company excepted. Would a common be a threat? Maybe, if they could nail me without being found out. But a fellow Mechanic? When I had never acted against my Guild? I hadn't done anything except excel at my work, ruin Ringhmon's plan to delve into my Guild's secrets, discover evidence that some Guild secrets had already been compromised, and then uncover a plot by commons who were using Mechanic equipment and skills. Those should have been good things!"

She shook her head, staring at the flames of the fire. "Yes, I'd also learned about you, and that Mages weren't frauds as I'd been taught, but my Guild didn't know that I had learned that. At least, I didn't think they did. So why the threats and the Interdicts against discussing anything? I needed to have the time to find out more." Mari shifted position, grimacing. "Blazes, my butt hurts. I think horses were designed as instruments of torture. And my thighs. You can't imagine how my thighs feel."

"I have tried to imagine how they feel," Alain offered.

Mari stared back at him blankly for a moment, then broke into laughter. "Alain, you don't just say something like that to a girl. Everybody knows men are thinking it, but they're not supposed to say it. We really have to work on your social skills."

"What are social skills?"

"They're...um...how people avoid saying what they really think. There's probably a better-sounding explanation than that."

"Lies?" Alain asked.

"No." Mari twisted her face in thought. "More like lubrication in an engine, to keep things going smoothly." She must have noticed his puzzlement. "That doesn't mean a thing to you, does it? We don't even use the same metaphors. How did we fall in love?"

"I did not choose to do it. It just happened," Alain said. "I have wondered myself how this came to be."

She studied him closely, then smiled. "I'm assuming you mean that in a good way. Where was I? My plan. I'd keep my head down, do as I was told, and learn more. The Senior Mechanics would stop seeing me as a threat, and all sorts of wonderful things would happen. Only they didn't. I kept getting sent farther south, and finally ended up in Edinton."

Her smiles and laughter were gone once more, replaced by moodiness. She leaned forward, picked up a stick dropped by those building the fire, and began drawing in the dirt before her. From Alain's angle, she seemed to making a map. "At that point, I figured I was being out-and-out exiled for a while. Very annoying, especially when I only wanted the best for my Guild. No explanation, just 'Follow orders, Mari.' I didn't have much to do—the leadership of that Guild Hall rivals that of the Guild Hall in Ringhmon for sheer idiocy and poor management— and the longer I was stuck there the more worried I got."

Mari stopped moving or talking for a long moment, her lowered head bent over the stick in her hands. "Long story short, I got lured into a trap. A Mage using that concealment spell tried to knife me. Then someone else tried to blow my brains out with a bullet."

"A Mage attacked you?" Alain asked, feeling a sick sensation inside.

"She tried. I knew they'd been watching me. I didn't give them any reason to try to kill me." Mari looked at him. "Did I?"

"It is my fault," Alain admitted. "Even though I have tried to keep them from finding out who you are, they still believe that you are dangerous."

She gave him another look, then shook her head. "From the looks of things, I'm mainly dangerous to my friends and myself. Just how much trouble did you actually get in because of spending time with me in Dorcastle?"

Alain looked into the fire. "My Guild did not believe that I had been with you in Dorcastle. The elders thought that the woman I had been seen with in that city was a common I had sought out because she resembled the Mechanic I had met in Ringhmon."

"Why would you want to find a common who looked like me?" Mari asked.

"For physical satisfaction." The simple statement would have created no reaction in a Mage, but he saw the outraged look on Mari's face and hurriedly added more. "I would not have done that. But the elders assumed that I did. I told you that they believed I was attracted to you."

"Alain, 'attracted to' doesn't bring to mind the idea of finding another woman who resembles me so you can pretend that you're—" She choked off the words, glaring into the night.

"The elders assumed that. I never wanted it. I would never do it. There is no other woman like you."

Somehow he must have said the right thing, because she relaxed. "But because of that belief of theirs," Mari said, "your elders thought you might look for me again."

"They actually thought that you would seek me," Alain explained. "They were very concerned that you would…" His "social skills" might need work, but Alain realized that he probably should not say the rest.

Too late. Mari bent a sour look his way. "What did they think I would do?"

"It is not that important."

"Alain…"

He exhaled slowly, realizing that Mari would not give up on this question. "The elders thought that you would seek to ensnare me, using your physical charms, and through me work to strike at the Mage Guild."

She stared back in disbelief. "Ensnare? They actually used the word ensnare?"

"Yes. Many times."

"Using my physical charms?" Mari seemed unable to decide whether to laugh or get angry. She looked down at herself. "I'm a little low on ammunition when it comes to physical charms, or hadn't these elders of yours noticed?"

"You are beautiful beyond all other women," Alain objected.

Mari rolled her eyes. "And you are seriously deluded. I hadn't realized how badly until this moment. You're welcome to your illusions on that count, but please don't assume that anyone else will share your opinion. So if other Mages had seen me near you, they would have assumed I was ensnaring as hard as my physical charms allowed? Do you have any idea how revolting that entire idea sounds to me?"

Alain nodded. "I think so. I know how I felt when the elders accused you of such a plan. I thought they had insulted you, that if they had known you they would never have suggested that you would do such a thing."

He had managed to say the right thing again. Mari relaxed a bit. "Well, apparently your elders decided my ensnaring skills were too powerful to risk leaving me alive. After their knife attack failed, I think it was Dark Mechanics seeking revenge for Dorcastle who took a shot at me. And then my own Guild..." Mari paused, her expression a mix of anger, anguish, and disillusionment. "They gave me orders to go to Minut."

"Minut?" It took a moment for Alain to place the name. "That is in Tiae."

"Minut is in what *used* to be Tiae," Mari said. "My supervisors claimed that a Calculating and Analysis Device had been abandoned there when the Mechanics Guild pulled out of Tiae. Do you know what a Cee A Dee is?" Alain shook his head. "What a Cee A Dee does is think. Sort of. It doesn't really think like a person does. It calculates. Does math problems, but it does them very, very fast. And that's all it does, though writing the proper ciphers lets you use math to figure out all kinds of things and track inventories and run simulations and..." Mari gave him a look. "You're bored."

"No," Alain assured her. "I always look like this."

"No, you don't. Not like that. But that's all right, because Cee A Dees are rare, and even a lot of Mechanics don't know much about them. You warned me about the one I was going to Ringhmon to work on, though it turned out what I had to fear wasn't the device itself but what was stored on it." Mari grimaced at the memories. "Anyway, my

Guild ordered me to go to Minut, claiming that there would be a strong escort waiting for me inside Tiae. Alain, I couldn't find any sign that an escort had been sent. I had never heard of any CAD abandoned in Minut, either. My Guild wanted to send me into Tiae to get rid of me."

Silence fell for a moment, then Mari shrugged. "So, everyone is trying to kill me. Except commons. How about you?"

He waved toward the remains of the dragon. "My Guild has decided to kill me as well." Alain told her of his being contracted as the sole Mage with the Alexdrians, of the ambush and retreat, concluding with the dragon. "It is clear I was meant to die. If not for you, and if not for General Flyn, I would be dead. Why my Guild did not simply kill me within the Mage Hall I do not know. But it seems that as with your Guild, they did not wish to do it outright, rather making it seem the byproduct of a normal tasking."

"Stars above, Alain," Mari said, her voice carrying anguish, "how can you sound so detached about that? Doesn't it bother you that your own Guild tried to kill you?"

Alain shook his head. "There is no surprise in it at all, merely confirmation of a possibility that I have considered more and more likely. The Mage Guild teaches all acolytes that any threat to the Guild will be dealt with in whatever way is necessary. My Guild has decided that I must die."

"But why? I was on the other side of the world, as far as they knew," Mari said. "Did they somehow track me, to know that I was coming this way? Or did they read my mind?"

"The first is possible, the second not." Alain looked into the fire. "Foresight on the part of some other Mage is possible also, seeing me as a potential future threat. But it may be that I betrayed myself. Since Dorcastle, my ability to suppress my emotions has diminished. I know feelings are showing, not in ways which commons might see, but clearly enough for Mages to spot. My elders could well have decided that I am ruined, that my contact with you has corrupted me beyond correction."

Mari looked at him, her expression miserable. "I'm used to some people in authority not being thrilled with me, but I've never thought of myself as being corrupting before. That's strange. Some Senior Mechanics said that about me, too, that I was a negative influence on other Mechanics. What does it take to corrupt a Mage, anyway?"

"I told you. They thought that you had attempted to seduce me. Perhaps they thought that you had already succeeded despite my denials that such a thing had happened."

Once again Mari stared at him, her face darkening. "I was under the impression that your elders thought I would try that at some future point. What did you tell them to make them think that I had already put my moves on you? Or that I had already hooked you?"

"Hooked?" Alain asked.

"Ensnared." Mari got the word out between clenched teeth.

"I told them nothing. That was the illusion they wished to believe, not thinking there could be any other reason for a female Mechanic to seek my company." Alain paused in thought. "A young and attractive female Mechanic, that is."

"Oh, right. The one with all of those physical charms."

"Yes," Alain agreed.

She gasped a laugh. "I was being sarcastic again, Alain. I hope that isn't the reason you've been attracted to me. Not the only reason, anyway."

"You are very pleasant to look upon," Alain said, and Mari's face flushed again. Had he angered her? "But my elders were foolish to think physical desire alone could corrupt me. It should not have been possible with all of my training, but I found that a single shadow was by far the most important part of the world illusion. That is what doomed me, so my elders were correct in thinking that you had altered my thinking. Not with your body or other physical temptation, but with who you were and the things you did." Alain made another effort to bend his lips into a smile. "I will never be able to return to what I was before I met you."

Her face as she stared at him now was tragic. "I hope you're not trying to make me feel better by telling me that, Alain, because if so it's not working. Because of me, your Guild wants to kill you."

"My Guild wants to kill me because my elders doubt my loyalty. They are correct to do so, because I have learned much from you, and remembered much from being with you, and will help you with the task you are fated to perform." Mari gave him a quizzical look, but waited as Alain continued speaking. "The road my elders dictate is a narrow one, and I no longer believe it to be the road to wisdom. I choose my own road. I choose to do the right thing, as you call it. I would not choose another companion for that road, and should you choose to walk that road with me, it would be..." His voice faltered, unable to put words to Alain's feelings, but he met her eyes, trying to let his feelings show. Perhaps he succeeded this time, because once again Mari blushed and bent her head.

"I don't deserve you," Mari muttered. "I leave a trail of destruction in my wake. Maybe I belong in Tiae where I can't do any more damage."

"You did not go to Tiae."

"No." Mari waved at the crude map she had drawn in the dirt. "It was pretty obvious I wasn't supposed to come back alive from Minut." She pressed lips tightly together and squeezed her eyes shut. "Alain, the Guild has been my only family for a long time. You expect families to have quarrels, disagreements, but it's not easy to accept the idea that your family wants to kill you."

"Our Guilds differ. Mine regards murder as but the fading of a shadow. Where did you go?"

"I rode out of Edinton but jumped a train north, traveling by various means through Debran and on to Danalee, hiding my jacket like I did in Dorcastle so I could pass as a common. An old friend of mine from Caer Lyn was at the Guild weapons workshops in Danalee. Have I ever talked about Alli? No? Sorry. I guess we've always had a lot of other things to worry about. Anyway, Alli was still my friend.

She didn't tell anyone I was there, but told me that there was a Guild alert out for me." Mari snorted in derision. "The Senior Mechanics were supposedly worried that something might have happened to me, claiming that I had decided to go into Minut on my own. I needed to talk to someone who had a lot more pull than Alli or I, but when Alli checked with the Mechanics Guild Academy in Palandur she found out that Professor S'san had retired suddenly a month earlier. What about Professor S'san? Have I mentioned her to you?"

"Yes, in Dorcastle. A Mechanic elder you respect for her wisdom."

"I couldn't believe she had retired, Alain. Professor S'san was old, but she hadn't slowed down at all. I would have sworn she had no intention of retiring. But there was my most reliable and powerful acquaintance in the Guild, abruptly sidelined." Mari gazed gloomily at nothing. "I really hope Alli didn't get in more trouble."

She poked at the fire with her stick, sending sprays of sparks on brief, brilliant arcs through the darkness. "So, there was nothing else I could do for myself at the moment. I swore Alli to secrecy and headed for Dorcastle, staying hidden as a common and taking ship from Dorcastle for Kelsi."

"Why did you not go to Palandur?" Alain asked.

"Because you were somewhere up here, and I had a growing fear that you were also in danger." She waved toward the remains of the dragon. "I was right. In Kelsi, I paid a common to go to the Mage Guild Hall, letting him believe that I wanted to hire a young Mage whom I had heard of whose services didn't cost as much as older Mages'. Because of what you've told me I knew the Mages in Kelsi would have known I was lying if I'd gone to them disguised as a common myself, but that common I hired thought I was sincere and so didn't show any deceit when he talked to the Mages. Those Mages told the common that you weren't available, that you had a contract in Alexdria. So I went there, where every man, woman and child was chattering about the secret raiding force which had recently left on a secret mission to secretly loot an Imperial town. And plenty of them were willing to talk about the young Mage who was accompanying that force."

Mari made a face. "Do you have any idea how much junk a military column leaves in its wake? It's like soldiers shed things as they walk. After picking up some medical supplies just in case a certain Mage had gotten himself hurt, *despite* his promise to me to take care of himself, I just followed the trail of trash at the best pace my horse could maintain until I heard gunshots ahead of me, and then I hustled faster, until I saw you facing that dragon. I dismounted, activated Alli's weapon, took careful aim, and conducted a successful field test of the device." Mari grinned. "I can't wait to tell Alli how well it worked, even though I have no idea when I'll see her again. Now, it's your turn. Tell me what you've been up to."

Alain took a moment to order his thoughts. "After we separated at Dorcastle, I took ship north as my Guild ordered. Since that time I have been moved from Guild Hall to Guild Hall, I suspect because many elders wished to evaluate me. I was closely watched everywhere." He shrugged. "I did betray much more feeling than I should have, especially when I thought of you and of our time together."

"Great." Mari sighed. "That should be sweet, except it meant that you were ultimately marked for death."

"Not right away," Alain said. "I was given no assignments, though I kept asking for one. I...I had difficulty having no one to talk with, as we had. There is only one Mage I think I could talk with, though not like with you, but I do not even know where Asha is."

"Asha." Alain could not make out Mari's expression. "You mentioned her a couple of times before." Mari hesitated. "Does Asha have dark hair? And is she a little shorter than I am?"

Her voice revealed that those questions had some deeper meaning, but Alain could not think what that might be. "No. Asha's hair is yellow. No. Golden. And she is about my height."

"Asha is a tall blonde?" Mari asked, her tone of voice shifting very quickly.

"Yes. Despite her skills, she had trouble with the elders because of her appearance."

"Her appearance?" Mari peered at Alain. "I thought Mages were taught not to care about their appearance."

"Female Mages are taught to disregard any sense of personal appearance," Alain agreed. "This was a problem for Asha. No matter what she did, she always looked very physically attractive." After a long moment of silence, Alain looked closely at Mari. "Mari?"

"What?"

"You said nothing."

"What would I have to say?" Mari asked in an outwardly casual voice that sounded oddly tense to Alain. "This Asha you keep talking about, this old friend of yours, is a tall, very attractive blonde. Why would I have anything to say about that?"

There had been times when Alain was an acolyte that elders posed questions to him, questions that seemed very simple yet had contained hidden meanings. Choosing the right answer could sometimes be extremely difficult. He wondered why Mari's last statement reminded him of that. "Should I not speak of Asha?"

Mari made a gesture which seemed uncaring, but the jerkiness of it implied considerable stress. "I don't care whether or not you talk about your tall, blonde, very attractive former girlfriend. Why should I care?"

"Asha...is a girl. We were never friends. Perhaps we could have been." Alain thought he should drop it, but felt a need to explain. "The first day after the Mages took us from our families and brought us to the Guild Hall, we were very young, and we spoke together. We could have been friends, I think, in time. But we were taught not to speak, not to help. There could be no friends. I learned that Asha was a shadow. She learned not to see me as real. Anything that might lead us from wisdom caused punishment. We learned not to be anything, not to care."

Mari held out one hand, touching his cheek. "I'm sorry. I forget the sort of things you went through. Sometimes I can be a real witch."

Heartened, Alain nodded, even though he was not sure what had just been happening. "Asha was not one of those female Mages sent to me to see if I would act as expected in a young male."

Her hand dropped abruptly, her eyes widened, and Mari's face got tense again, but surely not from embarrassment this time. "Female Mages? Sent to you?" she asked in what was almost a whisper.

"Yes." Alain nodded again. "To see if I would have physical relations with them. I showed no interest. This surely confirmed for the elders that I was somehow corrupted."

Mari breathed in and out slowly a couple of times, her tension subsiding. "Just what does your Guild teach about men and women?" she asked.

"That physical relations are meaningless, only a matter of satisfying the demands of the body, while no emotional relations are permitted."

"But you turned down all of these females sent to you?" Mari's voice was outwardly calm, but once again he could sense the tension underneath.

"Yes." Alain spread his hands helplessly. "I could not stop thinking of you, and when I did those others held no attraction."

She finally smiled. "Good."

"When I failed those tests, it must have been clear how far I had strayed from the path of wisdom," Alain continued. He noticed Mari's eyes narrowing again and hastily added more. "Wisdom as my elders see it, that is. A short time after the last such test, I received orders to go to Alexdria to accompany a military force. I understand now that the decision must already have been made that I must die, as my Guild had surely already put in motion the betrayal of the Alexdrian force and the large number of Mages to be arrayed against me."

Mari exhaled slowly, then drew in a deep breath. "Why didn't they just try to kill you? A knife in the back or something?"

"I am uncertain. I think my death may have been meant to send a message. Even a great Mage may be killed by a knife in the back at an unexpected moment, but if I died while on a routine contract, it could be blamed on my own failures as a Mage and my youth. It would be an object lesson on the dangers of succumbing to emotion, and a warning against granting Mage status to one as young as I. Then, too, I have heard discussions among the elders that the shadows of the Free Cities have been too bold of late and needed some rebuke to keep them under control. The total destruction of a force of that size would have had a strong impact."

Her expression had been shifting to dismay, and now Mari lowered her face into both of her hands, her voice partly muffled by them. "If you had done what your Guild expected you to do with those women, it would have lessened your Guild's suspicion of you. You didn't have any commitment to me, Alain. You had promised me nothing. You didn't even know whether or not you would ever see me again, since you say that vision in Dorcastle is only what might be some day. You would have had every right to do whatever you wanted with those women."

He gazed at her, puzzled at the change in Mari's reactions. She had seemed upset at the idea of him with other women, but now... "You wanted me to lie with other women?"

"No! Maybe." Mari kept her face hidden, but her voice was torn with conflicting feelings. "It would have kept you safe, Alain."

"I did not wish to do that so as to remain safe. Would you have lain with other men in order to protect yourself?"

"No!" Her hands came down and her head up, Mari glaring at him. "That's different. Completely different."

"Why?"

"Because..." Her glare deepened. "Because it is. But it doesn't matter now."

Alain frowned slightly, the visible reaction reflecting his extreme level of puzzlement. "You are angry with me because I did not lie with other women."

"*No*. You are *completely* missing the point. Just forget it. What happened after you turned down all of the Mage Guild's sluts?"

He did not understand Mari's reactions at all, but decided that pursuing the question would definitely not be along the path of wisdom. "I went to Alexdria, where I joined with the military force under the command of General Flyn, neither of us knowing that the fate of our mission had been already decided. Now you and I both know of the recent past of each other. What will you do, Mari?"

She licked her lips nervously. "Give thanks that you survived, thanks that this general was the commander of the Alexdrians, and thanks that I made it here when I did. After that? More data. I need more data. Exactly what is going on and why?"

"You seek to learn more of the oncoming storm?" Alain asked, thinking of the vision he had seen.

"Storm?"

"The danger," Alain said, casting his voice lower. "The chaos that threatens all this world. We spoke of it in Dorcastle, and you said you knew all about it, and what your role was to be."

"Oh," Mari said. "That stuff. Rioting in the cities, and random attacks by commons, and disproportionate actions by my Guild, and what's still happening in Tiae? As for my role, I know something must be done, but I don't know how to do it. I want to talk to Professor S'san. I found out that she's gone to live at Severun in retirement, so I'm going to go there and ask some hard questions and not leave until I get some decent answers." Mari looked down, her clasped hands twisting uncertainly.

"But Severun is deep within the Empire, and you cannot travel as a Mechanic if your Guild is searching for you," Alain objected. "A common without travel papers trying to enter and journey through the Empire will face many difficulties and dangers."

She still did not look at him, her face lowered. She brushed back her hair with one hand. "I've got some fake travel papers."

"It will still be very dangerous, Mari. But if you believe this must be done to fulfill your task, then I will do all I can to protect you."

Her head shot up and Mari stared at him. "Really? You'll come along? I didn't want to ask. It's too much to ask of you."

"If a friend is someone who helps, surely one who cares much more for another does even more," Alain said. "I only parted from you in Dorcastle because it seemed the best way to protect you from harm. I will not willingly leave you again. And I must assist you in what you seek to do."

Mari seemed to be trying to avoid crying, even though she was also smiling. "Alain, it's not something you must do. It's your choice, though I don't deny I am very happy with it." Mari paused, then spoke with careful control. "Please think about it before you commit to this, Alain. It will be very dangerous for you."

"Dangerous?" Alain asked. "My Guild already seeks to kill me. It would have already succeeded if not for you. But most important is ensuring your safety as best I can, and helping you to do the right thing. I will not leave your side again, I will assist what you seek to do, and I will not allow harm to come to you while I live. I do not have fake travel papers, though."

Mari looked embarrassed. "Actually, Alain, I have a set of fake travel papers for you, too. I was hoping..."

"You should have known this, Mari, that I would help you."

She was smiling again as she wiped her eyes. "Maybe I should have known. But I didn't, Alain. You are a Mage, and sometimes my memories of what happened in the Waste and in Ringhmon and at Dorcastle have seemed like some kind of hallucination. I didn't know how you would react when I found you. I was actually... Alain, I was afraid that when I found you I'd discover that you'd gone back to being like you were when we first met. That you'd just look at me as if I didn't exist and walk away. I should have realized that wouldn't happen. I should have known that you'd help without question. You keep saying that truth doesn't exist, but you are true. There's nothing false about you."

He felt very good at that moment, better than he could recall feeling in his entire life. "You will sleep beside me tonight?" Alain asked.

She looked surprised, then breathed a laugh. "I don't know exactly how you mean that, but the answer is no. We maintain our distance, Sir Mage, so that our desires don't get the better of our brains. You said that you're safer with me around, and I feel the same way about you. Just like before, whatever one of us can't handle, the other one can deal with. But I won't feel safe sleeping right next to you because I'm not sure that either one of us can handle that the way we should."

"You are right," Alain agreed.

"There. You told me that I'm right again. You may not have great social skills, but you know what to say to a woman." Mari reached over and retrieved her cup of stew, sipping at it. "It's cold. Yours must be, too. Sorry."

Alain picked up his and finished it off quickly. "Between the fire and your presence, I am warm enough."

She gave him a disbelieving look. "Who told you that line? Some of the soldiers that you've been hanging around with?" In the distance, the calls of the sentries sounded, reporting that all was still well. "I'm glad they're around us now, though. It's been a little scary sleeping out here alone." Mari made a face. "Blazes, it's been scary for months, every time I wanted to sleep, not knowing what might happen while I was sleeping. I could put wedges under my doors to keep out commons or Mechanics, but thanks to you I knew those wouldn't slow down Mages. I just had to hope the Mage Guild had lost track of me, too."

"Do you wish me to stay awake and keep watch?"

"Stars above, no. I can see how tired you are. Just having you near will be enough." She sighed, giving him a longing look. "But not too near. My physical charms might be too much for you, your touch might be too much for me, and then, hey, you'd be ensnared and I'd be worrying about maybe having to knit baby booties."

"I believe that I already am ensnared," Alain suggested.

"As long as you mean that in a good way. Alain, I'm exhausted. Do you mind if I lie down now? We can talk more in the morning." Mari wrapped herself in her blanket and lay down a good arm's length out of reach of him, though close enough to the fire to stay warm as the night air cooled. She blew him a kiss, her eyelids drooping, then closed her eyes, a slight smile on her lips. Mari must have been as tired as Alain, falling asleep within moments, but her smile remained in place.

He wondered how hard she had ridden to catch up with him and the Alexdrians. From what he had seen of her on horseback here and in the Waste near Ringhmon, Mari was not a natural rider. She must have suffered on that ride, but she had stayed in the saddle until she reached him.

Despite his own weariness, Alain remained sitting, watching her a while, seeing Mari's face relaxed in sleep, the gentle rhythm of her breathing bringing a sense of great comfort. He sat under the stars, absorbed in wonder at the marvels of this illusion others called the world, letting feelings he had once forgotten fill him.

She loves me.

In danger herself, she came to see if I was safe, pushing herself hard until she found me barely in time to slay the monster that was about to kill me. I should be unhappy about that, concerned that Mari ran such risks for me when only she can fulfill the prophecy that means everything to this world. But, perhaps, the same parts of Mari that brought her here in time to save me will also enable her to save this world.

I was taught that love did not exist, that like all else it is an illusion, yet today love saved my life.

I will never again leave her.

Chapter Six

Morning dawned chill, the heights around them blocking the sun's rays. Alain could hear the calls of Alexdrian sentries reporting all well, a reassurance that the Imperial forces had relied on the dragon to finish the job of destroying the raiders and not pushing up the pass themselves. Alain took another look at the massive carcass, still frightening even in its ruin. He could not imagine commons, or even Mages, choosing to follow on the heels of such a monster.

The fire had sunk into a few glowing embers. Alain had been trained not to care about personal hardship or discomfort and so ignored the cold in the air, but found himself concerned about Mari. He pulled out a few remaining branches from their supply of wood and got a small fire going again. Mari stirred, then opened her eyes and looked across the fire at him. "Yesterday wasn't a dream, then." She sighed. "That was the first night in a long time when I didn't have a nightmare."

Mari sat up, yawning and blinking. "I must look awful. I hurt all over and my mouth feels like my horse spent the night in there. Let me clean up and neaten up a little, then we'll eat something and go see your general."

The soldiers, busy getting ready to break camp, all maintained their distance, but Alain noticed that they often took quick looks at Mari as they talked among themselves. Mari acted as if she were unaware of them, though Alain could tell she was bothered by the attention. Two more cups of stew made up their breakfasts, brought by a pair of soldiers, one of whom eyed Mari with an awed expression while the other tentatively smiled at her before both left. After using water from a canteen she had brought to wash her face and rinse out her mouth, Mari spent a while straightened her hair and clothing. "Ready?" she finally asked him.

Alain ran one hand through his hair to comb it, twitched his robes slightly to settle them properly, then nodded.

She shook her head. "Guys have it so easy." Mari led Alain toward the camp, but halted several lance-lengths short of it. "Do you mind waiting here with me?" she asked. "I'm still a bit nervous around commons."

Alain nodded in response, not remarking on the falseness he had heard in Mari's voice. She was nervous, but not for the reason she had given him. "Will you ask these soldiers to join with you?"

"Will I—?" Mari looked at him the way she had soon after they had first met, when his simple statements of how Mages saw the world had baffled her. "Join with me? What does that mean?"

"You will need the assistance of commons—"

Mari laughed. "I'm not going to use an army to get through the Empire. I'm pretty sure I explained that we were going to sneak our way to Severun. It's too bad you can't make both of us invisible with that spell of yours." She gestured toward the carcass of the dragon. "Speaking of things disappearing, Alain, why don't those things vanish when they get killed? You told me that all Mage spells were temporary, only lasting as long as you could maintain them."

"That is so," Alain said, "but you must remember that dragons, trolls and similar spell creatures are not alive and so cannot die. They are a spell designed to maintain itself, mimicking a living creature. Because they imitate a living creature, they can be stopped by the same amount of damage which would kill a comparable living creature."

She raised a skeptical eyebrow his way. "That's consistent enough, but why don't they disappear once they've been pretend-killed?"

"Because they are imbued with enough power to sustain themselves," Alain explained. "It may be enough for a few days of activity, which for these creatures means intense action. That power does not vanish if they are stopped before the spell expires. It remains within them, slowly dissipating. The same amount of power which could keep a dragon moving and fighting for a few days would take many days to dissolve."

Mari stared at the ruin of the dragon. "So it decays. Sort of like a living thing, but faster. What does it take, a month?"

Alain made an uncertain gesture. "It depends. How much power was placed within the creature? How much did it use before being stopped? I cannot imagine the remains lasting more than a month at the longest, though. After that, everything is gone. Bones, muscle, it all fades into the nothing from which it came."

"From nothing to nothing?" Mari shook her head. "That really bothers me, Alain."

"It has always bothered me as well, though I could not betray such feelings in the past."

The soldiers must have passed the word of their presence there through the camp, because only a short time later General Flyn walked up, looking at Mari with uncertainty clear in his expression. "May I be blunt, Lady?" he asked her.

Mari shrugged. "I'm finding that plain speaking is too rare in my life, General. Feel free."

"Are you truly a Mechanic? Or did you acquire that jacket under circumstances I would be better off not knowing?"

"I acquired my jacket after an apprenticeship at the Mechanics Guild Hall in Caer Lyn," Mari replied. "I acquired my Master Mechanic status at the Mechanics Guild Academy in Palandur. And I'll answer the question you didn't ask, General. I'm eighteen years old, the youngest Master Mechanic in the history of the Guild."

"A young Master Mechanic." Flyn regarded her thoughtfully. "We have heard of a Lady Master Mechanic who burned down the city hall which was the pride of Ringhmon. This Mage and I discussed that incident a few days ago."

Mari shrugged once more. "I'm not sure why you would think I had anything to do with that, but I am sure that Ringhmon had it coming."

"Anyone who has dealt with Ringhmon would agree, I am sure, Lady," the general said. "You weren't in Dorcastle soon afterwards, were you?"

"Why do you ask?"

"A matter concerning dragons that weren't dragons. The Great Guilds have put out their versions of those events, but many rumors are making the rounds as well, speaking of a young woman whose description matches your own appearance. I did not place much credence in those rumors, but yesterday the Mage informed me that you had killed another dragon before this one. Was it you, Lady, who slew the dragon seen in the remnants of a warehouse before the Mechanics Guild declared it off limits to common folk?"

Mari looked around as if seeking a way to escape, then faced the general squarely. "I'm tired of lying to people. Yes. This Mage and I were responsible for the death of that dragon and the destruction of the warehouse."

"My role was small," Alain interjected.

"No, it wasn't," Mari said, her tone sharpening. "General, I'm trying to keep a low profile. I know that commons are talking about that incident. But I'd rather not have my name linked to it in ways that will get back to my Guild."

"We don't share such stories with your Guild, Lady. It seems you have done a number of remarkable things."

"Master Mechanic Mari will do many more remarkable things," Alain said, feeling a strange sense of pride in the way Flyn looked at Mari.

Mari covered her face with one hand. "Thank you, Sir Mage," she muttered from behind the hand. "That's very helpful."

"I have already promised not to tell any that you were here," Flyn said. "I will abide by that, but I cannot swear the rest of my command will do so for long. They will not tell any Mechanics or Mages, but sooner or later no matter what oaths they swear, they will have too much ale and tell friends who will tell friends, and thus word may nonetheless filter back to the Great Guilds eventually."

Mari looked glumly at the mountains beyond the general. "I expect a good head start, General. I *need* a good head start. You owe me that."

The general indicated the camp of the soldiers. "Lady, we owe you a great deal more than that. At least six men and women who would have died last night still live because of the medical supplies you brought and gave us freely. All of us here would probably be dead but for an act of yours, slaying that dragon, for which you have asked a ridiculously small payment. I assure you that I will do all I can to confuse your trail."

"Good. I've got another deal for you."

Alain saw wariness spring into Flyn's eyes. No surprise there. Centuries of poor treatment from the Great Guilds had left their legacy with the commons. Alain thought that Mari had noticed as well, but if so she let the general's first reaction pass without comment.

"That dragon-killer of mine," she said. "I've got another. It's easy to use. Would you like it?"

The general nodded. "You know I would, Lady."

"I should let you know that you'll have to keep any other Mechanics from seeing it. If they catch you with it, it would go ill for you. In trade for the weapon, I need more food and some water. I know you can't spare a lot, but I don't have much left and will need a few more days' worth. The Mage and I need that. But the biggest part of the price is this: that you tell everyone that Mage Alain slew that dragon but died in the process. No Mechanic was here and no Mage left this place alive."

Flyn's eyes went to Alain. "Sir Mage? Do you want us to report this to your Guild?"

Alain nodded. "Yes. Word of my death will be welcome to them."

The general hesitated before speaking again. "Sir Mage?"

"My Guild seeks my death, General. I have no doubt of this after the events of yesterday."

"I see." Flyn bowed to Alain. "Then we will do as you ask, reporting your demise with as much detail as your Guild elders could possibly desire."

"That will be of great service to me," Alain said, "though it will do little good. Any Mage you speak to will know you lie."

"I am aware of that, Sir Mage." Flyn paused to think. "But perhaps I can make them think the lie is elsewhere, by claiming that my men and I slew the dragon after it had finished you. The Mages will think you must have inflicted a death-blow on the dragon as it killed you and assume we're trying to take credit for an act only one of their own could have accomplished."

"That might prove an effective ruse," Alain agreed.

"Do we have a deal then?" Mari asked.

"Aye, Lady, we do, though as the Mage says, our lies may not fool his Guild for long. Nor, as with you, will all of my troops be able to keep from speaking of him when their tongues are loosened by drink. I will do my best to bind them to silence, though, and at worst to misdirect anyone asking after either of you. Do you then plan to depart together?"

"We do," Alain said.

Flyn scratched his beard. "If I breathe a word of this I will be branded the biggest liar in the history of Dematr, even including the Mages. Very well, Sir Mage. We would be glad to escort you and the Lady at least part of the way to wherever you go."

Mari shook her head. "I assume that you're heading back west. We're going east."

"Into Imperial lands?" Flyn gave her and Alain an alarmed look. "The legions are out, Lady. This is no time to try to cross the high plains."

"We have to, General."

He eyed her, then nodded. "Getting to Kelsi or going back through Alexdria would require backtracking, would it not, Lady Mechanic? And it's plain enough that you do not want to be found by your Guild, who you expect to be on your trail. Am I right? I know ways to Palla from here, from which you could get to Ihris."

"We need to go east, General." Mari had not raised her voice, it did not sound in any way harsher, and yet it rang with a finality that demanded respect.

"All right, then." Flyn pondered her statement, then pointed. "You would be captured for certain if you go back the way we came. Well, given what you two have done, not easily captured, and perhaps even able to fight your way through. But there would be a fight, and my guess is that you seek to enter the Empire without attracting the attention a battle royal would generate."

"That's right," Mari said. "We don't want to attract any attention at all."

"There are other routes east," Flyn advised, "some unknown to the Imperials. One I know of will bring you well north of our track before leaving the Northern Ramparts. It would require three days' march, about, from this point. The track is unsuited for any large force, and for horses as well, but two on foot could make use of it."

Alain nodded. "This seems to be wise advice, Lady Mari."

He had never called her Lady Mari before, but her sudden smile at him showed that she liked hearing her name said that way. General Flyn noticed that as well.

"Horses can't do it?" Mari asked the general, then looked toward her steed. "General, it seems I have a horse for sale."

Flyn grinned. "You'll need Imperial currency. Let me see what I can scare up."

When the general returned, it was with a substantial bag of coins. Mari frowned at it. "How much is in there?"

"I didn't count it, Lady Mari. Every man and woman contributed what they could. A good amount of it isn't Imperial coin, but you should be able to get it exchanged with the money lenders in Umburan, or wherever your destination lies."

Mari took the bag, obviously disconcerted by the weight. "I'm no merchant, but I know this is too much. I have no interest in cheating anybody, and I won't take money I haven't earned."

This time the general laughed. "Did you wonder that I asked if you were really a Mechanic? The troops insisted upon giving whatever they could, Lady."

"Why?" Mari demanded.

"Because they know you saved them yesterday, Lady."

Alain looked at the general. "There is something else that you have not said."

The general nodded, grimacing. "Serves me right for speaking half-truths in front of a Mage. All right, Lady, the full truth is not just that you slew yonder dragon before it could massacre every man and woman here. It's that the troops believe that you're the daughter of Jules, of whom legend has long spoken."

Alain had no trouble hiding his reaction to the news that the commons had guessed who Mari was, but unsurprisingly Mari had more trouble with it.

Mari stared at the general for a moment before managing to reply. "The daughter of Jules?" She laughed, trying to sound mocking, but Alain could hear the worry underlying that. He could understand that worry, if Mari was not yet ready for many to learn of her importance. "My parents were commons," Mari continued, "of no special note. Why would anyone think I am related to Jules?"

Flyn's own expression remained serious, his eyes on her. "My soldiers see that you wear the jacket of a Mechanic and have the skills of a Mechanic, yet you treat the common folk with courtesy. Though a day ago they would have declared it impossible, they see that you work with a Mage who has himself proven to be most unusual. They saw you stand watch over that Mage as he slept, protecting him just as you saved them. They know you expected the same treatment as them, and gave generously to save their injured comrades. And you killed a dragon with one blow, the sort of feat which Jules herself might have done. You are like no one any of them has seen or heard of, so they hope that you'll be the one, Lady, the one the prophecy speaks of, the one who has come at last to overthrow the Great Guilds."

Mari's expression shifted rapidly through what Alain thought was dismay, embarrassment and panic, though it could have been all of those things at once and more. He suddenly realized the actual reason for Mari's reluctance to be among the common soldiers. She had sensed their hero worship, sensed that they suspected who she was, and been greatly unsettled by it. "General," Mari insisted, "that is absurd. I don't know much about that prophecy, but I doubt that it says anything about Mages and Mechanics helping the daughter. Right, Alain?"

She had asked him, and Mari insisted on what she called truth, so Alain gave the answer he had learned in Ringhmon. "Though this is not known to commons, the Mage prophecy of old does say that the daughter will unite Mechanics, Mages, and commons to overthrow the Great Guilds."

"It does?" General Flyn said, astonished.

"It does?" Mari said in very different tones, then glared at Alain. "You are supposed to be *helping* me," she whispered to him angrily.

Mari turned back to face the general, composing her expression and her voice. "Regardless of what the prophecy said, I can't imagine why anyone would think I have any role in it. I'm a Mechanic. I fix things. I'm not exactly capable of overthrowing anything, nor am I as dangerous as some people seem to think I am."

The general gestured. "There's a dragon which might argue that last point, if it wasn't dead. And then there was Ringhmon, and Dorcastle—"

"Those had nothing to do with—" Mari looked to Alain, her expression reproachful. "What have you told him?"

"Nothing," Alain said. "Almost nothing, that is."

"Listen," Mari said. "I'm a pretty good Mechanic. That's all." Mari waved both hands before her in a warding gesture. "Now, if you will excuse me, I need to get my pack together." She walked off very quickly, leaving Alain and General Flyn.

Flyn gave Alain a shrewd look. "Your thoughts are hidden, Sir Mage. I would give much to know what you believe of the Lady Mari."

"I do not believe that she would approve of my telling you that," Alain said, feeling very uncertain. Since arriving, Mari had acted as if ready to reveal herself to these commons, but now she was denying who she was.

"But you have not only told me something not known about the prophecy, Sir Mage, you have also admitted that it exists. I am not aware that any Mage has ever done that." Flyn looked in the direction that Mari had gone. "I do not ask you to violate any confidences, Sir Mage, but if she is indeed that one, she will need all the friends she can get."

Alain intended saying nothing more, but his foresight came upon him again as Flyn finished speaking. A vision appeared before him: Mari and General Flyn on horseback, their mounts facing each other, Flyn saluting her with his sword. Alain sat on a horse as well, beside Mari. Vague shapes of other cavalry and soldiers on foot could be dimly seen in the background, at least one of the mounted figures also wearing the dark jacket of a Mechanic. A banner held by one of the cavalry bore the same design as Alain had seen on the armbands he and Mari had been wearing in his vision of the future battle at Dorcastle.

He blinked as the vision vanished, then looked at Flyn. Alain had seen himself in the vision, which meant it was something that might happen, a possible event if decisions and events led there, if he and Mari survived long enough. "You may play some role in the future, General. Your talents and your determination kept me alive. I would welcome your service to Master Mechanic Mari, protecting her as you protected me."

Flyn stared at Alain. "Have you...seen something regarding that, Sir Mage?"

"I have," Alain said, knowing that Flyn was asking if his foresight had provided any clues. "You may be, on some day to come, her general."

"I would serve no Mechanic, unless she was in truth..." the general began, his voice trailing off and a look of wonder dawning on his face. "She must be. I had not dared hope. What a miracle it is that I have lived to see this day, that I have lived to meet her."

"General," Alain said, "you heard Lady Mari. She does not want it known as of yet. You know the perils that she will face when the Great Guilds hear of her. Already Lady Mari faces many threats, but when she becomes known, the storm that threatens this world will bend every effort to destroy her."

"The storm?" Flyn nodded, his eyes on Alain. "You can feel it, too, then? Everywhere there is a sense that our world trembles and threatens to shatter from strains that have been pent up for too long. That also is so?"

"It is," Alain said. "Many Mages have seen warning of the storm, have seen it cloaking armies and mobs of commons, have seen it approaching swiftly, but the Mage Guild itself refuses to accept those warnings."

"How long, Sir Mage?" Flyn asked urgently. "How long until the daughter reveals herself? How long until the storm strikes?"

"I do not know," Alain said. "There is a sense of urgency in the visions that warns time is limited."

"And she goes into the empire?" Flyn asked, his voice despairing.

"To seek answers that she needs. And she will not do so alone. From this time on, I will be with her."

"That is a great comfort, Sir Mage." Flyn turned his head to look at where his soldiers were camped. "If she announced herself today, I have no doubt that my troops would immediately march with her. And I have no doubt that we would quickly be utterly destroyed. You are surely right that she needs secrecy for now. The daughter of Jules. Of blood or of spirit, I wonder? Surely both. But it explains her to me, Sir Mage. It explains that dead dragon over there. And since you two are clearly companions, perhaps it explains you as well. Who else could awaken the man beneath a Mage? Why did you tell me all of this, Sir Mage?" the general asked. "There is no more valuable secret in this world."

It took Alain a moment to answer, as he tried to understand the reasons himself. "I...trust you." Was that the right word? He tried to remember exactly what "trust" meant as the general's eyes flashed amazement. Alain's thoughts, his feelings, were very hard to express after so many years of being forced to restrain emotion.

"Thank you, Sir Mage," Flyn said. "I am beyond astonishment, but not beyond gratitude for your trust. I assure you that it is not misplaced."

Alain inclined his head respectfully toward the general, just as he would have toward an elder of the Mage Guild. An extremely inappropriate gesture from a Mage to a common, yet it felt right to Alain. "How is it that the commons do not know the lineage of Jules, if they believe so in the prophecy of the daughter?"

Flyn pointed toward Alain. "Because of the Great Guilds, Sir Mage. According to legend, the prophecy was made while Jules still lived. Somehow, she knew of it. It was kept secret as long as possible, but Jules and those close to her knew that it would leak eventually, and that when it happened the Great Guilds would ensure the destruction of anyone related to her. Before Jules died, her children were hidden among the commons in different places. It must have been hard on her, but it was the only way to keep them alive. None know the lineage of Jules, Sir Mage, for that was the only way to ensure the daughter of her blood could someday be born and grow to fulfill the prophecy."

Who had made the prophecy? Alain wondered. It must have been a Mage, for even though Mage elders disdained the legend, he had learned that most also sought to stamp it out with a fervor that bespoke belief, and the unconventional elder he had spoken with in Dorcastle had confirmed the prophecy had been made. But why would the Mage who saw the prophecy not immediately have told the elders of that long-ago day? Could that Mage have been like Alain, discovering a road that did not require obedience to elders?

Mari returned, her pack on her back, outwardly casual even though Alain could spot the tension beneath that facade. "Are you ready to go?" she asked Alain.

Before Alain could answer, Flyn unbuckled his sword scabbard, knelt, and held the weapon hilt-first toward Mari. "My sword is yours, Lady Mari, now and for as long as I live. Whatever you command shall be my law."

Mari stared at him, then gave Alain a suspicious look. "What did you tell him? Does he know who I really am?"

"He knows who you are," Alain said.

"Then I don't understand why—" Composing herself, Mari touched the hilt of the general's sword. "I don't expect to need a sword or a general, but thank you for your offer. Now, please get up. I don't like having anyone kneel to me. Please don't do that again."

Flyn stood, smiling grimly as he refastened his weapon to his belt. "You have done me the honor of accepting my offer of future service. If you ever need me or my sword, just send word. Now, let me tell you of the route you should take." He described the way, marking a piece of paper to make a map which Alain watched Mari study carefully. When Mari had memorized the path, General Flyn stepped back and saluted. "May the spirits of all who came before us smile upon your road, Lady. Keep her safe from the storm, Sir Mage."

The common soldiers watched them as Mari and Alain walked back eastward toward where the secret route would branch off from the pass. Mari kept her gaze set forward, her discomfort making it clear she was aware of being watched, though she occasionally looked upward with a puzzled expression as if searching for clouds.

Then one of the soldiers raised his sword and began banging it against his shield in a steady rhythm. The soldiers around him began doing the same, swords, pikes, crossbows and even the two Mechanic rifles slamming into shields over and over, the thud of metal on metal resounding from the walls of the pass.

Mari had spun around at the first noise, her face wary, then stared before turning to walk away again. "Why are they doing that? What does it mean?" she asked Alain.

"I have been told that it is a sign of great respect which common soldiers render to those who they believe have earned such a gesture," Alain replied.

"Oh," Mari sighed with relief. "Then it's for you."

He glanced back, hearing some cries of "The Mage" mingled with shouts of "The Lady!" General Flyn and his surviving staff stood rendering salutes to the departing pair. Alain felt his heart stir, gladdened that these commons felt he had earned such gestures, but he knew that the display was not solely for him. "They were also impressed by you," he told Mari.

"I doubt it. By tomorrow they'll have forgotten me."

She clearly did not believe that, but Alain let it pass.

It was not until they were out of sight of the soldiers and the noise of the salutation had faded that Mari gave Alain a sharp look. "What did you tell him? That general?"

"I told him of a vision I had as we spoke," Alain explained. "It showed him saluting you while I and soldiers stood by."

She rolled her eyes. "That wasn't much of a leap into the future. He did that just before we left. Talk about a self-fulfilling prophecy. That's all you two talked about?"

"That, and who you were. I did not speak of anything that you do not wish spoken of, but he guessed much from what I could say."

Mari made an angry noise in her throat. "I hate being on display like that. Look, all you commons, it's a Mage and Mechanic together! Do you think they're lovers?"

"Lovers?" Alain asked.

"In more than the emotional sense of the word," Mari explained shortly. "I didn't like that sort of speculation by others about my love life when it was about other Mechanics, and I like it even less now because there's almost a circus sideshow quality to the guessing-games. You didn't encourage that daughter stuff, did you? I cannot believe that you told him the prophecy included Mages and Mechanics."

"But it does," Alain said. "And you have told me that truth matters. I thought perhaps you had already heard that detail of the prophecy as well."

Mari sighed. "Alain, I'd prefer not to talk about that prophecy. I'm already under a lot of pressure, and talking about that makes it worse."

"I understand. I will not mention it again until such time as you wish to discuss it."

"Then we'll never talk about it again," Mari said, her voice firm. "The last few weeks have been rough. I did tell you that, didn't I? Rushing to find you, always worrying that I might be too late...let me relax for one day at least, thinking about nothing more serious than putting one foot in front of the other." She took a deep breath, visibly trying to relax. "He should have offered you his sword," Mari declared. "Just like those soldiers saluting you. You were the one who did so much to ensure they survived." They were walking side by side, and Mari gave him a smile. She seemed vastly relieved not to be the object of worshipful gazes from common soldiers any longer. "What are you thinking now?"

"I am resolving to be worthy of being beside you," Alain answered.

She laughed. "You don't sound like you mean it, but I bet you do. A lot of guys I've met were the exact opposite. They'd sound completely sincere but I knew they didn't mean a word of what they were saying." Mari looked around. "Here we are alone together again, just like in the Waste. That seems like a million years ago."

"It was just short of four months ago," Alain said. "At least this time we have enough water."

"Yeah." The smile was gone and Mari appeared tired. "I'm worried. I'm really worried. And scared, for myself and for you. Most of my life has been spent trying to learn and understand things. Now, for the first time, I'm not sure that I want to know the answers, because of what those answers may mean. But I don't have any choice, because our Guilds have already decided that you and I need to be dealt with because of what we're going to do."

"You wish to speak of the prophecy now?" Alain asked, surprised.

"*No*. What does— Will you just drop it? If those soldiers blab about me being that person we'll have half the world trying to kill us!" Mari calmed as she looked at him. "As it is, I don't know what I'd do if I was facing this alone. But I'd already be long dead in the Waste or in Ringhmon if not for you. It's funny, but there have been plenty of times I've thought about what might have happened if things had been different: if you and I hadn't met, or if you hadn't come with me when the caravan was attacked, or if you hadn't come into the dungeon in Ringhmon after me, or if I hadn't talked to you again after we parted in Ringhmon. You would think that would have made things simpler, and it would have, because whenever I consider what might have happened in those cases I come to dead ends. Literally. Knowing you has complicated things a lot, but without you I'd have the simplicity of the grave."

He thought about that. "This is also the case with me. You have saved me more than once. My path would have ended in more than one place without you."

Mari frowned, looking ahead now. "You know, it's because you're a Mage. I mean, you're a great person beneath that, but if you hadn't had a Mage's abilities I still would have died. Having a common with me wouldn't have gotten me out of that cell in Ringhmon, and having another Mechanic along wouldn't have helped either. If I'd been a Mage, with whatever special abilities I might have had, would it have kept you alive?"

Alain shook his head. "No. I do not think so. Your Mechanic skills, your knowledge, have been very important to our survival. It is as you said in Dorcastle. It matters that we have these different abilities. I do not know that they have ever been used to the same purpose."

"You remember that? You actually do remember everything I say, don't you?"

He took a moment to frame his words properly before saying them. "For many years, after I was taken from my parents to the be trained by the Mage Guild, I was told that only a few voices should be listened to. For many years, I listened only to the elders. When I met you, when you spoke to me, I realized that other voices should also be heard. Your words, your actions, showed me that what I been told for twelve years as a Mage acolyte was not all that was worth knowing."

Mari gave him a look that was hard to interpret. "So are you just accepting everything I say?"

"No," Alain said. "Simply accepting what I am told by anyone would just repeat the error. I pay close attention to what you say, and know what you say is always worth careful consideration, but each time I must decide whether it reflects a wisdom I should accept."

She grinned at him. "Good."

The sun had not risen much farther before they reached the cleft in the wall of the pass which marked the entrance to the hidden path. Mari squeezed through first, followed by Alain. This way was narrow and often difficult as it climbed and wove through the mountains, making for a long and tiring day of travel. "I suppose it was too much to expect this route to be a little easier," Mari complained after one rough stretch.

"But you always prefer the harder way," Alain pointed out.

"Why did I ever tell you that? And I never meant literally the harder way." They found a slightly wider area walled in by heights on three sides as the sun was setting and chose to camp there, sharing some of the rations that the soldiers had given them. "We are close to enemy territory," Alain said as darkness fell, "and my Guild may still have assassins on my trail. We should maintain a watch. I shall take the first one."

Mari nodded wearily. "All right. Wake me in a few hours."

"Hours?"

She managed to look even more tired. "I forgot. How do Mages tell time?"

"We watch the sun and the stars."

"Great. When the stars tell you that the night is about a quarter over, wake me."

"A quarter?" Alain asked.

"Oh, blazes," Mari said. "Couldn't your Mage elders have taught their acolytes any math at all? Wake me when you feel like sleeping."

✻ ✻ ✻

They were higher up and the night grew colder than before, but they could not risk a fire. Mari watched the sun come up with a hopeful expression. "We should be heading downward today and tomorrow, and the path is supposed to get easier until the final stretch that will dump us onto the Imperial plains."

They had been walking for most of the morning, and Alain sought for something to speak with Mari about. Since parting from Mari at Dorcastle, Alain had paid discreet attention to commons and Mechanics, and seen that they often spoke with each other, instead of following the practice of Mages, who only spoke when something had to be said. Alain wanted to speak about the prophecy, but Mari had made it plain that she did not want to talk about that.

But thinking of the prophecy and Mari's role in it reminded him of another vision, the one in Dorcastle, and something in that vision he had not understood. "Mari, could you tell me something?"

The path had narrowed, forcing Mari to walk ahead of him so Alain could not see her face, but Mari answered in a cheerful voice. "You want to talk? That's good. What is it?"

"What does it mean when a man and a woman wear rings?"

Mari suddenly stumbled, even though Alain could not see what might have tripped her. "Why do you ask?" she replied, in still-cheerful tones which nonetheless now held more tension.

"I have seen them, and I do not know what they mean."

"What kind of rings?"

"Plain gold. On both the man and the woman."

Mari stumbled again, and this time her voice was much more tense. "They mean that the man and the woman have pledged their promises to each other. That's why they're called promise rings."

"Promises?"

"They're married to each other."

"Oh." Alain must have let emotion sound, because Mari stopped walking, spinning about to face him.

"Oh? What does that mean?" she demanded.

"Perhaps it is something we should discuss at a later time," Alain suggested.

"I think we should discuss it now, Alain." Mari searched his face. "Why did you ask me about those rings? Did you really not know what they meant?"

"No, I did not," Alain said. "Mages do not marry. It was not discussed among us, and I did not recall anything about rings from my time before being forced to join the Mage Guild."

The tension seemed to drain out of Mari very quickly, leaving some other emotions that Alain was unsure of. She turned away and started walking again, seeming oddly deflated. "I see. Well, now you know."

Encouraged but also anxious over Mari's puzzling behavior, Alain kept speaking. "It was one of the things in my vision at Dorcastle of our possible future which I did not understand, so—"

"*Your vision?*" Mari twisted in mid-step to face Alain. "*The one at Dorcastle? The one with you and me in it?*"

"Yes," Alain agreed, feeling suddenly much more anxious. "Perhaps—"

"*We had rings on? You and me? Identical rings?*"

"Yes."

"*We were married in that vision and YOU DIDN'T EVEN MENTION IT UNTIL NOW?*"

Alain took two steps backwards, wishing at this moment that he had remained silent. "It appears so."

Mari was just staring at him, so many emotions showing that Alain could not sort them out. Her voice this time was very low and very intense and made Alain very nervous. "Didn't you think that was important?"

"I did not know what it meant."

"HOW COULD YOU NOT KNOW WHAT IT MEANT!?"

Alain tried to stand tall in the face of Mari's fury. "I am a Mage and—"

"I know you're a Mage! And I'm a Mechanic who should have had her head examined a long time ago!" Mari stared off into the distance, appearing stricken now. "We're going to be married?"

Obviously, this was the source of Mari's upset. Alain tried to reassure her. "The vision only showed what might be. One possible outcome. There is no need for us to do anything we do not want—"

"What?" She was staring at him again, her expression even harder to read. "What are you saying?"

"Just because the vision showed us married to each other does not mean that we have to ever—"

"You don't *want* to marry me?" Mari asked in a soft voice that nonetheless sounded extremely dangerous.

"I..."

"I'm waiting for an answer, Mage Alain."

There was only one possible way out of this that Alain could see. "If you wish to marry—"

"If *I* wish to? What about *you*? And maybe I *don't* wish to, Mage Alain." Mari had somehow gotten directly in front of him again, leaning in so that Alain leaned backwards. "Maybe I wouldn't marry you for all the jewels in the Imperial vaults!"

"But I do wish to marry you, Mari," Alain said desperately.

"Then why didn't you tell me what was in that vision? Was it supposed to be some kind of *surprise*?"

"You are being unfair," Alain said, finally getting his mental balance again. "I did not know the meaning of the rings, and we had little time to speak right after I saw the vision."

"You managed to mention a few other things! Something about armbands and some battle—"

"I thought the battle raging around us in the vision was far more important than the rings." Mari just stared at him. "Did this one err?"

She nodded, her face still rigid with multiple emotions. "That one erred. Boy, did that one err."

"Mari, nothing in that vision is fixed, nothing in it *must* be in our future. Everything depends on our actions, on our decisions." He looked back at her, the full import finally hitting him. "We...we may be married someday?" His voice sank, and Alain felt the unfamiliar motion of a smile forming on his lips, but in his amazement he made no effort to suppress the smile. "This may happen?"

Mari's face was relaxing as she watched him. "Yes, Mage. It may happen. Even now, it may happen. Don't ask me why, but it may happen."

Alain had to lean on the nearest boulder as emotions flooded him. "It was never to be in my future. Earlier we spoke of family, but I did not realize...now it may be. And with *you*."

She had actually begun smiling again. "If you play your cards right."

"Will you help me make that future happen, Mari? That part of it?"

Her hand rested on his. "I'll give it my best shot. Alain, I honestly cannot tell you yet whether I want to marry you. It would be a very big step, and we haven't actually spent all that much time together and... and there are some other issues I need to deal with. Big issues. But we'll see, Alain. We'll see."

The fury had passed. Mari was smiling at him again, then she turned to walk onward, humming what sounded like a merry song under her breath.

Alain followed, deciding not to try to talk about anything else for a while.

He had not realized how dangerous conversation could be.

CHAPTER SEVEN

Another night in the mountains, much lower down now. Mari sat watching the stars during her time on sentry duty. She had spent a lot of time doing that since Alain had talked to her about the stars: watching the stars, and thinking. *My Guild says Mechanics came from the stars, but discourages studying them. Why? What secrets do the skies hold? Was Alain right when he wondered if everyone on Dematr came from the stars originally? But how could that be possible? Whatever the stars are, the vast majority of them never seem to move relative to each other. If there's no apparent parallax, they must be incredibly distant.*

She gazed at Alain. His face, usually still emotionless during waking periods, was now relaxed in sleep. The Mage had trouble forming anything like a natural smile when awake, but sometimes at night Mari had seen a very ordinary and very comforting smile drift for a moment across Alain's face. *Married? I really haven't considered that. He saw it, though, us married in the future. What would it be like? What decisions do we have to make to get there?*

I don't know for sure yet, but I think I want to get there.

What if Alain had told me about those rings just before we parted at Dorcastle? I'd just realized I was in love. I hadn't really thought about a future with him. Marriage? I might have run screaming in the opposite direction. Knowing that possible future then might have made it not happen.

I've had months to think about it, months to realize that it wasn't just some crazy crush on a guy who needed fixing. Now I can think yeah, maybe. I heard those common soldiers who couldn't stop talking to each other about how brave he had been, how he had saved them. That's my Mage.

I wonder what our children would be like? I've never wondered that about a guy before.

An image of her mother came then, dimmed by the years, seen from the perspective of the eight-year-old Mari had been when she last saw her mother, and Mari felt suddenly cold. *No. No. Not if I end up like her, someone who could abandon and forget about her own daughter. I can't do that to Alain, to any children. Maybe it's better if he and I never get married, maybe it's better if I never have children.*

Though, honestly, the odds of either Alain or I staying alive long enough for that to be a possibility are getting worse all the time. Mari looked west, back in the direction they had come from. *And if those commons go around telling people I'm the daughter of Jules, we won't have any chance at all. Where did they get such a crazy idea? And why does Alain seem to encourage them sometimes? I know when he says they know who I am that Alain is talking about me being a Master Mechanic, and who I am inside, and his girlfriend. Not some mythical hero who's going to save the world.*

I mean, I want to fix things, and that may mean doing some very radical stuff, but that's not the same as...

Is it?

She tried to think about other things until she awoke Alain for his turn on watch, but Mari's dreams were troubled for the rest of the night.

When Alain woke her in the morning, Mari winced at the effort of standing. "Three days of riding, followed by three days of climbing. My thighs are never going to forgive me. According to General Flyn's map we should have one last difficult stretch and then reach level ground before this day is out."

Before starting out this morning she took off her Mechanics jacket, trading it for a coat such as commons wore, carefully packing away the jacket in her pack. Alain watched her, then exchanged his robes for common clothes from his own smaller pack. Anyone seeing them now wouldn't be able to tell that they belonged to the Great Guilds, or that a Mage and Mechanic were keeping company.

The path started out that day following gentle slopes, but by afternoon the trail had grown much steeper, plunging downward at so sharp an angle that they were climbing down rather than walking. Mari saw the narrow gap ahead with relief, and as the sun sank behind the Northern Ramparts again she and Alain stepped onto fairly level ground at the foot of the mountains.

Mari pulled out a large map she had bought back in Kelsi, spreading it upon a nearby rock. "Any idea how far north we are of the pass you used?"

Alain peered toward the south. "I see nothing familiar."

"I think we're about here," Mari suggested, tapping the map. "Flyn thought we would be far enough north to avoid any Imperial forces guarding the pass. That means we need to go east from here until we cross this stream," she continued, tracing the route with one finger, "then cut southeast to get back into farming country. According to the map, this area around us is supposed to be used for grazing herds, but I don't see any."

He gazed around, looking at the plains rolling gently off to the north, south and east. "It is autumn. The herds would have been brought in by now, taken to market for sale or slaughter, or moved to sheltered areas for the winter."

"How do you...? Oh. Your parents' farm?"

"Yes."

Mari hesitated, seeing how Alain was closing down his feelings, reacting to the pain of the long-suppressed memories this area was bringing out. His voice had, for a moment, softened and gained a more youthful quality, before a Mage's unemotional tones came back in control. "Alain, I—"

"Let us not speak of it now." He turned a troubled gaze her way. "Please."

She nodded, making herself smile. Because of his training as a Mage, Alain had incredible difficulty saying please, so it only came out when he expended great effort. That told her how upset he was right now. "Sure. Whatever you say." Seeking something else to talk about, she bent back to the map. "Anyway, if we run into any legionaries we'll say we're out hiking and show them our forged Imperial identity papers."

"What is hiking?" Alain asked.

"Walking for fun," Mari explained. "I mean, you're walking long distances, but not because you have to. For fun."

Alain gazed steadily at her. "Walking long distances, for fun. Are you saying a joke?"

Mari shook her head. "I know it sounds like that, but people really do it. Anyway, once we're back in farming country we'll hit the main road to Umburan and Pandin and can follow that all the way to Severun."

"It does not appear to be too difficult," Alain agreed. "But I remember being cautioned that maps carry their own illusions, often making appear simple a journey which is actually far more difficult in practice."

"Let's hope not." Mari bit her lip, folded the map, then reshouldered her pack with a heavy sigh. She felt helpless to do what she wanted to do the most, to give him comfort. All she could do was lean in and kiss him quickly, which did bring a spark of life back to his eyes. Giving Alain another encouraging smile, she led the way as they started walking away from the mountains.

Neither talked much for the rest of the day. Mari didn't know what to say, and suspected that Alain was trying to sort out his own feelings. They reached a wide, shallow stream with low banks as the last light of day faded, drawing a relieved gasp from Mari. "Just about where it should be. We're not lost." Tired out by the trip through the mountains, they stopped on the banks of the stream.

Mari took the first watch, looking out into the darkness, comforted by the presence of Alain and by the murmur of the stream, but also worried that the noise of the water could conceal the sound of enemies sneaking up on them. *Is this what the rest of my life is going to be like? Worrying about people trying to kill me? And I have to worry about Alain even though we're together again. It's because of me that he started remembering things, and that's good, but I can only guess how hard it must be for him sometimes.*

If only his mother and father weren't dead. If only I could take him back to them, so they could see what kind of man he has become and so he could have a family again. Surely Alain's parents wouldn't do what mine did. Surely they wouldn't reject him.

They didn't have much food left in the morning, but Mari expected to reach a populated area by nightfall. "Even if all we find is one farm house, they'll sell us some food and give us directions."

"Yes." Alain's voice had gone totally dispassionate once more.

"What's the matter? Tough memories again?"

He stared into the distance, then spoke slowly. "Yes. This area is similar to where I grew up, before the Mage Guild came for me. The memories it brings should be good memories," Alain answered, still outwardly emotionless, "but they bring hurt. It was much easier when I denied them."

"I'm so sorry." Mari watched him, feeling powerless to help again.

His eyes rested on her. "You bring me memories which do not hurt. You helped me remember things I should never have tried to forget. Thank you."

Mari smiled. "I remember the first time you said thank you to me and how shocked I was hearing it from a Mage. Now I bet you say that to all the Lady Mechanics."

"I do not talk to other Lady Mechanics."

"I know. That was a joke. I'm glad you're not sorry you got to know me. Let's get going. I don't like being alone out here. The sooner we can blend in with the Imperial population the safer we'll be. It's not hard to cross here," Mari added as they waded through the stream.

"We are fortunate," Alain told her. "It is more difficult downstream."

She felt a shadow cross her mind. "Where that bridge was? Where you almost died?"

"Yes."

"I'm really proud of you for that, but don't do it again. I'm being selfish. I need you." Mari waved one finger at Alain. "Don't be a hero."

He regarded her impassively. "Even if you need a hero?"

"That would be different. But we're going to try to avoid that from now on. We're going to be safe and quiet and no one is going to try to kill either of us for a while."

"You do not believe that."

Mari narrowed her eyes at him. "You know, I'm starting to realize that there are some disadvantages to being with a guy who can figure out how I feel about things. How about letting me have some illusions?"

"Everything is an illusion," Alain replied. "Today is my birthday," he suddenly added. "I am eighteen years old."

"Really?" Mari forced herself to smile again, wondering what Alain was thinking now. Maybe about his parents. Maybe about birthdays when he was very young, before Mages took him from his family to become an acolyte in one of their Guild Halls. So many hard memories, so many things in Alain's life which had been lost. What could she say? "Congratulations. I'm sorry I forgot to bring a gift."

He nodded, then the rigidity of his face finally cracked and Alain tried to smile at her. "Mages do not celebrate birthdays. They only mark them. But you have brought a gift. Your presence with me is a great gift, one greater than I had ever imagined."

Mari felt her face warming, wondering if she was blushing like a school girl. "You're easy to please, but thank you. I mean, you're welcome. Whatever. We'd better get moving. We have a long way to go today."

They spent a long morning tramping across rocky fields which rose and fell like lengthy ocean swells frozen in place. Aside from a few small abandoned sheds apparently used by ranchers during the summer, they had seen no signs of people or buildings. In part that was a relief, since Mari wasn't looking forward to encountering Imperial legionaries. But the emptiness also wore on her. She had spent most of her life indoors, within the rooms of Mechanics Guild Halls or the Mechanics Academy in Palandur, and in cities. The vastness around her now made her slightly dizzy at times.

By noon, though, Mari could see far enough across the landscape to spot in the distance the road they sought. "We'll be there before nightfall." She turned to smile encouragingly at Alain and then stopped, her smile fading, as she caught sight of the sky to the north. "That looks ugly."

Alain turned as well, his face growing rigid again as he studied the skies. "Those clouds look very bad, and they are moving fast."

"Yeah. This way," Mari agreed. "Is that the storm the general warned about?"

"No," Alain said, slight puzzlement in his eyes as he looked at her. "He warned of the storm of violence that threatened this world."

"Allegorical storm," Mari said. "All right. Those clouds aren't any allegory, though."

Alain shifted his gaze back to the north. "I have a memory, from my life on my parent's ranch, of being warned of clouds like that. I was warned to reach shelter fast if I saw such a sky. Run home, I was told. Run home."

Mari nodded, fighting a twinge of fear. "I don't see anything that looks like shelter. We'd better get walking faster."

They picked up the pace, heading for the road at the best clip they could sustain. At one point Mari saw riders and a wagon hastening down the road, still far too distant to hail for help. The lack of other traffic on the road was itself a glaring warning sign that the local inhabitants had already headed for cover.

All through the afternoon the clouds built, rising behind them in great roiling sky-mountains dark with menace. The sun vanished as the clouds blocked its rays and a chill wind came moaning down from the north. Mari and Alain paused long enough to pull what other protective clothing they had from their packs. Mari took another look at the clouds, thinking that what clothes she and Alain had weren't nearly heavy enough to deal with what that weather was bringing. After a moment's hesitation, she pulled off the shoulder holster that held her pistol and stuffed it and the weapon well down inside the pack as well. As a final precaution, they draped their blankets over their shoulders for more protection and so they could improvise head coverings if needed.

They altered their track a bit, bearing to the east as they closed on the road, and the wind shifted as well, coming around to strike them in the sides and the face. Mari gasped as the cold hit. "This is off the Bright Sea. Alain, how can there be a blizzard out of the north in the fall?"

"It is late fall," Alain stated, his face and voice betraying grimness. "Such storms are rare but not unknown. When they strike, they can be terrible."

"We need to get into shelter."

Alain swept his hand across the horizon. The land still rose and fell in slow gradients, but no sign of buildings could be seen. "All we can do is seek the road. If there is shelter, it will be along there."

Even though it wasn't yet sunset, the sky had darkened to an ominous gray tinged with yellow. The cloud cover had overtaken them now, reaching ahead to swallow the clear skies before them. To the north, the sky under the clouds was dark with curtains of falling precipitation. Mari and Alain walked quickly, still setting the best pace they could as the wind whipped at them.

Rain started to fall, large, hard drops spattering onto the ground and striking the two walkers. Mari wrapped her blanket over her head as best she could, knowing it would soon be soaked with the chilly rain but needing to keep out the cold. Within minutes, though, the rain changed to sleet, icy particles stinging their exposed skin.

Then came the snow. Big, fat flakes hurtling down under the wind's lash to quickly accumulate on the ground. Mari blinked her eyes clear, feeling an icy fear inside that matched the cold outside. *What have I done? We're here now because of me and we're stuck out in the open in a blizzard. What have I done?*

Alain shouted something and Mari looked down to see they had struck the road at last. Turning to follow the track, they leaned into the storm, plodding ahead and staring forward for any sign of safety. But the swirling mass of white kept them from seeing more than a lance ahead now. "Alain, I'm sorry!" Mari cried, unable to keep it inside any longer.

"For what?" he called back, the impassiveness of his voice a comfort now.

"For leading us into this. I saved you, but now I've led you into this and I don't know how we'll survive."

"Mari." His hand fell on her shoulder and gripped her. "It is not your fault. No one can predict these storms. And I chose to walk with you. I do not regret that."

"Alain, we're already tired and we have no idea how far it is to any shelter. We could walk past shelter in this storm and not even see it!"

"But we must keep trying," the Mage insisted. "Remember the Waste, when you would not let me give up. You were right then. To survive now we must keep moving."

Mari blinked away snow again and rewrapped her blanket head covering. "Yeah. I guess so."

They couldn't tell whether or not night had fallen, since the blackness had become so complete and the snow limited sight. Drifts began forming and blocking their way, so that before long they were slogging through snow past their ankles and in some places up to their knees. By now Mari couldn't even tell if they were still on the road or if they had wandered off to one side into the empty fields. The crunch of Alain's boots in the snow told her that he stayed just behind her, but otherwise the only sounds were the howling of the wind and the spattering of the snow against her.

Mari stumbled, barely catching herself in time to keep from falling. *I can't keep this up. Not much longer.* She squinted against the brutal wind. "Alain!" she shouted through lips gone numb. "Listen, if I fall, you keep going, you understand me?" He didn't reply. "Alain! Did you hear me?"

"I heard you!" he finally called to her over the moaning of the blizzard. "I will not leave you!"

"Listen, you fool, if I fall you won't be able to carry me! We'll both die out here if you stay with me!" A wild swirl of icy snow battered them, then passed on. "So if it comes to that you go! Just keep walking and get yourself safe!"

"No!" Alain's voice, which had barely carried over the storm before, came clearly this time.

"I'm not asking you! I'm telling you! I won't have anyone dying for me! Especially not you!"

"No! I would rather leave this dream in your company than continue to live in it without you!"

"*I don't care*, you wretched Mage!" Tears were welling in her eyes, freezing on her cheeks. "If I fall, *leave me!*"

"I will not take orders from a Mechanic!" Alain shouted. "And I will not leave you, just as you would leave no one behind. We will live together or we will die together and enter the new dream hand in hand."

Mari glared into the blinding sheets of snow and sleet being hurled at them, her anger bringing the first hint of warmth she had felt for a seeming eternity. "You're an idiot, Mage! Have I told you that?"

"I do not think so."

She realized he had sped up slightly to be next to her, then felt something on her arm. "What are you doing?"

"Tying us together so we will not lose each other in this storm. We should have done that already. I had forgotten, though. My father's words come back to me." He leaned his head close, but it was so dark and her eyes were so weary from the storm that all Mari could see of Alain's face was a blur. "We are in this together, no matter where it takes us."

"I don't want you to die!" she cried, tears once more fighting their way out against the wind and joining the ice on her face.

"And I do not want you to die. So we shall stay together, and we shall continue putting one foot in front of the other, until we either reach safety or we lie down together for the last time."

"You are such a fool, Mage. I love you."

Even over the storm she could hear the struggle as Alain tried to voice something he had been trained never to say. "I...I...love you."

"Stars above, you said it. You managed to say it." More tears, trickling out to freeze against her cheeks. Why now, when their lives seemed to have very little time left? "If you love me, then leave me. Leave me when I fall so that I can die knowing you still have a chance to live."

"No. We seem to be made for each other's company, so I will not deny destiny by ever leaving you."

She managed to rouse one last protest. "I don't believe in destiny!"

"Then I will believe for both of us. Do not talk anymore. Just walk."

And she did. Thinking angry thoughts of Mages too stubborn to pay attention to common sense, of boys so blinded by love that they wouldn't do what was obviously the necessary thing, Mari kept raising a foot, planting it a little farther forward, then raising the other foot. She pulled her head covering over her completely, trying to give her face what protection she could, and trusted in Alain to guide them while she muttered a continuous string of comments through numbed lips about his failure to be reasonable. Every step was an agony, but Mari kept going without any idea where she was getting the strength to keep lifting her feet and moving them forward, time after time. *I can't let him die out here. If I stop, he'll die. So I have to keep walking. Why is he doing this to me? If he'd just leave, I could lie down and sleep. Couldn't I? He said that he loved me. He said that he'd never leave me. Do I ever want to leave him again? Not if I can help it.*

Well, he may be an idiot, but he's my idiot.

I won't leave him and I won't let him die out here. A fresh gust of icy snow staggered her. *But if worse comes to worst, at least we'll die together. Like Alain said, hand in hand to whatever comes after this world.*

Chapter Eight

She walked on, step after step, for how long she could never say afterwards. Her leg muscles burned until she thought she couldn't stand it another second, and then they burned even worse. Her feet felt like inert sacks of sand, her lungs were seared with each breath of icy air she took, and her face seemed to be getting pricked with innumerable needles as the wind lashed it through the covering. The weight of her pack became unendurable, but she couldn't shed it with her arm tied to Alain's, so she hunched forward a little more and kept enduring the burden.

There came a moment in the endlessness of her torment when the wind slackened, as if they had come into the lee of some kind of shelter. Part of Mari noticed, but she couldn't rouse the rest of herself to do anything but keep walking. Then her boots clumped on wooden boards instead of snow drifts. Then there was a light and she finally stumbled to a halt with Alain beside her, raising arms that seemed barely able to function to lift the covering from her head. Blobs of lantern light. Alain raising one hand to pound on a door until the door swung open and more light spilled out. Vague shapes of people.

Without the need to keep planting one foot in front of the other Mari found herself swaying, every ounce of her either numb or screaming with pain and no strength anywhere. Her legs gave way and she started falling, staring blankly at the doorway of light. Alain could not support her and fell with her. Hands grabbed at her arms and then there was nothing but a deep dark where she could feel nothing.

✳   ✳   ✳

Mari woke surrounded by darkness and felt a moment's stab of fear, wondering if her last memories had been a hallucination and she had actually collapsed in the open and now lay buried beneath the merciless snow. Then Mari realized she could hear the sound of the storm still raging, but muffled. She blinked into the darkness, her weary eyes having trouble focusing, until she could make out walls around her which shook occasionally as a particularly strong gust hit. She turned her head, making out the dim outlines of a very small room. A little window in one wall showed nothing but the backs of storm shutters closed tight, small drifts of snow nonetheless penetrating to the inside. Mari was surrounded by a softness and a warmth that even her numb, aching body could feel. *I'm in a bed. We're safe. We?*

Where was Alain? Another bolt of fear went through Mari and she managed to prop herself up on one elbow, scanning the room. She almost missed him, then spotted Alain on the floor. He was rolled in a blanket, lying next to the bed, his face slack with exhaustion. Mari stared until she could be sure he was breathing, then collapsed back onto the bed and passed out again.

The next time she awoke the sounds of the blizzard had diminished a bit. A trace of weak light could be seen outlining the storm shutters over the little window. Mari lay still for a moment, staring up at the ceiling and wondering how someone could hurt this badly and still be alive. At least she was lying on a mattress, covered by a thick comforter. Then her conscience came to sit on her chest and stare accusingly at her. *I'm in a soft, warm bed. The guy who saved my life is lying on the floor.*

She pushed herself up again, seeing he hadn't moved from his place next to the bed. "Alain." Her voice came out in the barest whisper. She swallowed and tried again. "Alain."

The Mage stirred, blinking around with bleary eyes, then looked up at her. Too exhausted to maintain emotional control, his cracked lips bent in a small, slow smile. "Mari."

"Get in this bed."

"What?" Alain blinked some more.

"Get up here. I won't have you sleeping on the floor while I'm comfortable."

"But, Mari...your bed...you said...not too close..."

"Listen, you silly Mage, we're both fully clothed except for our boots, I hurt all over and can barely move, and the last thing on my mind is any form of exercise. Now get up here."

"But...you are sure?"

"Alain, if you don't get up here right now I'm getting out of bed and lying on the floor, too!"

That threat stirred him into motion. Groaning, Alain came to his hands and knees, then managed to pull himself up into the bed. He tried to lie right on the edge, as far from Mari as possible, but the bed was so narrow she had no trouble reaching out, grabbing him, and pulling him close, flipping the comforter over him as well as her. "Neither of us is a threat to the other's virtue right now, Mage." His body, tense at first, slowly relaxed in her arms. It felt good, even through the pain in her body. Holding Alain felt very good. "Why did I take so long to do this?" she murmured. "Are you all right, Alain? I mean, I'm sure you hurt as bad as I do, but are you all right?"

His voice sounded strained. "I will live. I will stay with you." His arm tightened around her for a moment.

"Don't get any ideas," she warned drowsily, already feeling worn out from her burst of effort. "We still have to wait. But I know I'm safe with you beside me here. Once I can move again, I'm going to kiss you. I don't care how bad my lips hurt. You're going to get kissed like you've never been kissed before."

"You are the only one who has ever kissed me."

"Let's keep it that way." She sighed, feeling a joy at his presence through the pain in her body. "You saved my life. I wouldn't have made it without you."

"Do you think I would have been able to keep going without you?" he asked.

Instead of answering, Mari smiled and snuggled her head against his shoulder, then surrendered again to her exhaustion.

❀   ❀   ❀

A noise startled Mari awake. Alain was no longer beside her. She saw a middle-aged woman standing near the narrow door to the small room, watching Mari with a smile. Mari looked around frantically. "Where's—?"

"Your young man?" the woman asked. "Getting a warm soak. He wanted to wait for you to awaken, but I told him the water wouldn't be getting any warmer and he needed it. From the way he looks, I believe he's still in shock."

Mari tried to gather her thoughts. *The way he looks? The lack of emotions showing! I have to cover for Alain.* "He...he's usually pretty impassive. That's just the way he was...brought up."

"Well, he smiled a little at you, so I'm sure he's not a Mage." The woman took a step closer. "I'm Jana. And I'm a healer. I took refuge in this inn, fortunately for you." The healer shook her head in wonderment. "Maybe it's because you're young. You came out of that in better shape than you had any right to. You and your man."

"My man? Inn?" Mari rubbed her forehead with both hands, trying to collect scattered thoughts. "The storm. We reached an inn?"

"That's right. I can't imagine how." The healer sat down on the edge of the bed and patted Mari's knee. "Even a Mage would have trouble finding a building in that blizzard." The healer leaned closer and whispered. "We've got a few of them sheltering here, too. Staying well away from everyone else, thank the stars." Then she straightened and spoke in a normal volume again. "But as I was saying, you and your man came out very well. A miracle, seems to me. How long had you been walking?"

Mari stared blankly at the wall. "I have no idea."

"Huh. Strange how things work." The healer leaned back slightly, gazing into the distance. "I've seen it before. People get caught on the plains. It's the footloose ones, the ones without anyone to live for but themselves, that seem to die. Folks with someone close they love, they somehow keep alive more often than the others. In some way that gives them some extra strength when they need it." She gave Mari an apologetic look. "I'm sorry. I've been assuming because I found you holding each other in the bed. You and the lad, you're traveling together like that?"

Mari nodded. *Like that. We don't have to remain at arm's length anymore. I can trust myself with him. At least when I'm totally exhausted.* "Yes. He's all right, too, you said?"

"He's in fine shape for a boy who almost died in a blizzard not much more than a day ago," the healer remarked. "You slept a good long while. How'd you come to get caught out there? The skies warned of it."

Still weary as she was, Mari couldn't think of a good lie. "We're not from around here."

"I knew that from the accent, girl. Where did you come from?"

"Palandur." That's what the forged Imperial identification papers said, anyway.

"Palandur! City dwellers! And you survived a blizzard on the plains near Umburan! That's one for the records." The healer spotted Mari's pack. "Can I get you some fresh clothing or anything else?" She reached for the pack.

"No!" Inside the pack, right on top, was her Mechanic's jacket. Deeper inside were tools and her pistol. If anyone here saw any of that, it would be very hard to explain. However, arousing suspicions wouldn't help either. For that reason, Mari instantly regretted her strong reaction. "I'm sorry."

But the healer just paused and then pulled her hand back. "Personal things in there?" the healer suggested with a small smile. "Two young ones out in bad weather, far from home, like they're running from something." Mari tensed as the healer continued. "What's the problem, dear? His parents or yours?"

Mari stared blankly at the healer for a moment. Then she got it. *She thinks Alain and I are eloping. That's as good a cover story as any. Better than most. Considering that our Guilds are the closest things we've both got to parents now, it's even true in a way.* "Both."

"Ah, the worst of both worlds. Are you eighteen?"

"Yes," Mari answered for herself, then remembered Alain's words alongside the stream. "Both of us are eighteen."

The healer shook her head. "Then you're both legal and old enough they shouldn't be trying to dictate to you. But I know sometimes it still happens. I won't pry for details." She sighed heavily. "Folks regret that sort of thing, you know, with time. The best advice I can give you is to offer them another chance some day. You and your man out there. Especially if a grandchild comes. Most people come around then."

Grandchild? Mari hoped her reaction hadn't shown. *A grandchild to the mother who abandoned me without a second thought?* Mari barely suppressed a shudder of apprehension and tried to keep her voice calm. "Thanks. I'll remember that advice."

"Good." The healer's face turned very serious. "Then I'll give you one more piece. Or maybe just a warning. Since you came in during the storm, you don't know who all's sheltering here besides you. A girl your age should know there's Mechanics staying here."

Once again, Mari had to fight to suppress her reaction. "Mechanics?"

"I can tell you're worried, and well you should be. A girl like you should be wary. Just like Mages, Mechanics have been known not to take no for an answer."

Mari had seen that, intervening when she could, never liking it, never allowing it to go too far in her presence. But she had heard stories, and now, without her jacket, she was as vulnerable as any common girl and she liked it even less. Her initial reaction had been fear of discovery, but following that came a greater sense of outrage.

Her eyes must have betrayed her anger, because the healer shook her head. "We have to endure it. You know that. Maybe it's different in Palandur with the emperor's eyes on them, but up here the Mechanics often do as they please."

"Mechanics don't care what the emperor thinks," Mari said in a low voice.

"That wouldn't surprise me a bit, but if you know them that well, you know enough to keep out of their sight. The women, too. Sometimes they want a personal servant for a while who they don't have to pay, or they just feel like humiliating us."

"I know," Mari said again, her eyes averted from the healer.

"Some bad memories, there?" the healer asked gently. "Sorry I brought them up."

"That's all right. Thank you. I'll exercise care." What were the Mechanics here like? Like the decent ones, or like the ones who enjoyed treating the commons as if they were slaves?

What would this healer think if she knew that Mari was a Mechanic? She would be afraid of Mari. She might well hate Mari. And both feelings would be justified by the healer's experience with other Mechanics. The knowledge made Mari feel slightly ill again.

The healer fussed over Mari a little while longer, then left with advice that Mari and her man get some food in the inn's dining hall as soon as they felt up to it. Mari sat in the small room, staring at the door.

After a while the door opened slowly and Alain stuck his head in, then managed another brief, tiny smile when he saw her awake. "I did not know if you were still asleep." He had put on fresh clothes, which clashed with the weariness still apparent on his face. Alain shut the door, then he just stood there, watching her with a very un-Magelike amount of anxiousness in his expression, looking somehow younger then usual.

Mari smiled back. "You've been smiling more. I like it. How do you feel?"

"I have been better, but have taken no serious injury and suffer no illness. You?"

"I think I'll be all right." She patted the bed. "Come over here and sit down. I want you close."

"Still?" The tiny smile flickered across his face again, and Alain came to sit beside her, his eyes on hers. "I wondered if you would regret taking me into your bed."

"Uh, Alain, that's not exactly what I did." He started to say something. "Yes, I know you slept beside me, and it felt wonderful to hold you. But we didn't sleep together."

Alain seemed baffled. "Yes, we did."

Mari sighed. "No, we didn't. We slept next to each other, which means we slept. 'Sleeping together' means the same thing as saying that a woman has taken a man into her bed, and both of those mean a lot more than sleeping has been going on."

Alain nodded, his face serious. "I see. Physical relations. Then if someone asks, I should say we sleep next to each other but not together?"

Mari was sure her startlement showed. "If anyone asks, you tell them that it's none of their business! What you and I do in bed, or don't do in bed, is our private affair."

"Private? Is this one of the social skills things?"

Are you sure you want to get in a very serious relationship with a Mage, Mari? "Mages don't understand privacy? The idea that some stuff is personal and doesn't have to be shared with other people?"

Alain appeared to be having trouble with the concept. "There are no other people. That is what Mages are taught. I have told you that. Why would a Mage speak to shadows of anything but what was absolutely necessary to say?"

"Oh. That makes sense, I guess. Don't Mages have things they keep from other Mages?"

"Secrets." Alain nodded. "We are not supposed to keep secrets from elders, but elders can order Mages not to tell things to other

Mages." His eyes lit with understanding. "Like the secrets I have kept about you. This is privacy?"

"Yes," Mari said. "Things you shouldn't tell other people."

"I will remember," Alain said.

For some reason, that made her giggle. "You know, you really are perfect. Except for a few things I can fix. Strong enough to keep me alive no matter what is trying to kill me, but willing to listen to me. What did I do to deserve you? And that reminds me. I owe you something."

She leaned forward and kissed him, wincing as her badly chapped lips met his, but didn't pull away. Her arms went around him, holding him tightly. The kiss lasted, and she felt his hands leaving her back and drifting downward. "Alain..."

The flash of disappointment was human enough that Mari was glad to see it. "No more. I understand."

"I don't expect you to like it, my love." She laughed. "Just respect it. Don't push me. I don't handle it well when people push me."

Alain's hand tentatively stroked her hair. He was holding her clumsily, unused to this amount of human contact and probably rendered more awkward by his feelings. "You are difficult. I already know that. I accept it, because it is part of you."

Mari smiled. "You might feel differently after living with it for another few months."

"I do not believe so. I would...what were the words you used? I would give you my promise now, if you would like that."

Mari went rigid. Her eyes locked on the fabric of Alain's shirt and her breathing speeding up. "You just proposed to me. Do you know that you just proposed to me?"

"Is that wrong? The blizzard made it clear in my mind. I wish to spend all my days with you. Just as the vision in Dorcastle showed."

She couldn't help smiling again, despite the anxiousness she felt. "Alain, I can't give you my answer yet. We need to know each other better. If we make promises now, we might regret it later. There's things about me that you don't know yet, that you may not like or may not be able to live with. I don't want you to feel bound to me by your promise, especially when I don't know what we'll face in the future."

"You are worried about a Mage feeling bound by a promise?"

She made a fist and rapped his shoulder. "You're not a Mage in that way. You're Alain. And yes, I don't want you ever to stay with me because you feel bound to me. I want you with me, but I want you there because you want to be there."

"That will never change," Alain said.

"Never say never, Alain. Things can change very quickly sometimes." Mari pushed aside the sudden feeling of sadness as thoughts intruded of the family she had once had. "Not that I ever want them to change for us, except for the better. But we're facing a...very difficult situation right now. We ought to concentrate on staying alive, and on getting the job done."

He nodded. "A task of great difficulty lies ahead. You are still weary and I have been keeping you from the bath the healer has ordered. Once you are better, we can go in search of the dining hall together."

"Yeah." The time in the bath would probably help her get her head together again, too. Mari straightened and stood cautiously, finding she was wobbly on her feet but could stand. "The healer told you about the Mechanics and Mages here?"

"Yes." Alain looked downward and to the side, as if he could see through the intervening floor and walls to wherever the Mages were inside the inn. "I already knew those Mages were here, for they are making no attempt to hide themselves. It is taking some effort for me to remain hidden from them, but I believe I am succeeding."

"I'd forgotten you said Mages could sense other Mages. Why didn't they find you when you were passed out?"

"Sleeping Mages send out few signs of their presence," Alain explained. "The elders of the Mage Guild debate the reasons, but we are taught how to maintain some shield of our presence without thinking of it, so perhaps that shield remains in place when we sleep. If the Mages are making no attempt to search for other Mages, they would be unlikely to sense me. My practice at hiding myself also seems to have improved my ability to conceal my presence at all times. I have been working at that."

"That's my Mage," Mari said with a grin, then noticed an almost-expression cross Alain's face. "What?"

"When you called me your Mage. I like when you say that."

Mari's grin widened. "Good. I'll do that more often. Speaking of Mages, though, how did you find this inn during the blizzard? Is that another Mage skill?"

Alain shook his head. "To find a building? A place? No. It is possible I sensed the presence of the other Mages here and unconsciously moved toward them. But I was so tired I do not see how I could have done that. It may have just been destiny," Alain continued. "Our fates may have led us here, just as they once led each of us to the same caravan."

"Mages don't believe in anything, but they believe in destiny?" Mari asked, knowing her tones sounded sarcastic again. "I'm sorry, but I'm the one controlling my fate, not some mysterious force called destiny."

"I do not disagree that our decisions matter," Alain said. "Mages speak of the road we choose to walk. I believe that we are given choices, places where decisions may be made to walk one road or another. We do not know what provides these choices, but we may call it destiny to give a name to that which is unknowable. Destiny offers the choices, but we choose the road."

Mari frowned in thought. "I hadn't thought about it in those terms. You mean like when we first met while the caravan was being attacked, you and I both had choices of whether to stick together or strike off on our own. Both of our futures would have been a lot different if we'd separated then. But why would destiny care about whether or not you and I lived, or ended up together?"

Alain shook his head. "Whether or not destiny cares—and if it cares, why it cares—is a question beyond the wisdom of anyone to answer for certain."

"I'm an engineer, Alain. I believe every problem has a solution, every question has an answer. I guess we'll learn our futures when we get to them."

His eyes were hooded with concern even she could spot. "The task before you is very dangerous."

"I already know that," Mari said, thinking of the Imperial security forces that would need to be avoided, the dangers from her own Guild, and whatever the Mage Guild might try. In their own ways, each of them wanted to be in control of things and tell everyone else what to do. "Not in detail, of course, but that's probably just as well at the moment."

"If you wish to speak of it," Alain began.

"There's not much sense in that, Alain," Mari replied. "I need to learn more before I know what to do. All you and I could talk about now is...our fears of what might happen."

"This is so," Alain agreed. "Mari, I must tell you, your calmness in the face of what you must do is the equal of the greatest Mage."

"Not a compliment I ever thought to receive!" Mari pulled some fresh clothing out of her pack. "Don't let anybody else look in my pack while I'm gone."

Alain nodded this time, his face reflecting concentration. "Privacy."

"Right. That and the fact that any common seeing the jacket and tools would know instantly that I'm a Mechanic."

The soak proved amazingly refreshing. Jana the healer had ordered some more hot water brought in to refresh the small tub, and Mari just sat in it for a long time letting physical and emotional stresses drain off and out of her. Finally, she managed to drag herself out of the bath. After that, the chill gusts of air that found their way through the inn's walls made it easy to dry off quickly and get dressed fast even though her muscles still protested mightily.

As she reached the door to their room, Alain opened it. "I sensed you coming."

"Yeah. How did you—? The thread?"

"Yes. It is very strong now."

That thread thing was a bit unsettling, but she would have to get used to it. Mari knelt by her pack, digging inside it again until she surfaced with her pistol and holster. "Can we be in the same dining hall with any Mages here without them knowing you're a Mage?"

"As long as I maintain my control and do not cast any spells."

"There's no chance any of them will recognize you?" Mari asked.

Alain gave her a questioning look. "Why would a Mage look at the face of a common?"

"Good point." Mari stood up, adjusting the holster and pulling on her common coat to hide it. "Hopefully the Mechanics at the inn will act the same way. We've got to eat." Her stomach felt like a vast pit now. "When did we eat last? At least a day ago."

The dining hall wasn't too hard to find. They just had to follow the scent of food and the roar of conversation. Every table was filled, but Mari's eyes went to two in particular. At the far side of the hall, a small group of Mages sat, anonymous in their robes with the hoods up, silent and ignoring everyone else. At a table as far away from the Mages as possible sat a larger group of Mechanics, talking loudly and dominating their half of the hall with their noisy arrogance just as the Mages dominated the other half with their mysterious menace.

Mari stood there a moment, uncertain what to do. As a Mechanic, she had grown used to commons quickly making room for her or simply joining a table with other Mechanics. But then a common woman at one of the tables closer to the Mechanics than to the Mages gestured to Mari and shoved her husband to one side on the bench to make room for Mari and Alain. "Thank you," Mari said, letting Alain take the outside where he had less contact with the commons and less chance to betray that he was a Mage.

The husband nodded briefly at her as he swallowed a bite. "I helped carry you in when you got here," he grunted. "Thought you were done for."

"Thank you," Mari repeated.

The woman shook her head. "What were you two doing out there on the plains?"

"Hiking," Mari explained. "We're students from Palandur."

"Palandur!" The woman seemed awed. "Have you seen the emperor?"

"At a distance," Mari admitted.

Before she could say more, a frazzled-looking server dumped a bowl of stew in front of her and another in front of Alain. "No more bread," the server said before leaving as quickly as she had come.

Mari couldn't help glancing at the Mechanics' table, where fresh loaves were steaming. The woman spotted it and nodded ruefully. "They're having to save what bread is left for the rulers of all creation over there."

"Hope they choke on it," her husband grunted.

"Hush! One of them might hear."

The woman kept talking, something about the emperor and how grand Palandur must be, while Mari started eating as fast as she could ladle in the stew. It looked as though the inn, overrun with guests seeking shelter from the blizzard, had simply been dumping anything available into the cauldrons of stew to keep them topped off. Mari didn't mind, though, since she was eating so fast she was barely tasting it.

Most of the way through her second bowl, Alain leaned close to whisper in her ear. "One of the Mechanics keeps taking quick looks toward you."

Mari's spoon froze in motion for a moment, then she managed to swallow and lower the spoon. "Man or woman?"

"It is a male Mechanic."

"Can I take a look without him seeing me looking back at him?"

"It would be difficult, since his glances are growing longer." Alain paused. "His companions have noticed. They are laughing and speaking loudly to him."

Mari didn't know whether to be relieved or worried. It sounded like the Mechanic had been watching her because he thought she was attractive, and his tablemates were now giving him a hard time. That was better than him recognizing her, but it could still be a problem.

The woman had noticed now, too. "Girl, one of them black jackets is looking at you. He's starting to get up. You'd best leave quick. You know what they're capable of doing."

"Thanks." Feeling shame at how the commons felt toward Mechanics mixed with worry now, Mari bolted to her feet, hauling Alain with her and walking quickly out of the dining hall. The roar of conversation had lowered considerably as the commons watched the little drama playing out, so Mari could hear the Mechanic's boots coming on fast behind her, hear the Mechanic's fellows urging him on with shouts of encouragement. She got through the door, shoving Alain ahead of her, then felt a hand on her shoulder as Mari reached for the pistol under her coat.

"Hold on," the Mechanic said.

Mari stopped moving as she heard the voice. *Can it really be him?* She spun around and looked at the Mechanic. "Calu. It's been a long time."

CHAPTER NINE

Calu stared at her, then grinned. "Mari? It is you. I kept looking at this girl, thinking she sure looked like Mari, and it's you. What's it been, three years?"

"About that. You must be twenty-one now, right? Look at you. All grown into a man and a full Mechanic." Mari smiled, letting her hand fall away from her weapon, then glanced at Alain. "Calu is all right. We were apprentices together at the Mechanics Guild Hall in Caer Lyn."

Alain, who had been watching tensed for action, relaxed a little.

"Apprentices together?" Calu smiled wider. "More like uncaught conspirators together. I heard you made Master Mechanic. Everybody was talking about that a while back." His smile turned wry. "Except the Senior Mechanics."

"Same old story," Mari said.

"Yeah. I'd wondered how you were doing, since I hadn't heard anything in so long, then I noticed you eating in there and wondered if it could be you. The other Mechanics thought I was checking out some common girl, but I just wanted to know if it was you for real."

"Oh?" Mari frowned at him. The Calu she had known never would have forced a woman, but that had been three years ago. "And if she hadn't been me? What would you have done?"

Calu smiled crookedly. "Asked her if she was your twin sister."

"I would have mentioned a twin sister if I had one, Calu."

"Maybe not if she was an evil twin sister. Blazes, Mari, you know me. I wouldn't have done anything, except maybe tell her I was sorry for scaring her."

Mari smiled, too. "You'd apologize to a common?"

"They're human, too, right? That's what you always said. You were always big on treating everyone with respect, and I didn't forget that." He gave her a curious look. "Why is there an alert out for you? Why aren't you wearing your jacket?"

Mari looked around. "I can't talk about it here, Calu. It's too dangerous."

"Dangerous? How can I help?"

She smiled again, despite her worry. Calu might be wearing a Mechanic's jacket now, but he hadn't changed in other ways since he was an apprentice. "Alain is helping me. I don't want you being in danger, too."

"Alain?" Calu nodded to the Mage, who nodded back stiffly. "Just Alain? Is he a common?"

"No..."

"All right, I understand. You can't talk now. How about later?"

"Calu, you really shouldn't get involved. Just don't tell any of the other Mechanics here that you saw me and—"

Calu shook his head. "No way, Mari. I'm still your friend, so I'm involved. What do think Alli would do to me if she heard I'd seen you and not helped?"

"Alli? I saw her in Danalee a little while ago."

"Lucky you." Calu grinned. "We're staying in touch but I can't wait to see her again. We told you about us getting serious."

"You did? When?"

"I know Alli sent some letters to you at the academy. We didn't hear back much, but we figured you were just too busy."

"No." Mari took a long, deep breath. "I only got a couple of letters from you guys. I'm sure I would have remembered Alli telling me about you two. I wrote to you. Did you see my letters?"

"One," Calu said. "Maybe two. Yeah."

"I wrote at least ten. Why didn't Alli mention that when I saw her?"

Calu shrugged. "We blew it off, Mari. We knew you were really busy, and how sometimes you'd get totally wrapped up in work and forget about everything else. We didn't take it badly."

"Thanks." Mari frowned, thinking about the oddity that a number of letters hadn't made it between Caer Lyn and the academy. Were lost letters part of the general breakdown of Guild functions that she feared? "Listen, if you're that determined to talk to me, we're on the top floor, in the last room. It's kind of tiny, but it's safe."

"All right. I'll come by tonight." Calu hesitated, looking from her to Alain. "You're both in there? So are you two together, or *together*?"

She reached for Alain's hand. "Together. Really, really together."

The grin was back as Calu looked at Alain. "Cool. You lucky dog." He saluted Alain. "You must be something, if Mari feels that way. All right, see you tonight, Mari. I'll tell my fellow Mechanics that I got a kiss from that common I was looking at." Calu twisted his face in thought. "I'll them you couldn't resist me, but I had to stay true to Alli since she's an expert shot. They'll understand." He winked and walked back into the dining hall.

Mari breathed a sigh of relief, then felt a stab of guilt. "I'm sorry, Alain. I shouldn't have agreed to meet with Calu and everything without asking you first. You're in this with me, so you deserve a say in things."

Alain nodded. "You know this Mechanic and I do not. He will not betray you?"

"Not unless he's totally changed in the last three years."

"Then I have no objection. I accept your judgment that we can... trust him." Alain frowned. "Trust. That is the right thing to call it?"

"Yes," Mari said softly. "Trust. Like you and I share. Did you realize that we trusted each other? I've trusted you since Ringhmon."

"I was not certain what it meant." He nodded slowly, and she saw the ghost of a smile again. "I told General Flyn that I trusted him. It was the right thing to say." Alain hesitated. "This Mechanic. He and you were friends?"

"That's right."

"Close friends?"

Mari couldn't help grinning. "Trust and jealousy! I'm teaching you all kinds of feelings. Come on. Once we're back in our room I'll tell you about Calu and my other friends at Caer Lyn. And yes, he was only a friend."

The rest of the day passed very slowly. Mari spent part of it talking about her experiences as an acolyte. *No, not acolyte,* Alain reminded himself. *Apprentice. Her Guild calls one who is learning an apprentice.* As Mari talked, she went from happy to wistful, finally winding down until she went to her pack, pulled out the metal things she called tools, and began doing mysterious things with them.

Alain sat watching her, memories of his time as an acolyte coming back forcefully. *I have no friends I can tell Mari about. I wish I did. Perhaps some of the acolytes from Ihris remember me, but how do they think of me? As just as a shadow whose path crossed theirs? How do I tell Mari more of my learning, of what I did and what was done to me? She would become sad, I think. I have seen her become sad when I mention some things about my training. And when I spoke of Asha before it bothered Mari. I cannot imagine why.*

The wind outside had diminished to a low rushing sound against the walls of the inn. Alain went into meditation, wishing that he could check his ability to cast spells now that he and Mari had become even closer. By the wisdom he had been taught, seeing shadows as other people should make his powers wither and vanish. He did not feel that that had happened yet; indeed during the fight to save the Alexdrians, he had repeatedly found more power in himself than he had ever experienced. But a spell to test it would be impossible to hide from the Mages also staying at this inn, so he must wait.

The light leaking in through the storm shutters had long since faded when a soft knock sounded on the door to their room. Alain jerked himself back to full awareness, watching as Mari drew her weapon and, holding it ready in one hand, cautiously opened the door enough to see out. A moment later she relaxed, opening the door to let in the Mechanic Calu and then locking it again.

Calu gave Mari a surprised look as she put away her weapon. "You're armed?"

"Yeah. I'll explain why."

"Can I see it?" Mari handed over the weapon without hesitating, and the other Mechanic turned it in his hands carefully. "This is a beauty. If Alli was here, she'd be drooling over it."

"She saw it in Danalee," Mari confessed. "I thought I'd never get it back from her. How come you two didn't end up at the same Guild Hall? I thought the Guild liked it when two Mechanics were interested in each other."

Calu handed back the weapon, looking annoyed. "I think it depends on the Mechanics. After you left Caer Lyn, most of the Senior Mechanics there seemed determined to break up what they called Mari's gang."

"You're kidding. I had a gang?"

"It surprised me, too. But when you think about it, Mari, a lot of the apprentices did listen to you, even the ones not officially assigned to you as group leader." Calu shrugged. "It sometimes seemed like some of the Senior Mechanics thought you were getting ready to start a revolution. Alli and I got tagged as part of your loyal band of revolutionaries, and we're both sure that's why we got sent to different Guild Halls."

Mari made an angry noise, clenching her fists. "They punished you two just because you knew me."

"It was our choice, Mari," Calu reminded her. "And we did pull our share of pranks and unauthorized activities, usually following some idea you came up with. Remember moving that one Senior Mechanic's entire office onto the roof one night?"

Mari grinned at the memory. "He was so mad. He deserved it, though, and we never got caught for that."

"Right. Now, are you going to tell me what's going on with you?"

"Do you want the short summary or the long story?" Mari asked.

"Short summary first."

"Sit down." Mari sat down on end of the bed as Calu sat on the other, then she took a deep breath. "The Guild is trying to get me killed."

Calu just watched her for a long moment, then looked over at Alain. "What about you?"

"My Guild seeks my death as well," Alain replied.

"Why?" Mechanic Calu's question was directed at Mari again.

"I'm not sure where to begin." Mari looked down at her hands. "The caravan? No. Ringhmon. What have you heard about Ringhmon lately?"

"Officially? The city is under a Guild Interdict for contract violations and scrambling to raise enough money to pay the fine and qualify for Mechanic services again." Calu gestured vaguely. "There are rumors that Ringhmon was doing worse things than contract violations, and other rumors that the emperor wanted to take advantage of that to launch another expedition in the south, but the Guild told him to knock it off. Were you involved with any of that?"

Mari laughed in a way that held no humor. "I caused it, Calu. I discovered what Ringhmon was up to and I reported it to the Guild."

"You also burned down the city hall," Alain pointed out.

"You helped," she retorted. Calu nodded, as if unsurprised to hear that Mari had burned down a building. "Contract violations?" Mari continued. "Do you want to know what Ringhmon was really doing? And before you say yes, I need to tell you that I'm under a Guild Interdict myself never to say a word of this to anyone."

The other Mechanic's expression was totally serious now. "If you think I should know it, I want to hear it."

"Ringhmon was trying to reverse-engineer Mechanic weapons. They were trying to figure out how to make their own."

Calu stared at her, his mouth dropping open. "They had the nerve to try that? But why? They could never succeed."

Mari's eyes were closed as she spoke. "Calu, do you remember something you asked Alli and me a long time ago? You wondered why, if commons can't do Mechanic things, we have to keep what we do secret from them."

"Yeah. I remember that night. Was that the first time Alli punched me, after I asked about that? I've wondered about it since then, too. What did I say? That it was like prohibiting us from teaching horses something."

"Algebra."

"Right!" Calu grinned for a moment before the happiness vanished into contemplation. "It still doesn't make sense to me, but like you wisely advised me then, asking about that would be a one-way ticket to the cells in Longfalls." He looked at her intently. "What all did you find, Mari?"

"I found evidence, Calu. A far-listener not made in any Guild workshop. A steam boiler without any Guild markings on it, operated by commons. And I was told, *ordered*, by the Senior Mechanics never to say a word about any of it."

"A boiler? You found an entire boiler? Full scale? With commons running it?"

"Yes," Mari said. "Did you hear anything about Dorcastle a few months back?"

"Just something about a Mage plot to blame our Guild for some extortion scheme." Calu jerked with surprise. "It wasn't a Mage plot?"

"No, it was these guys I call Dark Mechanics. I don't know who they are, but they can do Mechanic work, Calu, and even knowing they exist is apparently very dangerous for any Mechanic. The Mages didn't have anything to do with the plot in Dorcastle, though some Dark Mages helped put an end to the plot and almost put an end to Alain and me."

"Dark Mages?" Calu glanced from Mari to Alain. "Aren't all Mages kind of dark?"

"Not all of them!" Mari looked embarrassed by the force of her denial. "I mean, Mages aren't supposed to believe in anything, but they actually do believe in something they call wisdom which is supposed to help them gain more power. I mean, personal ability to do their spells. Dark Mages don't worry about that, instead doing anything that brings them money."

Calu was staring at Mari again. "How did you learn stuff about Mages?"

She gave him a helpless look, then turned her gaze on Alain. He knew what she was asking, and nodded to her. "You trust this Mechanic," Alain said. "I will trust him as well. I have seen no falseness in him."

"Huh?" Calu seemed baffled by Alain's words, then looked at Mari as she placed a hand on his arm.

"Calu, Alain is a Mage."

The Mechanic's eyes flared with worry as he stared at Mari, then shifted his gaze to Alain. "I saw him smile. I know I did. Is this some kind of sick joke, Mari?"

"Mari would not lie to a friend," Alain said, forcing himself not to tense in readiness at the suspicion and fear on the Mechanic's face. "She has saved my life more than once, and I will never harm her nor allow any other to harm her as long as I can fight to protect her."

Some of the tension left the Mechanic, then he looked at Mari. "I've heard they can control people."

"No," Mari denied. "They can't do that. Alain told me."

"Then he wouldn't object to leaving you and me here alone? Going as far away from us as he can so I can see how you react when he's not around?"

Mari gave Alain an embarrassed look. "Do you mind?"

Alain shook his head, standing with slow, casual movements, aware of the watchful way Calu was eyeing him. The Mechanic's suspicion of Mages was justified, after all. "Do you wish me to leave the inn, friend of Mari?"

Calu hesitated. "No. That would attract too much attention, with the storm still going on. How about down one floor and to the far end of the hall?"

"I will do this. How long do I wait?"

"Until I come and get you."

Alain looked to Mari, who nodded. "Please, Alain. I'll be safe here with Calu."

"I know this, or I would not leave." Alain left the room, closing the door carefully behind him to avoid making too much noise, then walked to the stairs, feeling for the presence of the other Mages in the inn. They were all on the ground floor, on the side opposite from where Alain had been sent by Mechanic Calu, and he could sense no spells being prepared by those Mages.

Alain reached the end of the hall one flight down from the room and waited. A small window gave a view of darkness shot by occasional swirls of white as blown snow was illuminated by the lanterns providing dim light in the hallway. Alain watched the snow, trying to calm his mind.

He was not sure how much time had passed when he heard the sound of Mechanic boots thumping on the stairs. He turned and saw Mechanic Calu coming toward him, wary but no longer fearful. Calu stopped directly in front of Alain, eyeing him. "You didn't say that you'd saved Mari's life a number of times."

"She is my friend."

"According to Mari, she's a lot more than a friend." Calu shook his head. "I owe you a lot for saving her, but how can I trust you?"

"Mari once asked me the same thing." Alain met the Mechanic's eyes. "I will tell you what I told her then: that nothing I can say will make a difference. You must judge my actions."

"She'd be dead now if not for you. That's pretty easy to judge. But what do you hope to get out of this? It's not like everything I've heard about Mages."

"My actions are not what Mages are taught. My own Guild is seeking my death because they believe that Mari has corrupted me." Alain had to think about the answer to the Mechanic's question, trying to put words to feelings which were still unfamiliar to him. "I hope to help Mari, to protect her from those who would harm her. Did she tell you who she is?"

"I know who she is," Calu said. "Do you mean, besides being Mari?"

"If she did not tell you, I should not," Alain said.

"Mari said something about fixing things," Calu said. "About how she needed to do it even though it might change the world."

"Changes to the world," Alain said. "To make it...right."

"People tend to have different ideas of what will make things right," Calu observed, rubbing the back of his neck with one hand. "But I've never heard anything from Mari that I disagreed with after I thought it through. It sounds like you feel the same."

"I do," Alain said. "But for me it is more than doing the right things. It is...is it a privacy thing to speak to you of how I feel about her?"

"Uh...no," Calu said. "Mari told me how she feels about you."

"Mari makes me happy. I want to be with her." He looked directly at the Mechanic Calu. "I had forgotten how to feel that way, and then I met her."

The Mechanic looked back, then grinned. "Either you're the best liar the world of Dematr has ever known, or you're sincere. She really believes in you. I'm going to be honest with you. That's what decided me. Mari is no fool. If she trusts you that much, enough to give her heart to you, then I have to trust you, too. But don't you ever let her get hurt."

Alain was not sure what to say, so he spoke carefully. "Thank...you. I will not ever hurt her."

"That's a bit different. Mari told me that you're trying to relearn a lot of things about people that your Guild tried to drive out of you, so as one guy to another, let me tell you that sooner or later you're going to hurt her somehow, no matter how hard you try not to. Just do your best so she'll forgive you when that happens. Let's get back to her room before somebody spots us out here." Calu gave Alain a curious look. "Why did you trust me?"

"I can tell when someone lies. You did not. You show strong feelings for Mari."

"Oh, uh, not that kind of feelings," Calu hastened to explain as they started up the stairs. "She's sort of like a sister to me. Has Mari talked about another Mechanic named Alli?"

"Yes. Alli is the one who is very skilled in the making of Mechanic weapons."

Calu laughed. "That's Alli."

"Did Mari tell you that she killed a dragon with a weapon that Mechanic Alli built?"

The Mechanic stopped walking for a moment, staring at Alain. "When did that happen?"

"About a week ago. It was a big Mechanic weapon, as long as Mari is tall, and with it Mari slew a very large dragon."

"Did she really?" Calu shook his head. "I saw a dragon once, not too close, fortunately, and my fellow Mechanics told me to forget I'd ever seen it. But I couldn't forget something like that." His grin came back. "And something Alli built killed one of those? That's my girl! It's a good thing Mari had that weapon, I guess."

"She knew she might need it," Alain explained. "After the difficulty we had slaying a dragon in Dorcastle."

"Dorcastle? Where she found the boiler? You killed a dragon there, too?"

"Yes. Mari..." Alain shook his head, unable to describe what Mari had done. "There was something on the thing you call a boiler, and Mari used rope to tie it, and the boiler became very loud and hot, and then destroyed everything around it."

Calu stared at Alain. "She tied down the relief valve. That must have been what she did. Mari tied down the relief valve on a boiler. Oh, I cannot wait to tell Alli about that. You helped her?"

"I found rope," Alain said. "But I cannot understand, cannot do, anything that Mari can do."

"Huh. Interesting."

Mari had a relieved smile on her face when they returned. "Satisfied, Calu?"

"Yeah." Calu pointed an accusing finger at her. "Why didn't you tell me that I'd won the bet?"

"What bet?" Mari asked, looking baffled.

"Several years ago, while we were studying steam, you and I got into an argument over which one of us would be the first to make a boiler explode. Remember?"

Mari looked embarrassed as she laughed. "Oh. That bet."

"And now I hear that you made a boiler blow up in Dorcastle. Pay up!"

She made a helpless gesture. "Calu, I can't remember what the stakes were."

"Something about the loser running naked through the courtyard of the Guild Hall."

"What? I didn't—" Mari bit her lip. "That was the bet, wasn't it? Calu, you're not going to...?"

Calu sat down, making a magnanimous gesture. "Because of our friendship, and because Alli would whip my butt if she found out I'd tried to insist you do it, I will simply accept victory as my reward. I was not the first to blow up a boiler. Mari of Caer Lyn was!"

Mari bowed toward Calu. "I admit it."

"I'm a better Mechanic than you are," Calu continued.

"The blazes you are! I blew up that boiler on purpose, not by accident." Mari looked over at Alain. "Do you have any idea what we're talking about?"

"No," Alain said. "But you are both clearly enjoying this. This is a friend thing, is it not?"

"It is," Mari agreed.

Calu looked from her to Alain and smiled. "We always said Mari could fix anything. All right. Now I know what's going on. What can I do, Mari?"

"Calu, keep your head down, stay quiet—"

"Let me clarify," Calu interrupted. "What can I do for you?" He looked over at Alain. "For you and, uh...Sir Mage Alain?"

"You may call me just Alain, if a friend of Mari's can be a friend to me also."

Mari was looking into a corner. "Calu, I'm on my way to talk to a Master Mechanic who I trust. She was one of my professors at the Academy. I need to find out more about what's happening to me and why, and get her advice on how to handle it. Maybe she can get this whole mess turned around and I can start working with the Guild again, instead of trying to avoid getting killed by it."

"If the Senior Mechanics were willing to send you into Tiae, I wouldn't hold my breath on some grand reconciliation happening. Are you going to take Alain in to see her, too?" Calu asked.

"Yes, because I want to see what she says about him and what he can do."

Calu studied Alain again. "Are you willing to talk about that? How you do that stuff? Or is it a Guild secret for you?"

"It is a Guild secret, but my Guild no longer can demand I keep its secrets. My loyalty now is..." He paused, trying to think that through. Who or what did he owe allegiance to, now that his obedience to his Guild no longer bound him? None of his training had offered guidance on that. The only alternative he had ever heard of was the Dark Mages, and he would not follow their path. He would need to make a new road.

Alain's eyes came up and focused on Mari. *Of course. I will follow her. She will show me a good road to walk.* "My loyalty is to my Lady Mari. To the right thing she seeks to bring about. What she asks, I will do."

Mari's face flushed even as she smiled at that, leaving Alain confused as to whether he had upset her or pleased her. But Mechanic Calu nodded. "I don't need to give you any advice when it comes to that, do I?"

"I do not know, Mechanic Calu. But I will answer what you asked me. The Mage arts are based upon the understanding that nothing is real, that all we see is an illusion."

Instead of appearing annoyed as Mari always did when he said that, the other Mechanic looked shocked. "Nothing is real?"

"Nothing is real," Alain repeated.

Calu turned to Mari. "Nothing is real!"

She glared at them. "It's bad enough when Alain keeps saying it. Why are you both saying it?"

"Mari," Calu answered eagerly, "did you get the letters where I told you that I'd been allowed to take those advanced physics courses but hadn't been allowed to pursue Master rating in them because of strict quotas? Yeah, I know it sounds weird that I'd be going for advanced physics when I had trouble with the simpler stuff, but something just clicked when I hit the high-end theories and models. And do you know what it all rests on? When you get down below the atomic level to the quantum level? It comes down to nothing is real."

"You've got to be kidding me," Mari said. "Mechanic physics says that?"

"At the fundamental level, yes." Calu pointed to Alain. "He said everything is an illusion. That's kind of what quantum theory says, that what we see and experience through our senses is just the way our brains organize things so it'll make sense to us. Can you believe it? The theoretical foundations of the Mechanics and the Mages are the same! We must go in totally different directions from there, taking completely dissimilar approaches to how we deal with the universe."

Mari shook her head. "That doesn't make any sense, Calu. How can arts like engineering be based on the idea that nothing is real?"

"No, it's the foundation, Mari. It's what explains how everything works, like electricity and light and friction and everything else.

171 Engineering follows the rules it does because of the way the universe

Engineering follows the rules it does because of the way the universe is organized." Calu grinned again at Mari's baffled expression. "I know how weird it seems. It's actually a whole lot weirder than it sounds when you get down to quantum level. I think if the Mechanics Guild had its way the whole thing would be banned, but it's considered too important to completely suppress, so only a very few Mechanics are allowed to learn about it." Calu frowned in thought. "But where could the Mages get the energy to do anything? The human body doesn't contain enough to create rapid changes like that. Mechanics get our energy from sources like electricity or magnetism. Is that what you use, Alain?"

Alain shook his head. "I do not know these words. We draw on the power which exists everywhere in greater or lesser amounts around us. A Mage can sense and channel this energy into a spell to change the world illusion. It also requires some energy from the Mage, so that creating spells quickly tires any Mage."

"Wow. Something like...heat transfer. Mari, remember those old plans for geothermal heating we found?"

"The ones the Senior Mechanics confiscated?"

"Right! There's heat in the ground, everywhere, and with the right equipment you can use that heat. So the Mages can make use of some other kind of energy, I guess. I would so love to research this stuff."

Alain studied the Mechanic, trying to understand Calu's enthusiasm. "Mechanics are so much in and of the world," he said. "Everything about it fascinates you and Mari. I was taught to ignore the world, but I find myself wishing I could feel so excited about what I saw and what I learned. I would...like to discuss these things more with you some day, Mechanic Calu."

Another grin. "If you're just Alain, then I'm just Calu." The smile went away. "But there's no way the Senior Mechanics would permit it. We're not allowed to learn new things, do new things, build new things."

Mari looked at Calu. "Maybe that should change," she said.

He looked back at her, and Alain could sense the sudden tension. "Seriously, Mari? Alli told me something about you years ago. She said 'Mari is going to change things some day, Calu.' And a little while ago, Alain told me that's what you were out to do. Change things. If anybody can, you can."

She gave them both aggravated looks. "Everybody expects me to do it! This is too important to start without having some kind of... of blueprint. And to have a blueprint, I need to understand exactly what's going on and why. I'm relieved that you two are getting along, but don't gang up on me. I wonder if Professor S'san knows anything about this quantum stuff? Calu, I might as well tell you what I can about our plans. Alain and I are heading for Severun."

"That means you'll have to go through Umburan and Pandin," Calu observed. "The Imperial road net always converges into a few big roads that go through the cities so the Imperials can track everyone's movements." Calu pointed to himself. "I'm at the Guild Hall in Umburan. Have you got Imperial identity papers?"

"Yes. Fake ones, of course."

"Good. From what I've seen since I got here, the Imperials regard any common west of Umburan as especially suspect. Once you get to Umburan and onward south and east, Imperial security will relax a little." Calu leaned back, furrowing his brow in thought. "We've got a coach taking us back to Umburan. How are you getting there?"

"Walking, I guess."

"You might be able to get a horse."

Mari flinched. "Don't talk about riding a horse, please."

Calu looked puzzled, so Alain explained. "Riding a horse hurts Mari's butt."

She flinched again. "Alain! Social skills! You don't talk about my butt to anyone else!"

Mechanic Calu seemed to be having difficulty, covering his mouth and coughing even though he was smiling. "Um...all right, then. I'll be in Umburan a few days before you two. That will give me time to see what I can find out."

Mari scowled at him. "Calu, do not put yourself at risk by asking around about me."

"I can be careful!" Calu said. "There's a Guild alert out for you, and that's a perfect reason to ask. 'I was at Caer Lyn with her, so maybe I help the Guild figure out where she is.'"

"I don't want you lying like a Mage!" Mari winced. "I'm sorry, Alain."

"For what?" he asked. "I have heard the saying, though it is not accurate. Those who believe truth does not exist cannot actually be lying."

"He's got a point," Calu commented. "Mari, when we were apprentices you used to say that we were all in this together. We still are. There's a bookstore about five hundred lances north of the Mechanics Guild Hall in Umburan. I'll be there around noon each day, starting a week after we leave here. It will take you at least that long to get to the city. Meet me in the bookstore and I'll tell you what I found out."

Alain could see Mari wavering. "I believe it would be wise to accept the offer, Mari. We must know as much as possible about what our opponents are doing if we are to reach Severun safely."

She nodded in defeat. "All right. Please be careful, Calu."

"Trust me. The blizzard is almost over. They're talking about us maybe leaving tomorrow, if the road is clear enough." Calu stood up, looking toward Alain. "You keep your eyes on her, okay?"

"I will."

Mari made a derisive noise. "He doesn't need any encouragement to look at me."

After the other Mechanic had left, Mari sat gazing at the door. "You are sad," Alain said.

"More worried than sad." Mari shook her head. "I keep getting other people drawn into my troubles. First you, now Calu. I don't have any right to do that."

"Mari, you say that you trust Mechanic Calu and that you trust me. Does that not mean you trust our ability to make decisions? You did not order us to do anything. We choose to walk the same road, to be your allies."

She thought about that for a while before shaking her head again. "You're right, but I still feel guilty. I know I'm always pushing people to do stuff, but why do they follow me?"

"Because of who you are," Alain said.

Mari rolled her eyes. "I just hope what I told him doesn't get him in trouble. I keep doing things that cause other things to happen. I just don't want anyone to be hurt."

"Those who wish to kill us may move against your friends in time anyway. It is best that they be warned. And if you do not keep trying, the storm will sweep away all."

This time, Mari glared at him. "Alain, have you ever heard the expression 'no pressure'?"

"No." Alain listened for a moment to the small sounds of the wind outside. "It is very late. We should sleep now in case travel is possible tomorrow." Alain moved to spread his blanket upon the floor.

"What are you doing?" Mari scowled at him and pointed to the bed. "I want you here, next to me. With your clothes on, and watch where you put your hands. I trust you and I want you close, but let's not press our luck." She put out the lantern, then held Alain close as he laid down beside her.

He had almost fallen asleep when she whispered softly to him. "Alain, if Professor S'san says I have to leave you in order to make peace with the Mechanics Guild, I won't do it. I just want you to know that. You'll never be alone again, Alain. Not while I live."

❄   ❄   ❄

By morning the sun was shining in a cloudless sky of brilliant blue, reflecting off the white snow in blinding glory. Temperatures were rising quickly. From the small window of their room Alain could see people walking past on the road, carrying their coats as they waded through the rapidly melting snow.

They waited until the Mages had left, three robed figures walking alone, the crowd separating to give them a lot of space. Then the Mechanics departed in a large coach with a common driving the horses as they plunged through the diminishing snow. Finally, with most prying eyes gone, Mari and Alain went down to see the innkeeper.

The innkeeper calculated their rate for the tiny room and the food they had eaten, adding in a "storm fee" which made Mari mutter something about profiteering. But they could scarcely complain, since the innkeeper had taken them in without knowing whether they would be able to pay anything. The healer was staying another day to help a mother who had given birth during the storm, and she accepted Mari's offering of payment gratefully. "Good luck," the healer called after them as they left the inn, "and may your parents see wisdom!"

Alain looked at Mari. "Our parents?"

"We're eloping," she explained.

"I had not known."

Mari laughed. "How long have you been hiding humor behind dry statements like that? Anyway, eloping is a good cover story. And you did propose to me. I don't intend to let you forget that."

Alain noticed his own spirits lift as he saw her happiness in being out of the inn and on the road in good weather. Mari was looking around at the melting snow drifts and the clear blue sky. "It's clearing almost as fast as it hit. Amazing. It's almost like that storm was aimed at us."

"Perhaps it was," Alain suggested. "To bring us to that inn, to come to some more understanding between us, to meet your friend Calu."

Mari seemed to be torn between more laughter and disbelief. "Oh, yes, destiny. I'd forgotten. Alain, if destiny chose to create that great big storm while we were walking across the plains a few days ago just to get us into bed together, then all I can say is that destiny engaged in some serious overkill of its own, though I'm sure the male in you regards that event as being of huge significance."

Alain shrugged. "Our sharing your bed may have been a minor step along the road we are to follow."

"Oh, yes, it was also so we would meet Calu!" Mari laughed. "I think that could have been arranged with a little less effort."

"You can be hard to direct at times," Alain suggested.

Mari shook her head, grinning. "Aren't you the diplomat?" Her grin faded, and she gave him a serious look. "That reminds me of something I've been meaning to ask. From what you've said of Mage schools, it's everyone for themselves there. Who taught you to be a gentleman? Way back when, the first days we were together, why didn't you start grabbing at me as soon as I was within reach?"

Alain felt the memories rushing in upon him, memories of solitude among many. "You are right. I was not taught to care for others in the Mage schools. I was taught that the wishes of others did not matter at all. Had I followed my teachings, I would have simply done what I wished with you and cared not for your feelings or whatever hurt it might have inflicted."

She gazed at him somberly. "More than one Mechanic takes the same approach when it comes to commons, though I never let it happen if I could intervene. I never thought it was right to treat commons, or anyone else, poorly because I always believed their feelings and their dignity mattered. But you were taught those other people didn't even exist, so what kept you honest?"

More memories of long ago, of animals and fields, of people he had spent years trying to put out of his mind. "My parents. My Guild tried to make me forget them, tried to teach me that they were only shadows, but always they stayed with me. Eventually, so strongly did the elders teach me to reject all that brought up feelings in me that I saw this as a weakness in myself, that I could not cease to care about them." Alain had to pause, breathing deeply. His eyes felt strange and watery.

Mari's hand gripped his arm and squeezed lightly. "Your parents must have been great people."

"They were." He whispered that, then looked up and spoke the next two words loudly before lowering his voice again. "They were. I will never try to forget that again. My father taught me to respect others, my mother taught me not to hurt others. It must have hurt them...so much...when I was taken by the Mages." He felt tears leaking out and rubbed them away.

Mari's hand left his arm and her own arm wrapped around his waist so that she held him as they walked. "I'm sorry, Alain."

"No. You should never be sorry, for if not for you I would have kept those memories out of mind. I would have continued to reject my feelings." He worked at it and managed to smile at her. "I think they would have liked you, Mari."

Her own eyes seemed watery before Mari looked away. "I hope so. Do you have anybody else? A brother or sister? Aunt or uncle?"

"No brother or sister. I had an aunt, my mother's sister, but I do not know what has become of her." Alain kicked at a mound of snow, knocking pieces along the road, enjoying the feeling of release from acting on his pain. "My grandmother will have nothing to do with me. She looked upon me and saw only a Mage."

"Maybe if she saw you now—"

"No. Her mind is fixed. I saw this. It hurt even when I would not feel hurt." Mari stayed silent, and Alain felt questions coming to him. "Mari, your mother—"

"We will not talk about my mother." Her voice had gone sharp and abrupt in an instant's time.

"Do you...hate her?" He had to know whether or not that was so, whether this was part of Mari.

He felt her arm tighten on him, not affectionately but with tension. "I told you I won't—No, I don't hate her. I can't. I tried, for years I tried to hate her, but I couldn't. My father, too." After a moment she spoke again, the words coming in a rush. "I just don't understand. I've never understood. How could they do that? How could they pretend that I'd never existed? How could they cut me out of their lives like that?"

"Perhaps—"

"No! Don't defend them!" Mari shook her head. "All the common parents did it when we were apprentices, just stopped writing and stopped caring. We were all so hurt and ashamed that we never wanted to talk about it. Now it doesn't matter why. I don't care about my parents anymore."

It was obvious that she was lying. "Can I help?"

"You can stop talking about them." Mari's arm tightened around him enough to hurt for a moment, but she did not seem to be aware of it. "I'm sorry. Just drop it, please. It's not your problem."

"Your problems are my problems now. Is that not so?"

Another tightening of Mari's grip, though this time it felt affectionate. "Thank you. But it's not really a problem. It's over, is all."

"May I ask if you had a brother or a sister?"

There was a long pause, then he heard the loss in her voice. "No. Just me. Just as well, don't you think? They couldn't do to any other child what they did to me. Now, not another word about that, Alain. Please."

He focused on the road, paying attention to the places where melting snow had exposed mud or the snow still lay drifted and must be walked around.

They reached a crossroads, traffic from the other road joining theirs, the surface under the snow now gravel, the snow itself packed down by the tread of many feet. Alain studied the snow, then spoke softly to Mari. "Part of a legion has traveled this way already. The boot marks are clear."

"A legion?" Mari looked down at the road worriedly. "I've seen legionaries at drill. I don't mind saying they scare me."

"They scare me as well. We must respect the threat from them." Alain looked back in the direction the legionaries must have come. "These were somewhere closer to the mountains, south of where we came."

It took her only a moment to understand. "They're part of the force that attacked you?"

"It seems likely, but that was a larger force than what I see traces of here."

"What does that mean?" Mari's eyes widened. "Some of them are behind us?"

"Yes." They sped up a little, but not by much because they knew they would be walking all day and because the growing density of foot travelers and horse or mule or oxen drawn carts, carriages and wagons made it hard to push faster than the flow of traffic. Alain found himself fighting down annoyance, and having to avoid showing his reaction when he was occasionally jostled or blocked by other people.

He looked around at the commons, some of them showing exasperation at the traffic, others just resignation. Beside him, Mari was doing a slow burn and plainly trying not to snarl at everyone and everything around them. "We have only been receiving the special treatment granted to members of the Great Guilds for a short time, and already we expect it," he told her. "How would this feel if we had been living with special privileges for many years?"

"Even more aggravating," Mari grumbled.

His eyes lingered on riders passing by, their progress a little easier because the crowds had to part before the horses.

Mari must have noticed his gaze. "If you really, really want to ride, we can try to get some horses."

"Your voice tells me that you do not really wish to do that," Alain said.

"I'd put it up with riding for your sake, but no, I wouldn't be happy. It's not that I don't like horses," Mari continued. "I mean, I like looking at them, and watching them run and everything. They're beautiful. But when I get in the saddle it's like I'm a misaligned part. I can't get comfortable or adjust right to the way the horse moves or anything. I think some horses laugh at me and others take pity on me, while some are just plain mean, but the truth is that I'm not a natural rider and probably will never be good at riding a horse. I'd rather walk for now."

"I was just thinking that we should continue walking," Alain said.

"That's what you were thinking while you were looking at those riders?" Mari asked skeptically.

"Yes."

"Liar."

"Like a Mage," Alain said, wondering if that was the right way to form a humorous response.

It must have been, because Mari laughed and wrapped her arm about his so that they walked side by side again.

They took a break around noon, standing to eat since there was nowhere to sit off the road that was not covered in snow or soaking wet. As they shared food and drink from Alain's pack, he felt a warning sensation. "More Mages are approaching," he whispered to Mari.

Her head came up in alarm. "Which way?"

"From the way we came. There are at least six."

"Can you hide from them?"

"I think so."

Mari frowned at him. "Get behind me. You should also physically hide yourself without being obvious about it. I'm not big enough to hide you, but maybe you'll be less noticeable that way." She took another look down the road. "I see some kind of banner."

The brass notes of horns sounded down the road, and Alain understood what the banners foretold. "The rest of the legion is coming. The Mages must be with them."

They could see commons hastily moving off the road now, going either right or left to clear the route for the oncoming legionaries. The speed and concern they showed made it clear what would happen to any common who was still in the way when the soldiers arrived.

Walking was impossible now with the shoulders of the road packed with commons and their wagons who had left the road, so Mari and Alain waited, he feeling exposed with Mages coming, even though Mari had positioned herself between him and the road. A sudden realization struck him then. *If they came for me, Mari would keep herself between them and me. She would be my shield.* The insight was both frightening and heartening, knowing that Mari cared enough to sacrifice herself for him but knowing that he could never allow her to be hurt. At such a moment, her status as the long-prophesized daughter mattered not at all. It was only because she was Mari. Alain redoubled his efforts to hide his presence from other Mages.

Cavalry led the column, but not very much of it. Alain, familiar with the makeup of Imperial forces from his schooling in the wars of common folk, wondered why more cavalry was not present. It was only as the first ranks of horsemen trotted past that he realized from the bandaged wounds on many of them that this was the same force which had ambushed and pursued the Alexdrians. *This is partly due to me. Their ranks are thin because I helped kill or seriously injure many of their comrades.* The pain that idea brought made Alain wish for a moment that he could still deny emotion.

Behind the cavalry came a long column of foot soldiers, the legionaries marching in ranks which filled the entire width of the road. The Imperial soldiers moved past, banners hanging almost limp in the mild breeze, silent except for the rattle of equipment, the clop of horse hooves, a drum pounding out cadence for the marchers and the sound of feet striking the road in endless repetition. The faces of the legionaries were weary, tired from the fight and from the march.

Alain could not help comparing the Imperial legion to the Alexdrian soldiers he had fought with, thinking that the Imperials seemed both grander and more lethal than the Alexdrians, with bright insignia and armor glittering in the sun and a practiced discipline to their movements. For the first time, he realized just how lucky he and the surviving Alexdrians had been to escape from these soldiers.

Then he felt a chill as two enclosed carriages came into view, their occupants screened behind curtains that completely covered the windows. The presence of the Mages inside the carriages glowed to Alain's Mage senses as he concentrated on hiding his presence from them. Those other Mages were not bothering to hide themselves, a good sign that they were not concerned enough to be alert for any signs of Alain's presence. These Mages were doubtless certain that he had died under the talons of the dragon.

Alain kept his eyes on the carriages, sensing that the first carriage had only two people in it, both radiating the power of potent Mages. Lightning and Dragon, surely, Alain thought, and both elders from the feel of them. He felt a moment of irrational pride that his Guild had felt it necessary to use two such powerful Mages against him.

Perhaps that moment of pride, the moment of distraction, betrayed him.

The second carriage held the six other Mages Alain had guessed at, those who had taken out the Alexdrian scouts without allowing them a chance to cry warning. As Alain watched that carriage pass, he felt a familiar presence among them.

The curtain over one window twitched open and a Mage looked out upon the crowd, her eyes going straight to Alain. He saw long blonde hair, blue eyes, and a familiar face of surpassing natural beauty. Asha. Her eyes met his, but her face remained impassive, as that of a Mage should. Alain stared back at her, knowing that she must have sensed his presence, as he had hers, perhaps because of his familiarity to her. She must have recognized his face. What could he and Mari do when Asha called out an alarm? With all of the Imperial soldiers at hand as well as at least seven more Mages, neither Alain nor Mari would stand a chance. *Perhaps I can draw all of the attention onto myself and Mari can escape. It will be her only hope for survival.* He tensed, ready to run away from Mari the moment Asha acted.

CHAPTER TEN

Asha's eyes stayed locked on Alain's for a long moment as the carriage drove past. Then Asha leaned back and let the curtain drop.

He waited, barely able to believe that Asha had not betrayed him to the Guild and the Imperials. But there was no alarm, no variation in the steady pace of the marching column, as the carriages of the Mages moved away down the road. Though Alain strained his senses, he could feel no sign that any of the Mages within the carriages were preparing spells.

Mari turned and gave him a worried look. "What happened? One of the Mages looked out and you suddenly tensed up, like you expected trouble."

Alain relaxed himself with an effort. "One of the Mages in the second wagon saw me and knew me," he explained in a low voice. Mari's eyes flared in alarm. "But she did nothing."

"The Mage who looked out toward us? Wait a minute." Her tone of voice went very quickly from alarm to umbrage. "Blond. Beautiful. Was that Asha?" Mari demanded.

"Yes, that was Asha."

"That was Asha."

"Yes," Alain repeated, wondering why he felt so worried by the way Mari looked at him.

"She has blue eyes," Mari said, pointing her forefinger at Alain. "You didn't tell me that she had blue eyes. And you didn't tell me she was beautiful."

"I told you she was very attractive. I did not mention the eyes because I did not think that was important."

"Not important?" Mari glared at Alain. "How old is she?"

"I do not know exactly. I believe she is perhaps two years older than me."

"Oh! Great!"

Alain watched Mari, unable to understand what was wrong. "She did not betray us, Mari. There is no need to be concerned."

"I'm not concerned!" Mari growled back at him.

"But—" Alain decided he should stop trying to explain. Mari was staring at the last of the Imperial forces marching past, her face unyielding. Alain watched them, too, wondering why Mari was so unhappy and why Asha had not betrayed him. Two women acting in ways he did not understand. Nothing in his Mage training had prepared Alain for this.

The last ranks of foot soldiers passed. Bringing up the rear came wagon after wagon, most being driven by farmers or merchants who had been pressed into service along with their vehicles and draft animals. Inside the wagons lay soldiers too badly wounded to walk or ride, sometimes moaning as the wagons jolted them. Mari leaned back to murmur to him. "They didn't get off easy either, did they?" Her bad mood seemed to have passed as quickly as the storm.

Alain just nodded. He wondered why he felt neither pride in having hurt so many of the enemy, nor revulsion in the harm he had caused to save the Alexdrians, just a melancholy at the sight of the suffering. "The Free Cities and the Empire have been waging war for centuries, to no purpose. Men and women die, but nothing ever changes."

"What a waste," Mari said. "But their deaths do accomplish something. They die to keep the world stable, so that the Great Guilds can continue to rule." She stared at the last wagons full of wounded as they passed. "What are you thinking now?"

"I am thinking that within a few years such deaths, such suffering, will occur on a scale so vast that all this world will be filled with it,"

Alain said. "And there will be no safe refuge for the injured or any others. Unless this world does change. That is its only hope, that one person can bring about change."

She looked over and back at him, somber and subdued. "Remember that 'no pressure' thing I mentioned? Why me, Alain?"

"I do not know."

"I already know how delusional you are concerning me," Mari told him, "but why does everyone else seem to think I'm either their great hope or really dangerous?"

He had no answer to that. Mari nodded resignedly to him, then gripped his hand. Together she and Alain joined the mass of commons once again clogging the road to Umburan in the wake of the legion.

✳ ✳ ✳

It took close to the week Calu had predicted before Mari and Alain reached Umburan, walking almost all the way since few wagons passing them had room for riders. By the time they limped into the city, Mari was rethinking her opposition to more horseback riding.

Mari had planned to pass through Umburan as quickly as possible. After she had learned about Alain's battle, that desire had been reinforced by worries about lingering too close to where the engagement had been fought. There were Imperials in Umburan who could conceivably have seen the young Mage accompanying the Alexdrians, and there were those eight Mages who might have been passing through or might live in the city's Mage Guild Hall.

But now she had to try to meet with Calu, and in any case by the time they reached Umburan the Imperial troops who had marched by them had already had plenty of time to monopolize all outgoing transport for the next few days. With no way out of the city except by walking—making them too slow and too easily intercepted by anyone looking for them—Mari decided it was just as well that they were planning to stay a while longer. Few would be leaving Umburan until the horses, wagons, coaches and other forms of transportation which had been requisitioned by the Imperial military were freed up for use by civilians again.

Alain, though, wanted to increase their risk. "I should go closer to the Mage Guild Hall to see if I can detect the presence of the Mage Asha," he argued.

"Why are you so eager to find this Mage Asha again?" Mari demanded, fighting off the aggravation she felt every time the name came up. "Catching up on old times is dangerous, and according to you she wouldn't be interested in that anyway."

"She may have important information," Alain said.

"I'm sure."

"Why does Asha concern you?" Alain asked.

"She doesn't concern me. Your old friends are no business of mine. All that I'm worried about is the danger to us." The small room they had rented in a hostel had thin walls, so they kept their voices low and tried to ignore the sounds that leaked in from the rooms around them.

"Your feelings do not match your words," Alain said.

"My feelings? My feelings are none of your business!"

Alain watched her for a moment with a puzzled air.

Normally Mari got joy out of spotting expressions on his face, but not right now. She schooled her voice to sound as reasonable as possible. "I don't think it's wise to seek out other Mages, particularly other Mages who were part of a group which recently tried to kill you. If there's going to be contact between you and other Mages, I would just prefer it happen a little farther down the road."

Alain sat silent for a little while, then nodded. "I do understand. It is hard for me to explain why I believe that Asha can be trusted."

"It's not all that hard to understand," Mari grumbled, thinking of the female Mage's hair, eyes and face.

"Perhaps you can explain it to me, then," Alain suggested.

"I don't think so." Mari checked the time. "I need to go meet with Calu."

Alain stood up. "I will watch from outside the bookselling place while you meet with him, to ensure no one approaches. There is a chance he is being watched by your Guild just as you were in Dorcastle."

"That's right. Thanks." Mari felt another of those pangs of guilt. She had been sniping at Alain over an old girlfriend of his, yet Alain was being perfectly reasonable about Mari's need to see Calu. "I'm sorry I've been a little on edge."

"A little?"

"Watch it." She unbent enough to explain. "I'm worrying about so many things: about the dangers to you and me, and what to do, and how to get to Severun, and...to be honest, I'm also dealing with some pretty powerful emotions that I haven't ever felt before, either. Sometimes I think they make me a little crazy."

They found the bookstore without too much trouble. Mari paused on the street, staring south to where the usual large plaza opened out around the Mechanics Guild Hall. Mechanics Guild Halls had been her homes since she was a small child. They had been her safety and sanctuary against the outside world, they had been where her friends and co-workers were. She had been educated and trained in them. To have those Guild Halls be a place where enemies lurked was very disturbing, as if a long-trusted friend or a stern but loving parent had changed inside to be a deadly foe. Mari could sometimes go for long stretches now without being conscious of not wearing her Mechanics jacket, but this close to a Guild Hall she suddenly felt naked without it. She belonged in that Guild Hall, she should be wearing her jacket, and there should be no doubts or fears within her.

That was what she had been taught as an apprentice. That was what she had once believed. Now, every certainty had been replaced by distrust.

Mari and Alain lurked in a shaded area until they saw Calu appear, strolling along until he entered the bookstore. "Do you see anything?" Mari asked.

"No. Nor does my foresight warn of danger."

"Good." She paused to look at him. "Thanks for putting up with me when I get hard to live with."

Alain bowed toward her. "I know that I am not always easy to live with, and I understand the no pressure you are under."

"You mean the pressure I'm under," Mari said. "No pressure means, uh, pressure...never mind. Thank you."

I will watch," Alain said. "Go meet your friend. What would be appropriate for me to say to him?"

"Uh...that you were sorry you had to stay out here keeping a watch for danger and couldn't say hello in person."

"Say that to Mechanic Calu for me," Alain said.

"Sure." Smiling despite her worries, Mari walked across the street and down to the bookstore with as casual a gait as she could manage. Her inability ever to manage the swagger employed by most Mechanics was a good thing, since it meant she didn't have to remind herself to walk like a common.

Partlyfilled bookshelves lined the walls and ran down the center of the store. Calu was standing to one side, screened from the view of the owner by a wall of shelves. Mari walked up next to him as if wandering through the store. "Hi, Mechanic."

Calu glanced over at her with a relieved expression. "You made it. Where's your, uh, Alain?"

"Outside, keeping an eye out for trouble. He said he was sorry he couldn't say hello in person."

"Did he really?"

"Yeah." Mari couldn't help grinning. "He really is trying to be human again."

"Good for Alain." Calu regarded her solemnly. "You need all the friends you can get right now, Mari. The alert on you has been upgraded to an arrest order."

"An arrest order?" She had been expecting it, yet it still felt like a punch in the gut. "Any reason?"

"For the good of the Guild." Calu snorted in derision. "And allegedly for your own good. We no sooner got back here after the blizzard than the Guild Hall supervisor called us in and asked us if anyone had seen or heard anything of Master Mechanic Mari of Caer Lyn."

Mari made a pained sound. "Senior Mechanics always pretended to forget to call me a Master Mechanic, but now that they're trying to get me arrested, they remember."

"The Senior Mechanic said that you had last been seen in Alexdria." Calu shook his head. "They also said that an expended weapon believed to have been in your possession was found in a pass leading into the Empire, so they thought you might've come this way. That's why they asked us if we had seen you."

"An expended weapon?" Mari winced. "Alli's dragon killer."

"Yeah, although needless to say the Senior Mechanic didn't mention finding a dead dragon near it."

"They just found one weapon?"

"Yup." Calu pretended to be examining some of the books before him. "But they also found a large group of Alexdrian soldiers, who first claimed not to have seen you. But they had a horse with them which matched the one you had bought in Alexdria, and when confronted with that and the evidence of the weapon they admitted they had seen a Mechanic heading south toward Kelsi. She was alone, these soldiers swore, and had traded horses for one of theirs since hers was worn out. They also said this Mechanic had asked them how hard it was to get a ship to Farland from Kelsi or Marida at this time of year." Calu glanced at her again. "I used to think that commons were so afraid of Mechanics that they'd always tell us the truth. Now I'm never going to talk to commons again without wondering whether or not they're lying to me."

Mari breathed a thank-you to General Flyn. Farland was as distant as any place on the Sea of Bakre could be, and almost the exact opposite direction from the way she had actually gone with Alain. She had a mental vision of General Flyn earnestly, politely, and oh-so-respectfully lying his head off to the Mechanics who had questioned him. "The Guild thinks I'm trying to get to Farland, then?"

"Yeah. We were asked if any of us knew anyone you might know there, and whether we'd gotten any letters from you." Calu took a book, pretending to look at it and shaking his head. "Mari, we got word of all this as soon as we got back here, which means somebody found out this stuff quickly enough to have it sent by long-distance far-talker and then relayed here. There must have been some Mechanics pretty close behind you."

Mari stared at the books before her, not focusing on their titles. "They must have been real close. Not much more than a day behind, I'd guess. I thought I had done a decent job of throwing off any potential trackers before I left Alexdria, but if I hadn't been moving fast they might have caught up to me before I reached Alain."

"Any idea why they didn't catch you after that?"

"Well, the commons lied to them, and Alain and I headed off the main pass, taking a small hidden route to the north. Anyone sent on east through the pass wouldn't have found us." She gave a heavy sigh of relief. "We thought we were just avoiding any legionaries ahead of us at the mouth of the pass, but we ended up sidestepping Mechanics coming up behind us, too."

"Lucky," Calu commented. "But it means the Guild was following you pretty well."

"I was wearing my jacket after I left Alexdria," Mari admitted. "I thought in Free Cities territory I'd be safer traveling alone as a Mechanic than as a common."

"Wrong."

"Yeah," Mari agreed. "Hopefully the commons and the detour and the blizzard threw the Guild off my track."

"I think so," Calu said, "since the Guild is asking everyone where you might be. But that means a lot of people will be looking for you, and the Guild is obviously keeping an eye out for you here in Imperial territory as well as elsewhere. The Senior Mechanics were all saying the Guild is worried about you, that you had gotten hurt in Ringhmon, hit on the head, and now might be irrational and in need of care."

"That's funny," Mari grumbled. "They weren't too worried about the lump on my head while I was still at Ringhmon."

"So," Calu continued, "you might say crazy things or believe crazy things, but if any of us saw you we were to either talk you into coming back to a Guild Hall with us or else go immediately and get some Mechanics to bring you back."

"I feel so warm and happy knowing how much the Senior Mechanics care."

He turned his head to face her. "Oh, they're worried about you, Mari," Calu assured her. "But what they're worried about is what you're doing. This is serious."

"I know. They tried to get me killed, remember?"

"I guess I was hoping you were wrong about that." Calu thought for a moment. "As far as I can tell without asking, they don't know about Alain. They think you're alone, but they're obviously worried about some other Mechanics joining up with you. They kept coming back to that, where your friends were and whether or not you'd be going to see them."

Mari sighed again, shaking her head. "I hope nobody gets in trouble just for knowing me. Did you tell them that you're a friend of mine?"

He gave her a sidelong wink. "I told them I used to know you. I figured they'd hear that quickly enough, anyway. I said it had been a long time since I'd seen any letters from you, though, which was true enough."

"Calu, I don't know how to thank you for telling me all this, but please don't stick your neck out anymore."

He made a face. "I'm not sure how much more I can do. The Senior Mechanics said we'll be getting a list of Mari's known friends soon, so I guess at that point they'll really get suspicious of me."

"My friends?" Mari leaned her forehead against the books in front of her. "Why do they have to be singled out?"

"You're not doing it, Mari, and I'm the only one of them who actually knows anything, right?"

"At the moment, yeah, but I got that weapon from Alli."

"Uh-huh." Calu made another face. "You didn't know it might get her in that much trouble, and you needed that weapon. Alli's a big girl, Mari. She can take care of herself. And if she needs help, I'll find a way to get to her." He paused again. "Can you tell me anything more about what you're doing?"

"You know where I'm going," Mari said, "and that's probably more than you should know for your own protection."

"Yeah, but what are you going to *do*, Mari? What the Guild is doing to you is wrong, the way innovation and technology are being suppressed is wrong, hiding the truth about Mages and these guys you call Dark Mechanics is wrong. Something has to be done."

She stared at the books before her, gaze unfocused again. "I don't know. I need to talk to Professor S'san. I need to learn more. I can't make decisions without more data, without having a better idea of what the results will be and what outcome I need to aim for. And to be honest, I'm not sure what I can do even once I find out what I need to know."

"Something has to be done," Calu repeated. "Did you know the long-distance far-talker in the Umburan Guild Hall is busted? I didn't mention that at the inn. They haven't been able to get it working for over a month now."

A Guild Hall long-distance far-talker broken and unrepairable. Mari shook her head in amazement. "A while back I heard the far-talker at another Guild Hall was out of commission for a couple of weeks. A month?"

"Yup. The Guild Hall in Umburan is dependent on written communications. We got that report on you by courier from the Guild Hall in Pandin." Calu gave Mari a look as if he didn't expect to be believed.

"They've told us here in Umburan to be ready to shift to continuous wave communications for good. You know, not voice, but that dot-dash code. The gear's less complicated. Did you ever meet a Mechanic named Yasmin? Yasmin of Westport. She's pretty sharp. Just one step shy of Master status herself. Anyway, her specialty is stuff like far-talkers. She came up with this idea for getting Umburan's big far-talker working, but when she presented it to the Senior Mechanics they took her notes and plans and told her to forget it. Yasmin was really unhappy."

"I'll bet," Mari agreed. "I know how she feels. Do you know why the Senior Mechanics killed her idea?"

"Because it involved a design change for some of the circuits. Innovation. All she wanted to do was alter some circuits to get the equipment working again, but that's prohibited. It's by the book or we don't do it at all."

Mari nodded slowly. "The Guild doesn't want change, but something has to change. Something big has to change."

"There's plenty of Mechanics who believe that, or are worried about it, but they can't get organized. They need a leader." Calu glanced at Mari again.

"Don't look at me! Why do people keep doing that? Why have people always been doing that?"

"There must be a reason." Calu grinned lopsidedly. "When you decide what to do, you've got your gang backing you up."

"Thanks. I've got a general, too. No army, but I've got a general."

"Really? I wish I had a general." Calu grinned again but the expression shifted back to a serious look. "The Guild Hall here could find out that I'm a known friend of Mari any day now, and then meeting with you will be too risky because they'll probably put a watch on me. You need to get out of Umburan as soon as possible. Avoid Guild Halls and see what this professor can tell you. I'm going to pretend I'm a naïve young Mechanic who believes that garbage about the Guild wanting to help you, and maybe that way I'll be able to find a little of what the Guild is doing and maybe lead them astray from finding you."

"Calu, please don't," Mari said. "If they find out you're doing that you could get in serious trouble."

"What was that? I don't copy you."

Mari tried to glower at him despite the elation his friendship brought her. "Alli will kill you if you get hurt playing spy against the Guild. Then she'll kill me for letting you get hurt. For both of our sakes, be careful."

He nodded. "Will do. Say hi to Alain for me. Tell him I'm counting on him to keep you safe."

"Calu...thanks. For everything. I was so afraid of what you might think of him."

"Alain? That guy will die for you, Mari. How can I dislike somebody like that?" Calu swung one hand out low toward her. "Good luck. Get the blazes out of this city."

"All right." She clasped his hand tightly for a moment. "See you. Stay safe. Don't take any risks."

"Yes, Lady Master Mechanic. I won't be anything like you."

She stuck her tongue out at Calu, he grinned once more, then Mari turned and walked out of the bookstore, trying to calm her nerves.

Alain waited until she rejoined him. "You are more worried now," he said.

"Yeah. I'll tell you everything he told me, but first we need to see how fast we can get out of Umburan."

❋　　❋　　❋

Another nerve-wracking day later, passage out of Umburan was reopened to civilians. There was a Mechanic rail line running southeast to Pandin, but given what Calu had told them that was simply too risky at this point. Instead, Mari and Alain stood in a long line to purchase tickets on one of the horse-drawn coaches making regular runs between the cities. The coach was noisy, cramped, bumpy and slow. Mari endured it, feeling guilty for forcing Alain to put up with the trip as well. She had noticed how uncomfortable he remained with human contact. Most human contact, anyway. He was getting much more comfortable with her touch, which was one of the few bright lights in her life at the moment.

But even the most tedious trip ends eventually. It was late afternoon when they reached Pandin. Mari stepped off the coach, wondering if her body would ever stop feeling stiff again. If she wasn't being put through heavy physical stress like hiking through a snowstorm, she was being forced to sit inactive in a hostel room or a crowded coach for hours on end. Her muscles kept getting completely different workouts and were expressing their confusion in uncomfortable ways. "You know what, Alain?" she whispered. "Life as a common is no fun at all."

"I was trained to endure hardship, but I agree."

She and Alain stopped to hoist their packs, waiting while the other passengers went past them and a few people came forward to meet some of the arrivals. Mari ignored them all, knowing no one should be expecting them in Pandin. A moment later, her expectations proved wrong.

"Lady Mechanic."

It took Mari a moment to realize that the man who had walked up to stand nearby had addressed her in a voice just loud enough to be heard by her. Then it took another moment to recall that she wasn't wearing her Mechanics jacket. She looked directly at him, not speaking, ready to run or fight if he proved to be from the Mechanics Guild. "Are you talking to me?"

Alain moved slightly to one side, giving him a clear shot at the man. Mari noticed him tensing the way he did before casting one of his spells. She glanced around, trying to spot any other people who might be working with this man, but couldn't see any.

The man smiled slightly. "I know you. I know you're a Mechanic. Let's not play games."

"Are you with the Guild?" Mari asked calmly. She searched the area again for signs of Mechanics ready to arrest her, looking for possible escape routes. Her hand twitched, wanting to reach for her pistol in its shoulder holster under her coat, but she held it down at her side. It seemed best not to reveal that she was armed, not until she understood what was going on.

Alain was waiting silently. Mari knew that if the man made a wrong move, Alain would strike.

The man shook his head. "No. I'm not with your Guild. If you'd like to know how I know you, and what I can do for you, come along."

"Why should I trust you enough to come along with you?"

"You wouldn't like the alternative." The man's smile was unpleasant this time.

Mari thought quickly. She and Alain were very exposed out in the open. If anyone had crossbows, or rifles, trained on them, both she and Alain could be killed very quickly. "All right. I'll follow, but you won't like what happens if you try to betray me."

The man looked over at Alain. "I saw you talking to him. You were with him at Umburan."

They had been watched for a while, it seemed, but whoever this man represented hadn't tried anything at Umburan. The Mechanics Guild wouldn't have hesitated, meaning this man didn't work for the Guild. "That's right," Mari said. "We're partners."

"Trying to build your own mob?" The man showed his teeth in a derisive smile. "Fine. We can always use another Mechanic." The man tilted his head to one side. "This way."

Mari glanced at Alain, trying to convey that he should pretend to be a Mechanic, and the Mage nodded back, indicating he would follow her lead.

Mari let the man lead her and Alain out of the large courtyard where carriages dropped off and picked up passengers. Once surrounded by buildings, she casually checked out the windows looking down on their path, trying without success to spot any snipers.

They followed the man all the way down the street, around a corner, across the next street, and into a restaurant with a discreet sign advertising its presence. Looking around offhandedly as they walked upstairs to the second floor, Mari realized that this was one of those places which catered to people who wanted privacy. Dining booths lined the walls, each having solid backs going up to the ceiling and each boasting a heavy curtain which could be drawn if desired. The man led her and Alain all the way to a booth against one back wall, then sat down.

Alain halted Mari as she started to follow, instead sliding in first so he was against the wall. Not certain why he had done that, she sat down next to Alain, looking coldly at the man. "What's this about?" she asked in a quiet voice.

The man shook his head, waiting until the waiter had asked for an order, then waiting again until wine arrived. He poured from a single bottle into glasses before himself, Mari, and Alain, then sat back. "I first saw you in Dorcastle," the man remarked.

"Oh?" Mari tried to look disinterested, pointedly ignoring the wine glass in front of her. "Were you a dragon?"

"I was helping with that little plan, yes," the man answered in a placid voice. "It was working pretty well, but then something happened to the warehouse we were using."

A Dark Mechanic, then. If nothing else, this contact confirmed for Mari that the Dark Mechanics had been watching her since at least Dorcastle. "Too bad it didn't work out for you."

He smiled back at her, but it was a thin-lipped smile lacking in any humor. "Yeah. Some nosy Mechanic found our barge, then some Mages attacked, then the whole warehouse blew up. But you wouldn't know anything about that."

"I might," Mari admitted, saying nothing else.

"We haven't figured out how the Mages found us," the Dark Mechanic continued, "but we think you were somehow involved in that, too. We lost some of our members and a lot of equipment. There were plenty of people who just wanted to get rid of the Mechanic who caused us so much trouble. You understand."

"I do. A couple of them took shots at me in Edinton."

Another insincere smile from the man. "They got disciplined for trying to nail the Mechanic without orders, and for missing their shots. Sometimes you can't win. But even though we had plenty of reasons to get rid of that Mechanic for good, a number of people thought that somebody with her smarts and her guts might be a very useful member of our organization, especially since she's having some problems with her own Guild."

"Problems?" Mari asked.

"Arrest order, as I'm sure you're already aware. It's funny to think that I could pick up a nice piece of change from the Mechanics Guild for hauling you to them."

Mari gave the man her own artificial smile. "If you tried, you might find that earning that reward isn't all that easy. You want me to join your organization?"

"It would be a mutually beneficial decision," the man observed, studying his fingernails.

That she hadn't expected. A recruitment offer. Mari wished she could look at Alain to catch his reaction, but didn't want to take her eyes off of the Dark Mechanic. "What organization is this?"

"The Order."

"The Order of what?"

The man shook his head. "Of nothing. Just the Order."

"And what does the Order do for a living besides tearing up things while making ransom demands?"

"Protection," the man explained smoothly. "We were asking for Dorcastle to pay us money to protect them from dragons or...other problems. There were negotiations under way with the city. The city was getting ready to pay a very nice sum when you ruined everything."

Mari gave him another insincere smile. "I can't tell you how sorry I am. You were blackmailing Ringhmon, too, weren't you?"

"That cost us a lot. We were ready to pay you back after you messed up our deal in Ringhmon. It's a shame our attempt to eliminate you failed."

"An attempt involving a wrecked train trestle?" Mari asked, thinking of how close the locomotive she was riding had come to going off the destroyed bridge. "I'm not that easy to eliminate."

A glint of anger showed in the man's eyes. "No, you're not. The Order decided to give you a chance to work with us instead of against us. You might want to give it serious consideration."

Mari nodded, thinking furiously about how to learn as much as possible from this man before trying to get out of this restaurant in one piece. "I'd need to know more about you. What does this Order do? What's its reason for existence?"

The man shrugged. "We've been over that. Profit."

"That's it?"

"What else?"

Mari grimaced. "If this Order truly knows the Mechanic arts, you could do a lot of good."

The man gave another one of his humorless smiles. "We do plenty of good. For ourselves."

"And no one else?"

"Are you trying to make me laugh, Lady Mechanic?" The man leaned back, giving her a scornful look. "Mechanics are taught to look out for themselves. We're just doing the same thing, only the Order is willing to do a few things your Guild won't. Or maybe I should say your former Guild. And now you're obviously getting ready to set up your own outfit, infringing on the Order's territory. Did I mention that doing that would be a very big mistake?"

"No," Mari replied in frigid tones, "you didn't. So, anything goes as far as the Order is concerned? Anything that might turn a profit? No matter the cost to someone else?"

The man looked as though he were pretending to think about her questions. Then he grinned. "That's right."

"And you expect me to join with you in this?"

This time the man shook his head, even though his nasty grin didn't waver. "No, Lady Mechanic. I don't expect you to agree to join the Order. I expect you to turn us down. I'm actually hoping you turn us down. It wasn't my idea to make you this offer, but I got outvoted."

Mari nodded, tensing and wondering how quickly she could draw the pistol under her coat. "What happens if I say I want to think it over?"

"You've got all the time you want," the man assured her. "Just as long as you're not planning on leaving this booth before you decide."

"I see." Out of the corner of her eye, Mari was noticing that several of the booths on the opposite side of the restaurant had curtains drawn. How many of those might hold other members of the Order? What weapons might they be armed with? The man's attitude made it clear that if she didn't agree to join the Order she wouldn't leave this room alive. But agreeing to go with him, even if she didn't mean it, would require placing herself totally in the power of the Order. That felt very dangerous.

Mari took a long, slow breath, then looked at Alain. "Have you made up your mind?"

He nodded, his face revealing nothing. "I am ready."

Chapter Eleven

"All right." Mari kicked out, her boot catching the man's ankle and drawing a yelp of pain. The man fumbled with the weapon he had been in the act of trying to draw as Mari grabbed the wine bottle and slammed it against his head. Watching curtains being yanked back on some of the other booths in the room, Mari began sliding out of her seat as the man slumped down onto the table. Before she could tell who was inside those booths, Alain had grabbed her and pulled her back inside their own.

"Close our curtain," he said.

Not waiting to ask, Mari used one hand to sweep the curtain to their booth closed, brandishing her pistol as she did so to dissuade anyone from rushing in immediately. "Now what? Why didn't you let me run?"

"There are better ways to leave."

Mari gave Alain a quick, puzzled look, then saw the wall beside his booth seat now had a hole in it, a hole large enough for them to get through. "I forgot all about that."

The thunk of handheld mini-crossbows firing echoed in the room and the curtain to their booth jerked as bolts tore through it. Alain was already sliding through the hole, then turned to help her. Mari ducked down as low as she could get as more bolts thudded into the booth. A moment after she had cleared the hole, it vanished as if it had never been. "That should slow down any pursuers," Alain remarked.

Mari impulsively kissed him. "I love you, my Mage."

Alain twitched one of his small smiles at the possessive term. "We have to keep moving and get away from here. Though they may not be able to figure out how we escaped, they can still launch a search of the area."

A couple of more thunks startled Mari, and she turned to see the very tip of one bolt sticking through the wall. "Let's hope they keep shooting into that booth for a while before they charge it." An ugly thought struck then. "We left that guy in the booth. He might get killed by his own people."

Alain gave her a dispassionate look. "Waste no concerns on him. When he spoke of the Dark Mechanic who shot at you in Edinton, I could see in him that he was one of those who tried to kill you there."

Mari couldn't help shivering. She had never before looked closely upon someone who had tried to kill her. "Thanks for not telling me that earlier." She looked around, seeing that they were on the upper floor of a laundry, with rack after rack of clothing hanging from rails on the ceiling. The distant sound of voices and splashing water warned of laundry workers laboring on the first floor. "It might be very hard to sneak past whoever is downstairs here, and if there's anyone watching the outside of that restaurant, they might see us leaving an adjacent doorway. Can you get us through another wall?"

"Yes, but the fewer walls the better. If we are going to run, I cannot afford to exhaust myself. Also, each time I use a spell, I risk revealing my presence to nearby Mages."

"We'll keep the walls to a minimum. Follow me." Mari started across the laundry, ducking down to scuttle under the rows of hanging garments. "I just wish I knew how those guys spotted us and knew we'd be on that coach."

"He said we had been seen together in Umburan," Alain noted.

"We were stuck in that town for days. Even though we stayed in our hostel room most of the time, someone must have seen me there, and after they watched us get on the coach, they called ahead to Pandin. I bet anything that the Order has far-talkers."

"Far-talkers?" Alain disentangled himself from the low-hanging hem of a long dress.

"Yes." Mari ducked under another row of clothing. She didn't see much sense in worrying now about some of the Guild rules that had kept her from talking to Alain in the past. "They're exactly what the name says, devices that allow us to talk across a distance. You've seen me use one, in Dorcastle. I've still got one with me, because as a Master Mechanic I was authorized to have one, and I thought it might be important at some point to have a far-talker."

To her surprise, Alain just nodded as if she had said something unremarkable. "The Mages have such things. There are those who can create spell creatures and send them to where we wish the message delivered."

"Uh, yes, but this is science, Alain. Far-talkers don't use spell creatures."

"What do they use?"

Mari wondered just how far across this laundry was as she ducked under yet another row of hanging clothing, then wondered how to explain far-talker transmissions to a Mage with no technical background at all. "They send, uh, these sort of invisible wave things."

"Invisible wave things?"

"Yes, waves. Of energy. The invisible waves carry messages."

Alain nodded again. "Like the spell creatures?"

"No, they don't really carry a message," Mari explained, "they, um, are the message."

"The message delivers itself?"

"Sort of. Yes. It's hard to describe." Why did science sound so much more mystical than the Mage arts? "Here's the next wall." She heard the voices downstairs pause and wondered if they had been speaking too loudly or if their footsteps had been heard. "How long will it take you?" she whispered urgently. *I'm asking someone to hurry up and create an imaginary hole in a wall. Sometimes I stop to think about this and it's scary.*

"Not long." Alain came up beside her, stood up in the gap between the last row of clothes and the wall, and took on a look of concentration. A moment later a roughly Mari-sized hole appeared in the wall. Mari stepped through cautiously, moving the pistol held in her hand back and forth in search of threats. This room was dark, with vague bulky shapes visible in the light coming in through the hole behind her.

Alain bent and turned to get through the hole. Once he was beside her the hole vanished, leaving them in darkness.

Not wanting to use her hand light, which might reveal their presence to anyone watching, Mari felt her way forward, spotting a rectangle of light that must mark the borders of a door. The door wasn't locked, so they opened it carefully, peering out into a deserted hallway.

"Unoccupied offices, I guess," Mari whispered. She led the way to the stairs and went down them, Mari wincing as each stair creaked with what seemed to be an incredible amount of noise. On the ground floor, a few small window openings were boarded up. "Great. How do we leave a boarded up building without someone noticing?"

Alain sighed. "Let us go to the back. If we cannot open a door there, I will make another opening." He seemed tired already.

"Let's hope we won't need to do that." Mari smiled at him. "Have I told you you're great to have around when bad guys are on the hunt?"

Alain managed another one of his smiles. "I can be useful in dungeons as well."

"True." They had to kick open an interior door before reaching the back. There Mari found a door locked from the outside. Grumbling, she pulled out a tool from her pack and hastily pulled the bolts from the hinges, then swung the door open backwards. Alain was watching her with a perplexed expression, plainly trying to figure out how she had done that. It was a source of unending amazement for her that a man who thought being able to walk through a solid wall was no big deal regarded the most simple mechanical tasks as mysterious and unfathomable.

The door let out into an alley, where Mari paused to look both ways, her pistol at ready. "Now what?"

"We can assume all ways out of the city will be watched."

"We can't afford to stay here, Alain. Pandin's already too dangerous for us."

"No, we cannot stay. But we can confuse our pursuers as to where we are going. I have thought of a plan, a stratagem."

"A stratagem?" Mari asked, impressed by his use of the term. "Really?"

He led them both out the alley and onto the street, walking rapidly back toward the coach station as Alain talked. "I am assuming someone may be watching for us," he assured Mari. "Let us get on the coach to Marida."

"We don't want to go to Marida, Alain!" Mari objected. "It's a seaport and we'd need to leave Imperial territory to get there. There'll be more spies and more Imperial security between here and there than anywhere inland!"

"We need only take the coach a short distance and then jump off to confuse our pursuers." Alain stopped speaking, staring ahead with a grim look in his eyes. "Then again, my foresight now warns of serious danger for us near the coach station. I do not think we will be allowed to leave that way."

Mari thought, running through options. "We have to get out of this city. Walking would be too slow, and...wait."

Alain looked at her. "I am already waiting."

"No, I meant— Never mind." She pointed in a direction where a smoky haze was visible over the city. "There's one way out that the Order will never suspect we'll take. We'll get on a train."

"A train?" Alain followed as Mari began walking rapidly toward the Mechanics Guild train station. "A Mechanic train such as we rode from Ringhmon? But your Guild seeks to arrest you."

"Yeah. Which means it would be crazy for me to walk into a Mechanic Guild train station. Which also means no one will expect me to do that," Mari explained, wondering to herself whether that actually sounded like a smart plan.

"But then—"

"I'm not wearing my jacket, Alain. My Guild thinks I'm still wearing it, they think I'm traveling alone, they don't think I'm in the Empire." Mari smiled in what she hoped was a confident way. "We should be okay. Just a couple of commons. The Mechanics here won't look twice at us."

Mari turned casually away from the ticket booth as she spotted the poster with an all-too-accurate drawing of her face on it just inside where the Apprentice selling tickets could easily see it. The Guild had been more efficient than she had expected. "Time for another plan," she muttered to Alain.

Gazing around the station, Mari saw that it resembled other Mechanic train stations. No surprise there, since the Guild had a mania for standardized design. The main difference from the train stations farther south was that up here the locomotives used coal to fire their boilers rather than the oil employed in the southern Empire and the Bakre Confederation. Instead of oil tanks, this station had large coal bunkers.

But if this station was otherwise just like the stations she was more familiar with... "I've got another idea. Follow me and try to look casual and unconcerned."

"That was easier to do before you announced that you had another idea," Alain said.

"Very funny," Mari said. "Lots of Mages in the world and I get the one with the hidden sense of humor. I've done way too good a job of teaching you sarcasm."

Mari led the way to one side, where crates, barrels and bags were stacked awaiting transport in freight cars. She slid smoothly in among the freight, ducking slightly so she was concealed behind the stacks, then moved rapidly toward the train just beyond.

There weren't any guards, just as Mari had expected, because no common would risk getting close to a Mechanic train except to board the passenger cars. She studied the nearest freight car, looking up and down the train. A small cluster of Mechanics and Apprentices was visible at the rear of the train, standing around talking before boarding the passenger car there. Up front, a single Mechanic and one Apprentice were fussing with the steam locomotive. No one was looking her way. Mari pulled out her Mechanics jacket and put it on, stuffing the common coat into her pack. "Stay here," she cautioned Alain, then stepped out from cover.

The door to the freight car was locked. Mari glanced up and down the track again, wondering what the odds were of getting the lock picked without anyone noticing. *Even though right now I look like just one more Mechanic, it's still too risky because no one should be popping open any of these cars right now. How can I get us inside this thing without being spotted?* She looked up, then beckoned to Alain. "Come on."

It took her five steps to the rear of the freight car, then Mari swung in between cars to where the small ladder leading up the back was located, pulling Alain behind her. She started climbing, glad to be hidden from the Mechanics at the front and rear of the train, pausing only to gesture Alain to climb after her.

The top of the freight car felt hideously exposed, but was actually screened right now from anyone close to the train. The lock on the small top-access door was also closed, but easier to pick than the side door would have been. Mari popped the lock in a few seconds, then beckoned Alain again, getting him down inside the freight car and following quickly. She stopped when only her head was still out in the open, listening and looking for any sign that someone had noticed. Reassured, Mari lowered herself into the freight car, swinging the door shut after her.

The car was almost full of freight, but that left plenty of room for the two of them. The sides of the car were supposed to be solid, but the car was old, the wood had shrunk and warped, and therefore there were numerous small gaps through which light and air could enter. "Welcome to our ride to Severun," she whispered. "Stay very quiet until the train starts moving."

Alain sat down on a crate, watching her. "We will travel in this wagon?"

"Yeah," Mari agreed, looking around for a less uncomfortable spot. "It'll be fast and no one will see us in here. Unless this car contains freight to be offloaded before the train reaches Severun."

"I see." Alain waited for Mari to continue, then finally spoke again. "What will we do if that happens?"

"I'll think of something."

"All right."

She stopped to look at him. "That answer satisfied you?"

"Yes."

Mari smiled at him, settling down onto the top of another crate. "Thanks."

It took a while for anything to happen after that, Mari and Alain sitting quietly and listening to the Mechanics outside calling orders to each other. One Mechanic apprentice came walking down the outside of the train rattling doors to ensure they were locked. He couldn't have seen them inside the car unless he had shined a light through one of the gaps and put his eyes up close, but she didn't relax until he had moved on. Mari wondered if she would have recognized the apprentice if they had met face to face. The idea depressed her, and she slumped against the nearest crate, eyes downcast.

Alain's hand touched hers, and when Mari looked up he tried to smile at her. She forced a return smile and he seemed to understand her mood, nodding silently, then leaving her to her thoughts.

The train whistle screamed, then the car jerked forward into motion. The outlying districts of Pandin rolled past as the locomotive began picking up speed and were replaced by the low hills on the northern side of vast Lake Bellad. Mari settled back and tried to rest. The crates weren't exactly comfortable, but compared to the crowded coach from Umburan this was almost luxurious. She finally fell asleep, lulled by the motion of the train.

She awakened sometime later when she felt Alain's hand on her arm.

"Something is amiss," he warned.

Mari stared around. Judging by the angles of the rays of light slanting in through the gaps between the sideboards of the car, the sun was much lower in the sky, but the train was still moving at a good clip. "What?"

"I do not know. I sense a Mage nearby and rapidly getting closer, though how this could be I do not understand since we are traveling so fast."

"He's in front of us somewhere," Mari explained patiently. "The train is moving toward this Mage—"

"The Mage is behind us, Mari."

Mari just stared for a moment. "The Mage is rapidly catching up with a train? What's he doing? Flying?"

"Flying? Of course. That explains it." Alain looked up. He didn't look worried, but that didn't mean anything, since even now Alain rarely let his feelings show.

Before Mari could say anything else the freight car shuddered and rocked, its wooden top bending and creaking alarmingly. Mari stared in shock as the wood overhead burst inward at one point, driven by an enormous bird's beak. The beak withdrew and an equally enormous bird's eye peered into the opening, twitching back and forth as it searched for something.

"It is a Roc," Alain explained in that same impassive tone of voice.

"Blazes!" Mari yelled, hauling out her pistol. Before she could fire, the eye jerked away, then the beak reappeared, tearing a bigger opening in the roof of the freight car. "Is it after us?"

"Probably," Alain agreed, his voice still unnaturally calm. "It is possible that I am still not good enough at hiding my presence from other Mages, but more likely my use of spells in Pandin led another Mage to find me and follow us long enough to determine that I had gotten on the train. The Mage riding this Roc—"

"There's a Mage riding it? That's real?"

"Nothing is—"

"Don't say it!" Mari flinched as broken wood showered downward and the roof of the freight car sagged alarmingly. "There's a giant bird being ridden by a Mage on top of this car and it's trying to kill you? That is insane!"

"It may be trying to kill you as well," Alain corrected.

"Great! Why did I get involved with a Mage? What do we do?"

Alain had been concentrating, and now Mari felt a gust of heat. The broken wood around the opening the Roc had been widening burst into flame and the giant beak jerked away. "That should discourage it." Alain noted.

"You set fire to the freight car we're inside and there's a giant bird outside trying to kill us!" Mari tried to calm herself as the car rocked violently again but fortunately didn't jump the rails. "Can you kill a Roc?"

Alain hesitated. "I can certainly try to harm the Mage riding and controlling it. I would rather not, though."

Mari stared again. "Why not?" she finally asked.

"Rocs are not like dragons or trolls. They have more the seeming of natural creatures, and the Mages who create them have ties to the Rocs."

It took her a moment to process that. "You don't want to kill the Mage or his giant, murderous pet bird."

"The Mage is female, I think," Alain corrected.

"Excuse me. *Her* giant, murderous pet bird." Mari looked up. The fire was spreading, but had at least driven away the Roc. "Will it leave now that the car is on fire?"

Alain frowned slightly in thought. "I doubt it. We would need to startle the creature beyond the Mage's ability to control it and also find a way to hide ourselves."

The freight car jolted again and part of the flaming roof fell into the car as huge talons punched through the still intact part of the roof. "That does it," Mari snapped. She raised her pistol and fired through the roof. A deafening squawk sounded and the freight car jerked once more, the talons vanishing and leaving ragged holes in their wake. "We've got to get out of here." How to startle a giant bird? How to drive it away? The answer suddenly seemed obvious. "We've got to get to the engine."

"The what?"

"The locomotive!"

Alain nodded, his Mage composure infuriating to Mari at the moment. "The Mechanic creature at the front of the train."

"Close enough." Mari holstered her pistol, making sure the holster was fastened shut, then climbed up some crates to get right under the opening which the Roc had torn in the car. The fire was still blazing but the dry wood wasn't generating much smoke, the flames pale in the late-afternoon sunlight as they ate at the freight car. Mari studied the wreckage carefully. "The bird knocked a big enough hole in the roof that we can get out, and the fire is on the downwind side. We just need to jump up and onto the still intact part of the roof at the front of the car." The freight car swayed wildly, the land rushing past on either hand. The train had increased speed to a dangerous velocity, probably trying to outrun the Mage creature.

She jumped up and forward, through the hole and outside onto the top of the freight car, skidding for a heart-stopping moment before she could stop her movement and cling to the oscillating roof. Alain landed beside her, missed his grip and began sliding off the roof. Mari grabbed his arm, going flat to grasp a good hold with her other hand. She felt a whoosh of air and something hard brushed her back, followed by an enormous, disappointed squawk from the Roc.

Mari caught her breath. Alain was still half off the roof, his feet dangling in open air, Mari's right hand locked onto his arm and her left hand gripping the other side of the roof.

Moving with strong, careful movements, Alain pulled himself up and next to her.

Mari swallowed, nerving herself. The locomotive was apparently running full out, wind was buffeting them, and the roof of the freight car kept swaying and jerking beneath them. Clouds of dirty smoke mixed with bits of flaming coal from the locomotive billowed over them, bringing up frightening memories of the fire in Ringhmon's city hall and limiting their ability to see the Roc somewhere overhead. Hopefully it would hide them from the Roc as well. "Follow me!" she yelled to Alain over the wind, then forced herself up despite her fears and scuttled forward.

There were three more freight cars between them and the locomotive. Mari wondered what the passengers farther back on the train thought of the Roc's attack, especially the Mechanics in the last passenger car. *Mages are frauds. That's what the Mechanics Guild insists, and that's what you've always been taught. How are you going to rationalize a giant bird tearing apart the train you're riding on? You'll be told not to talk about it, just like I was. You'll be told to pretend it never happened. Will any of you find yourselves unable to do that, and in the same trouble I got into?*

She reached the end of the roof, gazing across the gap to the next freight car. It wasn't all that far. An easy jump. Easy if the train wasn't thundering along the track as fast as it could move and the cars weren't threatening to jump the rails at any moment and the wind wasn't tearing at her and a giant bird wasn't somewhere above doubtless getting ready to dive on her again.

Mari jumped, landing with her boots sliding for purchase on the roof and her hands scrabbling for a hold, any hold, and her body starting to fall sideways toward the ground tearing past in a blur and... she got a hold and gripped it so tightly her hand hurt.

214 ❀ *Jack Campbell*

Looking back, Mari saw Alain watching, his own eyes betraying an unusual amount of apprehension. "Come on!" she yelled. "This is easy compared to facing a dragon!"

That brought a trace of grimace that might have been a smile to Alain's face, then he jumped, his body crashing into her. Mari wrapped one arm around him, the other keeping its hold. Alain got himself set, then glanced up and back. "Down!" he shouted.

Mari, who had already started forward again, flattened herself onto the roof of this freight car. She heard and felt another whooshing over the roar of the train. A tremendous creaking sounded just overhead and she realized it was the sound of the Roc's feathers shifting in the wind. A shadow flashed past, Mari swearing she saw the Roc's wing brushing the top of the car ahead of them, then the massive bird was curving up and away to prepare for another strike.

Despite her terror, Mari found herself momentarily frozen in admiration as the smoke from the locomotive parted to give her a good glimpse. The Roc seemed much like a hawk with a slightly elongated neck, but a hawk so large that the figure of the robed Mage on its back seemed no bigger than that of a small mouse compared to a real hawk. The creature swept the air with its huge wings, moving with a titanic grace that left Mari smiling involuntarily at its graceful flight. The Mechanic part of her mind told her that no bird could possibly be that big and still fly, but the rest of her didn't care that something so lovely was impossible. "All right," she yelled at Alain. "I know why you didn't want to kill it."

She got up into a crouch and ran, not stopping when she reached the gap to the next car this time but leaping across without any pause that might let fear master her. Once again she felt her feet sliding out from under her and once again Mari managed to get a handhold in time.

Alain followed, landing clumsily and squinting into the wind, one hand trying to bat away the hot cinders pelting them. "Have you done this before?" he shouted over the rushing wind.

"Run on top of a moving train? No!"

"I do not want to do it again."

"That makes two of us." Mari gazed upward, searching the sky and spotting the Roc winging over for another dive. "Come on!"

Another run, right to the edge of the first car in the train and over to the tender without stopping. Mari dropped onto the tender, landing on lumps of coal that shifted under her and bruised her painfully. She rolled to one side, wincing as the coal lumps dug into her.

Alain came down and hit hard, staring at her and gritting his teeth. "I did not know we would be jumping onto rocks this time."

"It's not rocks. It's coal," Mari told him.

"It feels like rocks and it looks like rocks."

"Rocks don't burn! It's coal!" Mari heard something and tugged Alain down. "Watch out!"

The Roc swept past again, its beak stabbing down and narrowly missing them. Mari stared after it. "If this keeps up, I'm going to kill that thing! I don't care how beautiful it is!"

"I understand your feelings," Alain assured her.

Mari scrambled down the slope of the coal to the cab of the locomotive. Two apprentices stopped frantically shoveling coal into the boiler for a moment to gape at her. The Mechanic driving the train was looking forward, his face set in desperate lines.

Mari pulled herself next to him. "We need to scare it!" she yelled over the roar of the boiler and the clashing of the locomotive's drive wheels.

The other Mechanic jerked his head over to stare at her, his face white with fear. "You made it up here from the passenger car? Who are you?"

"I'm...never mind now! Just trust me!"

"You know how to stop that thing?" the Mechanic demanded. He was well past middle age, Mari could see now, probably not far from being able to retire after a lifetime of quiet train trips across the Empire.

"Yes!" *I hope.* Mari scanned the skies again. "Here it comes."

Alain was near the back of the cab, eyeing the boiler with nervousness so plain that Mari could spot it easily. In Dorcastle he had seen what an exploding boiler could do. Or perhaps he still believed the locomotive to be a creature like a Mage troll or dragon, something that could go into an out-of-control rampage if the Mechanic commanding it made a mistake.

The Roc came arcing down, talons extended this time as if it intended to pluck her and Alain from the locomotive cab. Mari tried to keep breathing as the vast shape of the Roc grew rapidly in size. Fearing she had left it too long, Mari yanked down the whistle lanyard and held it.

The whistle of the locomotive screeched like a banshee, even louder than usual because of the high pressure in the boiler. The Roc jerked upward, its eyes flaring with fear, wings backing frantically as the huge bird broke its descent and tried to flee this awful thing shrieking as if a dozen Rocs were in torment.

Mari grinned and gave Alain a thumbs-up. "It worked."

"It will be back," he advised. "We have to keep it from coming back."

"How—?" Mari coughed as another wave of harsh smoke swept across them from the locomotive's smokestack. "That's it!" She turned on the apprentices. "Smoke! We need as much smoke as you can make!"

"Lady Mechanic," one of the apprentices gasped, "we're already putting out a lot, and we'll slow down if we lower the fires by making them smoke more."

"You can't outrun that thing! But you can drive it away with smoke! Do it!"

Both of the apprentices looked to the Mechanic driving the locomotive, who nodded hastily. They started reducing the airflow to the fire, causing tremendous clouds of black smoke mixed with a swarm of glowing cinders to billow out of the stack. Within moments Mari was coughing, her eyes smarting.

Alain was beside her. "This reminds me of something," he got out between his own coughs.

"I remembered it first." They had almost died from smoke inhalation during the fire in Ringhmon.

"And, just like that time, we have to escape," Alain added.

She gave him a baffled look, then realized Alain wasn't just referring to the Roc. Caught up in the need to drive off the Roc, Mari had forgotten that if these apprentices or that Mechanic recognized her they would try to arrest her. If she and Alain were still in this locomotive when it stopped—and it would stop as soon as possible to deal with the burning freight car before its flames spread—one of the Mechanics from the passenger car at the end of the train might well recognize her.

Mari leaned out as far as she could on the side opposite the engineer, squinting against the smoke, tears running down her face from the irritation. "There's a small bridge up ahead," she said, putting her lips close to Alain's ear so the others wouldn't hear. "There's a creek under it. I think."

"You think?"

"Yes! Get ready!" Mari looked around frantically and found what she knew would be in the locomotive cab: a big mailbag with a water-resistant seal for Mechanics Guild dispatches and packages. The apprentices and the other Mechanic were engrossed in staring out the other side of the locomotive in search of the Roc as Mari tore open the bag, stuffed her pack inside, then resealed it.

Grabbing Alain's arm, Mari shoved him to the side of the locomotive. "Good luck!" She gave him a quick kiss, then as the low trestle and the ditch that hopefully marked a creek or stream hove into view, Mari launched them both off the side of the train.

The drop seemed terrifying, whatever lay beneath them impossible to make out through the smoke and with their eyes watering so badly.

❄   ❄   ❄

Mari slogged through the shallows at the edge of the stream, feeling like a rat someone had beaten and then tried to drown. Her foot slipped in the mud and Alain caught her to steady her.

"I never knew water could feel so hard," Alain observed.

"It's softer than dirt or rocks," Mari grumped.

"Or coal."

"Or coal," she agreed. "Just be glad there actually was water to land in."

Alain gave her a look. "You told me there would be water."

Maybe it was just her imagination, but his voice sounded accusing. "No, I didn't! I clearly said I *thought* there was water." He paused to think, then nodded. Mari's defensive irritation vanished under a wave of remorse. Alain had, after all, trusted her enough to jump off a train without being certain what they were jumping into. "I'm sorry."

Her Mage actually smiled back slightly in response, bringing an answering grin to Mari's lips. Still smiling, Mari sloshed through the last shallows and up onto the bank of the stream. She more fell than sat, bracing herself on her hands to stare upward and in the direction the train had vanished, leaving a huge cloud of dirty smoke in its wake. "I think I can still see the Roc. It looks like it's following the train."

Alain nodded, looking tired. "I am concentrating very hard on hiding myself from the senses of other Mages."

"Can I help?"

"I do not think so."

"Oh, yeah, I'm a distraction." Mari sagged back down to lie full length, closing her eyes and breathing deeply from exertion. "I guess it's safe to say that your Guild knows you're alive. They really picked you up because of those two spells you did in Pandin?"

Alain nodded again. "To another Mage, it would be as if I were standing in an open area, shouting my name."

"We need to be more careful about using your spells, then. You think that Roc might have been after me, too?"

"It tried to seize you," Alain said.

"Yeah, it did." Mari gave him a startled look. "It went for me first. Why would it go for me before it went for you?"

He gestured slightly, as if the answer was obvious. "My Guild must suspect who you are. That is a bad thing."

"If it means giant birds are going to try to kill me, I have to agree," Mari said, trying to shake the sensation that the whole thing had been some bizarre hallucination. "Do they think I'm going to ensnare more Mages?"

"Yes," Alain said.

Mari felt her face warming. It was absurd, but for a moment the implications of that upset her more than the recent attempt to kill her.

"They expect you to gather more allies," Alain explained. "As the prophecy said. Mechanics, Mages, and commons, united to change this world."

"I'm not—" Mari's eyes locked on the sky past his shoulder. "Stars above, it's coming back. Quick! Under the bridge!"

They helped each other up, then both hastily waded back into the stream and under the shelter of the stone bridge which seemed far too small at the moment. Mari and Alain huddled up against the buttress on one end of the bridge.

She started to lean out to look up, then glanced at Alain. "Can you tell where it is?"

Alain was frowning in concentration. Then he raised one hand and pointed, the forefinger slowly traveling as he followed the motion of the Roc.

"It's going back north," Mari said, waiting until Alain's finger was pointing well past the bridge. She finally leaned out then, peering upward and seeing a dark shape in the sky swooping low over the track. "That Mage figured out we jumped, but doesn't know where."

Alain gazed to the west. "The sun will set in a while. We can travel then."

"The Roc won't see us?"

"They do not see well in the dark at all. It is one of their greatest weaknesses."

She grinned with relief. "It's nice to know that your Mage stuff follows its own rules, even if those rules are things that my Mechanic training say are impossible. All we have to do is stand in the water under this bridge until the sun sets." Mari's smile faded as she looked down at her boots, submerged in the creek. She sighed heavily, then awkwardly pulled off her boots and socks, piling them onto a projecting rock shelf. Hopefully they would dry a little. "It's going to be a lot of fun walking long-distance across country in wet boots."

"It will?" Alain asked. "I know little of fun, but walking far in wet boots does not seem a thing to desire."

"I was being sarcastic again, Alain." He was looking upward and north, plainly still trying to track the Roc, so she slumped back against the stone and shivered as the water chilled her feet. "Now I know what a mouse feels like when a hawk is cruising overhead."

What seemed a very long time later, the sun finally set and light faded enough for Alain to believe it was safe. The Roc had stayed searching in their general area until sunset, crossing over the bridge several more times without spotting them, but when full darkness fell the Roc and its Mage headed south at a good clip.

Mari staggered out of the water, her feet numb, and pulled her pack from the dispatch bag. Even though the waterproof bag might be handy in the future, it was too bulky to carry and also had "Mechanics Guild" printed on the side in big letters. There wasn't any sense in making it too easy for her Guild to find them. Mari went back into the stream far enough to wedge the bag against a rock as if it had come to rest there. "With any luck the apprentices and the Mechanic in the locomotive will think this bag, and you and I, got knocked out of the cab by accident or by the Roc. Or maybe they'll think we went back to the passenger cars. Thank goodness that train didn't back up looking for us."

"Perhaps the presence of the Roc persuaded your train not to do that."

"It's nice to think we got one benefit from that monster." Mari dug out a pair of dry socks, but then had to tug on her still-wet boots, hoping that any blisters she picked up tonight wouldn't be too bad.

She shrugged, trying to make herself feel accepting of things she couldn't change. "Sooner or later one of the people in that locomotive may realize the female Mechanic who joined them looked a bit like that Master Mechanic Mari the Guild is looking for. Maybe not. Things were really hectic in that locomotive cab, and the Guild may be so busy trying to get every Mechanic on that train to forget they saw a Roc that the matter of who the female Mechanic was falls through the cracks. My Guild will surely also be sending blunt signals to your Guild that there better not be any more attacks on trains. Hopefully it'll be several days before everything is sorted out and somebody guesses it was me. Let's get moving. We need to get into Severun and then out again before my Guild's Senior Mechanics put two and two together. I don't want to follow the tracks. Do you have any idea which direction Severun is in?"

Alain looked upward, studying the stars. "That way," he said, pointing. "It should take us toward the road. Or do you wish to avoid that as well?"

"No. If we find the road, we can try to hitch a ride." Mari looked up as well. "My Guild discourages us from ever studying the stars. You can use them to tell your way at night?"

"Yes," Alain said. "Some stars move, but others stay fixed."

"I wish I knew more about that." They started walking, Mari gazing upward and to the south even though she didn't see how she could spot a Roc at night if the creature returned. "Can Rocs carry just the one Mage?"

"Some can. Others are larger and can carry up to three or four additional people. You may not remember, but I once asked you about riding one with me."

"Going on a date with you, riding a giant bird," Mari said. "I admit at the time I didn't expect that to ever happen. I didn't see how Rocs could be real."

"They are not real," Alain said.

"Right." Mari tried to laugh. "Nothing is real. Maybe you and Calu should go on that date."

"Why would I— Sarcasm?"

"Uh-huh." Mari did laugh briefly this time. "Well, my Mage, someday maybe we will ride a Roc together. If it's not too dangerous."

"Dangerous? May I ask you something about these Mechanic trains?"

"Trains? Sure," Mari agreed. "What?"

"Why does anyone travel on such hazardous things? I have been on two journeys on them, and both have nearly ended in disaster. Travel by Roc seems much safer by comparison."

It took Mari a moment to think up a reply. "Usually, trains are safe. When you and I aren't traveling on them, that is. Most of the time they get where they're going without any disasters taking place."

"Are you certain?" Alain asked.

"Well, that's what I've heard."

"I was afraid for a while that you intended making that device explode just like the one in Dorcastle," Alain added.

"Huh? No, I never planned on that! Not this time. I don't usually deliberately make steam boilers explode."

Alain nodded as if relieved to hear that.

"I don't know why every man I meet thinks I get a kick out of blowing up steam boilers," Mari grumbled. "Or burning down buildings."

"As you once told me," Alain said, "it is important to stay on your good side."

"Yeah. I guess that's true. Have you ever forgotten anything that I have said to you?"

Alain paused to think. "Not that I can recall."

She laughed, wondering if the Mage had intended that as a joke or not, and linked his arm with hers as they walked.

They headed east toward Lake Bellad, since Mari's map had shown the road ran closer to the lake than the rail line did. The moon was not near full, and the path overland required most of their attention to avoid obstacles. A chill wind was blowing down from the north, bringing with it uncomfortable memories of their narrow escape from the blizzard. But no clouds threatened this time, just the steady march of winter overtaking the more comfortable days of autumn.

Mari was limping when they reached the main road running south to Severun at midnight, but they kept going to put as much distance as they could between them and the site of the train attack. Eventually Mari stumbled to a halt, her feet and one ankle on fire. "I'm totally exhausted. There's some high grass over there. Let's get hidden in it and sleep."

Alain nodded, betraying a great deal of tiredness as well. The grass wasn't the worst outdoor bed they had endured, but occasional foot or horse traffic on the road made enough noise to rouse them. Neither of them slept well. Dawn was just graying the sky when Mari got up, feeling almost as bad as she had after narrowly surviving the blizzard. "If anything or anyone attacks us today, I'm going to kill them," she vowed.

"I will help," Alain croaked in a hoarse voice.

Fortunately they were able to wave down a passing wagon, buying seats amid the bales of cloth in the back and settling down to sleep some more, well concealed by the fabric.

Two long days and a succession of begged and purchased rides later they arrived in Severun, dropping off from their latest wagon in a business area where no one would be looking for passengers arriving. "Better late than never," Mari sighed. "Let's find Professor S'san's home."

Alain gave her a look in which hesitation was unusually easy to see. "Mari, before we see your elder, I think it would be wise to check to see if Mage Asha is at the Mages Guild Hall here. We must find out, if possible, whether my Guild believes I died on the train, and what my Guild knows of you."

"Alain." Mari put one hand to her forehead, trying to rub away a sudden headache. "Don't you think that's too dangerous? What if this Asha did betray you later on? What if she is the reason the Roc attacked that train?"

He thought, then frowned slightly. "Establishing contact with Asha is the only way to find out why she did not announce my presence on the road to Umburan. Asha sensed me even when I was concealing my presence as well as I can. If she is indeed hostile to us, she could lead the Mages in this city to the home of your professor in search of me."

"But—" Mari glowered down at the cobblestones of the street. Showing up at Professor S'san's home with a bunch of Mages in pursuit, or maybe another dragon on their trail, would be a disaster. "All right. Fine. We'll go look for your old girlfriend."

He gave her one of those questioning looks. "I thought I had explained that while Asha is a girl, she was never a friend."

"You did. Never mind. Let's just get this over with."

Mari followed Alain toward the Mage Guild Hall. *He's right. I know he's right. But why did Alain have to end up being friends with and needing to talk to the only drop-dead gorgeous, blue-eyed, blonde-haired female Mage in the entire history of the world? And he says she's a few years older than me, which probably makes her seem even more attractive to guys Alain's age. How can I compete with someone like that? Serves me right for getting involved with a Mage.*

Alain gave her a glance. "Did you say something?"

"I hope not," Mari mumbled. "No," she added in a louder voice. "How much farther?"

"Not far." Alain stopped walking, his head slowly turning to gaze down a side street. "Mage Asha is here. She is making no attempt to hide herself at all, as if she wants me to find her."

Oh, great. "What do we do?"

"Let us wait for a short time here." Alain turned his head slightly. "Or perhaps we should go wait near the Mage Guild Hall."

"Alain, no one lingers in front of a Mage Guild Hall," Mari explained patiently. "They're afraid some Mage will pop out and turn them into a toad or something."

"No, that is impossible," Alain assured her. "No spell can change a person directly."

"You told me that before, didn't you? Why not? I thought we were all supposed to be illusions."

"Shadows," Alain said. "I was taught that other people are shadows on the surface of the world illusion. But while Mages can change many aspects of the world we see, no spell can directly affect any person. I can make a hole in a wall, but I cannot make a hole appear in someone where their heart should be. This is a matter which the Mage Guild has never resolved, but I was told the elders believe it reflects our inability to fully divorce ourselves from others. If we were able to completely disregard all other humans, then we might be able to use spells on them. I do not know if this is so. It is only what I was told."

"But why does everybody think that Mages can do those things?" Mari asked. "I mean, if they think Mages can do anything, that is."

Alain's small smile came and went. "The Mage Guild sees such beliefs as being to its advantage. They increase the fear with which the commons regard Mages." He looked down the street again. "Mage Asha has left the Mage Guild Hall."

Mari watched as Alain's head slowly pivoted, as if he were a cat following the track of an invisible prey. Then Mari saw the robed shape of a Mage appear around the corner, walking their way. The Mage pulled back her hood, golden hair spilling down her back, but otherwise did nothing but keep walking toward them, her face an emotionless mask.

Alain just stood and waited, so Mari did as well, trying to keep her hand from jerking up to grab hold of her pistol. If Mage Asha really were hostile, there might be very little time to deal with her if she attacked.

The female Mage came even with them, then walked past, giving no sign that she had noticed them. Alain waited until Asha was a few lance-lengths beyond them, then beckoned to Mari and began following, roughly matching Asha's pace.

As a result, Mari got an unwanted but prolonged look at the female Mage's long blonde hair falling to her waist and the seductive sway of her hips as she walked. *I can't believe it. She's even got a great rear end. I am so completely outclassed here.*

They followed her along the street until Asha turned off toward the city park. The journey continued until they reached the forested park area, then through ever-diminishing pathways that finally ended in a small bower shaded by low-hanging branches that blocked sight in all directions. There, Asha stopped and turned to await them, her face still betraying no visible emotion.

As they walked toward the expressionless female Mage, Mari could feel herself tensing, fearing an ambush. She had some idea how to handle threats posed by other Mechanics. She had no ideas at all how to deal with a surprise attack by several other Mages with the powers that Alain had demonstrated.

CHAPTER TWELVE

Alain kept walking, his face showing neither worry nor any other emotion, until he stopped just before the female Mage. "Mage Asha."

He had reverted to full Mage behavior, Mari noted nervously, his voice as impassive as his face. "Don't lose yourself, Alain," she muttered.

Asha inclined her head very slightly toward him. "Mage Alain." If Asha had taken any notice of Mari's presence, she didn't show any sign of it.

"This one has been trying to find you," Alain explained, "to discover why you did not inform the other Mages present when you saw me on the road to Umburan." He might have been asking about the weather in Kitara, for all the feeling in his voice.

"I knew you," Asha stated blandly, her face still showing nothing, "from the days of our acolyte training. Your presence was clear to me, though the other Mages did not feel it."

"Why did you not tell the others?" Alain asked.

"I had no instructions to do so."

Alain nodded. "Were you among the Mages who assisted the Imperial ambush of the Alexdrian raiders west of Umburan about three weeks ago?"

Asha nodded back. "I was."

"Did you know the Guild had assigned me to be the Mage for the Alexdrian forces?"

"I did not."

"I was the only Mage with the Alexdrians."

The female Mage stayed silent for a moment before replying. "Only you? There were ten of us with the Imperials." Was it Mari's imagination that some trace of surprise, of upset, had finally entered Asha's voice?

"Ten." It was Alain's turn to pause, as he absorbed that information. "I was not told. The Mage who cast lightning attempted to strike me during the battle," Alain continued with a deadpan voice and no expression. "A direct attack on me. The dragon Mage then sent his spell creature up the pass with orders to kill me first."

Asha hesitated again before replying. "I did not know these things. Do you say, Mage Alain, that our elders have decreed your death?"

"I believe this is so."

Mari watched the two Mages converse, feeling a growing sense of disbelief and disquiet. They were discussing, quite literally, matters of life and death. This was apparently their first reunion in some time. Yet their faces and voices gave no clue to the emotions they felt, gave no clue to any emotions at all. It was both eerie and disturbing. *I'd forgotten that Alain could be like this. I'd forgotten what he was like when we first talked in the waste outside of Ringhmon. Watching this is downright scary. What if there had been another Mage along with the caravan? What if I had seen him conversing with another Mage then, the two of them so blasted inhuman? I never would've spoken to him, even if we'd still ended up fleeing together. He, they, would've been too creepy. Even if I'd just seen other Mages talking together close up then I bet I would've felt that way. But I never have.*

Alain talks sometimes about destiny bringing us together. I think that's nonsense, but then again if we hadn't both been alone when the caravan was destroyed, if we both hadn't lacked actual experience with members of the other's Guild before that, we wouldn't have talked. We wouldn't have seen beneath the exterior we thought we knew and caught a glimpse of the real person beneath. Things would've been a lot different.

Thanks, destiny.

Asha was gazing dispassionately at Alain. "A Roc Mage arrived here a day ago with a tale of having attacked a Mechanic creation. I saw that she was hiding something from us when she spoke of this."

"That Mage too tried to kill me, and Mari as well."

"Why would the Guild seek your death, Mage Alain? Did you act against the Guild?"

"I did not act against the Guild before the attempts to kill me. I believe that the elders ordered my death because I had come to know this woman." Alain indicated Mari.

Mari nodded at Asha, then decided someone here ought to act human and smiled politely. "Hi. Nice to meet you. How are you doing?"

The female Mage looked at Mari for just a moment as if she was gazing at a rock, not returning the smile or any other expression before turning her attention back to Alain and speaking only to him. "She is not a Mage. Why do you know a common, and why should the Guild be concerned by this?"

"She is a Mechanic."

News that would have aroused outbursts of emotion in a conversation with Mechanics or commons merely caused Asha's eyebrow to twitch. "Why are you with her?"

Perhaps it was because Mari had been around Alain, gaining experience with detecting emotions which were mostly hidden, but she thought that Asha's voice rose infinitesimally in disbelief at the end. Not that anyone else would probably have noticed. Listening to the Mages' emotionless conversation did have one benefit, Mari thought. She couldn't hear or see any negative feelings about her in the impassive words of Asha.

"I am with her," Alain said, "because she is important."

"I do not understand. She is a shadow. She cannot be important."

"She is to me." Alain paused. "She is to this world. She defines the world I see."

That actually caused a visible flash of surprise on Asha's face. Mari was so busy staring at Alain, aghast at what sounded to her like a very exaggerated description of her importance to him, that she almost missed Asha's reaction. The female Mage looked at Mari a little longer this time, then shook her head. "I do not understand how a shadow could lead you to believe this, Mage Alain."

Mari couldn't help noticing that the female Mage was talking past her, as if only the two Mages were present. She would have gotten angry except for her own training as a Mechanic to do the same to Mages and commons whenever she was around them. It didn't make sense to blame Asha for acting the same way that Mari had been instructed to act.

Alain stood perfectly still for a moment before answering Asha's question. "I believe this because I have seen it. And because...I love her."

This time the astonishment on the female Mage's face was plain enough that Mari could see it with no trouble. Then the amazement vanished, replaced by a hint of clear sorrow. "Mage Alain, you have lost your wisdom."

"No, Mage Asha, I have found a new wisdom."

"You were a strong Mage. Your powers have been lost."

Alain shook his head. "My powers remain."

The female Mage regarded him for a long time before speaking again. "You do not lie. What you say should not be possible, according to what we were taught."

"What we were taught is wrong."

To Mari's surprise, Asha looked at her again. This time she addressed her directly. "Mechanic, what is your purpose with the Mage Alain?"

Mari took a deep breath, amazed to be discussing her private feelings with a female Mage. "I love him. He loves me. We want to be with each other, to protect and help each other, to do some important things, to make each other happy."

"That is not possible," Asha said, without feeling yet conveying distress.

Looking at her, Mari had a growing feeling that the female Mage was bewildered, trying to understand what she was being told and unable to grasp it.

Alain reached to touch Mari's hand. "This Mechanic faced and slew the dragon sent against me, else I would have died under its claws. She has saved my life more than once, at the risk of her own."

"That was a mighty dragon," Asha said without feeling. "You did this for Mage Alain, Mechanic?"

"Yes."

"Why?"

"I told you," Mari said. "I love him. I may marry him. Maybe. But I won't let anyone hurt him."

Asha stared at Mari for a while, her face once again betraying no emotions. "When we were acolytes, newly come to the Mage Guild Hall in Ihris, Mage Alain once tried to catch me as I fell. He was punished for this." Her gaze went to Alain. "We talked. In the first days. Before such things were driven from us. He was...he could have been...someone..."

"A friend," Alain said.

"Friend." Asha seemed to be looking inward now, as if searching for memories lost in time. "What does this mean?"

Alain's voice took on more feeling. "It is someone who helps."

"Helps?" Asha suddenly inhaled strongly. "I remember. When all else was gone...Alain...helps...helped...me."

"We were taught to forget this," Alain said. "Master Mechanic Mari reminded me of what it meant. She has reminded me of many things. She must do something of great importance. Will you help me now, Mage Asha?"

Her gaze rested on Alain, then went back to Mari. "This Mechanic helps Mage Alain. I will help, too. I will not betray you to the Guild, Mage Alain."

Alain bowed toward her. "Thank you, Mage Asha."

Mari saw the female Mage blink in momentary confusion. "I had not remembered those words. Did she teach you them?"

"Yes."

"She has saved your life," Asha said dispassionately.

"Many times."

Mage Asha turned back to Mari, then tried to speak, her lips struggling to form words that seemed stuck inside her. "Th...Th..."

"Uh...you're welcome." Mari spread her hands, feeling awkward and uncertain. She had felt tears starting as Asha tried to speak words which had been forbidden to her. What had it been like for Asha? Close enough to see her well now, Mari could spot on Asha's face the marks of the same kinds of treatment that Alain bore. Old scars and other signs of the harsh teachings that Alain rarely spoke of. This woman had suffered just as Alain had. "Thank you, Mage Asha, for being a friend to Mage Alain."

"Friend?" Asha gazed into the distance. "I have not heard that word for so long a time, Mechanic. I have no friend."

"Yes, you do," Mari said impulsively. "You've got Alain. He's your friend. He's told me about you, and he thinks about you and he...he cares about you, I think. And...and if you want...you have me. Any friend of Alain's is a friend of mine. My name is Mari."

Those brilliant blue eyes pinned her. "Mari. This is what Mage Alain calls you?"

"Yes."

"You have saved his life before, but he may yet die because of you."

"I know." Mari's words came out in a miserable whisper this time.

"Yet he chose you over the wisdom he and I were taught." Asha reached out very slowly with one hand, until her finger pressed lightly against Mari's cheek for a moment. "If you are no longer a shadow to Mage Alain, then I will try to see you differently...Mari. I will find out what I can of the Guild's plans for Mage Alain, and give what warning I may. If Mechanic Mari can face a dragon for the sake of protecting

Mage Alain, I can scarcely do less." She turned those brilliant blue eyes on Alain, the ends of her blond hair swinging around her hips as her head moved. "I will do what I can for Mage Alain."

Mari hoped the jealous feelings that hit her again didn't show.

Asha turned back to Mari. "I have much to think on. I have been taught that all is false, and that Mechanics are doubly false. Yet I see no lie in you or in Alain when he speaks of you. Will you betray Mage Alain?"

"I'll die before I do that," Mari replied.

"I see that again you do not speak falsely. There is much I must consider. A different wisdom. Now I must go. Other Mages in this city might wonder why I linger here and sense Mage Alain near me. I will find out what I can, then I will seek Mage Alain wherever he may be." With another long look at Alain, the female Mage walked away without any word of farewell, quickly disappearing among the foliage.

Alain stared in the direction Asha had gone. "I had not known she remembered my trying to catch her."

Feeling awkward, Mari cleared her throat. "How old were you?"

"It was within a few days of arriving at the Guild Hall. I was still five years old."

"So Asha was seven?"

"I believe so."

She could stay jealous of that gorgeous female Mage, or she could accept that Asha could be Alain's friend. "I'm not surprised you tried to help. Even when we first met, you still managed to remember what help meant."

Alain looked downward, his face revealing some distress to Mari. "I find I have doubts of Asha, worries that I cannot trust her. She does not remember what trust means."

I'm glad you said that and not me. I'm already feeling too catty as it is. "You could be trusted before you remembered that word."

Alain gazed in the direction the female Mage had gone. "Perhaps Asha will remember feelings."

"Yeah," Mari said. "She apparently already remembers feelings about you. What were these talks you and she both recall?"

"A few words, in moments when we were not watched by Mages or older acolytes." Alain looked down, his gaze distant with memory. "The only traces of companionship we had in those first months, before we learned to deal with feeling nothing. Before that, when I despaired, her words gave me hope."

Mari thought Alain sounded regretful but also resigned, as if speaking of something which might have been but was forever lost. "You didn't love her? Even a little?"

Alain glanced at Mari. "I was too young to think of such things. I had no sister, but I felt as if she were one."

"A sister? You think of a woman that gorgeous as a sister, but you fell in love with me?"

"You are more beautiful than Asha. I see this inside of you as well as outside."

Mari shook her head. "Have I told you that you sound totally crazy sometimes? You expect me to believe that she never lit any fires in you, and I did?"

"Yes," Alain replied, his tone faintly bewildered as he looked at her. "Asha never changed the way I saw things, as you have."

That reminded her of something. "What did you tell her about me? That I define your world or something? I couldn't believe you said that."

Alain nodded. "You define the world I see. Yes. I needed to explain what you mean to me in terms another Mage would understand."

Mari could feel her lips quivering but tried to fight off laughter. "Alain, I 'define the world' for you? That's too much."

"Too much?"

"It's so sweet, it's nauseating."

Alain pondered her words. "What is wrong with that statement? I see the false world through my own illusions. You are now my reference for those illusions. Why should that make you feel ill? You define the world I see."

Maybe it was relief that the meeting with Asha had gone well, or at least had not turned into an ambush. Maybe it was also relief that Asha and Alain hadn't betrayed any romantic feelings for each other—not that they had betrayed many feelings of any sort. Maybe it was Alain's apparently sincere inability to see how his words sounded to someone who wasn't a Mage. Whatever it was, Mari couldn't stop it any more, breaking into open laughter. "I can't stand it. Oh, Alain. It's just...just... sickening!" Mari kept laughing all the way out of the park.

❇   ❇   ❇

The long walk to the home of Professor S'san gave Mari time to sober up except for an occasional giggle, which appeared to be a relief to her companion. "Alain, you do know that I never laugh at you, right? I always think of it as us sharing a joke."

Alain had a serious expression as he nodded. "This is part of what love means, is it not? To share things? But sometimes I do not understand why you find something humorous. Is that also part of love? To not understand everything about the one you love?"

"My Mage," Mari said, "truer words were never spoken."

Mari's former teacher lived on a hill in an apartment facing the waters of Lake Bellad. The building itself looked to be a little more than a century old, but that could be deceptive, since the simple, clean lines of its two stories and balconies facing the lake were of a style which had been used off and on for hundreds of years. From the top of the hill, those on the balconies could look down across the rooftops of a stretch of Severun until the lake's bright blue waters began. The surface of the vast lake continued on to the horizon, vanishing into a gray haze in the distance.

"Nice spot," Mari commented. "Professor S'san used to talk about Lake Bellad sometimes. She really liked Severun, so I wasn't surprised when I found out she had retired here. That she had retired was a surprise, but not that she came here afterwards. No, the odd thing is that she's not living in the retirement area of the Severun Guild Hall. There aren't many Mechanics who live among commons when they retire."

"They are like Mages, then?" Alain asked. "Elders live in the Mage Guild Halls until they pass from this dream."

"Right." Mari looked around, evaluating the neighborhood. "This looks like a decent area to live in, but still, it's odd. Why choose to live here after spending your entire life in a Guild Hall? It's lucky for us, though. If Professor S'san had chosen to retire inside a Guild Hall, with no reason to go outside it, then talking to her might have been impossible."

"Perhaps that is why she chose to live here instead of in a Guild Hall," Alain suggested.

"But that would mean...that Professor S'san expected me, or other Mechanics, to need to talk to her without the Senior Mechanics knowing. Alain, can you see any sign of danger?"

Alain shook his head, looking around carefully. The neighborhood was a quiet one, with little foot or wagon traffic at midday. "I can sense no Mages near. Neither my eyes nor my foresight warn of danger."

"I can't see any sign that my Guild is watching the place, either. The bureaucratic wheels inside the Mechanics Guild leadership must still be turning slowly, and haven't gotten around to tracking my former teachers."

Inside the building, they went up the single staircase and then walked along a narrow corridor lined with doors until they reached the apartment with the number Mari was seeking. "I don't know how she'll react to you, Alain, but Professor S'san always struck me as smart and open-minded."

"I can pretend to be a common."

Mari hesitated, then shook her head firmly. "No. I'm not ashamed of you. If Professor S'san is the person I think she is, she'll accept you. If she doesn't accept you, that's her loss."

Mari knocked, waiting.

"You are worried," Alain murmured.

"Not worried. Nervous." Before Mari could say anything else, footsteps sounded, then the door opened and an older but still vigorous woman dressed in casual clothing and a Mechanics jacket looked out.

Professor S'san rested her eyes on Mari, not speaking for several seconds, then nodded. "Mari. This is a surprise."

Mari felt a strange combination of affection, respect and anger as she gazed at her old teacher. "I thought for once that somebody besides me ought to be surprised."

S'san twisted her lips in an ambiguous expression, then focused on Alain. "And who is this?"

"The only reason I lived long enough to get here."

Professor S'san nodded once more, looking unhappy. "It wasn't supposed to happen that way, Mari. You know that there is an arrest order out for you?"

"Yes."

"I have no intention of acting on that order, Mari. Please come inside, if you still trust me enough to accept my hospitality."

Mari nodded, beckoning Alain to follow. The apartment wasn't spacious, but Mari saw that Professor S'san had set it up to mimic her old offices at the Mechanics Guild Academy. A desk dominated one side of the living area, facing a couple of comfortable chairs and a sofa. Beyond the sofa lay a small kitchen with a coal-fired stove for cooking and heat, and past that a door doubtless leading to the bedroom. Just as in S'san's old office, everything was in subdued earth tones, with straightforward lines and angles rather than elaborate decoration. Missing from the walls, though, were the Mechanics Guild citations and technical drawings which the professor had once displayed. In their place, the apartment walls held only a few paintings showing the ancient port of Landfall and some ships at sea with all sails set.

Mari stood stiffly in the center of the living area, realizing that faced with her old teacher she had fallen right back into her habits as a student.

S'san gestured toward the sofa. "Please sit, you and your nameless companion."

"His name is Alain," Mari said.

"Just Alain? A common, then? A hired bodyguard?"

"He's not a common and he hasn't been hired!" Mari replied, her voice sharp.

S'san raised her eyebrows at Mari. "Did I insult you, or him?"

"No. Not exactly. But...how much can I trust you, Professor?"

S'san sighed heavily. "That hurts a great deal, Mari. Not that you asked the question, for you have every right to do so. No, what hurts is that you have cause to wonder whether you can trust me or anyone else in the Guild. I am ashamed and angry that it came to that." She met Mari's eyes. "I will not betray you, Mari. I may have held some things back, but I will never lie to you or knowingly allow you to come to harm."

Mari felt some of the weight come off of her, but found herself glancing at Alain.

"She does not lie," Alain said.

S'san's eyes glinted with anger. "I am not accustomed to having my word questioned or the accuracy of my statements evaluated by people unknown to me."

"I'm sorry, Professor," Mari said. "After everything that has happened, I don't know who to trust anymore. But I know I can trust Alain."

"And what makes this Alain such an expert on the subject of truth and lies?" S'san asked, her voice sharp.

Mari felt herself quailing under the disapproval of her old instructor, but stiffened her resolve. "I'll introduce you, and that will provide your answer. Professor S'san, this is my friend and companion, Mage Alain of Ihris."

A long silence stretched, then S'san took a couple of steps closer to Alain, studying his face. "A Mage? You show more feeling than I would expect."

Alain nodded slightly. "Mari has reawakened my feelings."

"Oh?" S'san fixed a demanding look on Mari. "What sort of feelings?"

"We're in love," Mari replied. "Don't give me that look, Professor! This Mage, this *man*, has risked his life for me more than once and saved my life more than once. While the Senior Mechanics and others were plotting my death, this Mage stood beside me and protected me and stayed true to me."

Her old professor nodded abruptly. "It's not my place to judge personal decisions, Mari, but I will suggest that you avoid taking any impulsive steps. The odds are very much against it, but the Mechanics Guild may yet be persuaded to reinstate you. This all may perhaps be fixed, but not if you are consorting with a Mage."

"I trust this Mage," Mari said, putting all the resolve she could into those words. "I do not trust my Guild anymore. If I have to make a choice, I'll stick with Alain."

"You can't make decisions like that based on emotions."

She had never imagined talking back to S'san, but Mari did it now. "You sound just like a Mage yourself."

"You'd certainly know, wouldn't you?" S'san retorted.

"Yes, I would! Because I refused to accept what I had been told, I examined the problem, and I did my best to find out the underlying truth! Isn't that what you taught me to do?"

S'san gave Mari a hard look, then nodded. She went to the door giving way onto the balcony, testing it to ensure it was closed and locked, then sat down, her expression changing to distress. "Yes, I did. I thought that would be for the best, for both you and for the Guild. Your professor failed."

"You..." Her emotions tangled, Mari finally sat as well, beckoning Alain to join her on the couch. "Professor, I need to know what happened and why."

"You have a right to that," S'san agreed. "But there are things we shouldn't discuss in front of a Mage, Mari. His Guild is an enemy of our Guild."

"I no longer hold any allegiance to the Mage Guild," Alain replied. "I follow Lady Mari."

Mari nodded, feeling pride mingled with her anguish. "My Mage is threatened with death by his own Guild, his *former* Guild, professor. His loyalty is to me."

"*Your* Mage?" S'san sat back and laughed shortly. "You continue to amaze me, Mari." She watched Alain again. "Has he told you any of his Guild's secrets?"

"Yes. He's told me and...another Mechanic."

"Interesting. And wise of you not to name this other Mechanic. If I don't know who he or she is, I can't be forced to reveal their name."

"Professor, Mage spells really work," Mari said. "You must have known that as well as I do now."

"Of course I did. I'm not one of those fools who think that by ignoring reality you can make it go away. Though I suppose that's a weak argument in the eyes of a Mage."

Alain shook his head at S'san. "What you call reality does not exist. A Mage does not ignore anything. A Mage places a smaller illusion over the greater illusion."

To Mari's surprise, her old professor actually smiled at Alain's remark. "You make it sound very simple, Mage. Excuse me, Sir Mage."

"It is simple in idea, Elder," Alain replied, "but very complex to apply. Achieving the ability takes much work and concentration."

S'san's eyebrows rose. "Elder? Isn't that a term of respect among Mages?"

"Yes, Elder. Lady Mari has spoken often of you to me."

Another smile. "Has she spoken of the Mechanic arts to you?"

"Yes." Alain made a frustrated gesture. "She has tried to explain some things, and I have seen her at work. But I cannot understand how her arts work. They are very mysterious and complex, and endure much longer than any Mage spell."

"Mysterious?" S'san glanced at Mari.

Mari nodded. "He can't even figure out how to use a screwdriver, Professor. Something about Mage training makes them incapable of grasping the sort of things we do. But he can do things I can't even imagine being able to accomplish."

"Interesting." S'san looked back at Alain. "You say the works of Mages cannot last a long time?"

"That is so," Alain said. "A spell lasts only so long as concentration, strength, and power endure. Then the illusion returns to its prior state."

S'san nodded thoughtfully. "Hmmm. Like an electric light. Shut off the current, and there is no sign it ever gave off illumination. That explains some things. One of the arguments used by the Mechanics Guild to claim that Mages are frauds is that it is impossible to point to any artifacts, to any permanent changes created by them. I had wondered at this myself. Mari, I wish I had a few weeks to pick the brain of this young man."

"But why hasn't the Guild already done that?" Mari demanded. She glanced out the window looking toward the lake, wondering how much warning they would have if the Guild were watching them here and preparing to charge in to arrest her. All she could do was hope that Alain's foresight would provide some notice of the danger. "Why hasn't the Mechanics Guild tried to understand how Mages work, instead of insisting that they are frauds against all of the evidence?"

"Why haven't I done it? Because no Mage would speak to me. Why hasn't the Guild ever done more? Because, Mari, they're avoiding that which they cannot explain." S'san gave Alain another long look. "Our technology cannot explain what the Mages do. There are two ways to respond to that. One way would be to research and to study, to learn more, to expand our knowledge or at least admit that there are things currently beyond our understanding. But the Mechanics Guild has clung to power for this long by refusing to allow new research and controlling all technology. I don't know how the initial decisions about the Mages were made all those centuries ago, but it's easy enough to guess. Our Guild leaders back then decided that what they couldn't understand—the Mages—couldn't be allowed to exist. But the Guild couldn't destroy the Mages. Oh, it tried. That surprises you? Yes, there was open fighting at one time. I know that much. But the Mages couldn't be wiped out of existence, so eventually the Guild decided to *pretend* they didn't exist. It's been that way for I don't know how long."

Mari gripped the arm of the sofa. "Why did you tell me the Mages were fakes?"

S'san shook her head. "I never told you they were fakes, Mari."

"You didn't?" Mari frowned, thinking back. "No. You didn't, did you? A lot of other Mechanics did, but you never talked about that, and when somebody else did, you didn't comment on it. But then why didn't you tell me the truth?"

"I was trying to protect you." The professor took a deep breath, seeming to shrink in on herself as she exhaled. "How many lies could I expose without dooming you, Mari? You had to learn gradually, like other Mechanics do. I knew you wouldn't be satisfied with official explanations, that you would be smart enough to navigate the dangers of learning the truth." S'san's gaze sharpened again. "At least, I thought you'd be smart enough."

"My smarts were busy trying to keep me alive," Mari shot back. "Despite the best efforts of the Senior Mechanics, I did manage to stay alive."

"Do not doubt that I am very grateful for that," S'san murmured, looking away. "Mari, I honestly did not know the lengths to which the Senior Mechanics would go. I feared you might be sent into dangerous situations, but no more so than any other Mechanic. I never suspected that you would be deliberately exposed to peril by setting you up to be kidnapped on that caravan to Ringhmon—"

"What?" Mari leaned forward, her body rigid. "Deliberately? The Guild wanted me to be kidnapped?"

S'san nodded, her expression hardening into anger. "They kept it very secret, but the Guild leadership had some knowledge of what Ringhmon was up to. They wanted to hammer that city, but claimed they needed more proof. So you were set up, placed in that caravan, alone, with the full knowledge of Ringhmon, bait for the commons who would see you as an irresistible target."

"Bait?" Mari's ears were buzzing as she stared at S'san in shock. "My Guild used me as bait?"

"Yes. *I did not know*, Mari. I swear it."

"She speaks the truth," Alain said.

Mari reached to grasp his arm with her free hand, grateful for that confirmation even through her growing outrage. "They wanted Ringhmon to kidnap me, to kill me, to give them the evidence they needed to put the city under an interdict. Stars above, Professor, no wonder the Guild Hall supervisor in Ringhmon was so unhappy with me! I wasn't playing my role!" Mari knew her voice was rising, but she kept talking. "I hadn't let myself be kidnapped! Or killed! When I was captured I escaped! I wasn't cooperating with the Guild's plans at all! The Guild wanted my dead body!"

"Mari—" Professor S'san began.

But Mari kept talking, overriding her professor, something she would never have imagined doing not long ago. "I trusted the Guild! I was loyal to the Guild! I never would have done anything against its interests. Yet the Guild was willing to sacrifice me like a cheap game token. If it hadn't been for Alain..." She looked over at him. "How's that for irony? My Guild's own actions led me to know a Mage, and to learn some of the truth behind my Guild's lies. I suppose I should be grateful that they tried to use me as bait. Otherwise I might have spent many years laboring loyally for people who deserve no loyalty."

S'san nodded in the silence that followed Mari's outburst. "You have every right to be angry, to feel betrayed. You *were* betrayed. The Guild didn't need your body as evidence of wrongdoing by Ringhmon. The

Guild doesn't need any evidence to do whatever it wants. But it offered a way to get rid of someone who worried the Senior Mechanics."

"Why?" Mari demanded. "Why did I worry the Senior Mechanics? What did I do?"

"You did nothing except what any loyal Mechanic should do. What worried the Senior Mechanics was what you were: smart, with an agile mind, a natural leader who acquires followers the way most people pick up spare change. They feared that over time you would gain enough strength to challenge them, to challenge the way they believe the Guild must be run. That's why the Senior Mechanics tried to get rid of you in a way that would tar the commons with the guilt for your death, turning your death into a reason for anyone sympathetic to you to become more loyal to the Guild and also reinforce support for maintaining a hard line against allowing any change. Never forget that most of the Senior Mechanics are certain that they are right, and that makes them willing to do anything that they believe to be necessary."

The professor bent her head toward Mari. "I am very sorry, Mari. If I had known, I would have warned you. I swear it, though perhaps you have little faith now in my own vows as well."

Mari sat without speaking, emotions tumbling through her, finally fixing on one thing she could be sure of. "You didn't have to admit that to me, what the Guild had done. But you did. You're too honest for your own good, Professor."

S'san nodded somberly. "Perhaps. You and I probably share that fault. Did you wonder why I had retired?"

"Yes, I did."

"Once word got out of what the plan had been," S'san explained, "there was quite a blow-up among the senior ranks of the Guild. Some, such as myself, were appalled. All too many others were willing to excuse the betrayal of you as necessary for the good of the Guild. I was outvoted, to put it mildly. But everyone in the senior ranks knew that if the rank-and-file Mechanics heard the truth, there would be very serious consequences. Most of them would be shocked by the betrayal. So, I was given the choice of retirement here, in exchange for swearing to say nothing, or retirement in a cell in Longfalls. I chose here, where I have been discreetly trying to find out where you were, and trying to come up with an idea to help you, though nothing has come to me."

S'san covered her face with both hands. "I don't consider myself bound by oaths forced under duress, so I'm telling you the truth, but I have failed you, and I failed my Guild. Its current leaders are too shortsighted, too ruthless. We cannot continue doing the same things, but they refuse to change. Perhaps we are all doomed."

Mari didn't know what to say, finally looking helplessly at Alain.

The Mage had been watching S'san. "It is not hopeless. A new day can come to this world."

"A Mage offers hope?" S'san laughed harshly. "It's come to that."

"Professor," Mari said, "the reason I didn't die at Ringhmon, the reason the kidnap plot failed, the reason I was able to escape when the commons in Ringhmon imprisoned me, was because of this Mage."

"Indeed?" S'san sat up a little straighter, intrigued. "I had heard something about a Mage, but as someone tangential to everything that occurred in Ringhmon."

"He was central to it all," Mari said. "I'm sure you understand why I didn't report that to my superiors. I could scarcely tell them that a Mage had helped me escape from the dungeon under the city hall and helped me burn the place down."

"He helped you escape from a dungeon? How very romantic."

"Yes. That's...probably when I started falling in love with him."

"In love." S'san bent a skeptical look on Alain. "And when did you start falling in love with Mari?"

"I have thought on this," Alain said, "and decided it began when first I met her, but I did not understand what was happening to me until after she threw me out a window."

"She threw you out a window?" The professor shook her head. "Mari has always been fairly awkward around boys, but throwing one through a window is a bit much even for her. Still, I suppose that might have been what was necessary to get the attention of a Mage."

Alain nodded. "It did get my attention. I should add that Mari was saving my life when she did that."

"Men tend to like that in women." S'san raised an eyebrow at Mari. "I told you that you impress people. Even a Mage found you memorable the first time you met."

"The first time we met," Alain added, "Mari was preparing to...what is the word? Preparing to shoot me."

"He was a Mage," Mari said. "I wasn't exactly looking at him as boyfriend material back then."

"I see," S'san replied. "Mari, most girls trying to discourage a boy wouldn't go so far as to shoot him and throw him out a window."

"It didn't work, anyway," Mari said, torn between irritation and fascination at the way Alain and S'san were almost joking about her. The last thing she had expected was for S'san and Alain to not just get along but actually seem to have some kind of rapport.

"It's just as well," S'san observed. "I was worried for a while that you might end up with Professor T'mos, but as I expected you dodged that bullet."

Mari felt heat in her face and wondered how badly she was blushing. "Professor T'mos? He was at least twenty years older than me. He could've been my father!"

"Wiser women than you have looked for second fathers when they should have been looking for partners," S'san said. "And more than one older man has looked for a girl they could regulate rather than a woman who could partner them. It was very foolish of T'mos to think that Mari of Caer Lyn could be regulated by anyone, but T'mos always did let his ego override what intellect he possesses. What happened after you threw this young man out a window?"

"We stayed in touch, and after Ringhmon Alain helped me clean up the mess in Dorcastle, though as far as I know the Senior Mechanics have never realized his role in that."

"The Mage was at Dorcastle, too?" S'san was thinking, her eyes intent. "The Guild has been busy seeking some mysterious other Mechanic they believe assisted you there despite your denials. The Guild Hall at Dorcastle has been turned upside down seeking the guilty party, and the maltreatment of anyone believed sympathetic to you is of course backfiring against the Guild leaders."

Mari felt another one of those pangs of guilt. "People shouldn't be suffering because of me."

"That sort of sentiment is why you make a good leader and why people follow you. Unfortunately, Mari, there's nothing you can do to help them at this time." S'san made a face. "I heard that you had disappeared from Edinton. What made you decide to run?"

"I was ordered to Tiae," Mari said, surprised that she could it so calmly. "On my own."

"Tiae? Alone?" S'san shook her head angrily. "Smart girl. You wouldn't fall for being sent into danger twice. But now the Guild is seeking you. At least they haven't called out the assassins."

"Assassins?" Mari asked.

"Yes. I know little about them, except that they exist." S'san paused to think. "I can understand your fears, but from what I've been able to find out the Senior Mechanics aren't trying to kill you now, Mari. At one time they wanted you to be killed by someone else, but now they want you alive. Safely in their custody, but alive, so that they can question you, find out what you're doing, who your friends are, and what plots might be underway."

"Plots?" Mari demanded.

"Oh, yes, Mari, they assume that you are out to overthrow them and seize control of the Guild."

It took Mari a few moments to realize that she was staring at S'san, her mouth hanging open with shock. Mari managed to bring her jaw up again, but her voice was strident with disbelief. "I have never sought power. I have never—"

S'san was shaking her head again. "Mari, what matters isn't what *you* think or are planning right now, it's what the Guild's leaders believe you are thinking and planning."

"Yes," Alain said. "Your professor speaks wisdom. The illusion your Guild leaders see is what guides their actions."

"You have a fine mind, Sir Mage," S'san approved. "That's a very good way of putting it."

"You know," Mari said in steadily rising tones, "I was hoping that you two would get along, but I didn't expect you to gang up on me!"

"Mari." S'san had leaned forward, her old posture as an instructor. "I'm trying to help you identify the problem and come up with solutions. The first priority, as you have already concluded, is keeping yourself free and alive. But that, at best, maintains the current situation. What do we need for a solution?"

"A clear understanding of the problem," Mari replied, feeling as if she were back at the academy.

"Exactly."

"The Guild is lying," Mari continued. "Lying about Mages. It's also lying about or denying the existence of non-Mechanics who can do Mechanic work."

"That's true," S'san agreed. "You ran into them at Dorcastle. You were doubtless placed under an interdict to say nothing about them. And, being you, you kept digging."

"They tried to recruit me," Mari reported. "In Pandin. They call themselves the Order."

"Oh, yes, the Order. It's been a good while since I heard that name spoken openly." S'san cocked a questioning eyebrow at Mari. "And they failed, I assume."

"They're evil, Professor, using the Mechanic arts purely for personal gain." Mari paused, a new thought coming to her.

S'san saw it. "Have you connected the dots, Mari? Did you consider the differences between the Order and the Senior Mechanics who run the Guild, and realize that at the current time the difference is purely one of scale? Oh, the Senior Mechanics claim they're controlling technology and limiting it and charging as much as possible for it for the good of all, and many sincerely believe that to be so, but somehow 'the good of all' translates into wealth and power for them. They don't want to risk losing that. I imagine that is very different from your Mage elders," she said to Alain.

Alain shook his head. "An elder told me that most of the Mage elders seek only to preserve their own power, and will ignore or battle anything which threatens that power."

"That shouldn't surprise me," S'san said. "Mage elders are as human as the rest of us, it seems. In any event, Mari, the Order is much smaller than the Guild. Its members live like rats in the woodwork, impossible to eradicate but constantly being hunted and slain."

Alain nodded. "If they were strong enough, they would make their presence known openly, and your Guild could do nothing."

"Exactly, but they'll never reach that kind of strength." S'san spent a moment looking closely at Alain. "Mari did choose someone with a mind as sharp as hers, though different it seems. But you're as young as she is, surely."

"I recently turned eighteen."

"Impressive." The professor settled back again. "I suppose you've come here looking for answers, Mari."

"Yes," she said firmly. "What is happening, Professor, and why have I been targeted by the Senior Mechanics?"

"It's very simple, really, and yet also very complex. Mari, how do you keep a system totally stable and unvarying?"

"Totally stable and unvarying?" Mari shook her head. "You can't. There's wear and tear. You need to repair and replace. You can't just maintain it in the same shape with the same components forever."

"It's like a living organism in that way," S'san agreed. "What happens to a living organism that stops growing? It dies. The Mechanics Guild has been dedicating its efforts to keeping everything exactly the same. It wouldn't allow change or growth. And so, for centuries, it has been slowly dying. You remember the ancient far-talker I once showed you? It was much lighter, smaller, and when it still worked it was far more capable that anything the Guild makes today. That is an example. The technology that lets us build such a device is crumbling, so the Guild is forced to use ever-cruder methods to try to achieve the same results. The tools to make the tools are failing. Keeping them working would require innovation, and as you are painfully aware, innovation is not permitted."

"But they can't possibly believe such a system can continue," Mari insisted.

"My dear child, that system has continued for century upon century. How do you convince them that it's going to fail when they can argue that it has yet to fail? It would be like arguing that the sun is not going to rise tomorrow. The sun always rises."

"The Mechanics Guild must have been different once," Mari said. "How did we ever get the technology we have? At one time, and for a long time, the Guild must have encouraged trying new things."

S'san made a frustrated gesture with one hand, as if she were trying to grab an answer out the air. "That's so, but I have never seen any trace or evidence of that period. All record of it has vanished from the minds and the documentation of Mechanics and commons alike." She glanced at Alain. "Do the Mages know anything of such a time?"

"No," Alain said. "I have never heard or read in Mage Guild records any account of a time different from now. As I have told

Mari, though, the history we share begins with a strange abruptness, the first cities springing to life as if from nothing. I do not know the meaning of this."

"You're also not the first to make note of it, Mage, though I am pleased that you have seen and thought about the issue." S'san sighed, looking weary. "I never found the answer, and I now suspect no answer is to be found through any available means. My hope for you, Mari, was that you would gain approval or authority to pry open the vaults in the Mechanics Guild headquarters and use the forbidden technical texts in there to jumpstart the Guild."

Mari had to take a moment to understand that statement. "Open the vaults? How would I ever have the power to open the vaults?"

"If you worked your way up, achieved a high-enough standing and accumulated enough allies—both of which were well within your abilities—then you could have achieved such power." Professor S'san made an angry gesture this time, her hand slashing through the air. "You weren't given the opportunity. I was quite upset with you at first, Mari, believing that you had gone tearing off in the wrong direction and burned every bridge out of sheer stubbornness and impulsiveness, but I practice what I preach when it comes to thinking. I looked into everything as best I could, and it became obvious that the Senior Mechanics had also seen your potential, seen it well enough to decide them to eliminate you before you threatened their hold on the Guild, before you threatened to cause the change they now fear more than destruction."

S'san let out a long, sad sigh. "You were trapped, Mari. I am astounded that you managed to escape with your life. And I am guilty of not anticipating that you would face such perils."

"You were obviously worried about me," Mari said quietly, opening her coat to show the pistol she wore.

"You've still got it? Good." S'san shook her head. "I wasn't worried enough." Her eyes rested on Alain. "And this is a further complication.

Mari, things are very bad with the Guild right now, but fixing the situation is not impossible. You do need to stay out of sight while your friends work on it. However, I don't know of any way the Guild will ever accept the idea of your companioning with a Mage."

Mari felt a flare of anger. "He's not just my companion! I love him! And he loves me!"

"Love?" S'san looked away. "Mari, I don't doubt your sincerity, and he may use the word, but what does a Mage know of love?"

Alain answered before Mari could. "It means she is my world. It means nothing is more important. It means I will die before I let her be harmed."

S'san gave Alain one of those demanding looks Mari remembered so well from her classes. "Do you love her enough to leave her, if that is in her best interests?"

"Professor—!" Mari began.

"Let him answer, Mari."

"My own feelings are not as important as her safety," Alain said. "That is why I left her at Dorcastle even though I wanted to be with her. To try to protect her."

Mari turned a triumphant look on S'san. "See, Professor? He knows what it means."

"Yes, he does," S'san murmured in a thoughtful voice. "What have you done, Mari? Well, would you leave him?"

"No."

"The Guild—"

"To blazes with the Guild! I will not leave the man I love to try to make nice with a bunch of Senior Mechanics who have already tried to have me killed!"

S'san looked at Alain again. "How do your Guild leaders feel about all of this, Sir Mage? Mari said you had been threatened with death?"

"That is not quite accurate," Alain replied dispassionately. "The elders of the Mage Guild do not make threats. Another Mage could easily tell whether the threat was one they intended to follow through on, or simply an attempt to intimidate. The decision must have been made that I am a danger to the Guild, and since then they have tried to kill me more than once. The last attempt involved a Roc."

"It's a giant bird that Mages can create," Mari explained. "Big enough for a person to ride. I know it's impossible, but I saw it. It tried to kill both of us."

"A giant bird." S'san nodded. "I've seen a few, Mari. One of those things Mechanics aren't supposed to admit to seeing. They're lovely, aren't they?"

"Yeah, when they're not trying to kill you. Professor, what was the end game here? You just wanted me to fix the Guild?"

"That's enough, isn't it? As the Mechanic Guild's abilities decline so does its strength, and with that goes the stability of the world. You must have heard about some of the things going on, the commons increasingly restive. Do you want all of Dematr to end up like Tiae? That's what happens when the Guild leaves commons to their own choices."

"Are those the only alternatives?" Mari demanded. "Things as they are or else anarchy? Have you ever walked among the commons as if you were one of them, Professor? They're very unhappy. They hate their overlords, and that means us. Many of the commons I've met seem to be decent people, better than the Mechanics Guild leaders, anyway. And the flat-out denial of truth by our Guild is indefensible."

"Stars above, Mari, what are you thinking?" S'san asked. "I wanted you to strengthen the Guild because the Guild is what holds this world together."

"The Guild holds the world in chains!" Mari erupted. "We've been talking about how trying to keep technology under control is slowly killing the Guild by causing its technology to crumble. Can't you see the same is true of the wider world? Yes, the Kingdom of Tiae fell apart in a series of civil wars and remains in chaos. But that was because the Guild's system failed there and the system doesn't know how to fix it, so Tiae just keeps falling farther into barbarism every year. How long before the same problems start causing the Confederation to crumble, and then the Alliance and someday the Empire? The Guild has tried to keep the entire world the same, unchanging, and the world is choking to death!" She stopped, startled by her own words. "I guess I am a traitor to the Guild now."

S'san's voice was troubled. "The Mechanics Guild has done many things I don't approve of, but this world is the devil we know. Anything else could easily be far worse."

"Mari, may I speak of the storm to come?" Alain asked.

"Uh...sure," Mari said, not certain what he meant.

"The storm moves toward us swiftly," Alain told S'san. "You speak as if the available possibilities include the Mechanics Guild remaining in power. This is not so. Within a few years, order will begin to collapse everywhere. The Mage Guild and the Mechanics Guild will be destroyed along with everything else, unable to stand against the fury of forces pent-up for too long."

S'san looked at Alain, startled. "You are predicting the end of the world?"

"The end of the world as it is known," Alain said, his unemotional tone of voice contrasting oddly with the dire nature of his words. "The destruction of almost all that exists, and the death of many, many of those who now live. I have seen this, as have other Mages."

Mari managed not to reveal her surprise. She and Alain had discussed the troubled state of the world, and he had described the looming danger as a storm before, but why had he never mentioned having foreseen this storm of devastation? And why had he asked her permission to bring it up now as if it was something she already knew about? But that was something to ask about later. "Professor," Mari said, "if you believe this is the best possible world, then why did you want to change things? Because you did. You had no idea exactly what would happen, but you encouraged me to think in ways that would lead to a change in the way things are. There's no telling what releasing that banned technology would do to this world. Why did you hope for that if you think change is wrong?"

S'san sat without speaking for a long time, before finally shaking her head. "I always said you were a great student, Mari. Now you've caught your teacher in an error. I did try to have it both ways, didn't I?" After another long pause, Professor S'san shrugged. "Not that it matters anymore. The vaults of the Mechanic Guild won't be accessible to you now, Mari. Without that lever to accomplish change, I don't know what one person can do."

Alain spoke into the silence that followed. "One person can lead many others."

"Ah, yes," S'san said. "Mari already has a Mage. That's something the world has never seen, a Mage and a Mechanic working together. I'm sure that's something that your Guild never claimed to have predicted," she told Alain with a sardonic smile.

"It was in the prophecy," Alain said. "That one would unite Mages, Mechanics, and commons in one cause."

"The prophecy?" S'san asked. "Which one?"

Alain looked at her, apparently asking permission again, but Mari shook her head. "Nothing that matters to us," she insisted.

S'san leaned forward again. "Why don't you trust me with that information? I may still be able to help you."

Mari sighed, letting her aggravation show. "Oh, it's that daughter of Jules nonsense that the commons believe in. Just because I killed a dragon—"

"It was your second dragon," Alain pointed out.

"And you don't have to keep telling everyone that! Just because I killed a dragon to save Alain and happened to save all these commons, too, and then I gave them some medical supplies and talked to Alain and acted like a human being instead of a Mechanic, those commons thought I was—that I was her!"

S'san gazed at Mari intently, then at Alain. "The commons believe in that prophecy, but I was always told it had never actually been made. Yet this Mage just spoke of it as if it were real."

"Nothing is real," Alain said. "But the prophecy was made."

"Alain!" Mari said, her voice sharper than she intended.

"Mages, Mechanics, and commons in one cause," S'san mused. "Do you already have allies among the commons, Mari?"

"No!"

"She has a general," Alain said, "sworn to her service."

"Stop helping, Alain!" Mari said as she glared at him. Why was he doing this?

"So." S'san had brought one hand up to her chin as she thought. "Mari, there has long been a tremendous irony in that the two Great Guilds, while hating each other, have effectively worked together to the same end: to keep the world stable. Both have used the commons to achieve that goal, dividing the commons against themselves. Whenever any powerful number of commons has tried to rise against the Great Guilds, another powerful group of commons has been found to oppose them and do the bidding of the Great Guilds in exchange for some temporary advantage. If your idea is to form an army of commons—"

"What?! I never said anything about—"

"It won't work." S'san shook her head, eyes still intent. "Not without something that would allow that army to prevail against everything that the Great Guilds and the commons who ally with them could throw against it. If you had been able to access that banned technology in the Guild vaults, get the tools that technology must offer, it might have held the advantage you needed. But without that, your army can't win."

"I don't have an army!" Mari almost yelled. "I don't want an army! Why would I want to start another war?" But Alain gave her a look, and Mari knew why. In her mind she heard again the words he had spoken at Dorcastle, words engraved in her memory as Alain told her of his vision. *You and I are on this wall, again...a mighty battle rages around us.* Another war? One she would somehow start? The idea was terrifying.

"I have told you my advice on the matter," S'san said, unaware of the memory that brought a tightness to Mari's chest. S'san paused, her face troubled. "The daughter of Jules."

"Professor, I—"

"I'm not saying you are her, Mari. But that title—the belief of the commons in the one they accept as that person—is a very powerful variable. How that will affect the equations which govern this world I am far from wise enough to know. That hope alone, that the daughter would someday free them, may have helped keep the commons quiet longer than any other factor. Rather than revolt en masse, the commons have waited for her to appear." The professor paused, then shrugged again. "I cannot guess how that might change things. Mari, here is my other advice, for whatever good it is. The stars above know that my plans thus far have been utter failures, so you need not feel obligated to do as I suggest. Find somewhere quiet, somewhere you can hide while new plans are formulated. That may be for a long time, unfortunately, as I have few ideas at this point. The Guild wants you, and the Guild will seek out everyone who might be your friend or ally to see if any of them can lead the Guild to you."

Mari felt that tightness in her guts again. "You're in danger because of me."

"You were set up to be kidnapped and possibly killed partly because of what I taught you!" S'san raised an imperative forefinger. "We know a bit more about the problem now, but the solution, if there is one, remains unknown."

Alain gave her a look, one in which Mari thought she read some meaning, but she focused on S'san as the professor spoke, pretending not to notice Alain's gaze.

"If you die or are captured and then disposed of," S'san was saying, "I know how that sounds, Mari, and I'm sorry, but we must assume that is what we're dealing with—if you are gone, then there may not be any solution. Dematr may continue its slow slide into darkness, with all the world gradually becoming like Tiae, the Great Guilds controlling less and less as they cling to what they will not change."

"It will not be slow," Alain repeated impassively.

S'san slapped her chair angrily. "Fast or slow, I can offer no other suggestions or advice at the moment. I will continue to explore the chances of the Guild forgiving and forgetting, of seeing that some change must come, but regard that as unlikely at best."

"I won't renounce Alain," Mari said. "That is off the table."

"I understand. As your professor, that distresses me. As a person, it gives me hope. Maybe what this world needs is someone who won't do whatever they think is necessary to make things be the way they want. Now, you can't linger here or in this city. I recommend you get out of the Empire and go as far west as possible. There are places where the hand of the Guild is a little weaker. The forests around Landsend or the mountains north of Daarendi. Perhaps you'll have a better chance there. You have already lingered here too long. I do not think the Guild is watching me constantly, but I know I am under suspicion. You should leave quickly, though I wish you could stay and talk, you and this intriguing Mage of yours."

Mari stood up, her eyes on Professor S'san. "Thank you, Professor."

S'san blew out a disdainful breath. "For helping to guide you into this mess?"

"Yes," Mari said, surprised to realize she was sincere in saying that. "You tried, where others are content to ignore truth and reality. I can't fault that. And if you hadn't taught me the way you did, perhaps I wouldn't have gotten to know a certain young male Mage. Will you be safe?"

S'san made a face. "That's hard to say. No one can tell what the future holds, unless you believe in that fortunetelling the Mages do. What they call prophecies, like that about the daughter." She directed another look at Alain. "What do have to say about that?"

"Foresight provides warning and visions, though it is unreliable," Alain answered. "Its meaning is also often unclear."

"Why would it be unclear?" S'san asked.

"There is only a vision," Alain said. "It may be...what is the word... an allegory, such as a vision of an oncoming storm, that must be interpreted. But even a clear picture provides no understanding of how the events in the vision came to be, what decisions led to it, or what is happening outside the range of the vision. I have also come to understand that the person you see in the vision of the future, if it is you, may not be the same person you are. If a year ago I were to have seen a vision of myself at this moment, I could have neither interpreted nor understood any part of it. Why do I not wear my Mage robes? Who is the young woman beside me and why does she smile upon me? Who is the Mechanic and why do I speak with her? Where am I? Why did I come there? Though an accurate view of the future, the vision would offer no answers, only questions."

S'san had been listening very closely. "Remarkable, yet also completely logical. A picture of the future lacks all context, so by the time you can understand a vision of the future, you're there. It provides no useful information, you say?"

"It can," Alain corrected. "It may show a possible event. The decisions made can lead to that event, or lead to something else."

"Oh, Mari," Professor S'san said, "if I could have only a week with this Mage to see how much I can learn! But I won't imperil either of you by insisting on that. In a week, who knows what might have happened to me?"

Alain shook his head. "I have had no visions regarding your fate, Elder S'san."

"If it's a dire one, I have only my own mistakes to blame. Forgive me, Mari," S'san said in an unusually quiet voice. "My errors placed you in grave danger."

Mari walked forward to hug her old teacher. "You have not just my forgiveness but my thanks for what you've taught me. I have a lot of thinking to do. Since you taught me how to think well, maybe I'll make the right decisions."

But as the door closed behind her, Mari could see nothing ahead. Momentary optimism, fleeting hope, dissipated into nothing as she thought of her situation. "All of these people think I'm going to make some huge difference," she said to Alain. "Including you. But how? It's impossible. I'm out of options. It really is hopeless."

CHAPTER THIRTEEN

They left the apartment building quickly, walking back toward the center of Severun. Alain kept searching for danger, but at some point he realized that his watchfulness was making him look suspicious. Thereafter he tried to appear less interested in the world while still watching. Not as disinterested as a Mage, but like the commons around him and Mari. The Imperial citizens they passed were absorbed in their own business, and the local police had their attention fixed on the people carousing in taverns along the way. At one point Alain saw a couple of Mechanics in the distance and nudged Mari, but she gave the two a disinterested glance as they disappeared down another street.

Within moments after leaving S'san's place and expressing her fears Mari had sunk into moody silence. She walked without another word until Alain spoke to her. "What should I do?"

"Nothing." Mari shrugged. "There's nothing anybody can do. I already said it. It's hopeless. All we can do is hide, while the entire world goes to blazes."

"Perhaps when we talk we can come up with some ideas."

She stared down the street they were on, shadows stretching across it as the setting sun dropped lower in the west. "I don't know. There are certain hard realities here, Alain. I can't change them by wishing and hoping. You can't change them, either. This isn't something as simple as...all right, I was going to say as simple as walking through solid walls, but that doesn't make sense."

Mari shook her head, gazing morosely down toward the waters of Lake Bellad. "Professor S'san taught me never to give up on a problem, to keep trying different things until I found a solution. But I don't know if any different things exist to try. And I admit that it shouldn't be surprising by now to find out that my Guild deliberately allowed me to be placed in peril for its own ends, at a time when I had done nothing against my Guild, but it still hurts. It also reinforces that anything I try now would not only likely be futile but also might end up causing harm to people who know me. While I was in there with Professor S'san I could pretend that there might be hope, but now? What else can be done that won't be futile?" Mari fixed her eyes on the ground passing beneath their feet. "Let's find a safe place to sleep. I'm tired. Very tired."

Alain steered them by a cafe first. Mages were taught simply to take what they wanted from commons too frightened to resist, but Mari had shown him the basics of ordering and paying for meals, so he was able to buy some food and drink while Mari stared silently into space beside him. He made her eat despite the scowls he earned from Mari for his efforts. Only then did he head for a hostel, finding a plain but clean one a fair distance from Lake Bellad which had plentiful vacancies with the winter coming on. Mari had to check them in, since Alain had not yet learned how to do that.

She roused enough to ask for privacy, for a room without anyone in the rooms next to it, a request the clerk granted with a smirk at Alain. But once in the room, Mari sat down glumly in a chair with a view out the window to the lake, where nothing could be seen in the darkness after sunset but the flickering torchlights of fishing boats and other watercraft, gliding like ghost beacons across the surface of the water.

Alain sat down near her. "We need to make plans. Where do we go now?"

"It really doesn't matter, does it?" Mari shrugged. "Pick a place. Maybe Cathlan. Blazes, Alain, I don't want to spend the rest of my life hiding."

He felt the tug of urgency that had first appeared when he saw the vision in the desert. "We cannot afford to hide. There is no such time to waste."

She glanced at him, then quickly away. "Then you should make the best of what time is left. Maybe if you left me, you could get back in good graces with your Guild. That way you could be with Asha."

The words startled him. "Why would I leave you to be with Asha?"

Mari shook her head, looking drained. "Only you of all men would ask that question."

"You would not leave me in the hopes of gaining forgiveness from your Guild. Why would you expect me to leave you? I have promised to stand by you and assist you in bringing the new day. We can make plans in the morning if you prefer that. A night's sleep—"

"Won't make any difference," she interrupted with a bitter voice. "There's no place left to go and no reason to go there except running for our lives. And for what? To live hunted a little longer? This isn't a game there's any chance of winning any more."

"There must be a way to win."

"You keep saying things like that. Mari will change the world! Where did you get that idea?" Mari slumped a little lower in her seat, glaring out at the night.

"You have told me you know of your role in the prophecy. I understand why you have not wanted to speak of it, but—"

"What?" Mari stared at him. "I told you what?"

"That you did not wish to talk about your role as the one who will fulfill the prophecy to overthrow the Great Guilds."

"When did I—WHAT?" Mari gazed at him wordlessly, stunned.

"The prophecy," Alain tried again. "You kept telling me you did not want to speak of it, and that you already understood what you were fated to do."

"Fated? Me?" Mari gulped for air before she could speak again, her words coming fast. "That prophecy was a long time ago. Why would anyone think it connects to me? Aside from deluded commons, that is."

"You said you knew about what I had seen," Alain said, growing more confused. "Each time I brought it up, you—"

"What you had seen?" Mari stared at her hands, then back at him. "About me?"

"Yes. The vision clearly indicated that you were the one. She who could stop the oncoming storm, who could bring the new day, who would fulfill the prophecy of the daughter."

Mari's mouth hung open. Her eyes were locked on him and she appeared to be struggling to breathe. Alain, alarmed, jumped to his feet and ran to her. "Mari!"

She drew in a convulsive breath, followed by several more. "When?" Mari finally managed to say.

"When will you fulfill the prophecy?"

Mari suddenly shot to her feet and glared at him. "No! When did you learn this?"

"In Dorcastle."

"*In Dorcastle?* And this is the first time you've mentioned it?"

It was Alain's turn to stare at her, wondering why she was so angry. "No. I tried to speak of it there, and you told me not to. You said you already knew."

"I—" Mari couldn't breathe again for a moment. "You know, I'm pretty sure I *would remember that!*"

"But I have brought it up again and again and each time you have said it did not need to be discussed!" Alain realized he had actually spoken with force.

"I didn't mean— That was— You never—" Mari sat down abruptly, as if her legs had lost all strength, her expression horrified. "Tell me. Tell me everything."

He sat down as well, feeling both confused and awful, though Alain was not sure why. "In the desert, after we had joined the salt traders, I saw a vision focused on you. I did not know what it could mean. It showed a second sun above you, and striving against that sun a swiftly moving storm whose clouds were made up of angry mobs and clashing armies."

Her eyes were still locked on him, but Mari did not say anything.

"You and I had ceased speaking with each other once we found others, so I could not tell you of it then. It was not until I reached Dorcastle that I found an elder who would tell me what the vision meant," Alain continued. "This elder was not like the others. She warned me against speaking of it to anyone else, because, she said, it revealed that the daughter of the prophecy had come, that she was the one whom I had seen the vision focused upon. That an awful storm approached our world, one that would cause it to descend into chaos and destruction as the commons erupted in uncontrolled fury after centuries of servitude. The elder said the forces making up that storm would try to destroy the daughter, because she was the only one who could change the world and overcome the forces which threatened the world. She told me that, as you and I talked of in Dorcastle, the anarchy in Tiae is a sign of what is to come everywhere unless the storm is stopped.

"I tried to speak of it to you when we met at the restaurant, and you told me you already knew what I wished to say, and there was no need to say anything."

Mari finally spoke again, her voice ragged. "Wait. What did you say? Exactly what did you tell me?"

Alain tried to remember. "I said it was about you, and about me, and the future—"

"Oh no!" Mari slammed both of her palms against her forehead. "You— You— I thought you wanted to talk about you and me being together in the future!"

"I did, because I knew you would need my help, my protection, in order to fulfill the prophecy—"

"No! No! No!" Mari was angry again, glowering at him. "What you said sounded like a romantic discussion, like you wanted to talk about us being serious and committed to each other, and I was not ready for that so I told you..." She gasped, sagging back against her seat, looking stricken. "No. I can't be her."

"Mari?"

"I want to be angry with you. I want to be very, very, very angry with you," Mari said in a whisper. "But I remember some things, times you started to say things and I thought... Oh, no. Alain, couldn't you tell that I didn't really know what you wanted to talk about?"

"No," he said. "I could not." Alain wondered what his own face and eyes might be revealing now, because he could no longer think to control them. "You did not know? All this time you did not?"

She looked back at him, and must have seen something there that calmed her anger though not her distress. "You really did think I knew. Why did you think I didn't want to ever talk about it?"

"It is such a huge thing," Alain said. "Such a difficult thing."

"Yeah," Mari said in a faint voice. "Huge. Difficult. Alain, you said your Guild knew who I was."

"Not that way," he hastened to say. "They knew you were the Mechanic I had seen in Ringhmon. They did not know you were the daughter—"

"Don't call me that."

Alain tried again. "The elder I spoke with would not have betrayed you or me. I am certain that my Guild did not know. If they did, they would not have sent a single Mage with a knife to try to kill you in Edinton. If they even suspected, they would have used every Mage in Edinton and every spell they possessed, or they would have waited until you came to me to ensure they killed both of us."

Her eyes stayed on his. "Maybe they expected me to join you on that Alexdrian expedition that was attacked, so that dragon could kill both of us."

"That...is possible," Alain said. "But the Roc tried to kill you first, so it may be that the Mage Guild now suspects who you are."

"That's what you meant when were talking after we were attacked on the train?" Mari was blinking, her expression shifting from horror to dismay to disbelief and through all those emotions again. "My Guild, your Guild, they'll kill me in a heartbeat if they find out about this. The Empire...what would the Empire do if they got their hands on me now? My life isn't worth a speck of dust."

"But you are fated to fulfill—" Alain began.

"Stop that! That's simply ridiculous!" Mari jumped up and began pacing, her hands moving wildly as she talked. "How could I be her? Do I look like her?"

"Mari, you had already decided to change this world—"

"That's different!" She spun to face him. "That didn't make me...her."

Alain stood up slowly and spoke with care. "You are still Master Mechanic Mari of Caer Lyn. You will always be that person. All the prophecy says is that you are also the daughter. It is not you. It is only part of what you will do." His voice faltered and he fought to steady it. "Mari, I...am...sorry. If I had suspected that you did not know, I would have found a way to tell you before this."

She looked away from him, out the window facing the lake.

He waited, wishing he could see her face. Outside noises came faintly to them, and on the lake the lights of boats moved leisurely across the water, but Mari remained silent and motionless as even the stars swung unhurriedly overhead. Through the window, Alain could see the moon very slowly crossing the sky, forever chased by the two small dots of light known as the Twins.

"Alain," she finally said, "can you imagine what this is like for me? It's not just that so many people will want to kill me, but the idea that I'm some...I don't even know how to say it. If I believed for even one minute that you have deliberately avoided telling me about this until now, I...I don't know what I would do. But I have been trying to remember every conversation we have had, and I can see how you and I thought we both knew what the other meant, when actually we did not."

"What can I do?" Alain asked.

"Just tell me one thing." She finally looked at him again, her face drawn, eyes haunted. "Are you with me because of that? Did you stay with me in that blizzard because of that? Because I'm...her?"

Alain shook his head. "I resolved to be with you before I knew of that. I thought of nothing but you during that blizzard. I would be with you now and always even if that vision had never come to me."

Mari began laughing and crying at the same time, a mix of emotions that dismayed Alain as he watched it.

"You're not lying," she said. "You really mean it. Oh, Alain, what am I going to do?"

"What you were already planning on doing," he said, feeling helpless.

She shuddered with the effort of regaining control, took in a long, slow, breath, then exhaled, her expression calming somewhat. "My plans just hit a brick wall, Alain, remember?" She wiped her eyes roughly. "You heard Professor S'san. Even if I had an army, it couldn't prevail. What you call the storm would blow it to pieces before it could get strong enough. And what would I do if I had an army? Do you have any idea how absurd that sounds to me? I wouldn't know the first thing about leading an army. I don't know how to fight battles. Where would I get an army, anyway? And why would an army follow me?"

"You wish me to say what I believe?"

"Yes," Mari said, "and from now on if I say let's not talk about something, talk about it anyway."

"Then I will say that from what I saw in the Northern Ramparts," Alain said, "someone believed to be the daughter of Jules could raise an army of commons simply by calling for it. The same forces that would help drive the storm—the anger and the frustration of the commons—would cause them to flock to the—to the one they believe could save them."

Mari was still breathing deeply, still looked stricken, but she was also frowning in thought. "Redirect the force? Employ it for useful ends instead of destruction? I can understand that. It makes sense. We talked about attitudes and emotions among the commons as being like pressure in a boiler. If it just keeps building with no outlet, then the boiler explodes. But if instead I use that force to accomplish work..." She bit her lip. "How can they believe that I'm that person, Alain?"

"The soldiers of Alexdria were eager to believe it," Alain pointed out. "I was told by General Flyn that long ago the children of Jules were hidden among the commons, so that when word of the prophecy reached the Great Guilds they could not slay every child in the line of Jules. No one knows who carries her blood."

"How many centuries ago was that, Alain! How many daughters would have already been born to the descendents of Jules, and how thin would that blood be by now?" She started pacing back and forth through the room again, though this time in a much more controlled way. "Even if blood mattered, when it came to what a person could do! It's ridiculous. Me, the daughter of Jules. Am I a pirate queen? Am I an explorer? Have I founded any cities or countries? Have I fought the Empire itself to a standstill? I have nothing in common with Jules. I can't afford to believe such a thing. You know me better than anyone except myself! How can you believe it?"

"Because I know you," Alain said. "You are smart and you are brave. You help others find new strength. You give them hope. You do not give up."

She stopped and stared at him. "Alain, I am scared. I'd gotten used to the idea that my Guild and your Guild were hunting me, but that is nothing compared to what will be sent against someone who claims to be that person."

Alain nodded. "I know. I long ago resolved that I would die to defend you. That will not change."

"Oh, great. So if I die, you will, too. That doesn't actually make me feel better." Mari flung her hands toward the ceiling. "Just what do I do now? You heard Professor S'san. Her whole plan hinged on my getting access to the Mechanic Guild vaults and the banned texts inside them. That's impossible now. What can I do without that knowledge?"

"These texts exist only in those vaults?" Alain asked.

"Yes! At Mechanics Guild headquarters in Palandur! Supposedly kept safe for use in emergencies when the tech in them might be critically needed, but no Mechanic believes those texts will ever actually be made available, no matter what happens. Everything is so tightly guarded we'd need an army to get at them. A very big army. That's even if a Mage were helping me get through some of the defenses. I wouldn't put it past the Senior Mechanics to destroy those texts if they thought I was trying to get them."

"Palandur?" Alain shook his head. "That city is not much more than a century and a half old. Surely there was once another headquarters for your Guild. Might something not still be in that place and perhaps not as well protected?"

Mari laughed bitterly. "The old headquarters was in Marandur, Alain."

"Perhaps that is the answer."

She gave him a startled look. "Marandur? How can Marandur be the answer? I don't know all that much about it, but I do know that after the city was destroyed the Emperor Palan declared it off-limits for all time. It's an automatic death sentence to set foot inside the old city. Even Mechanics were warned not to mess with that prohibition."

"Yes," Alain agreed. "But you do not know the story? The history of the end of Marandur?"

Mari finally sat down again, still looking very worried but eyeing him with interest. "Please tell me. It was some kind of rebellion, but that's all I know."

The change in her mood heartened Alain. "A fanatical underground movement arose. It gained thousands of followers who worshipped their leader. The Imperials had become complacent and did not realize how powerful this group had become. Over time, the rebels by trickery lured away the legions which normally guarded the capital and in a bold nighttime stroke seized Marandur, closing the gates before the legions could return. They captured most of the Imperial family along with the capital city." He shook his head. "Then, as the returned legions watched along with Prince Palan, who had by chance been out of the city, the rebels brought the Imperial family to the walls and murdered them all."

Mari made a noise of disbelief. "I'm not the smartest person in the world, but even I know how stupid that must've been. Everybody talks about how loyal the legions are to the Imperial family."

"Yes. Palan proclaimed himself the new emperor and ordered the legions to retake the city at all costs, ensuring no rebels survived. Many Mages were called upon to assist in the assault, and I assume many Mechanic devices must have been used as well. The city was destroyed, building by building, as the legions advanced and the rebels fought to the death."

He paused, his thoughts dark. Once the story had seemed interesting but removed from him, something that could not stir emotions he no longer acknowledged having. But Mari had made him see that other people were not just shadows, and now the thought of the suffering disturbed him. "No one knows how many citizens of the city died during the retaking of Marandur. But when the assault was over, every rebel had been slain as they fought to the last, and the city was a wasteland of ruins populated mostly by the dead. That was when Palan decreed that Marandur would stand as an eternal monument to the costs of rebellion. After giving any survivors a very short period to leave, the ruins of the city were declared sealed on pain of death, a quarantine enforced by Imperial soldiers ever since. Palandur was built as the new capital." Alain pointed at Mari. "Some artifacts and wealth were removed from the wreckage of the Imperial palace, but by the emperor's decree no one else was allowed to bring objects out of the ruins of Marandur."

She took a moment to realize what that meant. "The vaults at the original Guild headquarters. I was told that the rebels overran the Mechanics Guild headquarters, which was blamed on the guards not being alert. That's why apprentices get told about it, since apprentices stand the routine security watches in Guild Halls. The Guild Hall in Marandur was certainly badly damaged, if not destroyed, when the legions retook the city, but the vaults might still contain manuscripts. If the Guild had copies elsewhere—and there are always supposed to be copies of important documents—and if the Guild believed that the ones in Marandur had probably been destroyed anyway, it might not have contested Palan's decision. Blazes, the Guild would have known that the Empire was keeping everyone out of what was left of Marandur, the legions inadvertently guarding those old vaults better than even the Mechanics Guild could have. If those vaults are still sealed, which they well could be because they would've been very strong, those manuscripts might've survived intact." Mari was getting visibly animated as she spoke. "It's possible. Alain, it's just possible. I can open those vaults, given time."

Mari clenched her fists, gazing toward one wall. "Maybe...maybe the technology in those vaults could change things without a war. Maybe that army you saw me with would never be used. Maybe the big battle in Dorcastle wouldn't have to happen. That's possible, right?"

"That is possible," Alain said. "The visions showed only possible futures."

"And we're already together again. Oh, Alain, this could give me the tools I need to fix things without some kind of war happening. The prophecy doesn't say there will be a war, does it? It just says the Great Guild will be overthrown."

Alain nodded, thinking. "As far as I know, that is correct. But will either the Mage Guild or the Mechanics Guild surrender without fighting?"

"I don't know," Mari said. "I have to try." She looked at him, a different kind of worry visible now. "But it's an automatic death sentence from the emperor to go to Marandur. That doesn't matter as far as I'm concerned, with so many people who will want me dead when they discover about that prophecy. But you...I can't let you be sentenced to death as well."

"I am already under a death sentence from my Guild," Alain reminded her. "It would not matter if that were not so, for I meant what I said. If you die, it will only be because I have already fallen protecting you. If you go to Marandur, I will go also."

Mari looked at him for a long time, then to Alain's surprise smiled in a very sad way. "I'm such an idiot. Do you know why? Because you and I are going to Marandur. I still don't believe that I'm that person, but I'm going to keep trying to fix things." Mari came over to hold Alain tightly. "You're forgiven for not telling me."

"I tried," Alain said, once more bewildered.

"In your own silly Mage way, yes, you did," Mari agreed. "But you have to promise me something."

"Anything," Alain said.

"Never say that," Mari insisted. "I don't own you. I don't have any right to ask you to promise anything I want. But this one thing I need you to do. Please promise you will not call me that name. I can't control what other people do, what other people might say, but I need to remain Mari in your eyes. Not...her."

"I promise, Mari."

She started laughing softly, alarming him again. "The word of a Mage. I just got a Mage to promise me something."

"Many people would not understand why you bothered," Alain said, relieved. "Do you feel better?"

"No. I'm in denial right now. I'm scared and overwhelmed and my mind is racing. But," she paused and looked at him. "You're here. You just gave me hope. You also just scared the blazes out of me. I'm no longer sure that I'm the most difficult person in this relationship."

"I remain sure of it," Alain said.

"Did you just make a joke?" She pulled away a little and stared at him, smiling more like she usually did. "Are you making fun of me, Mage?"

Alain couldn't remember how long it had been since he had laughed. The act was completely alien to Mages, to the training he had endured since he was a small child. But now he laughed, the sound rusty and halting, yet he knew it was a laugh, and it felt so good to be laughing and holding Mari that Alain wondered what Mage art or other promised reward could possibly be worth giving up such things.

Mari looked at him, blinking away tears. "You're laughing. What a wonderful sound. My Mage is laughing. Our Guilds want to kill us, everybody thinks I'm somebody I'm not, and we're going to a ruined city where the Emperor has decreed any trespassers must die. And we're happy. Do you want to leave for there tomorrow?"

Alain stopped laughing long enough to answer. "Certainly."

Then the moment vanished as they both heard an odd sound, like a distorted voice.

Mari flung herself away from him, toward her pack. Digging in the pack frantically, Mari surfaced in a few moments with the boxlike thing Alain had seen her use to call other Mechanics in Dorcastle. He heard a strangely raspy voice speaking in barely audible words. "I repeat, Master Mechanic Mari, please respond. Your Guild is concerned for your safety. If you will please come to the Guild Hall here in Severun we will ensure you are taken care of and that you are protected. Please respond—"

Mari did something to the Mechanic device and the voice cut off. "We're not leaving in the morning. We're leaving now. Somehow my Guild suspects that I'm in this city. Get everything together. I want us out of here as fast as possible."

CHAPTER FOURTEEN

Fortunately, packing required nothing more than throwing a few things back into their packs and then heading for the door. The room had been paid for already, so Alain just had to wait while Mari tossed the key into a slot at the owner's door, then they both hastened out of the hostel. "We go south," Mari said. "Marandur is that way, and neither one of our Guilds will expect us to go south from here." She felt dazed from the many emotional ups and downs of this day, which obviously had not ended.

The daughter? Her? How could she possibly be that person? Mari shook her head violently, trying to drive the thoughts away. *Focus on here and now, on getting away from my Guild here, or that prophecy might end badly in a few hours.*

Alain looked back for a moment, toward the waters of the lake, and came to a momentary halt. "I see a black haze when I look to the north. Danger comes from the lake."

"Mechanics?" Mari asked, tugging Alain back into motion and increasing their pace.

"No. Mages, I think. It feels like that. They must be coming to Severun on one of the lake ferries or ships."

"Blast! My Guild seems to have figured out we're here, and so has your Guild. How did they find us?" Mari looked around. "More importantly at the moment, how do we throw them off our track?"

"Asha," Alain said suddenly.

"What? Do you think she betrayed—"

"No," Alain said. "She is close to those on the lake. Her presence shone brightly for a moment. She must have been ordered to assist the Mages coming here, but she deliberately let her presence show so strongly. She has tried to warn us that the other Mages are coming."

Hearing the clop of hooves and the rumble of wheels on the paved streets, Mari looked ahead to see a carriage approaching at a rapid clip along streets nearly deserted at this late hour. She took Alain's arm and pulled him into the nearest doorway, waiting in the shadows there as the carriage rattled past. "They're in a hurry to get somewhere. Let's—Get back!" Mari pushed Alain into the shadows again as a second carriage appeared and rushed down the street past them. "We can't run without drawing too much attention, but let's walk as fast as we can. I couldn't see who was in those carriages, but the drivers sure looked like Mechanic apprentices to me."

Alain stayed with her as they walked, but glanced back once. "Why would your Guild have warned you if they were sending Mechanics to take you?"

She frowned at him. "That's a good question. That message tipped me off. It was pretty dumb of someone to—" Mari paused, looking straight ahead now as she thought. "Maybe that wasn't a mistake. Maybe someone warned me just like Asha warned you." Who did she know in Severun besides Professor S'san? If Calu had been sent to Umburan, perhaps some of her other old friends had been sent here.

Or someone she had never met? Like the Mechanics who had confided in her their own doubts and worries about the Guild?

The two- and three-story shops and homes on either side of the road were mostly dark or with only a single window showing light from a lantern or candle inside. They had made it a fair way along the street, the road still climbing along the long slope leading down to the lake behind them, when Alain held out a cautioning arm. "I see police ahead."

"Oh, great," Mari groaned. "We have to worry about Imperials tonight, too."

The two Imperial police walked at a leisurely pace as they approached, but when Mari and Alain were close one of them held up a restraining hand. "A bit late to be out, citizens. Papers."

Mari tried to look meek as she handed over the fake identity papers. The officer scanned them slowly, while Mari wondered how close behind various pursuers might be. "Palandur," the Imperial officer finally said. "Why are two citizens from Palandur wandering the streets of Severun at night?"

"We're visitors seeing your city," Mari said.

The two police officers exchanged glances and both smiled in a smug way. "This looks suspicious, don't you think?" one asked the other.

"Definitely," the second agreed. "You two will come with us for a little talk down at the local station."

Mari had no trouble understanding what the Imperial cops were doing. It was the same sort of thing which she had seen certain apprentices and Mechanics do to more junior apprentices on a whim, using their power to enliven an otherwise dull period of time by harassing someone unable to resist. One of the trade-offs which Imperial citizens suffered for their sense of security was dealing with police who had few practical limits on their powers.

She tried smiling beseechingly at the two officers. "Please, we're just passing through the city and will leave soon. Two fine officers such as yourself—"

"Resisting us?" one of the officers asked the other. "She's resisting answering questions."

"Yup," the second agreed.

Alain gave Mari a look. She knew that his spells could handle these officers, but that would betray his location to the Mages coming in from the lake. Her pistol could also deal with the officers, but the noise of it would draw the Mechanics chasing her. Mari looked over the Imperial police officers again, in their leather chest armor, each armed with a short sword and a hardwood club. There didn't seem to be any alternative to threatening them with her pistol and hoping they wouldn't force her to fire.

Mari nodded to Alain, then gave the two Imperial officers a pleading look. "I'm sorry, I forgot. There's something else I need to show you." She raised her hand toward the pistol concealed under her coat. If she could overawe them with that weapon, keep them quiet while Alain tied them up—

Her hand had closed about the grip of the pistol, but before she could draw the weapon a series of rapping sounds resounded from far down the street in the direction of the hostel Alain and Mari had fled. Both of the Imperial officers focused their attention down the street, listening. "Mechanics?" one questioned, then pointed a finger at Mari and Alain. "Did you two see any Mechanics up to anything down that way?"

"We saw some closed carriages go past us moving quickly," Mari replied. "Really quickly. They almost ran us down." She managed to inject some righteous indignation into her voice along with the meekness expected of Imperial citizens speaking to anyone in authority.

The first officer turned on his companion. "I told you we should've checked on that! Now there's a bunch of Mechanics in the Viryen District breaking into houses and hostels down there!" He shoved the identity papers back at Mari. "You two get the blazes out of here."

Mari stuffed the papers back into one of her pockets, grabbing Alain's arm as they walked rapidly onward.

Alain looked back to see one of the officers kneeling, hardwood club in hand, to rap out a reply to the first message on the stones of the street. Then the two Imperial police set off running toward the lake. "I had not realized before that commons employed such methods to communicate over distances," he remarked.

"I didn't know about it, either," Mari said. "I've heard that kind of rapping at times, but I haven't been out among commons that much and when I was I never paid attention. It's a clever system, using those clubs to tap out simple coded messages that carry a long distance, especially at night when there's not as much background noise. I wonder how many Mechanics know that commons keep track of our movements using systems like that? In any case, it got us out of that mess before I had to use my weapon. There was no way I was going to let us be hauled in so some bored Imperial cops could practice interrogation techniques on a couple of citizens from out of town."

Despite her hold on him urging Alain along, Mari felt Alain pausing again. She spun to tell him this was no time to wait around and saw Alain looking steadily to the north.

"The Mages are moving...that way," Alain said. "Along the lake. I just sensed Asha again. She must be more cautious in her attempts to warn us. The Mages with her will surely notice that she is dropping her defenses for brief periods."

"That way?" Mari swung her arm along that direction. "West. Why are they going west?"

"We must assume that something, or someone, has caused them to search in that direction."

"Asha," Mari said. "You were right. She's helping us."

Alain frowned very slightly as Mari got him walking quickly south again, a sign of how deeply he was concerned. "The Mechanics knew not only that you were in the city, but in which part of the city as well. From what the Imperial police officers said, the Mechanics are breaking into the hostel where we were staying or somewhere near there. Can Mechanics sense the presence of other Mechanics, just as Mages can sense Mages?"

"No," Mari said. "I have no idea how they found us, which is very worrying. I don't believe that Professor S'san betrayed us, and even if she had she didn't know where we were staying tonight. Maybe we gave ourselves away by how we acted, or maybe some Mechanic we didn't notice recognized me and followed us."

"If they believe you are in this city," Alain suggested, "then they will also be going to the home of your elder. They will believe you came here to see her."

"Stars above, you're right." Mari aimed an anguished look in the direction of S'san's home. "We can't go warn her. They're probably already there. Oh, Alain, what am I doing to my friends?"

"You are doing nothing to your friends. These are the actions of others. The blame for those actions does not rest with you."

"No matter how many times you say that, I won't believe it." They reached a high point in the street and looked back a final time toward the lake. Mari bit her lip, gazing north in distress. "Is there anything else from Asha?"

"No. I sense nothing now from any other Mage."

Mari pulled her far-seers from her pack and focused them to the north, then pivoted to look south in the direction they were going. Nothing was visible in either direction but darkened streets and buildings dimly illuminated by streetlamps burning coal. In one place behind them to the north, a few more lights were visible, but it was impossible to see anything in detail. "Far-seers," she explained to Alain. "They have lenses in them which make far-off objects much easier to see." She was putting them away as she spoke. "It's risky for me to use them when anyone else might see me, because only a wealthy common or a senior military officer could afford far-seers, but I wanted to see if anything was visible."

"I saw these with the Alexdrian soldiers," Alain said. "I do not understand the Mechanic spell which makes them work, but the commons found them valuable. Did you see the Mechanics?"

"Not directly. There are some more lights down there, but the lights are staying around where we were. The Mechanics are probably searching every possible hiding place in the area of that hostel and the buildings around it." Mari bent her head in thought. "Since my Guild knows or strongly suspects I'm in this city, it wouldn't be safe to try heading south by train."

Alain actually revealed relief at her words. "I would prefer not to risk a train again."

"Trains really are usually safe, Alain."

"Your Guild and mine may be watching the horse-drawn coaches from Severun as well."

She blew out an exasperated breath. "You're probably right. We'll have to walk until we're well clear of the city and then try to get rides on passing wagons again. That's the only way to avoid being spotted at the coach stations, and the Senior Mechanics will never suspect that anyone would be willing to walk when they could ride." Mari settled her pack. "Let's go. It's going to be a long walk tonight."

They had been trudging along for a while, having reached the southern stretches of the city, when Mari gave a brief laugh as an incongruous thought struck her. "Jules was a sailor. If I'm a daughter of Jules, why do I have to walk everywhere?"

"Do you enjoy sailing?" Alain asked.

"I've hardly ever been on the water." Mari shrugged. "Alain, no offense, but I will never believe that I'm actually descended from Jules."

"What you believe is less important than what others believe," Alain suggested. "The illusion they see is very powerful."

Mari sighed. "I haven't exactly spent my life to this point aspiring to be a powerful illusion." She noticed Alain looking back north again. "What's the matter?"

Alain didn't answer for a few moments. "I am...worried about Mage Asha. Her attempts to warn us and misdirect our pursuers could have placed her in great peril."

Mari turned to him, guilt and gratitude mixed inside her. "Alain? I hope she's all right."

"Your professor?"

"Your friend. Asha. It was very brave of her to risk herself for us that way."

Alain's voice held a note of wonder that she had rarely heard before. "I have two friends?"

"Yes," Mari said, "if you mean Mechanic Calu and Mage Asha. I am more than a friend."

"You are much more than a friend, my Master Mechanic."

Feeling tremendous relief as they walked past the indifferent guards at the south gate of the city and out into the open country beyond the city walls, Mari couldn't help a brief giggle. "Alain, you, and only you, are allowed to call me just Mechanic."

❋   ❋   ❋

A little before dawn, and with the city well behind them, Mari and Alain found an area not far from the road which was sheltered by a large stand of trees. Staggering with weariness, they made it well into the trees and then collapsed onto the ground next to each other. By the time Alain awoke, the sun was well up in the sky. He sat up carefully, trying not to disturb Mari, then went back toward the road, seeing that it was now covered with considerable traffic. Being one of the main roads within the Empire, the route was paved with massive stone blocks and stretched wide enough for wagons to pass each other and the foot traffic with no difficulty. Even if he could not have seen the road he still would have known it was near from the scent of the manure from the various draft animals baking in the sun's heat.

Mari came up beside him, looking haggard. "Any sign of trouble?"

"No. We should not have difficulty blending in with so many foot travelers, wagons, and carriages using the road."

She yawned, then winced. "Do your legs hurt as much as mine do?"

"I do not know. How could I know?"

Mari closed her eyes and sighed heavily. "That's another rhetorical question, Alain."

"A question which is not to be answered."

"Yes. And yes, that is kind of an odd thing, now that you've pointed it out. Let's see if we can find a wagon that'll let us pay for a ride, preferably a wagon with cargo we can hide ourselves among."

Alain looked north, watching the sky. "Do you feel the wind? Winter comes marching from the north, but we remain a step ahead of it."

Mari shivered. "They don't have blizzards down here as severe as they do up north around Umburan. I would have noticed if anything like that hit Palandur. But I'm not thrilled at the idea of slogging through a regular snowstorm, either. Those can be plenty bad enough. Let's try to get to Marandur before then."

"We must not mention our destination again," Alain cautioned.

"Fine. You're right. Let's go." She walked out toward the road and Alain followed, seeing that their appearance attracted little attention from the passing traffic.

About noon they managed to buy seats in the back of a big wagon hauling freight southward. Mari wedged herself and Alain between some of the crates so that they were almost invisible to anyone on the road, then fell asleep.

Alain stayed awake longer, watching for danger, but finally succumbed to tiredness himself.

He awoke much later in the afternoon when the wagon rolled to a stop. Gazing out cautiously, Alain saw an inn offering water and food. "Need anything?" the driver leaned back to ask. "I'm just getting something for me and watering the mules, then we're off, so make it quick."

Awakening Mari, Alain got his aching body out of the wagon, grateful for the moment for his Mage training at enduring hardship. "I sense no Mages nearby, so I will go first to see if it is safe." He went into the inn, buying some wine and travel food, and finding an irrational pleasure in knowing how to do such a simple task for commons. But as he turned to walk back to the wagon, Alain saw two Mechanics lounging near the passenger coach stand. Both carried the large Mechanic weapons that Mari called repeating rifles. The commons were either ignoring the Mechanics or casting worried glances their way, so Alain also pretended not to be aware of them.

"The station is watched," he warned Mari, describing the Mechanics. She glared at him. "How the blazes am I supposed to relieve myself?"

"I...do not know."

Mari had to wait until the wagon was well down the road, jumping off to dart into a patch of bushes, then running to catch up to the wagon again as Alain watched anxiously. For some reason she appeared to blame him for her inconvenience, but the wine and food Alain had purchased put her in a better mood. "We'll have to stock up on supplies before we leave the road for...our destination," Mari remarked. "I don't think we can count on finding anything there."

He thought about that as the wagon rumbled through the last light of day. What would a city destroyed and then abandoned for more than a century be like? The thoughts brought no comfort, and Alain was glad for the distraction when the wagon turned into a drover's station for the night. He and Mari got a tiny room in the drover hostel and slept in each other's arms. So much human contact had taken some getting used to, but now he found himself wishing he could hold her more. It sometimes took great effort not to move his hands to places where Mari had told him not to touch her. But as Alain lay, feeling her breathe in her sleep next to him, he remembered her distress in Severun, and how badly he had wanted to help, and how little he could do. Being told that she was the daughter of the prophecy had been a hard thing to take, an awesome responsibility to be told of.

In some ways, Alain realized to his sorrow, Mari would always be alone, no matter how closely he held her or how hard he tried to help.

✳   ✳   ✳

Even with frequent purchases of rides on wagons going in the same direction, the need to rest at night and keep an eye out for Mages or Mechanics or Dark Mechanics meant it was still close to two weeks before they reached the place where Mari could see the Imperial road taking a wide turn toward the new capital of Palandur. At that turn, the old route to Marandur was easy to spot, though the paving had been buckled by more than one hundred and fifty years of deliberate neglect. Grass, shrubs, and trees were intruding on the old road, some of the trees quite tall now, but its path remained obvious.

So did the Imperial watchtower at the place where the old road and the new diverged. Unlike the watchtower on the northern plains which Alain had described seeing, this tower was of stone, looking stout enough to stand for a thousand years. The sentries on the tower looked bored, but they kept their eyes on the road traffic.

Standing next to the tower was a huge stone, the side facing the road cut flat and polished. Deeply engraved on the stone were words formed of letters so large as to be easy to read from the road. "To All Who Pass," Mari read out loud to Alain, "Know The Price Rebellion Will Pay. Only Death Lives In Marandur Now, And Death Will Claim All Who Go There Or Dare To Raise Their Hand Against Their Emperor. Palan, Emperor."

"Death lives in Marandur?" Mari remarked despite the knot in her stomach the words brought. "The emperor could've used an editor."

"Were I the emperor's editor," Alain replied, "I doubt I would find much to criticize in the emperor's writing."

Mari and Alain walked on past the turn-off with idle glances at the old road, then went back to watching their fellow travelers for signs of danger. Over the last week sightings of Mechanics on watch along the road had lessened as they went farther south, and then ended except for infrequent sightings of Mechanics who were clearly traveling to destinations in comfortable carriages and paying no attention to others on the road. As hoped, Mari's Guild apparently had not expected her to come this way, but Mari covertly watched the Mechanics as they passed, her feelings by turns wistful and worried. She should have been one of them. Now they were hunting her.

The occasional Mage had passed them as well, but Alain must have become very good at hiding himself from other Mages because none of them paid any attention to him. Had Asha succeeded in making the

Mage Guild believe that Alain had gone west from Severun? Mari felt another guilty twinge at the thought. Despite his advice to Mari that she should not feel guilty for the dangers faced by others, Alain himself clearly felt responsible for anything that might happen to Asha. One time he had tried to talk about that to Mari, but she had been moody and the conversation had ended quickly, Alain appearing let down and Mari mentally kicking herself. The next day she brought it up, let Alain talk out his worries, and they both felt better afterwards.

It seemed that they had thrown their Guilds off of their track, at least temporarily. But that still left the Imperial troops enforcing the ban on traveling to Marandur.

Later in the day they passed a roadside stand selling food and watered wine, so they filled their packs before moving on. They walked until darkness fell and made sure no one was observing them, then turned left off the new road and headed straight for the old, making their way carefully through the night.

They were moving across an open area between patches of woods when Alain grabbed her arm and forced Mari down flat in the grass. Though uncut, the grass here grew not much higher than their ankles, leaving them far too exposed even when hugging the ground. Mari lay unmoving as the muffled clatter of armor and weaponry merged with the soft rustling sounds of legs striding through the grass. The half-full moon provided plenty enough light to see the shapes of the Imperial legionaries trudging by maybe fifty lance-lengths to one side of her and Alain.

Mari held her breath, one hand on her pistol under her jacket. *If I have to use this, we're dead. The sounds of the shots will draw every legionary within thousands of lances.* The legionaries didn't seem to be searching, though, instead slogging wearily along with the attitude of soldiers who have done the same thing too many times with nothing ever happening. None of them glanced in the direction of Mari and Alain, and after some heart-stopping moments the patrol was past its closest point to them and moving away.

Finally drawing a breath, Mari lowered her face to the soil. "This is going to be a long night," she barely whispered to Alain.

"They cannot patrol the entire area between here and Marandur in strength," he said. "Even the Empire does not have sufficient troops or wealth to keep such a large garrison in place. Once we get past this band of defenses we should find areas that are less well guarded."

"I hope you're right, my Mage."

They dodged another patrol before dawn, then holed up in a shallow ravine cut by a stream, huddled against the raw earth of the banks as they tried to get some rest, one of them always awake and on watch as the other dozed.

No Imperial patrols disturbed their day, though, and as the sun sank to the horizon Mari and Alain started out through the dying light, quickly stumbling across the old road. Mari came to a halt on its verge, seeing that the road showed no sign of use for several decades at least. "They have troops around Marandur itself enforcing the quarantine, but they're not using the old road to supply them or move them."

Alain gazed at the old road, his expression uncharacteristically somber. "The emperors believe they have the power to force their illusions on all others. This is part of that. The road itself is declared dead, never to be used, and no one dares dispute the Imperial will."

"Not much better than the Great Guilds, is it?"

"No, I do not think so. When you seek allies among the commons, Mari, I believe you should look to those who do not blindly accept the authority of their leaders."

"Too much failure to accept authority and you end up with anarchy, like in Tiae," Mari pointed out.

"That is so," Alain agreed. "But as you told your elder, there is much that lies between total control and anarchy. The leaders of our Guilds and the rulers of the Empire would have us believe that only those two extremes exist, but I have been among the Free Cities and you have been in the Confederation. Their governing systems are not perfect, but they work while still allowing their people freedom."

"Freedom?" Mari turned to Alain, surprised. "I've never heard you use that word. Hardly anybody uses it."

"I was taught that freedom is an illusion, only one more illusion which distracts from the path of wisdom." A flare of some deep emotion showed in Alain's eyes. "But I have felt freedom, Mari, as I walked the road beside you, and I know it is no illusion. The will of the Great Guilds, of the Emperor, those things are illusions, and their images will not endure."

She stared at him. "At times like this I really remember why I fell in love with you. You know, since you told me about...about the prophecy, I've been thinking more about overthrowing the Great Guilds, and I've realized that's not a goal. That's just something you do on your way to somewhere else. But where? What is the goal, what is it that would replace the Great Guilds? And you just said it. Freedom. To think, to act, to do new things and to make what we do matter. All my life I've wanted that. I bet most other people do, too."

"A new day?"

Mari looked away, feeling uncertainty fill her. "I still don't see how I can do that, Alain. And I have to wonder why things are like this. It's been bothering me all the way down here from Severun. You may noticed I've been a little preoccupied."

"I have noticed," Alain said.

"Aren't you the diplomatic one," Mari said. "I have to wonder. Was freedom tried and did it fail? Is that the history before the history we know? Or has it ever been? Why are things as they are now? Is there a reason? Would freedom be a mistake?"

His brow creased ever so slightly, the equivalent of a major frown from a non-Mage. "I cannot believe it would be. I have been a servant to those who demand absolute obedience, and I am now free. I know which is better."

"Me, too. But does that give me the right to make that decision for others? Do entire societies, do worlds, work better that way? I need more data, Alain. That's one of the reasons we're going to Marandur. Maybe along with the banned technology there will be some banned histories." She frowned at him. "I know that not-a-look of yours. What are you thinking and not saying?"

"I…" He struggled with a word before getting it out. "Hope. I…hope you decide that freedom is the answer."

Mari gave him her best reassuring smile. "No matter what we find, Alain, I will not believe that the answer is anything like the Empire."

His eyes rested on hers, concern easy to see. "There may be many who want you to become an Empress."

"Oh, please!" Mari laughed at the absurdity of the idea. "I will guarantee that is never, *ever* going to happen. Can you see me on a throne?" Her laughter died as an awful thought struck her. "Have you? Have you seen me on a throne?"

"No," Alain said. "I have never had such a vision."

"If you ever do," Mari said, "that is one future we will ensure does not happen."

They veered off from the old road and a bare path alongside it that revealed the trail sometimes used by the legionaries. After getting far enough away from the road, they turned to walk parallel to it, watching constantly for more Imperial troops. The road to Marandur cut across a series of slight hills and shallow valleys, so as Mari and Alain traveled they caught sight of the old city while on the higher ground and then lose the view as they moved down into the low areas. The result was to create a series of images, each offering a slightly closer view and more detail than the next.

When first they sighted Marandur the city looked almost beautiful, gleaming in the distance under the last rays of the setting sun. From far away, the city could have been intact. Only the lack of any kind of haze over the city hinted that no people lived or worked there. A living city was always crowned by a haze made up of smoke from fires to heat and cook and work, and from the dust thrown up by the movement of people and animals, just as a living creature breathed out warmth. But the sky above Marandur was almost crystal clear, like that above a vast cemetery where no one moved or drew breath. Mari felt a chill at the sight, and she moved to walk a bit closer to Alain. "Hold on."

She stopped walking, pulled out her far-seers, and studied the city. Under the magnification of the far-seers, gaps became apparent in the great walls. Towers were truncated, the upper stories fallen into the streets below. The huge gates lay sprawled next to the entrance they had guarded, an entrance with no traffic and lacking any sign of life. Mari moved the far-seers slowly as her head turned, spotting the ragged walls of lesser buildings standing vacant. In all the great city, it was hard to find any place where a roofline or a wall or even a window presented lines unbroken by damage.

Mari shifted her gaze to the area just outside the city. A watchtower stood a few bowshots outside the gates, the reflected glint of the setting sun on the armor of sentries easily visible. "There are towers all the way around as far as I can see," she told Alain, "close enough to each other that even at night I bet they can spot us if we tried to walk between them. There are sentries walking rounds between the towers, too. It's a very good security barrier. I tell you, Alain, the Empire is a bloody-handed and despotic state, but they sure know how to build things right. How are we going to get past those sentries?"

"We must not linger on the higher ground," Alain cautioned. "It will make us to easy to see. We must get close enough to study the defenses and spot any weaknesses."

"Fine with me." Mari stayed close to Alain as she put away the far-seers. They went down into the next low area and quickly lost sight of the dead city.

There were more rises, and even though Mari and Alain stayed low and moved quickly across the crests of the high areas, each successive look gave them a better view of the city as the moon rose, its pale rays shining on the dead metropolis.

Outside the city, watch fires had been set at regular intervals, illuminating the ground and the outside of the broken walls. "I can't see any gaps in the Imperial defenses," Mari whispered to Alain. Even though they were still a few thousand lances from the Imperial watchtowers, she felt very exposed. She glanced up at the sky, where the stars were paler and the moon was close to setting. "It's not long until dawn. I don't want to try anything in daylight."

Alain pointed toward a small patch of trees to one side of them. "That is wise. Those trees will offer a little cover during the day. We can lie among them, observe the Imperials, and make plans."

Mari looked. "Why haven't the Imperials cleared those trees?"

"It is a small patch, merely saplings, and more than a long crossbow shot from the towers. Still, the Imperials will probably clear it sometime during the winter to provide a little extra wood for their fires."

They moved cautiously toward the small stand of trees, constantly watching for any sign that some Imperial sentry had glanced backwards and seen them. At one point, Alain came to an abrupt halt and stared into the darkness. "I sense a Mage, but he or she is distant, somewhere else among the defenses."

"You can hide from that Mage?"

Alain nodded. "I believe so. The other Mage is not attempting to conceal his or her presence, and is so far off that I think a low-level spell would not be spotted, or if spotted the Mage could not reach here in time to know who had been casting it or why."

"A spell?" Mari asked. "What spell?"

"My spell that bends light. If you hold me tightly and stay close to me, it will protect you as well. If we wait until night falls again, then use it only when we reach the area where the fires show everything, we should be able to get past the patrols without giving the distant Mage enough time to react."

"You want to make us invisible? Even though I've seen you do that, it's still hard to believe that's possible. Are you sure that other Mage won't know it's you doing the spell?"

"Yes. Not at that distance."

"I don't see any other way in, so I guess we'll have to risk it." She looked over and grinned at him. "Your plan requires me to hold you tightly all the way into the city? Shame on you, Mage."

Alain gave her a slight smile back. "I am not saying I will not enjoy it, despite the danger."

They reached the saplings and lay down close to each other, screened as well as possible from anyone coming from the Imperial lines around the city. "I can just see the top of the Imperial watchtowers while lying down," Mari said. "We're going to have to stay as still as possible when daylight comes."

It was a very long day. The thin patch of woods offered little cover, and the ground was scattered with drying leaves, making it hard to shift position without causing the leaves to crackle in a way that sounded far too loud. Mari managed to fall asleep now and then, only to awaken with a start of fear that she had been making noise. "Do I snore when I'm sleeping?" she finally whispered to Alain.

He didn't answer.

"Alain? Are you awake?"

"Yes," his reply finally came. "I just do not know which answer would be right."

"Just tell me!"

"Sometimes."

"Sometimes?" Mari moved her eyes enough to glance at Alain. "Loud or soft?"

"Sometimes."

"Does it ever bother you?"

Alain hesitated again. "Sometimes."

"Are you going to give me any plain yes or no answers to this?"

"Not if I can avoid doing so," he replied.

"I guess you're learning social skills." Mari watched an insect clambering across the dead leaves in front of her nose. A chill breeze was coming down from the north again, but she was afraid even to shiver for fear the motion might be seen from one of the guard towers. "I wish we were talking about this in bed. A nice warm bed in a nice warm room and nobody trying to capture or kill us."

"That would be nice," Alain agreed.

"Do you remember the first time we slept nearby each other? On that ledge looking down on the wreckage of the caravan to Ringhmon?"

"I will never forget that."

"Would you have stayed there if you had known you'd end up with me here?"

His voice was barely audible. "If I had known I would end up with you, no matter where, then I would have known that night what happiness was."

She smiled despite the situation they were in, then tried to get some more sleep as the distant calls of the Imperial sentries echoed off the walls of the dead city.

They waited in the small patch of woods for full night to fall and the bustle of activity involved in lighting the watch fires to diminish, then waited a while longer for the sentries to lapse into the boredom of another night of guarding a dead city. Finally, Alain rose into a crouch. "The other Mage remains far from us in another part of the Imperial lines, but we should wait to use my spell until we must. The less time I am revealing my presence, the better. But remain close."

"Not a problem," Mari assured him, wincing as she tried to stretch out stiff and sore muscles. As night had fallen, the eerie silence and emptiness of the city had become more unnerving. Alain's presence was even more comforting than usual. "Let's head for that gap in the city wall there. It's about equally distant from the guard towers on either side, and looks like it extends low enough for us to climb in easily."

They went out into the open, hunched over, moving slowly and carefully toward the guard towers. All of the Imperial sentries, their postures relaxed, were once more facing toward the city. She wondered at that, since it implied that the Imperials were more worried about someone leaving Marandur than they were about someone entering. Why? But the open ground and the fires between the towers and the walls made it almost impossible for anyone trying to enter as well, so in practical terms the sentries' focus inward made little difference.

As Mari and Alain got closer to the towers, they began to hear snatches of conversation. The legionaries were talking about their homes, their families, their girlfriends and boyfriends, how bad the food was, and what they would be doing once they got off guard duty. Mari listened, realizing how human these Imperial men and women were, yet also knowing they would not hesitate to kill her and Alain in the course of following their orders.

Alain stopped short of the guard towers, beckoning Mari over. She wrapped one arm tightly around him. "Both arms," Alain breathed at her.

"You're doing this on purpose," Mari mumbled under her breath, but she brought the other hand around and hugged him with that as well, clinging to his back as tightly as she could.

Alain held still for a moment, then Mari saw her view blur slightly. He started walking slowly so that Mari could keep pace and her hold. It was awkward walking with both arms around Alain, but the sight of the watch fires burning ahead was enough to keep Mari clinging to the Mage. They reached a point from which they could watch a patrol walking between the towers. Mari held her breath, staring straight at a legionary who seemed to be looking right at her. No, right *through* her. The Imperial soldier showed no sign he had seen Mari. The patrol passed, then Alain went ahead again. Mari found herself breathing as shallowly as she could, trying to make as little noise as possible, even though the Imperial soldiers made plenty of noise themselves tramping through the grass.

She relaxed a bit once they had gotten past the line of fires, then almost fell when Alain stopped abruptly. He bent his head over and back to breathe his words in her ear. "Mage alarms. I do not see any way around them. We will have to go through. It will be difficult to avoid the alarms and maintain my spell to keep us hidden. Do not distract me."

Mari waited, trying not to do anything distracting. It was very hard not to move while holding Alain tightly, very hard to keep breathing shallowly so the motion of her chest rising and falling against Alain's back wouldn't be too obvious to him. She could feel his own breath coming more heavily. Was that because her body was pressed tightly against him, or because the exertion of maintaining the spell was wearing on Alain? There wasn't much she could do about it if Alain was being distracted by her, but as Mari thought about it she doubted that was happening. She had seen how the often-brutal training Alain had undergone as a Mage acolyte had taught him how to block out physical discomfort and distractions. More likely he was being tired out by the Mage spell. Despite Alain's attempts to explain to her, she had never been able to grasp exactly how tiring doing spells was for a Mage. But she knew it took work, and she wished right now that she could lend some of her strength to him instead of just standing here uselessly.

"Now," Alain whispered, and started moving ahead. She kept locked onto him, matching his slow steps with her own as Alain moved through alarms which Mari couldn't see. Alain had described them to her as looking like gossamer spider web strands drifting through the air but confined in one area. Getting through them undetected required Alain to use his mind to move the strands enough to each side to allow him to pass through the gap that created, without pushing so hard that it alerted the Mage monitoring and maintaining the alarm.

Their progress felt agonizingly slow. The grass and brush here were a bit higher, impeding their progress. To Mari it felt like the noise they made as they moved through the vegetation must be echoing loudly enough for the Imperials to easily hear, but the crackling of the watch fires must be hiding the sounds Mari's and Alain's motion made, and the flickering shadows would make the movements of the grass harder to see.

Mari's back itched, anticipating the impact of a crossbow bolt or, ultimate irony, a Mechanic-made rifle bullet.

Alain stumbled and she almost fell, barely catching herself, managing not to drop and pull the Mage down with her. He stood a long moment, his breathing louder and more strained that it had been before, then carefully moved ahead again. She concentrated on anticipating and matching his movements, her head resting against his back while she tried to will some of her strength into him.

There finally came a moment when Alain stopped, wavering where he stood. "We are through the alarms," he gasped. "We must get through the gap in the wall."

"I'll help hold you up. Keep moving." Mari did her best to support Alain now, as the two of them staggered the rest of the way to the wall. Once there, at the foot of the break in the wall that they had aimed for, Alain leaned against the broken stone.

"I will hold my spell while you climb over me. It will help hide you in part until you get inside. Then I will follow."

She hated to do that, but recognized the wisdom of Alain's instructions. Mari unwrapped her arms from about him, her joints and muscles stiff with the effort she had been expending, then took a deep breath and scrambled up his back and into the gap in the wall. Once screened from being seen from the outside, Mari turned. For a moment, she could see only the gap and the reflected flames of the fires beyond, then Alain popped into view most of the way inside the breach in the wall.

Grabbing his arm, Mari helped pull him inside, listening fearfully for any sounds which would show that the Imperials had spotted Alain. But no shouts or trumpet calls resounded, and after crawling over broken stone fragments and rubble they reached the inner side of the wall and dropped down to the forbidden streets of Marandur.

"There are no sentries inside the walls," Alain gasped in a low voice. "We can be sure of that much."

Mari stared at the jagged ruins poking their battered faces into the night sky. If ever a place seemed right for haunting by the restless spirits of the dead, it was Marandur. "What could have created this wreckage?" Mari panted, worn out from mental strain and physical effort. "This much damage? It can't all be due to Mechanic weaponry, though after so much time and neglect it's hard to tell."

Alain slumped down to a seated position, his back against a solid portion of the wall. "There were trolls employed. They are awful creatures. And dragons. The destructive power of Imperial ballistae and catapults cannot be ignored, either."

"I'm not happy to be here now, but I'm sure glad I wasn't here then." Mari sat next to him, putting one arm around Alain again, staring into the dark ruins. A little light from the Imperial watchtowers came through the break in the wall, but it only served to illuminate enough of the old wreckage to emphasize their spookiness. "Alain."

"Yes, Mari?"

"I want you to be honest with me. Do Mages know anything about ghosts?"

"Ghosts?" She couldn't see his expression in the dark. "Mages are taught that this world is a dream, Mari. When we die, my elders said, we go on to another dream. Ghosts are but the memory of those who have gone on."

"So...are you saying they do exist? Or they don't?"

Alain sat quiet for a minute. His breathing was steadying, but he still sounded worn out. "You know Mages can change the illusion if they believe they can. As far as I know, even memories can appear to live if one believes hard enough."

She shivered, even though the wall behind them blocked the breeze from the north. "Are they dangerous?"

"Not unless you believe they are."

"Blast it, Mage!" Mari hissed. "I want you to reassure me! This isn't something I can fix with a hammer or a slide rule!"

"Oh." It was somewhat comforting to be able to hear the regret in Alain's voice. His outward emotions were displaying more clearly the longer he was with her. "I did not understand," Alain explained. "The dead cannot harm us, Mari, unless we give them the power to do so. Then they act out their worst impulses through us, guiding us to do things which hurt ourselves and others. This is not Mage teachings. It is the lesson of the history I have read."

Somehow that wasn't as calming as she had hoped for. "I for one have no intention of letting the dead force me to do things that hurt us. We can't move through this debris at night. It would be too dangerous. We'll have to wait until daylight."

He nodded, the gesture betraying how tired Alain was. "Resting would be wise in any case, I think. We will need our strength."

Mari rested her head on Alain's shoulder and tried to sleep, but the slightest sound would jerk her awake. She knew the ruins had to be home to many wild creatures, from mice up to feral dogs, but that didn't make it any easier on her nerves when she heard a pebble roll somewhere or the soft pattering of tiny feet. When she finally fell asleep for a while, she did so with one arm around Alain and one hand on the grip of her pistol.

CHAPTER FIFTEEN

Dawn came eventually. Mari stood up, blinking and feeling rotten. *A bed. I used to sleep in beds all of the time. Someday, when all this is over, I'm going to wake up every morning in my comfortable bed and give thanks. I'll never take a bed for granted again.*

The sound of a rock fall came from somewhere inside the city, rattling her nerves. "Alain? How are you?"

He looked into the city, rubbing his face. "I have slept better."

"Me, too. Excuse me while I find a convenient ruin to do my business behind, then we can eat."

When she got back, Alain was standing braced against the wall. The huge stone blocks making up the fortification would have seemed invincible if not for the ragged breach in them that loomed just beyond Alain. "We need to find good shelter tonight," Alain said. "Somewhere we feel secure enough to rest."

"Good shelter?" She ran her gaze across the vast landscape of ruin that stretched ahead of them. "I hope the remainder of the city is in better shape than this. Otherwise we'll be camping out in the open so we don't have to worry as much about a wall falling on us."

They ate and drank, Mari thinking that the food tasted dusty, as if the ruins were already working their decay on it. "All right. Let's go. Can you handle the distraction of me going first?"

Alain looked as ragged as Mari felt, but he managed one of his tiny smiles. "I will be grateful to be able to see something nice amid all of this wreckage."

"Just keep your eyes on your feet occasionally. I don't want you walking into a hole while you're staring at my rear end."

The banter heartened Mari a little and they started off, trying at first to stick to one of the main roads of the city, but finding that so choked with rubble that it was easier just to follow whatever path offered the least resistance. "The destruction seems horrible at the walls, but I can see buildings that are more intact farther inside the city," Mari remarked. "Why do you suppose that is?"

"I would guess the rebels first tried to defend the walls and the buildings closest to the walls, and held out long enough to cause the devastation of the areas they were in. Once the walls and the defenses behind them crumbled, subsequent fighting was less intense though still awful." Alain shook his head, then hastily reached out to grab the remnants of a brick wall as the debris under his feet shifted.

Mari looked down, seeing shards of white bone mixed in with the broken masonry. "How many bodies lie unburied here? Ugh." Then she saw something else. "Alain. There's a path."

He looked in the direction she pointed. They approached cautiously, seeing it was a beaten trail through the wreckage. Mari knelt to examine it. "This wasn't made by animals. Those look like sandal prints. I think. It's pretty crude cobbler work. And some bare feet. Human."

"Those prints cannot be too old," Alain said.

"No. Certainly not a century and half old." Mari looked up at the partial buildings around them. Empty windows stared back like the eyeless sockets of skulls. "I guess everybody didn't get out of Marandur before the emperor sealed it off. Maybe some of the inhabitants survived. Maybe rebels who managed to hide out until the legions left. Over one hundred and fifty years trapped in a dead city...I don't think I want to meet these people, Alain."

"I agree. Now we know why the Imperial sentries focus so much of their attention inward. Where should we go from here?"

Mari stood, pivoting slowly as she studied what could be seen. "Too bad nobody sells maps of Marandur any more, but that's banned, too. The Mechanics Guild Hall should be near the center of the city. In the oldest cities, that's where all the halls are located, and Marandur wasn't too much younger than Landfall. Can you see any sign of an aqueduct?"

"Aqueduct?"

"Something that looks like a thin bridge. Aqueducts carry water to cities."

Alain shook his head. "The Ospren River cuts through Marandur. Would the city have needed an aqueduct?"

Mari squeezed her eyes shut and slapped herself lightly. "No. I should've figured that out. That means the Mechanics Guild Hall should be somewhere on the banks of the river."

"How will we know it?"

She looked around, then found what she sought and pointed. "See that strand of wire hanging there? Electrical wires to send power through the city would've come out of the Hall. We need a big building with lots of wires visible. Once we get close enough I'll be able to know it's the Mechanics Guild Hall by the design features. All Guild Halls have standardized hallways and things like that."

Alain nodded. "Why?"

"Why? Why what?"

"Why are these things standardized, as you called it?"

"Because..." Mari wondered how to describe it to a Mage. "It's easier to build things if they follow certain rules every time."

"It gives you comfort?"

"No. Well, okay, I guess it does. But that's not the reason. It's more efficient."

Alain nodded slowly, then shook his head. "Efficient?"

Mari tried not to slap herself again, this time out of frustration. "It means doing things the best way you can. Like when we needed to go through that Mage alarm thing and you had to maintain the hiding

302 ❀ *Jack Campbell*

spell. It would have been more efficient to concentrate on one thing at a time, but of course you couldn't do that."

"Oh. Why do Mechanics have so many words for things?" Alain asked. "Mage Guild acolytes are told that Mechanics believe giving names to everything grants them power over things."

Mari grinned. "Are you serious?" Then she thought about it. "Maybe there's truth to that. In order to do science or technology you need a lot of special words. In a way it does give us power over things. Change of subject. Do you want to look for the Mage Guild Hall, too?"

"No." Alain didn't seem to think the issue even needed to be discussed.

"There's nothing there you need? Or want?"

"No. There would not be."

"All right, then." No sense following that dead end. Times like this reminded Mari of just how different Alain's training and experience had been. "Let's get away from this trail before anyone who uses it comes along, and see if we can find our way to the river."

As the sun rose higher and began heating the rubble, their surroundings became almost uncomfortably warm, especially since little wind found its way into the ruined city. At one point they startled a little herd of small deer, about the size of dogs, which stampeded nimbly off through the piles of debris. Occasionally Mari spotted a wild cat watching them from some high vantage point. Birds nested everywhere among the broken buildings, their discarded feathers and messes covering the debris in some places. About noon they saw roughly a dozen dogs running across a wide street some distance away. Mari and Alain veered off in the other direction to avoid meeting the pack. By then the route had cleared considerably, with buildings relatively undamaged by battle but worn and disintegrating from decades of abandonment.

Tough grass had sprouted in many places, and wiry bushes could be seen anywhere enough dirt had gathered, including on the upper stories of buildings blown open to the weather a century and a half earlier. Sometimes they would find a tree shoving its way up through the buckled pavement. Every once in a while, a slow rumble in the distance announced the collapse of something somewhere in the city. Everywhere they found traces of the former inhabitants, or of the soldiers and rebels who had died in the act of mutually destroying the city. Mari tried to avoid walking on the splinters of bone, but sometimes the patches lay too thickly to avoid and then she just tried to close her mind to it. One time she slipped, almost turning her ankle, as an old, heavily corroded Imperial helmet rolled underfoot, exposing the crumbling skull still resting within it.

They took a break at noon, sitting in the shade of a partial wall. Mari glanced at Alain. "Is this affecting you in any way? I can't tell."

Alain shrugged. "There is a lot of dust. It is hard to keep crawling over all of this wreckage. I am not enjoying myself, if that is what you are asking."

"I don't mean just that." She gazed down the street as a small flock of birds swooped by. "It's really strange in a way. It's so quiet, and there's animals and birds and plants. Almost idyllic. Except it's a huge graveyard."

He nodded. "I was thinking how people create this illusion of a world. How many people labored to create the illusion of a city here—these buildings." Alain waved his hand at the ruins. "Then other people worked to create another illusion, that of death and destruction. Their illusion has triumphed. That is the illusion the Emperor Palan sought to maintain, and it has endured thus far. Someday the last remnants of the last building will fall to dust, the grass and the trees will grow everywhere, and then that illusion too will be gone, and it will be as if no man or woman ever laid hand to this spot."

"Why, Alain," Mari said, startled, "that's almost poetic."

"Do you mean that? I was never taught to use words artfully," Alain responded.

"You must be a natural, then," Mari remarked.

"Should I say thank you?"

"Yes, that would be appropriate."

"Thank you." Alain looked around, shaking his head. "I have seen no sign of humans since we saw that path, though, and that worries me."

"Me, too. I'd hate to think they might be spying on us and setting up an ambush." Mari checked her water bottle, then took a small swig. "Hey, we're rationing water again. Remember that? If I never again go back to the desert near Ringhmon it'll still be too soon."

"At least we survived the experience."

"Yeah. Do you think the water here is safe? There's got to be wells and cisterns still intact enough to hold something, and it has been a long time since things I don't want to think about were dumped or fell into them."

Alain shook his head. "I would not trust it. You see there are still many places where grass or trees do not grow. Old poisons must still abide here. The river should be safe, though. It flows from clean lands to the east and then through the city, constantly renewing itself."

"Yeah." She pulled herself up, studying the route ahead. "I think we need to bear right a little for the shortest route to the river."

"I would advise staying on this side street. The way you are looking is too exposed."

She sighed. "I'm tired, but I see your point. All right. Let's see how far we can make before sunset. I'm *not* walking around this place in the dark. Even if I wasn't worried about unseen humans and other predators, this wreckage is treacherous. We'd probably end up walking into a big hole that used to be a basement or something."

But they almost immediately encountered a maze of destruction so jumbled that it slowed progress to a crawl. Climbing to a precarious perch on a high mound of rubble, Mari could see the same devastation running off to both sides for long distances. Making her way back down a sliding slope of broken brick, she told Alain. "This is at least as bad as the stuff near the walls."

"It is probably what is left of the inner defensive line of the rebels," Alain suggested.

"What were they doing all the way from the walls to here?" Mari groused. "I thought that wreckage marked heavy fighting."

They still hadn't caught sight of the river by the time the setting sun was touching the top of the ruins to the west, though at least they had gotten clear of the area of total destruction. Alain pointed out a nearly intact storefront and led the way inside. Mari pulled out her hand light and searched the dim interior. "The front room doesn't look bad, and there's some kind of counter or divider still intact here. We can get behind that and be invisible from the street."

Whatever the store had once sold must have been looted long before, the remnants having since crumbled into piles of decay. They cleared a small area of the floor behind the counter in the angle where two miraculously intact walls met, Mari feeling relief at the lack of human remains here. She and Alain ate cold rations, drank sparingly, and then huddled together against the chill that night brought on, not wanting to risk the light and smoke a fire would create. Mari closed her eyes, feeling worn out and achy. "I'm hope I'm not too tired to sleep. Hey, Alain? Guess what we're doing."

He turned his head to look at her. "What are we doing?"

"Cuddling together on the first night of our visit to the old Imperial capital. Isn't it a wonderful vacation?"

"You are making an illusion to place over that of this city?" Alain asked. "Perhaps I will make a Mage of you."

"Not likely," Mari said. "So, how do you like it in my illusion?"

"The accommodations leave something to be desired," Alain said, "and the travel arrangements have been wanting. But I cannot fault having you along with me. The only thing that would make things better would be if this was our honeymoon."

"Men!" Mari said with a snort. "Move your hands, Mage. No, not there. All right, that's better. I thought you'd be too tired to be thinking about that kind of thing."

"You have a way of bringing it to my mind, even here."

"You'll get over it," Mari told him.

"It seems I must, for now," Alain said. "Try to sleep. I can no longer sense any other Mage nearby, so I have set a small alarm spell on the entrance to this place which should sustain itself until close to morning, if not full daylight. It will reveal little trace of itself to anyone searching for signs of me."

"Thanks." She raised her head enough to kiss him. "I'm a lucky girl, even if I am in the middle of a dead city with two Great Guilds after my hide and now an Imperial death sentence added to the measure." Mari closed her eyes again, wondering how long it would take to fall asleep in the middle of this dead city.

She was so tired she must have passed out quickly, but at some point in the night something caused Mari to jerk awake. The room lay in almost total darkness now, barely illuminated by the moonlight outside which revealed only the vague shape of the counter they were huddled behind. A heavy chill lay leaden in the air around them, making her glad for Alain's warmth next to her. Mari lay still, breathing slowly, listening as carefully as she could, wondering what had awoken her, feeling incredibly grateful for the barrier between them and the broken front of the building that gave onto the street. Faint sounds came, the sort of noises insects or small rodents might make. The thud of Mari's pulse pounding in her ears seemed almost deafening by contrast.

Every once in a while she could hear the far-off sound of debris shifting slightly, marking the movements of small creatures, or the slow centuries-long collapse of the city's ruins, or possibly the progress of larger beings accustomed to negotiating the rubble. Possibly humans, though how human such persons would be after living all their lives in this awful place was an open question.

Glancing over at Alain required Mari to turn her head slightly, which she did with great care, afraid of making the slightest noise in the eerie quiet that enfolded the ruins of Marandur. Alain was sleeping peacefully, no sign of worry on his face. Surely if there was any immediate danger, Alain's Mage alarm would provide warning.

Mari closed her eyes again, trying to calm herself. None of the noises appeared to be nearby. But if anything in this world was haunted, it was these ruins. Her imagination too easily conjured up images of vengeful spirits stalking the empty streets of the dead city. How many had died here? Not just the rebels who had chosen their fates and the legionaries following their orders, but the countless men, women, and children caught in the middle of the fight? There wasn't any way to know how many victims there had been. "I'm sorry," Mari whispered in the barest voice she could manage.

Alain stirred slightly and she leaned into him, willing Alain to be silent again but finding immense comfort in his presence. She imagined being alone in these ruins and almost shuddered at the thought. A night alone in Marandur could surely drive someone insane.

Would the ruins of the Mechanics Guild Hall feel haunted, too? What would those dead Mechanics think of her and what she wanted to do? Would they feel remorse for their actions when living, or would they seek to protect the secrets they had kept in life?

Jules herself might have walked these streets, centuries ago when Marandur had been a living city and the capital of the Empire. Mari had learned a little more about Jules in the last few weeks, curious about the woman. After all, if Alain and the old prophecy were right, that ancient hero had been her distant forbearer. Before heading west, Jules had been an officer in the Imperial fleet. Different accounts offered different reasons for her leaving Imperial service and becoming an explorer and a pirate. The truth was probably long lost, though Mari fantasized for a moment about finding some ancient records lying amid the rubble of the city. *Am I doing the right thing, Jules? Should we have come here? Are you really my blood ancestor? Can anything about that blood help me know what to do and how to do it? It seems like total superstition, but is there any truth to it? I need all the help I can get.*

Why am I doing this? Not because I'm supposed to, according to that prophecy. To stop the storm? Yes. But that's like overthrowing the

Great Guilds, just a step on the way to something else. For freedom? That's a big thing. This city...this city is a monument to how the world works, the world controlled by the Great Guilds. The Great Guilds didn't prevent this. All they could do was help destroy the city.

Freedom. But what if freedom caused this disaster in the first place? What if those who argue that the Great Guilds need to control the commons to prevent more dead cities are actually right? Something has to change. The world has to change. Otherwise there will be a lot more cities filled with the dead. If Alain is right about that storm he talks about, every city will end up like this within just a few more years, as the world the Great Guilds have wrapped in chain breaks out and breaks up. But is freedom the answer? Or will it just lead to the same outcome, as every place turns into Tiae anyway? How do I know?

The unnaturally quiet ruins offered no answers. Mari stared out into the darkness for a long time before her eyes drooped shut from exhaustion and she fell into a mercifully dreamless sleep.

When she opened her eyes again, the pale light of dawn was visible over the counter. The sun had risen on their second day in the dead city.

❁   ❁   ❁

They waited until the light was good enough to illuminate any dangerous spots in the ruins, eating cold food and drinking sparingly for a cheerless breakfast, and then started out again.

Progress was better than the day before, though still not easy. They stumbled across one relatively clear street and were able to follow it for a little way before finding the wreck of an Imperial siege tower lying athwart the road. That forced them back into a warren of alleys and side streets choked with debris, further slowing their progress. They finally stopped beforea small plaza, an open space with little wrack of battle littering it. Alain shook his head. "Must we cross this? It is open to easy sight of anyone in those buildings surrounding."

Mari wiped sweat from her forehead, the moisture smearing the dust on her into a muddy streak on her forearm. "We can't go back. And I am not going into any of those buildings."

"No. That would be far too dangerous, even if nothing but the dangers of decay lurked within them." Alain stared around the plaza. "My foresight reveals nothing at this time, but my instincts tell me we are being watched."

"Me, too. We're making plenty of noise getting through this mess. They could track us by that racket alone." Mari checked her pistol. She needed both hands free while scrambling over the rubble, but wanted to be sure she could get the weapon out fast if needed. "Let's go."

They made it across the plaza without incident, even though the blank faces of the surrounding buildings watched Mari and Alain with silent menace. Mari breathed a sigh of relief as they entered the next street, where piles of debris formed an irregular series of barricades which needed to be climbed over. They were about halfway down that street and crossing a small open area between obstructions when a rock fell ahead of them, rolling down a long slope formed by the collapse of one side of a building. Alain froze. Mari yanked out her pistol and searched the wrecked buildings rising in one or two crumbling stories around them. "What is it?" she asked him.

Alain pointed. A man was visible ahead, standing in shadow between two piles of debris. All three of them stood still, the man silent and motionless, Alain and Mari watching him and searching their surroundings for others.

Finally, the man moved, stepping into the light. Mari fought down a shudder of revulsion. It was impossible to tell how old he was because his body and hair were caked with filth. He wore a ragged strip of fabric as a sort of loincloth, crude-looking sandals on his feet, and on his chest the type of breastplate Imperial centurions had worn more than century ago. Looking every day of its age, the pitted and corroded breastplate also sported a large hole which could have been made by either an antique crossbow bolt or a Mechanic bullet.

Mari took in all that in a moment, focusing on the broken sword the man held in one hand. She pulled back the slide of her pistol to load a round, clicked off the safety, then leveled her pistol at him while steadying it with both hands, hoping that the process was sufficiently threatening to deter the man and any unseen companions he had. "Stop right there, unless you want that armor to get another hole in it."

The man stopped, then opened his mouth in what could have been a smile but wasn't, the gesture revealing that a lot of teeth were missing. "Give up or fight. Don't matter to me. You fight, we kill you slower." His accent was archaic, the words slurred from sloppy pronunciation.

"We?" Alain asked.

The man gave a low, shrill whistle. There was a stirring of the rubble on all sides, and others came into view, each wearing a combination of badly aged cast-off clothing and pieces of armor, and each carrying a weapon in various stages of corrosion or breakage.

Mari shook her head, hoping her voice would remain steady, her weapon staying fixed on the leader. "I've got enough bullets in this Mechanic weapon to kill every one of you. Leave us alone and we'll leave you alone."

The man seemed amused, showing another gap-toothed smile, and Mari realized the expression was actually more like the snarl of a wolf. "We already dead, girl. Didn't ya know? Dead born to the dead. Emperor say so." He spat to one side. "What can you do?"

"Right now you may be officially dead, but you're not really dead," Mari replied. "I can change that." The man took a step closer. Aiming carefully, her weapon steadied in both hands, Mari fired at the battered wall next to the man. The sound of the shot was amplified by the small hollow they were in, echoing repeatedly off the broken ruins to all sides. A chunk of the wall shattered, spraying the man with fragments. "I missed you on purpose. That was a warning. The next shot will blow your head off."

The man bared what teeth he had, the snarl fiercer, looking up and to one side. Mari kept her eyes and her pistol sights on the leader as

Alain followed the gesture. She felt a sense of warmth that told her Alain was building a ball of heat in one hand.

There was a crack of breaking masonry, then Alain spoke with a Mage's total calmness. "A man in a broken window, with a short spear. Both man and window are now gone. You deal with a Mage, commons. Depart or die."

Mari took a deep breath, keeping her weapon sighted on the leader. To her own surprise her voice remained firm. "You heard my Mage. Try anything else and I'll kill you where you stand."

The leader shook his head. "I already dead, woman." He raised the broken sword and lunged forward. Mari could hear sounds all around as his followers also charged.

Her mind numb, Mari lowered her sights to make sure they were centered on the leader's breastplate and fired. He staggered, swaying to one side, then got his feet under him again and tried to keep coming. Mari fired again, her shot this time cracking his ancient breastplate in half as he dropped to the dusty rubble. She could hear Alain hurling fire to her right, so she spun left, firing again as another man scrambled toward them. The shot missed but she got off another immediately, this one knocking him down. Pivoting again, Mari lined up on a third man and put a bullet in his belly. He was still screaming when she fired three times at a fourth enemy, a woman who was very close and diving with a rusty dagger at Alain's back. The hits drove the woman back and to the side, to fall like a broken doll.

Mari couldn't see any other targets to the left so she spun back to the right, checking each man she had already dropped. The wounded man seemed unable to get up, but picked up a broken brick and heaved it at her as she turned. Mari flinched as the brick hit her shoulder, then closed her mind to what she was doing and fired one more time.

Silence fell. Alain spoke into the quiet as he sheathed his long Mage's knife under his coat. "All on this side are dead."

"Here, too," Mari gasped. "Are we safe?"

"For the moment."

"Good." With trembling hands she ejected the clip in her pistol, loaded a new one, set the safety, returned the pistol to its holster, then went to her knees and got sick, losing everything she had eaten that morning and what felt like some of last night's meal in the bargain. Once that was done she knelt there, shaking like a leaf, until she felt Alain's hand on her shoulder.

"It is hard," he said. "These are the first you have killed?"

"Y-yes." She was trying not to think about what had happened, to keep her mind blank, but revulsion still roiled through her.

"It is hard," Alain repeated, his voice carrying compassion she could hear. "I have never forgotten the first time I had to kill others, and then I believed them to be but shadows."

"We didn't have any choice," Mari muttered, wiping her mouth with the sleeve of her coat. "They didn't give us any choice. Why didn't they give us any choice?"

"That is right," Alain said, his voice soft. "We had no choice. We did not seek the fight and we tried to avoid it."

She clenched her teeth, then stood up, Alain steadying her. Mari's mouth and throat were sour with her vomit but right now she felt like hurting, letting the pain distract her a little from the sight of the bodies about her, the memories of bodies falling as she fired her pistol. "We— we need to move. Get away from here before more of them come. The sound of this fight must've been heard all over the city."

He didn't argue, and had probably already reached the same conclusion, Mari thought, but had given her a few moments to cope with her reactions to the first time she had been forced to use the pistol to shoot other humans. "Stupid. Stupid people," she gasped, half sobbing. "Maybe they didn't have any reason to fear dying. But they didn't have to make us kill them." Fighting down another tremor in her arms and legs, Mari followed Alain, glancing back once to see the bodies sprawled on the rubble, a few small fires set in the ancient wood by Alain's spells sending up thin columns of smoke.

A voice in her head nagged at Mari as she scrambled over the next pile of debris. She realized it was her old friend Alli, who had taught her to shoot and sprinkled the lessons with lots of advice. *"Always reload any time you get a chance, Mari. You don't want to get caught with an empty weapon."*

Alli, back then it was just fun, blowing holes in a paper target. It's no fun at all when the target is another person. It's just awful and frightening and terrible. But thank the stars above that you taught me how to use a pistol. I don't even want to think about what those creatures would have done to me.

Mari tried to focus on the rubble they were climbing over to help block out the horror filling her, but took advantage of a level stretch to reload the clip she had ejected from the pistol, wondering whether the barbarians would be sensibly discouraged by the killing of their comrades, or would keep coming after her and Alain. "The legionaries must have heard those shots, too. They'll report them. They won't come inside the city, though."

"No, they will not enter the city." Alain thought, then shook his head. "Perhaps there will be no report, either. Declaring that they had heard the sounds of your weapon would mean admitting someone had gotten into the city past them. I would not be surprised if the legionaries find another explanation for the noise, one which they would not be required to report to their superiors."

"Something big collapsing, maybe? Beams of wood snapping?"

"Yes. Whatever illusion they need to convince themselves of in order to avoid placing themselves in serious trouble with their superiors. Mages are not the only ones who try to make the world illusion into a different form. Sometimes it is necessary for everyone." Alain looked back at her for a moment. "Are you all right?"

"I'll survive, Alain. Thanks for asking." Mari drew in a long trembling breath as they crested the latest pile of wreckage and headed down the other side. "Let's not talk unless we have to. More of those savages might hear. I'll be all right. Because I have to be."

They moved as quickly as possible for a while, not worrying much about the noise, trying to put as much distance as they could between themselves and the place where they had fought. Alain seemed wearier than he should have given their pace, causing Mari to worry until she mentally kicked herself for forgetting that his spells tired him out. Another battle might leave him too exhausted to move for a while. That was something else to worry about.

Once Alain stopped in his tracks and gestured off to the side. Mari followed without question, assuming his foresight had this time warned of some danger ahead.

Because of the ruins blocking their view, they stumbled onto the banks of the Ospren River without warning and stood, trying to catch their breaths. Mari walked to the cracked edge of the river wall, looking each way down the river. "All of the bridges have collapsed. No surprise there, unfortunately."

Alain nodded, gazing watchfully back the way they had come. "They were probably badly damaged during the fighting. Is your Guild Hall on the other side of the river?"

She pulled out her far-seer and studied the far bank of the river, checking out each ruined building in turn. She scanned past one a short ways downriver from them, then turned the far-seer back to take another look. "That's a hydroelectric generator if I've ever seen one. It's beat to junk and corroded like there's no tomorrow, but I'm sure of it. The Guild Hall did get blown to blazes if one of the generators is out in the open." Mari pointed. "That's the place we want."

Alain blew out a long breath. "Getting there may be difficult. Especially since I fear our trail can be easily followed by the inhabitants of Marandur. We may not have much time before more of them arrive."

Mari studied the river. The water flowed clear, impeded only by the broken stubs of bridge supports, marching in ragged columns toward the opposite shore, and the remains of the fallen bridges themselves, which in some places poked above the surface. Aside from that, the only things visible in the water were the decaying stumps of masts from boats and ships sunk long ago. From what she could tell from the wrecks, the river hadn't silted up in the long time since the Imperials had last dredged it, remaining deep enough that small ships could probably still navigate it. As far as Mari could see, the Ospren River spread widely between its banks, its waters running with a steady current that carried occasional pieces of driftwood past at a decent clip. Swimming obviously wasn't an option even without taking into account the weight of her pack. "Deep, wide, and fast, and we're on the wrong side of it. We need a boat."

"I cannot create one, if that is what you are asking," Alain advised.

"Maybe I was hoping for that." Mari stared around at the ruins of the waterfront. "Most of these places seem to have been burnt out as well as blown apart. But if we can find a warehouse door that wasn't burnt and hasn't decayed into uselessness, maybe it'll serve as a raft." She started walking along the edge of the water, peering at the battered buildings and rubble for large pieces of wood. Fortunately, the very edge of the river wall near the water was almost clear of junk, probably having been swept clean occasionally when the river flooded in the Spring.

Alain followed, his own eyes going back frequently to check on their trail. "They are not in sight yet, but they will see us crossing," he observed.

"Fine. As long as they don't have boats to follow us with," Mari snapped. "Hey." She darted toward a gaping opening, tugging at some large pieces of wood still fastened together. "It's part of an old warehouse door."

Alain lent a hand and they pulled it free. The Mage eyed the cracked wood dubiously. "Will it hold us across the river? Will it even hold us and stay afloat?"

"Do we have a better option?" Mari asked. As she waited for Alain's answer, they heard rubble falling a short distance upriver in the direction they had come from.

"Not unless we want to fight again soon," Alain agreed.

It took both of them to shove the old door to the river. Mari climbed on first, balancing with difficulty, then going to her hands and knees. "We're not standing up on this trip," she advised.

Alain nodded, began to join her, then paused. "We should get paddles of some kind." But as he turned back a thrown rock struck less than a lance-length away from him, thudding into a rotten crate. "Then again, perhaps we need to trust to luck." He sat down on the door and then used his legs to shove off from the shore as hard as he could.

Mari hung on, her arms and legs quickly drenched as chill river water washed over the makeshift raft. But the raft didn't sink, supporting them as the river's current carried them out toward the center of the water and down toward the remains of the nearest bridge. "We need to try to catch ourselves on the remains of that bridge and pull ourselves across the river," she yelled over at Alain. "Otherwise we might get swept completely out of the city." She didn't want to think about what would happen to them if the Imperial sentries saw a couple of people on a raft drifting out of Marandur.

"All right," Alain called in reply.

A moment later, Mari heard the *plunk* of something small and heavy hitting the water. Looking back, she saw more barbarians on the riverbank, still too close for comfort and all of them hoisting rocks and bricks from the endless supply around them. She could see dark objects arcing toward her, following them with her eyes until they landed around the raft, sending up splashes that soaked any parts of Mari and Alain that had remained dry up until then.

"They have bad aim and little strength," Alain told her. "That is not surprising. They probably get barely enough to eat to survive, and in the warren of the ruined city, they surely fight normally at close hand by ambush."

"Does that mean we're safe?"

"Not yet. I think I remember something about being in water. Swimming, it was called?" Alain put his feet in the water and began kicking, helping shove the raft farther from the river bank.

Mari kept her eyes on the approaching bridge, trying to judge their chances of snagging some part of the wreckage. But a wide stretch of river ran free between two supports, and the raft was heading straight down the center of that. Cursing, she tried using one hand as a paddle to propel the raft toward some of the debris sticking up above the river, but made far too little progress. The current swept them through the gap and downstream. "Okay. Let's aim for the next bridge. It's a big one. Probably used to be the main bridge for the city. There should be lots of wreckage sticking up far enough for us to use."

Their pursuers had been left far behind now, small shapes on the riverbank, as Mari did her best to aim the foundering raft toward a bridge support, cutting across the current with the help of Alain's kicking in the water. For a long moment she feared they would fall short, but then the raft hit, almost knocking her off as she grabbed for handholds, the worn stone and masonry cold and slick from river water and algae. A hard lump formed in her stomach as she imagined getting thrown from the crude raft into the river, having to abandon her pack with her jacket and her tools, struggling through the cold water but perhaps not making it, sinking slowly into the darkness of the river, her spirit becoming one more restless wraith haunting the ruined city.

Mari gripped the shattered bridge support so hard her hands ached, taking deep, shuddering breaths.

"Mari?" Alain's voice was close by. "Are you all right?"

"Yes," she gasped. "No. I'm scared to death."

"I am glad I am not the only one." His voice held no trace of humor. Mari turned her head enough to stare back at him. "Are you really?"

Alain nodded, his face tight with strain, his clothes drenched. He lay on the other side of the small, improvised raft. "I do not swim all that well, and I am tired, and this raft is...not very good."

"Alain, I'm too scared to move. There's just been too much. The storm and the trip south and the Dark Mechanics and Professor S'san and the prophecy and this awful, awful city and—" She tried to still her shaking. "You know." He nodded again, silently. Mari closed her eyes, trying to block out the world for a moment, but she kept seeing an image of Alain. *He trusted me. He got on this raft. He's counting on me. I have to get him to safety.*

Thinking about someone else made her own fear subside a little. Mari forced her eyes open, staring at the ruined bridge support just before her face, then moved her head to look where they needed to go. There were plenty of rough spots ahead. Plenty of places to grab and hold. It wouldn't be easy, but it could be done. *Just keep telling yourself that. You can do this. It's gotten you through life this far and it's going to get you to the other side of this river.*

She focused on her left hand, willing it to release its death grip on a protruding brick. And finally it did, jerking free. She scrabbled the fingers along the surface of the column a short distance, to a place where some bricks had fallen, leaving an opening she could latch onto. Shivering, Mari wrenched her right hand free, bringing it up to grab a hold near her left hand. The raft swayed and grated sidewise along the bridge support a little. Seeing another handhold a little farther down, Mari lunged for it and grabbed on there. The raft moved a little more.

She found that once she had started moving, keeping going was hard but not nearly as hard as starting had been. The raft swung alarmingly under her knees as she pulled it along, Alain helping where he could from the back and using his legs to push the raft when he could find a spot to rest a foot. They came to places where branches and other debris had piled up against the bridge supports, and yanked the raft around them. In one of those piles, Mari found a stout branch long and light enough to be useful as a pole and passed it back to Alain.

They cleared one column. Mari stared down into the rushing water, seeing the layer of broken bridge remains lying beneath the surface here. *If you're the daughter of Jules, then your ancestor sailed unknown seas. You can get the rest of the way across one lousy river.* "Don't let me fall off," she said to Alain, then slid down so her upper body was resting face down on the raft and her feet dangled into the water low enough to reach the submerged rubble. Step by step she walked the raft across the gap, the cold water biting into her legs and hips and grabbing at her as it raced past through the opening.

"Let me take the front now," Alain suggested as they reached the next bridge support.

Mari shook her head, keeping her eyes fixed on the next stretch of wreckage. "We can't get by each other without losing the raft. It's barely together as it is. I'm all right."

After the fight through the gap between supports, pushing along the solid surface of another support seemed easy, even though her shivering was increasing as the cold water stole the heat from her body. She pushed her fears back a little again with thoughts about heat-sinks and fluid dynamics. The next gap between supports wasn't too hard, with the remnants of the fallen bridge so close to the surface Mari could brace herself against them. Then another column, another gap...

She thought the raft might be sinking lower, the ancient wood soaking up water and losing its ability to float. Pieces broke off occasionally, whirling away in the cold water and quickly lost from sight. Her shivering had grown so violent that Mari wondered if that alone would break the decayed wood. *Don't think about it. Just keep going. You can do this.*

Mari bumped up against a flat surface and just stared at it blankly. Alain's hands were on her shoulders, then his arms were around her waist, helping her up a short, steep slope that abruptly leveled out onto a flat surface littered with the leavings of battles over a century gone. They were on the other side of the river, on the clear area edging the river wall. Mari huddled into a tight ball, her clothing soaked, shaking uncontrollably from the cold.

A warmth grew around her, surrounding her body as if she were encircled by gentle fires. Mari yanked her eyes open, astonished, to see Alain kneeling nearby and staring at her. "W-what are you d-doing?"

He spoke slowly, concentrating on his effort. "I am making the air around you heat up. Not enough to harm, just enough to help."

"I—I kn-knew that h-having a M-mage for a b-boyfriend would c-come in handy s-someday."

She just lay there for a while, the heat soaking in, her shivering subsiding and her breathing growing calmer. "Alain, I know this takes a lot of work. Please stop. I'll be all right now." Getting her arms under her, Mari pushed herself up to a sitting position.

Alain looked weary but he was smiling at her, the expression clear enough that anyone might have noticed it. "You are a brave and remarkable woman, Mari."

"I'm not half as brave and remarkable as my Mage is." Feeling embarrassed by his praise, she forced herself to her feet, then offered Alain a hand. "Come on. We need to keep moving, just in case those sub-humans have another way across the river."

He took the hand and stood up, almost overbalancing her. But she managed to stay up, too, then laughed. "Hey. We forgot to fill our water bottles."

"Other issues had our attention. Can it wait?" Alain asked.

"Yeah." Mari pointed. "The current carried us downstream. The old Mechanics Guild Hall should be right over that way." Walking along the edge of the river at the best pace they could sustain, they saw the building they sought once they had climbed up and over a pile of rubble where a waterfront building had collapsed outward.

Mari led the way, her eyes searching the remains of the old Guild Hall. "Yes. That's definitely it. What happened to it?" She paused to rest, breathing heavily under the weight of her pack, hands resting on her legs. "It looks like... I bet they did."

"Did what?" Alain asked. He was standing beside her but once again looking back the way they had come. "I do not recommend spending a lot of time unmoving like this, Mari."

"I know." Mari straightened. "I think my Guild blew up the place. Maybe after the rebels captured it. The way the walls have fallen outward in several places make it look like internal explosions did the job." She started walking. "There should be a couple of ways down to the basement vaults. If we're lucky one of those will still be usable."

As they got closer, Mari pointed off to one side, where once-impressive buildings had collapsed in on themselves long ago. "That must have been the old Mechanics Guild academy. It looks like it was once identical to the one I attended." Mari shook her head, overwhelmed by a strange feeling, as if she were a ghost haunting the ruins of a place where she had lived long ago. "It's so bizarre, seeing that. Less than a year ago I left the living, breathing buildings of the new Guild academy, and now here are identical buildings wrecked over a century in the past. It looks like they were gutted by fire." She swallowed, imagining the chaos, the destruction, places she would have recognized, hallways which would have seemed familiar, all sharing in the death throes of Marandur.

"It happened many years ago," Alain said, his calm voice a comfort. "Your imagination gives new life to what has long been dead."

"So I need to stop thinking about it." Mari turned her face grimly from the brooding ruins of the old academy, concentrating on picking out a path to the tumbled remains of the old Guild headquarters next door.

When they reached the front of the building after crossing the rubble-littered courtyard, Mari found a solid wall of debris where the main entrance had stood. Working their way around to the side entrance, they discovered it too was completely blocked where part of the upper stories had simply slid down on top of it. Crossing her fingers, Mari led the way to the back entryway.

There she stopped for a moment, unable to believe their luck. Then she took another look. "Somebody cleared this."

Alain studied the ruins before them. "You are certain?"

"I think so. It must've been quite a while ago, but look at the way some of the wreckage has been shifted to clear the entry." Mari knelt to examine the dusty surface. "I don't see any sign that anybody has used it in a long, long time, though." Moving carefully, she started forward, crouching to get past low areas in the cleared passage. The light dimmed as they went inside and down, so she paused long enough to open her pack and extract the hand light. Her pack was as watertight as Mechanic art could make it, but a little moisture had made its way inside during the river crossing. Fortunately, the hand light was dry. Mari clicked it on, then started walking again. Alain followed close behind. Mari could see he was still devoting most of his efforts to watching their trail for signs of pursuit.

She paused to study the ruins, running her light across their surroundings. "I could be wrong, but it looks like there were two stages of destruction. Part of this looks like it collapsed, then the rest came down on top of it later." Mari frowned as she turned sideways to slip through an area where the path was barely still open. "The second collapse came after this path was cleared, though. I'm sure of it."

The first door they came to had long ago fallen off its hinges. The second had been shoved aside, its splintered remnants heavily coated with dust. Mari froze as something creaked alarmingly somewhere overhead in the wreck of the building and a fine haze of more dust trickled down from the bent ceiling above them. An occasional scuttling noise marked small creatures fleeing from Mari and Alain's approach, but nothing large seemed to have laired here. Mari sniffed, catching the faded scent of industrial chemicals, wondering if the poisons liberated by the destruction of the building had kept it free of invading plant and animal life. "Don't touch anything unless you have to," she cautioned Alain.

Moving ahead again with great care, they reached the steel door leading to the basement area. It, too, lay askew, but had been wedged to one side to help support the cracked door frame. Mari pointed to old, dark smudges on the ceiling. "Soot. Somebody was down here using torches." Or somebody had been down here burning something else. How much soot would have been created by priceless technical texts turning into ash? She tried not to think about that possibility, feeling sickened by the idea of so much knowledge being destroyed.

The stairs leading downward were slick with dust but otherwise sturdy enough. Mari took a moment to bless her Guild's obsession with excavating foundations, basements and subsurface stairs from solid stone whenever possible. Reaching the bottom, she gave Alain an anxious look. "The vaults should be right up this way." She wondered why she whispered, then realized she felt worried about noise somehow causing further collapse of the ancient ruin. Then, too, there was a sensation of disturbing a place where living humans were no longer welcome.

She picked her way across the floor, increasingly concerned at the signs that there had been a lot of foot traffic here, even so long ago. At one point she paused, seeing something sticking out from under a fallen mass of material. Mari knelt, touching a rifle barrel so badly rusted that a portion of it disintegrated under her finger. "Standard-model repeating rifle. It looks like it was identical to the ones today. The same weapons used in this siege over a century and half ago were employed by the bandits who attacked us in the desert waste. It's like we're part of the same story."

"Perhaps we are," Alain said, his voice also hushed.

Finally they reached the vaults. Mari shone her light on the big metal doors, all of them sagging open. Their massive hinges, heavy enough to support the doors, had nonetheless bent under the burden of decade upon decade of holding up their weight. "The vaults have been open for a long time," she whispered. "But they don't show any signs of being forced. Someone had the keys and the combinations."

Mari stepped to the entry of one vault, moving the light from side to side, seeing empty shelves and vacant drawers left hanging open. Dust lay heavily everywhere, all of the drawers corroded so badly that it was probably impossible to move them now.

Somebody had been here before them. A long time before them. Their entire ordeal had been for nothing. She checked the other two vaults, seeing the same vacancy. Running her light along the floors and ceilings of the vaults, she could not see any signs that fires had burned here in the past, one small comfort in the midst of her distress. "At least they didn't burn the texts, but my Guild must have somehow managed to get them out of the city before the emperor's ban took effect. The texts must be in the Guild's vaults in Palandur, where we'll never be able to get to them. This entire, horrible journey was a waste, Alain."

"I am sorry. It was my idea."

She turned to him, fighting back tears. "It was a good idea. It just didn't work out." Without another word, she headed back the way they had come. Mari took the route almost carelessly this time, only caring about getting out of the ruin as fast as possible. She didn't stop until they reached the open again, where she stood blinking up at the late afternoon sky and wiping her eyes with one dirty coat sleeve.

Mari was turning to blurt out her disappointment again to Alain when a sound came from somewhere in the dead city on this side of the river, a long, low whistle. Moments later another whistle came, from back along the way they had come down the river. A third whistle sounded in reply, this one farther inside the city.

Alain shook his head. "The hunt is on. We are the prey. We need to find a place where we can defend ourselves and we must find it quickly."

CHAPTER SIXTEEN

Mari and Alain fled along the riverbank, where the going was easiest. Every once in a while another whistle would sound, the direction of the signal telling them that a net was slowing closing around them. Once again, Alain let Mari find the path while he watched behind them, wondering how much strength he still had after a long day of exertion.

"How are you doing?" she asked.

"I am all right," Alain said.

"And I'm the Queen of Tiae," Mari retorted. "Alain, how are you doing?"

"I have few spells left within me," Alain admitted. "I am amazed that I have even that much after all this day has held, but it is not enough to fight off a mob of savages. We could stop and rest in hopes of rebuilding my strength more quickly, but that would just allow these human hounds to catch up with us faster."

Mari had been silent and depressed since they left the ruins of the Mechanic Guild Hall. "Listen, Alain. I don't need much strength to use my weapon, so we'll depend on that as long as possible. If they pin us down and we're trapped, use everything you've got left to try to stop them. If that doesn't work, I'll save the last two bullets for us."

He wanted to argue that grim logic, but the thought of what the barbarians might do to Mari if they captured her alive silenced his protests. "If they can be stopped, I will stop them," Alain vowed. "You must live. You must save this world. Mari, if I hold them while you keep running—"

"I'd get caught really fast," she said. "We both know that. If we split up, we're both as good as dead. We'll—" A sudden gasp from Mari brought Alain spinning to face front. She had reached the top of another pile of debris and was staring ahead. "Alain, look."

He climbed up beside her, seeing a wide, open area, then a brick wall significantly smaller than the city walls but still twice as tall as any man. "What is it?"

"I don't know. But look! That wall's been repaired in places. I'd swear it." Mari was fumbling out the thing she called a far-seer and placing it to her eyes. "Yes. Repairs. That's the first sign we've seen of somebody fixing and maintaining a structure in Marandur."

He followed her pointing arm, seeing the sections where lighter patches of brick marked more recent work. "A wall which has been kept standing means it might still be defending something. Do you think there are people inside who are using it for protection from the types who hunt us now?"

"It could be. Can you see? They've also been clearing the open ground in front of the wall. The vegetation has been cut and burnt." Mari was peering around frantically. "But I can't see the gate. There's got to be a gate." She jerked in sudden recognition. "It's the university. If Palandur was modeled on Marandur, then this would be the old Imperial university. I didn't see that at first because everything around it is wrecked and lifeless, but it's in the right place relative to the Mechanics Guild headquarters and the Guild academy."

Another pair of whistles sounded behind them. "If we cannot see the gate, let us go look for it," Alain urged.

"If it's like the university in Palandur, the gate should be over this way." Mari scrambled over the top of the pile of wreckage, sliding down in a shower of dust and small debris. Alain followed as she ran toward the wall at an angle, away from the river and across the open area.

"It's a bit separated from the rest of the city by a park that surrounds the university walls," Mari gasped as she ran. "It's not a park anymore, but it used to be. All of the trees are gone now and the paths must be covered by dirt and grass. But when there were trees here it must have been just like in Palandur. Can you see those buildings inside the wall? Some of them look intact."

Alain, using his attention to watch the ground and the ruins of the city behind them for danger, made a noncommittal sound. Another whistle sounded in the ruins facing the open area, just slightly ahead of Alain and Mari. Alain spotted a shape moving there and created a fireball, placing it near the dimly seen barbarian to cause an eruption of stone and broken wood. The entire building sagged, then collapsed in a prolonged roar.

The effort weakened him.

As if she had sensed that he would need her, Mari had already spun about and grabbed his arm, placing it over her shoulders as she kept moving. "Stay on your feet! They're that close?"

"Some of them are." Alain stumbled again, then got his feet under him with the help of Mari's support. He wondered how many more fireballs he could manage before the effort would be too much. Certainly he could risk no more before they reached cover.

Mari had her arm tightly about his waist, locking them together and supporting Alain, though she was still staring toward the wall. "Hang on to me," she said, urging them both forward at the best pace Alain could manage.

Another set of whistles sounded. Mari pulled out her Mechanic weapon with her free hand, pointed it toward the blank, ruined facades of the buildings facing the open area and fired, the crash of the shot sounding very loud and sparking panicked birds into flight.

"Can you see them?" Alain asked.

"No. Even if I could see them I couldn't hit them at this range. But maybe I can scare them into keeping their heads down." She put the weapon back inside her coat and tugged at Alain. "Come on, my Mage. You can do it. It can't be much farther to the gate."

If it is much farther, we will not make it. Alain concentrated on

328 ❀ *Jack Campbell*

keeping his feet moving, knowing speed was their only hope now.

Mari gave a gasp of joy. "There it is." She pulled him in toward the wall at a sharper angle, their feet crashing through the dry grass which had grown since the last burn-off and now stood knee-high in places.

Alain looked in the direction Mari was guiding them, seeing a large gate of heavy timbers reinforced with wide bands of metal, sealed shut to bar entry inside the wall. Sentry towers stood at either hand, but no one was visible standing guard.

They staggered to a halt before the gate as another set of whistles sounded, making it clear that their pursuers now had them boxed in. Mari pounded on the gate, yelling. "Inside the wall! Let us in!" No reply came. "Alain, can you get us through that door?"

He shook his head. "I am too tired. A small hole, perhaps..."

"That won't do any good! This thing has to be locked with a heavy bar of some kind. Inside the gate! Please let us in!" Still no answer. He could hear the desperation growing in Mari's voice. "Alain, can you set fire to the door? If we can hold them off long enough for the fire to eat a hole in it—"

Her words cut off as a crossbow bolt flew down from one of the sentry towers to thud quivering into the dirt nearby. A figure was visible in that tower now, looking down at them. The lowering sun lit him up well enough to see that his clothing was frayed but neat and his armor polished. Unlike the barbarians, he was also clean and shaven. As Mari watched, the sentry picked up another crossbow and pointed it at her. "Go!"

Mari pointed toward the city. "They'll kill us!"

"That's not our affair." His words were also archaic in accent, but clear. "We don't meddle in the city beyond our walls."

"You can't do this! You can't turn away people who need safety!"

The figure gestured, and several more men and women appeared on both sentry towers, all aiming their own crossbows. "We don't take in anyone from the city."

"We're not from the city, you blasted common idiot!" Mari shouted. "Didn't you hear the shots I fired? How many working Mechanic weapons do you think there are in this blasted, hateful, smashed excuse for a city?"

"Mari," Alain said through his attempts to catch his breath, "that may not be the best way to gain their cooperation."

The guard hesitated, then brought his crossbow to his shoulder. "You lie. We heard the sounds, but no one here knows what a Mechanic weapon sounds like. I will not warn you again. Go or—"

"Wait!" Mari turned to Alain. "Quick. Get your robes out and put them on." She was kneeling as she said it, pulling open her own pack. "Hurry!"

Alain did, finding the carefully folded robes, yanking them out and hastily donning them. By the time he was done Mari had her Mechanics jacket out and had traded her coat for it. Then Mari looked up at the sentry towers again. "You must remember what this jacket means and what those robes mean. I am Master Mechanic Mari of Caer Lyn. This is the Mage Alain of Ihris. We are not from Marandur. Please let us in."

Alain could see the figures above staring and pointing. The one who had first spoken came to the edge of the tower to gaze down at them. "A Mechanic and a Mage? Together? What has happened in the world to bring this about?"

"If you want to know," Mari shouted back, "you'll have to let us in."

Unexpectedly, the man grinned. "A fair trade, it seems. It has been a long time since this place has seen any members of your Guilds." He called down to someone inside the gate. "Open! Quickly!" Then to the other figures on the sentry towers. "Keep watch for the barbarians!" They raised their crossbows and aimed out across the open area toward the city.

Mari reached and grabbed Alain's hand. He gripped hers tightly in reply, hearing sounds on the other side of the gate. Slowly, it creaked open a small distance. Mari grabbed her pack and darted for the opening, dragging Alain along. He had just enough room to get through the gap behind her, pulling his pack in last, then they were inside and several people were hastily pushing the gate shut again and sliding a heavy beam across the back to seal it.

Mari threw her arms around Alain, laughing with relief, then kissed him hard. "I told you we'd make it, my Mage," she said, breathless from the kiss and their exertions.

"You were right, as always, my Mechanic." He held her tightly as well, then looked around to see faces staring at them in total bafflement. "We will have a lot to explain to these people," Alain murmured to Mari.

❊　　❊　　❊

The furnishings were old and worn, most of the windows boarded over, and candles provided only a weak illumination, but the large room still felt like a paradise after even a few days amid the ruins of Marandur. Mari and Alain were both seated in chairs facing one side of a long table. Several men and women were seated along the other side. All wore the robes of professors among the common people, though those robes showed signs of long wear. "I am Wren of Marandur, Master of the Professorship of the University of Marandur in Marandur, by grace of the emperor," a woman with gray-streaked hair announced. "Together with these others, we are the masters of the university. Who are you?"

Alain let Mari talk. She smiled politely, indicating Alain. "As we told your people at the gate, this is the Mage Alain of Ihris. I am Master Mechanic Mari of Caer Lyn."

"Ihris. Caer Lyn," another of the professors noted in a drained voice. "How long has it been since those cities were represented here?"

"You know that as well as the rest of us," Professor Wren replied tersely. "Tell me, Lady Master Mechanic, how did you come to be here?" Listening to her was like reading the words of someone from almost two hundred years before. Which, Alain realized, in many ways she was, since the university had been isolated for so long.

"We entered Marandur from the north two days ago," Mari said, speaking in a firm voice as if she were the one in authority here and merely bringing the commons up to date on her activities. "After coming through the city and crossing the Ospren River, we came under attack by those savages who still live in Marandur. Fleeing them, we came upon your wall and knew civilized people still lived there."

The professors waited for a moment after Mari finished as if expecting more, then Wren spoke again. "Why did you enter Marandur? Does not the emperor's ban still stand?"

"Yes," Mari admitted, "it still stands. We had business in the city, seeking something I sought to find in the ruins of the old Mechanics Guild Headquarters."

"Something important enough to bring a sentence of death upon the pair of you?" asked a third professor, perhaps the oldest of the group. "What could this be?"

"I sought manuscripts from the vaults. But they were gone."

The professors all kept the same expressions, but Alain, used to watching Mages trying their best to conceal emotion, could see something flicker across the faces of the men and women facing them. What could it mean? "Do you know anything of those records?" he asked.

Another, stronger flicker, even as Professor Wren shook her head with every outward appearance of regret. "No idea, I am afraid."

The direct denial revealed clearly, to the eyes of a Mage, that she was lying. But why? "That is unfortunate," Alain said, deciding to wait and learn more before confronting the professors over their lie.

Wren nodded, her movements quick with nervousness. "You, too, are concerned with Mechanics Guild records? Tell us, Sir Mage, what brought you along with the Mechanic? Was this by order of your Guild? Has some remarkable event caused the Mechanics and Mages to be reconciled?"

Alain shook his own head, realizing as he did so that he was once again adopting the mask of a Mage to conceal his own feelings. "Our Guilds still dislike and distrust each other. I came with Lady Mari for reasons of my own."

"You *embraced* her!" another female professor exclaimed in bewildered tones. "She did the same to you! She kissed you! And your ages! You're both very young. If you had not already demonstrated your powers as a Mage, if she had not already given proof of her status as a Mechanic, we would not believe it."

Mari sat silent, her jaw clenching with stubborn pride. Alain could see her face hardening at the mention of her youth. He gave the woman professor a bland look, his voice still betraying nothing. "I have come to enjoy the company of this particular Mechanic."

All of the professors stared back, then one slumped in his chair. "The world outside our gates has gone mad."

Mari exhaled slowly, then looked at them with cool authority, becoming even more the Mechanic as she posed her own question. "What of you? Everyone was supposed to be gone from Marandur. All of Marandur was supposed to be a place of death and ruins. Yet here we find life and purpose."

Professor Wren nodded. "Our ancestors chose to disregard the edict of the Emperor Palan to leave this city. They had all sworn an oath to the old emperor, you see, to remain in these offices for life, and most of them interpreted that phrase literally as applying to the buildings. The university hadn't been too badly damaged in the battle compared to the rest of the city, because the rebels did not occupy it. Our ancestors never found out why, they just gave thanks."

Wren shrugged. "There was discussion that surely the Emperor Palan didn't mean to include the university in his edict. By the time everyone realized that he did, it was too late for those who had tarried. Here they were, here they stayed, and as they wed and had children, here we came to be. We have kept the form of the university all these years, making the most learned and senior among us the professors and masters, while most of those living here are labeled students even though they devote far more time to the tasks of survival than they do to studies."

"Have you ever tried to petition subsequent emperors?" Mari asked. "Surely if they knew—"

"Emperors do not accept petitions from the dead, Lady Mechanic," a professor stated with a coldness born of lack of hope. "We would need to be alive to have such a petition considered by the emperor, and we cannot be alive until the emperor considers such a petition. To the Imperial bureaucracy, such a dilemma is an unfortunate byproduct of the rules by which they operate, but certainly not in their eyes grounds for changing those rules."

"Of course," another one of the university masters added, "the fact that the Imperial sentries slay anyone they catch trying to leave the city is also a problem. We haven't tried finding volunteers to carry such a petition for some time, since we don't care to waste any more lives."

Professor Wren spoke again. "You are trapped here now with us. We regret that, but we have managed to keep much of the university's stock of knowledge intact. If you desire learning, it can still be had here."

Mari shook her head. "I'm a Mechanic. What I needed was those manuscripts from the Mechanics Guild Hall. Without them, I can't do what I need to do."

Once again Alain saw the hidden reactions among the professors, confirming his earlier belief. *They are hiding something. They know something about those things Mari seeks. Do I confront them now? No. I will wait and speak with Mari of it. She knows more than I do of these records, and together we will better determine how to respond to the deceit of these Masters.*

Professor Wren nodded regretfully. "There may be something else we know that can help in your task. What is it you need to do?"

Mari gave the professor a flat look, speaking with calm certainty. "I need to change the world."

✳   ✳   ✳

Later that evening, they joined most of the remaining inhabitants of the university in the former faculty dining hall. The old student dining hall was far too vast for the roughly five hundred people who still lived inside the walls. They were served a sparse meal which the thin frames of the professors and the other inhabitants of the university made clear was the norm, It consisted mostly of potatoes and a few other vegetables grown inside the walls, leavened by a few scraps of meat from the meager flock of chickens and herd of pigs that the students watched over. Alain, experienced in such a diet from his days as a Mage acolyte, recognized it as one that would keep people alive, but not much more than that.

Afterwards, Alain sat on the bed in the small private student quarters he had been given. The single candle lighting the room danced in the cold drafts penetrating the aging walls and window frame, causing shadows to shift and flow. The masters of the university, either out of propriety or because they could not imagine a Mage and a Mechanic wanting to share a room, had given them separate quarters.

He knew Mari had come to his door before her soft knock came. The thread between them seemed to be ever-present now. Mari had her pack with her, avoiding Alain's eyes as she entered. "I didn't feel like being alone. Is it all right if I stay in here for a little while?"

"It is all right," Alain said. Mari was keeping her face averted, but he could see enough to spot a tangle of emotions chasing each other.

She sat down at the desk, facing mostly away from him, her pack on the floor. "So...you're doing all right?" Mari asked.

"I am. Are you well?"

"Sure," she replied, the tenseness underlying the word denying it. After a long, quiet moment, Mari yanked open her pack and pulled out a small packet, then reached under her jacket to bring out her weapon.

Alain watched as she brought out small tools and brushes, as well as a little bottle that smelled of oil. He had seen Mari do what she called "cleaning" the weapon, a task which always seemed to bring her comfort. But this time her hands shook as she worked, shook so badly that she kept dropping things, until Mari finally stopped, staring at the pieces of her weapon where they lay on the desk. "Alain? Can I...can I sleep in here tonight?"

"Yes. You did not need to ask."

"I just...it's been an pretty rough day. The ruins and...and the river...and getting in here and...I...I don't want to be alone."

"Of course." Alain felt that he should be doing something, but did not know what.

Mari came and sat down next to Alain, still not looking at him. "Do you want to do more?"

"More?"

"Than sleep. I mean...you know...if we're trapped here. We might as well stop waiting."

He watched her, trying to figure out her meaning, then it dawned on him and a strange feeling flooded him. "Mari, why do you offer this when I know it is important to you to wait?"

"It's just...not that important anymore. That's all. Do you want to?"

"Yes." Alain wanted to reach for her, touch her, but he stopped himself. She was still looking off to one side, away from him. "I do not think you want to."

"I said I did, Alain!"

"It does not feel right." Something was very wrong. He could sense that much.

Mari breathed deeply, then wrapped her arms about him, her face against his shoulder. "My brave, wonderful Mage. How many men would have turned down that chance? Can we go to sleep now? Just sleep?"

The student bed was narrow, but there was enough room for them both as long as they held each other. Alain could feel the tension in Mari after she blew out the candle, but it did not seem to be tension born of physical strain. Plainly exhausted, Mari fell asleep fairly quickly, her body relaxing in his arms, but her breathing occasionally ragged. Concerned, Alain took longer to sleep, but finally drifted off as well.

He woke in the stillness of very late night, feeling Mari thrashing in his arms. Alain focused on her face, dimly visible in the weak moonlight filtering through the room's window. Mari's eyes were closed in sleep, but her mouth was open, distended, her expression that of someone screaming. Yet no sound emerged. There were only the jerky movements of her body and the silent scream caught in Mari's throat.

Alain had never felt so frightened as he did then. "Mari! Mari!" He shook her as he called her name and Mari's eyes flew open, looking about wildly before they finally met his. "What is wrong?"

She started crying, then buried her face in his chest, her voice muffled. "Alain...Alain...don't let go. I keep seeing them. I keep seeing them."

He knew, then. "Those we had to kill. Mari, they gave us no choice. If we had not fought, they would have killed us, and I am certain our deaths would have been much slower and much more painful than the deaths we gave them."

"It doesn't matter, Alain! Will I forget them? Tell me I won't always see them!"

He felt a certainty that Mari, who had never wanted falsehood, now wanted a lie. "You will not always see them."

"You're lying," she sobbed. "I can tell you're lying. Tell me again."

"You will not always see them." Alain had never felt so helpless as he held her, Mari's tears wetting his chest. "Mari, the memories do fade some. They are not easy to live with, but you can. That is so."

She shuddered but didn't say anything else, her grief pressed against Alain as she cried silently. He kept his arms around her, trying to offer what comfort he could, wishing that General Flyn had been wrong or given greater reassurance rather than a harsh truth. *It is a hard thing.* And now Mari bore that burden as well.

✳   ✳   ✳

He could not recall falling asleep again, but Alain finally woke to morning light and the occasional soft click of metal against metal. Mari sat at the desk once more, her hands much steadier as she worked methodically with her weapon. She did not seem to take any pleasure in the task, but continued as if it were something that must be done.

Alain watched silently until Mari had finished and put away the small bag of tools. She held the weapon in her hand, looking at it, then after a long time Mari holstered the weapon under her jacket.

Mari had not looked at him, but now she spoke. "Good morning."

"Is it?" Alain asked.

"I...have to deal with it, Alain. Thank you for being there. Thank you...for being you."

"I can only be me. I wish I could be more when you need it."

She turned to look at him, smiling sadly. "I couldn't ask for more. I meant my offer last night, Alain."

"You did not."

"All right, I'll admit I was a bit overstressed and I'd probably be regretting it this morning. But I wouldn't have blamed you, and I really do want to be with you."

"I know that. The right time will come." Alain sat up, watching her. "You can talk with me. I know the feelings you have."

Mari grimaced. "You've lived with them since that ambush on the way to Ringhmon, haven't you? And I didn't have any idea. I'm so sorry. Maybe I could handle this better if I knew what to do next. How can it end here, Alain? Trapped inside Marandur because there's nowhere else to go and nothing else we can do? What I had to do yesterday...if the world falls into chaos, how many more people will die like that or have to kill like that to survive? It can't end here. I don't care whether the prophecy or your vision about me is true or not. I have to change things. I have to stop...that storm." She shivered, wrapping her arms about herself.

Alain, experienced in ignoring physical discomfort, finally realized how cold it was in the room. He stood up and draped the blanket about Mari's shoulders. "There is something I did not have the chance to speak with you about last night. When we dealt with the masters of this university, I saw some deception in them."

"Deception?" Mari whispered the word, her eyes going to the door. "Danger?"

"I do not believe so. Each time you spoke of why we had come to Marandur, of the texts from your Guild, I saw deception in the faces of the masters of the university. They know something of these texts, something important which they did not reveal."

"Really?" Mari pulled the blanket tighter about her, eyes intent with thought. "Why didn't they say anything? Any guesses?"

"There was fear and worry in them along with the deception."

"Guilt?"

"I do not think so."

She shut her eyes tightly. "How do we convince them to tell us whatever they are withholding? It'd be easier to figure out if we know why they're withholding it."

"Is this a trust thing?" Alain asked.

"It might be." Mari gave him a questioning look. "How do we get them to trust us? What can we do?"

Alain shook his head. "I do not think my Mage skills can offer much for the people here."

"I can tinker with a few things, but these people don't have lots of Mechanic equipment." Mari shivered again. "It's already cold and it's just going to get colder as Winter hits. I hope you don't mind if I keep sharing your bed."

"I have never objected to that."

Her smile seemed more natural now. "No, you haven't, and you also haven't taken advantage of it." Mari's gaze went to a metal object under the window. "I'm glad you can keep me warm. These buildings were designed to use steam heat, and that steam plant must not have worked since the last Mechanic left."

"These buildings are warmed by Mechanic devices?" Alain asked, surprised.

"Yeah. They're not being heated that way now. We didn't see it last night, but there's a steam boiler somewhere that heats water and sends the steam to all the buildings. Or it would if it was working."

"Could you make that Mechanic thing work? That might cause the masters of the university to trust us more."

Mari's eyes widened, then she actually grinned. "My wonderful, wonderful Mage. What a great idea." She jumped up and came over to hug him tightly. "Thank you."

He knew she meant much more than the idea he had just given her, and that made Alain feel much better than he had since last night.

Hope was a strange thing. He could give it to Mari even while wondering if it still existed. Perhaps that hope was false like everything else, a mere illusion, or perhaps it was as real as he was now certain Mari was as well.

CHAPTER SEVENTEEN

It wasn't until Mari left the room that she realized the inhabitants of the university probably knew that she had spent the night with Alain. Her pack had been left resting next to his in the room. She felt a surge of embarrassment, then defiance. *Let them think what they will. I'm not going to explain or justify myself to anyone, not when I've done nothing wrong. I'm tired of people who think the worst of me.*

As they walked toward Professor Wren's office, she felt the silence more strongly than usual. Normally it felt right just to be with Alain, not necessarily saying anything. But now the lack of words weighed on her. "You know, Alain, I can't operate a boiler all by myself."

"I did not know that," Alain said.

"Well, I could for a little while, but I need to sleep. I'm going to need help. I'm going to need to train people." Mari looked around. "And the only people here are commons."

"When you spoke with Mechanic Calu, you said you thought commons might be able to do Mechanic work," Alain pointed out.

"You remember that? Yeah. Those Dark Mechanics we've encountered. Where do they come from, anyway? The Mechanics Guild is supposed to find everyone with Mechanic talents when they're still kids." She walked a few steps more, thinking. "Maybe there is a talent, but it's not all there is. I mean, the Dark Mechanics don't have the Mechanics Guild's rules. They could build new stuff if they wanted to, but they don't seem to have done so. Maybe they can do basic work but lack the talent to design new things."

"Basic work?" Alain asked.

"Like turning wrenches and tightening screws. Reading gauges." Mari glanced at Alain. "Commons use simple tools all the time, even though they don't recognize them as tools. Levers, for example. They operate rifles. They work pump handles. I've always been told commons can't go beyond that, but if there was ever a place to test that rule, it's here."

She felt a sardonic laugh coming and let it out, drawing a look from Alain in which both surprise and concern were apparent. He had a right to both, after last night. *Please let it get better. If I have to deal with that kind of nightmare every night, I'll go insane.* "It's all right. I was just thinking that I may be about to break one of the most important rules of my Guild. But what are they going to do to me besides what they are already trying to do? I can't change the world without running a few risks."

Alain actually managed to look skeptical. "A few risks?"

Mari laughed again, the sound feeling strange to her still. "You know, like trusting a Mage."

"I understand," Alain said. "I have also run risks against the teaching of my Guild. Why has my closeness to you not harmed my Mage powers? I was taught that being able to cause temporary changes to the world requires believing that the world I see is false and that other people are part of that illusion. Yet I feel more strongly every day that you are real, that you cannot be an illusion, and my powers have not diminished."

Mari felt uncomfortable at that, at the idea that Alain's feelings for her might have limited the powers he had sacrificed so much to attain. "Maybe that's because you believe in this illusion of me that isn't real," she tried to joke. "I bet you really do believe that I'm the daughter of Jules."

"I am certain that you are the... You told me not to call you by that name."

"Sorry," Mari said. "That wasn't a deliberate trap. I guess I can say it, because I don't really believe it, but if you say it, I would know you believed it. Because you think I'm this impossibly wonderful person who can do anything. I've heard you tell people that."

"That is not an illusion," Alain said, his voice perfectly serious.

"If I thought you really believed that, I'd run away right now," Mari said, keeping her own voice just as serious. "That's too much for anyone to live up to."

"You are more than you think you are," Alain said, "but perhaps that is what makes you more."

She rolled her eyes at him. "It's too early in the morning for me to think that through. Promise me that you won't go around telling people here that I'm...her."

"I promise," Alain said. "Can I tell them that you can be difficult?"

He had made another joke. Mari smiled at Alain. "I think they'll figure that out on their own soon enough."

※   ※   ※

Mari faced Professor Wren, master of the university. It felt good to be wearing her Mechanics jacket again, good to be recognizable to everyone who saw her for what she could do.

That wasn't all that felt good. Yesterday she had said it straight out. *I want to change the world.* What had made her decide to say that? Had it been experiencing the horror of Marandur, which was a product of the way the world was? Whatever the reason, Mari felt real relief at having accepted that goal, even though the goal was still a vague one. Except for overthrowing the Great Guilds. The only way to change the world was by doing that. *So it seems I'm accepting the role of the daughter even if I can't believe that I am really her.*

Even better, after the haunting horror of last night, had been waking in Alain's arms and knowing she had the strength to keep going. Start small. Finish cleaning the pistol and reassemble it. It had been hard to pick up the weapon after that, its familiar feel in her hand become strange and menacing. Alli had talked about that, too, when she was teaching Mari to shoot, but Mari hadn't really paid attention, hadn't really understood. *Shooting these is fun,* Alli had said. *Designing them is cool. But, really, Mari, they only have one purpose. They exist to kill things. You can't ever forget that.* And so Mari had holstered the pistol, knowing that she had used it only when no alternative existed, and knowing that she would use it again only for the same reason.

Then Alain had given her another gift with his suggestion. Now her mind seized upon the idea of fixing that old boiler, training commons in its use, creating instead of destroying. "Professor Wren, I'm going to take a look at the steam heating plant for these buildings."

Wren blinked, her expression concerned. "We have not tampered with the Mechanic equipment, if that is your worry."

"I want to see if I can fix it," Mari stated. "Get it working for you before winter comes."

"Do you think you can?" Wren's face lit with amazement. "But we have little money and we understand the works of Mechanics are always very expensive. We cannot afford to pay."

"You saved my life and the life of the Mage Alain. We're benefiting from your hospitality now. Why don't we call that even?" Mari's eyes challenged the professor to debate further.

But Professor Wren slowly nodded. "You have a remarkable amount of self-possession for a woman your age, Lady Mechanic, if you don't mind my saying so. Your...behavior is also not what we were told to expect should Mechanics ever come here again. Are all Mechanics like you?"

"No." Mari let it stay at that for a moment, then realized she owed Wren more. "I'm different. Treat any other Mechanic, assuming you meet any more of them, with care until you learn their attitude."

"I will remember that, Lady Mechanic. I will find some students to show you the way to the building where the heating system is located."

The handful of students Wren quickly rounded up eyed Mari with unconcealed wonder and peppered her with questions. "You have seen the world?" "You are a Mechanic? An actual Mechanic?" "That man is a Mage?" "What is it like out there?" "Have you seen the sea?"

Mari answered patiently, while thinking how odd it was to deal with commons who had never been taught to treat a Mechanic with respectful silence. Partly that was a relief, because these commons didn't have the barely hidden hostility with which Mari had become too familiar, but it was still disconcerting. The fact that the "students" ranged in age from several years younger than her eighteen-almost-nineteen years to decades older only made it feel stranger. She asked some questions back, learning that the students engaged in a lot more than learning things they would never get to apply. They tended the crops growing inside the wall, took care of the small but important herd of farm animals, stood sentry on the wall, and kept the wall standing when parts of it started to crumble.

It took some effort to access the building holding the steam plant. Time and the elements had swollen the wood of the door so that it had to be pried loose from the frame. The heating plant was set in a building surrounded by a cleared area, roughly centered between the main offices and living spaces of the university. She knew that was intended to provide a little safety if there was an accident in the heating plant, but even eyeballing it told her the offset was too small, that a boiler explosion would cause serious damage to the other buildings. Someone had sidestepped the safety requirements when they located this steam plant here, but that would be in keeping with what she had seen of Senior Mechanics so far. For all of their avowed devotion to following the rules, Senior Mechanics somehow always found justification for doing whatever they wanted.

Mari braced herself for what she might see inside the building, then strode in like she owned the place.

Although, as the only representative of the Mechanics Guild in the city of Marandur, she actually *did* own the place, Mari told herself.

The windows, heavily grimed by time and the elements, didn't let in enough light. Mari flicked on her hand light, drawing exclamations of awe from the students, and began examining the equipment. To her surprise, the steam plant looked to be in decent shape under a coating of dust. "Do any of you know anything about this? Did it just stop working or did someone shut it down?"

The students exchanged baffled looks. "All we know is that it used to provide heat a long time ago, ma'am. We were told never to enter this building."

Ma'am. They had her feeling like an ancient with at least, oh, thirty years of life behind her. "The proper title is Lady Mechanic. Or just Lady." They mumbled quick apologies. "I'm going to need a lot of hands in here. People to get this dust wiped up and the windows cleaned so I have enough light to work by. Can you get me some more help?"

Before she could say another word they had all dashed off in different directions, their threadbare hand-me-down garments flapping behind them.

Sighing, Mari turned back to the steam plant and started inspecting it. To her pleasant surprise, the tool lockers were all still stocked. She had been wondering how she would cope if the big wrenches were missing. Even better, the tools had been carefully stored away, wrapped in oiled cloth. The boiler appeared to be intact, with no signs of corrosion, meaning all of the water had been drained from the system before it was abandoned. Everywhere, the plant showed signs of having been carefully shut down and prepared for a long-term period of hibernation. *Who did that? Why would the Mechanics who presumably left this place in a big hurry have bothered? But somebody did it, and it'll make my job a lot easier. If there had been water left in the boiler to corrode the insides for the last century I probably wouldn't have been able to fix this thing at all.*

Her helpers returned with large numbers of others in tow. Mari had estimated that roughly five hundred survivors inhabited the university, and more than half of them seemed to be here, itching to help. Fortunately, she had plenty of experience directing apprentices. Breaking the students into teams, she soon had them working at various tasks, removing the grime of more than a hundred years of disuse from the steam plant and the building it rested in.

"You should eat." She turned to see Alain standing near, a water flask in one hand and some food in the other. "It is past noon."

"It is?" Mari blinked up at the sun. "I guess I got lost in my work."

He sat next to her as she wolfed down the food. "The professors have been complaining that all of their students are gone," Alain said. "Even those who are supposed to be working on preserving food for the winter or repairing the wall are in here. Only the wall sentries have remained on duty."

"That's not my fault." She gave him a glance, wondering if Alain was just passing on the information or if he found it amusing. "What've you been doing?"

Alain shrugged, then gestured around. "Observing. I have walked around to see what I can see of the area inside these walls. I could find no evidence of what we seek. Also, I did some tests on my Mage skills, which is why I am resting again."

"Tests?" Mari asked around a mouthful of food. "What kind of tests?"

"I was trying to see if I am losing specific spell abilities, or having spells lose power. I could not do this when I might be detected by other Mages, but within this city I am as safe from that as I can be, short of being far out at sea."

She swallowed, feeling the food sticking in her throat at Alain's words, and took a long drink to clear it. "I thought you told me that you weren't getting weaker."

"I did, but I wanted to see how strong my skills are now, and whether every skill I once had is still present," Alain said. "Though I had to use my powers to the utmost yesterday, I have not been able to practice my skills to determine their limits since we met in the Northern Ramparts, and my attachment to you has grown since then."

Mari stared down at her food. "I can't imagine losing my ability to do my work. I'd feel terrible if your falling in love with me caused you to lose some of your abilities."

"You did not make me fall in love with you, unless this is some power of yours over men which you have not told me of."

"Not to my knowledge," Mari replied with a grin. "I have no idea why you fell in love with me."

"Your modesty is surely one of the reasons," Alain said.

Mari snorted. "You did think I'd placed some spell on you, remember? Back in Ringhmon?"

"It seemed the only reasonable explanation," Alain said. "How could this female Mechanic have wrought such changes in me? She must, I thought, have more power than any Mage. I was right."

Mari felt her face warming again and laughed to cover up her embarrassment.

"I have not become weaker," Alain continued. "In Ringhmon, you showed me how to find that place inside where strength may be found when none remains."

"I...what?"

"You know of it," Alain insisted. "You have used it. Back in Ringhmon to save me, later during the blizzard, and on the river yesterday, and other times. But more than this, being near you has not weakened me. I have never been stronger. A few months ago I could not have cast all of the spells I did yesterday. I would not have had the ability or the spell strength."

"Being in love with me is making you stronger?" she asked, disbelieving. "That's sort of every girl's dream come true, but I didn't expect it to actually happen with anyone."

"I think, yes, you are making me stronger. I still know the world is false. What I believe to be real is you. Another person. That alone is supposed to cripple my ability to view everything as false." Alain's frown was obvious enough that anyone could have seen it. "I am thinking about this. About what it may mean. There is something false about the teachings of my Guild, something completely flawed. I must learn what it is. And then I must discover actual wisdom."

Something really hit her then for the first time. "Any Mage would expect to lose their powers if they fell in love? You thought being in love with me would cause you to completely lose your Mage powers? You believed that would happen?"

"Yes. Why did you ask the same question three times?" Alain wondered.

"Because...it wasn't the exact same question! You thought you'd lose all your powers, and you still kept caring for me?"

Alain nodded, that tiny smile appearing again. How she loved to see that smile. "Of course. What were my powers compared to you?"

"Alain, that's..." Mari blinked rapidly, staring at the ground and rubbing at her eyes as she felt tears starting. "I never thought any guy would want to make that kind of sacrifice for me."

"I have shown that I was willing to die with you. This is much less than that."

Mari shook her head. "No, you silly Mage. It's much more. Dying from danger can be easy. It happens so fast, you know? But deciding to live every day of the rest of your life knowing you've given up something very important for someone else...that's hard. I wouldn't have asked you to do that, Alain. Not if I'd known. You realize that, don't you?"

"I believe that I always did," Alain replied. "Perhaps I was not aware of it before now, but somehow I knew." He studied her, his eyes betraying some concern. "It is well that I did not tell you earlier. You might have denied any feelings for me in an attempt to...save me from myself."

Mari couldn't help a short laugh. "All right. But I'm going to feel very guilty if someday you do lose your powers because of me." Mari brushed her hair back with one hand, realizing again just how much responsibility came along with her love for Alain.

"You should not feel guilty," he insisted. "It is my choice. Perhaps someday I will see the effects my Guild warned of, though I have no reason to believe that will happen later if it has not happened already. For now, is there anything I can do to assist you?"

Mari watched Alain for a moment, thinking of the person he was inside. Who could have guessed a Mage could be like that? "Do you know anything about the operation, repair or maintenance of steam heating plants?"

Alain took the question absolutely seriously, of course. "No, I do not think so." He looked toward the building holding the steam plant. "You keep calling it a plant. I expected to see something like a tree, but it looks to me more like one of the Mechanic boiler creatures you have also called it."

Mari couldn't help laughing again. "It's not that kind of plant. I'm sorry. Mechanics give different meanings to some words. But you're right, it is centered around a boiler like those on a locomotive or the one we blew up in Dorcastle."

Alain's alarm was uncharacteristically easy to spot. "You must take care, then."

"Relax! I made Mechanic rank as a steam specialist. I know this stuff." She smiled ruefully. "Though given your experiences with boilers I can see why you're worried. Believe me, I'm being careful. Now, what can you do? The best thing, I think, is to get plenty of rest and in your spare time keep looking around. Oh, and check the histories they have here. Maybe they still have things that aren't available any more to the outside world, something about history before what you know, or even something referencing those Mechanics Guild texts. If we find something like that we'll have grounds for asking the masters about the manuscripts in a non-confrontational way."

"All right," Alain agreed. "Though I will enjoy the task of searching these histories, and it seems wrong to enjoy myself while you labor so hard."

"My Mage, I am having the time of my life. Trust me." She leaned in and kissed him. That felt so good that she kissed him again, longer this time.

"Ma'am?"

Mari jerked away from Alain, seeing that some of the students had approached while she was...distracted with Alain. Her face once more flaring with the heat of embarrassment, she barely managed to keep from snapping at the students as Alain stood up. "Yes? What?"

"We have finished the job you gave us, ma'am," the oldest announced eagerly.

Mari winced. The student was at least twice her age. "Lady Mechanic!"

"Yes, Lady Mechanic," the students all chorused, looking abashed.

"I'll see you later, Alain. Now, do you guys want to learn how to use tools?" Her stomach tightened as she said it. Actually teaching Mechanic arts to commons was something she would have thought inconceivable a year ago. It still felt wrong. But with everything else she had learned since then, this might prove important as well.

They gathered around her eagerly. In their isolation, none of the students knew how revolutionary a thing Mari was about to do. Mari found herself hesitating, realizing that this truly was a point of no return.

She bent to pick up the largest of the wrenches, one that could be adjusted to fit different widths. "This is called a mankey wrench."

"Why?" a student asked.

"That's its name. Big wrenches are mankey wrenches."

"But," another student asked, "what does mankey mean?"

"It means it's a big wrench," Mari replied. "I don't know where the name came from. I've never heard of anyone or anything called a mankey except these tools, and no Mechanic I've talked to has any idea why big wrenches are mankey wrenches, but the name is an ancient one so remember it." She raised the heavy tool in both hands. "Mankey wrench. Who wants to learn how to use one?"

By the time dinner call sounded her students had acquired an impressive array of skinned knuckles, bruises, and abrasions from slipping and misapplied tools. But they were using the tools effectively enough if not perfectly. The cleaned-up steam plant lay gleaming under the last rays of the setting sun, its fittings checked and tightened. "Tomorrow we need to go over the delivery pipelines running from here to the buildings to make sure they don't have loose fittings or holes. Which after all this time they certainly will. Then we check all the steam heating pipes in the buildings for the same thing. Then we come back here and check this set-up again." She had just described the sort of drudgery that made apprentices groan, but the students were staring at her with wild-eyed enthusiasm. Amazing.

She and Alain ate alone, Alain doing all of the talking as he described the histories he had read so far. "I have found nothing yet which tells more than the histories I have already seen. On the other matter, I have learned nothing else."

They went back to his room together, Mari's mind so full of steam plant mechanisms and operating requirements that she forgot to ask Alain if it was all right to stay with him again. But he didn't raise the issue. It wasn't until she was lying down beside him that the memory of her offer the night before suddenly popped back into her head. What if Alain...?

But as his arms came around her, Alain's hands came to rest one between her shoulder and one in the small of her back. Both halted their movement, not roaming around or seeking a way inside her clothing. "Alain?" Mari murmured.

"Yes?"

"You are so special. Thanks."

Exhausted from her day, Mari fell asleep quickly, barely having time to worry that the dreams of the night before might return.

She woke up in the middle of the night, something dark inside her fading dreams retreating as Mari fixed her eyes on Alain lying beside her, sleeping peacefully. Her heart was pounding and her breathing rapid, but they began to slow as Mari calmed herself. Somewhere outside, beyond the walls of the university, barbarians roamed the dead city of Marandur, but as Mari snuggled next to Alain she realized that she had never felt so safe.

If she dreamed again that night, she could not recall it the next day.

That next day proved less tedious than she had feared. The enthusiasm of the students was infectious. Before long, Mari was actually feeling like an eighteen-year-old herself again, pumping her fist at the sky as each section of piping checked out good or was repaired and patched where necessary. She noticed Alain watching her occasionally, his face impassive but his eyes smiling in a way she could recognize now. He looked younger again, too.

At the end of a busy and incredibly exhausting week, she stood watching as the fires were lit beneath the boiler. It felt odd to know some of the wood in the fuel bunkers had come from abandoned buildings on the university grounds that were being slowly cannibalized, but if the buildings were coming down anyway from disrepair or old damage they might as well serve a useful purpose. The rest of the wood had been harvested from buildings outside the university and from small trees growing in the ruins of the city. There were wells on the grounds, so water wouldn't be a problem.

Alain stood back, watching with what she could have sworn was a proud expression. Her pack of student leaders, the ones she had chosen as the work progressed because they showed the best aptitude, were gathered close around as she explained the operation of the boiler. "The most important rule is to never let the pressure get too high. If it gets too low, buildings will get a little cold. But if the pressure gets too high, the boiler will explode, people will die, and this plant won't be working again no matter what you do."

"You mean, it will look like out there?" one of the students asked, pointing toward the ruined city.

"Yeah. Pretty much. Trust me. I purposely over-pressured a boiler smaller than this and it blew apart a really large building." The students watched her with wide eyes, but none asked why she had blown up a boiler. It was a bit disconcerting to realize that like Alain, these students just seemed to accept that Mari would sometimes blow up stuff.

Mari went over the safety rules again and again, thanking fate that her students could all read the Mechanic warning postings on the walls. The pressure built steadily, the relief valves started hissing at the right points in the process, and Mari took her students over to crank open the valves to feed steam to the still-occupied buildings where classes were held and everyone lived and worked. The steam hissed out and she waited for shouts of pain or alarm as major leaks announced themselves. But the checks of the pipes had done their job, and to her own surprise Mari heard nothing but whoops of excitement. There would be plenty of smaller leaks to patch, but this was a low-pressure system so that wouldn't be hard. Wearisome, but not hard.

She spent the next few hours supervising the students, making sure they watched the boiler and the fuel and the water, adjusting the flow of steam as necessary. There was an art to anticipating when to increase or lower the fuel supply, but some of the students were picking it up quickly.

When Mari staggered away from the steam plant, it was well after midnight. Leaving the building that housed the boiler, she heard a prolonged cheer go up. Staring across the open area outside the building, she saw apparently every inhabitant of the university applauding her.

Turning to flee the adulation, Mari saw Alain standing there, openly smiling as much as she had ever seen. "Get me out of here," she pleaded.

"As you wish, my Lady Mechanic." Alain waved off the crowd of well-wishers, taking her back toward their room. "How do you feel?"

"Totally worn out. Totally marvelous. I did it! I made it work! I taught all those commons how to do it! They can! I was right, Alain! They can do that kind of work!" She hugged him fiercely with one arm as they walked. "I'm so happy and excited! And you suggested it! Alain, if we were promised right now you'd get a night you'd never forget."

"You did not have to tell me what I will be missing this night," he responded, the tiny smile flickering on again to take any sting from the words.

"Sorry, but I can give you this." Ignoring the fact that they were still outside, Mari stopped, turned Alain to face her and kissed him passionately, again and again. Somewhere she continued to hear cheering and hoped it was still for the steam heat and not for the show she was putting on, but she didn't really care. Alain didn't seem worried about it, either.

❋   ❋   ❋

The masters of the University of Marandur stood behind the same table they had occupied the night Mari and Alain had arrived. Alain watched them, trying not to look too tired; Mari had kept him up half the night describing over and over again what she had done to get heat into the buildings once more. Alain had understood practically nothing Mari had said but had listened and nodded at what he hoped were the right places. He must have succeeded, since every once in a while Mari would stop her explanations long enough to kiss him for a while before jumping into another rapid and incomprehensible recitation of Mechanic work.

Overall, it had been a very enjoyable night, given that both he and Mari had as usual remained clothed the whole time, and the masters of the university had been diplomatic enough not to comment on Mari and Alain's obvious state of sleep deprivation.

"Lady Master Mechanic," Professor Wren said. "We owe you more than we can say. The most serious threat to our existence has been the cold of winter, and you have given us a way to fight that."

"It was my pleasure," Mari replied.

Another professor spoke. "Professor Wren says that you did not request payment for this service."

"That's correct." Mari looked down the rank of professors. "Make no mistake, I gained some important knowledge by what I did. But I also wanted to do something because it was right, not because it would profit me."

The masters shifted in their seats, gazing at each other and murmuring in voices too low for Mari or Alain to hear.

Finally Professor Wren addressed Mari again. "You told us that you wished to change the world, and that you sought manuscripts from your Guild's old headquarters. Is that truly why you seek these manuscripts?"

"It is." Mari looked in the direction of the nearest window, then gestured toward the ruins of the city beyond the university's walls. "Things must change. The world is headed for a fate like that of Marandur, only multiplied countless times. I need the technology in those manuscripts if I am to have any chance of altering that."

Wren looked at Alain. "And you, Sir Mage, do you agree with this goal of Lady Mechanic Mari?"

Alain nodded. "I agree with her. It is my goal as well, to do what is right."

A male professor leaned forward, clasping his hands on the table before him. "To do what is right? We have weighty responsibilities, Sir Mage. Not everyone agrees on what is right. How do we know this Mechanic's words are true? How do we know that she does not serve other ends than she proclaims?"

"What other proof can we ask for?" Professor Wren said, looking at her companions. "We have seen what this woman did freely, without any compulsion, without knowledge of any reward we might give her."

Yet another professor spoke, his tone challenging. "I will accept that, but still I must know this answer. Do you act against the emperor, Lady Mechanic?"

"No," Mari replied.

"But you defied the emperor's ban to come here."

Mari fixed the man with a cold look. "There's a new Imperial capital down the river from here. The city's name is Palandur. If nothing is done, then someday, someday not too far in the future, maybe only a few years, Palandur will suffer the same fate as Marandur. Cities in Tiae have already fallen prey to chaos and lawlessness. Some day soon, that rot will reach the Empire, and Landfall will crumble, and Palandur, and Severun, and Umburan, and there will be nothing but barbarism like that outside your walls from one end of Dematr to the other. I want to prevent that."

His voice impassive, Alain added one more sentence. "Is such a goal contrary to the welfare of the emperor and the Empire?"

"And what of your Guild, Lady Mechanic?" asked a female professor. "How do they feel about this goal?"

Mari met the woman's gaze. "Many Mechanics know that something must be done."

"But does your Guild approve of your mission?"

"No." Mari spoke quietly, with only a trace of defiance. "But change is necessary if this world is have a future."

The woman spoke again with careful deliberation. "You would... overthrow...your Guild?"

Mari took a deep breath, then nodded. "And the Mage Guild. It must be done."

The masters of the university gazed at Mari with the expressions of people who had just seen a myth come to life before their eyes. Alain saw reaction to Mari's words ripple down the ranks of the masters, then the professors returned to quiet but animated discussion among themselves.

Finally Professor Wren spoke in a clear voice. "We have decided. We have decided to trust in you. I must now confess that we have kept something from you. It was because of a promise made long ago. But your actions and your words have proven that you are the person we have been waiting for. Perhaps...perhaps the person all of Dematr has been waiting for. The manuscripts you sought from the Mechanics Guild Hall...we have them safe here."

Alain felt Mari quiver and her hand tightened convulsively on his. "Intact? Readable?" she asked.

"Yes, though we have never read them, in keeping with that promise. Please follow me. There is something else we must show you first." Wren led the way for Mari and Alain along some long passageways, the rest of the professors following silently. She finally stopped at a door which opened under protest, as if it had been sealed for a long time. The professor bowed Mari inside.

She stepped in, pulling Alain with her. He saw a room like the ones they had been assigned to sleep in, but this room bore numerous personal items, all heavily coated with dust. Mari was examining the objects with intense interest, then something caught her eye and she lunged past Alain. He turned to see a dust-covered Mechanics jacket hanging there.

Professor Wren cleared her throat apologetically as Mari stared at the jacket. "When the ban was put in place by the Emperor Palan, one Mechanic remained. He had been ordered by his Guild to ensure that the destruction of the Mechanics Guild Headquarters begun by the battle was complete, and to ensure that the manuscripts vaults were destroyed as well, before leaving the city with the last of those allowed to do so. He would not destroy the manuscripts as ordered. Instead he came to our ancestors after the city had been sealed, telling us what still lay there and begging the university's help in rescuing it from destruction. Our ancestors agreed, and only after all of the documents had been taken from the vaults did the Mechanic set off some more explosions which finished leveling the Guild Hall. This knowledge of events has been passed down from that time, and none of us doubt its accuracy."

Mari had found a sheet of paper, brown with age, sitting in the center of the desk. She read the words on it out loud. "To the Mechanic who comes here someday. Greetings. Do not think ill of me because I did not follow the Guild's orders. The manuscripts we have saved are the Guild's past and the future of our world. I could not see such knowledge destroyed. Use these texts wisely. If you should go to Midan, tell the family of Mechanic Dav that he died content, having done what he deemed best for all, Mechanic, common, and even the Mages, for we all share this world." She closed her eyes, then looked at Alain. "Mechanic Dav of Midan. Don't ever let me forget that name."

"I will not," Alain promised.

Mari looked at the masters of the university. "The future of our world."

Professor Wren spoke again. "Yes. When you said that, it erased our final doubts, because you echoed the words of the man who saved those manuscripts long ago. It was Mechanic Dav of Midan who kept the steam plant running for many years after the ban. But when he grew old he said he had to stop it and prepare it to last until someone else could start it again. He is buried in a place of honor." She gave a small, sad smile. "When we heard a Mechanic was at the gate, we feared you had finally come from his Guild to find out whether he had followed the last orders he had been given. Mechanic Dav had left instructions that we needed to be sure the next Mechanic who came was a good person before we let them know what he had done. He did not want his work to have been for nothing. He did not want his Guild to destroy what this world needed."

"He was a very good Mechanic and a very good person," Mari said, her voice tight. Alain saw tears welling in her eyes. She wiped her sleeve across them, then faced Wren. "I'm proud to wear the same type of jacket he did, and let me tell you there have been times in the last few months when this jacket brought me no pride at all. But now I know I share it with someone like him. Where are the manuscripts?"

"In our safest storage area. We will show them to you now."

Alain followed Mari, seeing the tension rising in her as they went down stairways and through stout doors, at last stopping before a heavy entrance below ground level and sealed tightly. Professor Wren gave her the key, then stepped back. "This is yours. We hope what you find here will aid you in your task."

The other professors left, but Wren paused, studying Mari as she put her weight on the key to turn it in the reluctant lock. Mari leaned into the door to push it open, revealing a room lined with shelves bearing rows of bound texts. "Lady Mechanic," Wren began, "I am familiar with certain legends. Are you...?" She took a deep breath, then spoke again. "Are you truly a Mechanic? Or are you one who wears the seeming of a Mechanic but is much more? The...daughter of someone famous in history?"

Mari gave Alain a resigned look. "I am who I am, Professor. I'm just trying to do what I think is right."

Wren nodded. "Those who study legends never expect to actually meet one. I do not know if you are that woman in truth, Lady Mechanic. But I hope that you are. A changed world could someday free those in the university as well as the common folk in the wider world."

"I understand." Mari waited, staring into the room, as Wren left to follow after the other professors.

Alain spoke quietly to her. "The masters of the university are right. This is yours. I will go elsewhere."

"Thank you." Mari shook her head, her expression disbelieving. "It's hard to believe that I can look at the banned manuscripts from the vaults of the Guild. Nobody ever expects to see those. Nobody. But all of those texts are here."

"I will keep watch." He walked to the end of the hallway and sat down on the stairs, looking back once to see that she had gone inside.

When he thought it was about noon, Alain went to get food and drink, returning to find Mari engrossed in a text laid on the table before her. She did not even notice him until he had set the lunch in front of her. "Alain? Look at this, Alain." Her voice was hushed. "It's talking about something called coherent light. A lass-er, they call it. It's astounding." She stared at him. "This is so far beyond what the Mechanics Guild is using that I can barely grasp it. These manuscripts are filled with terms I can't understand. I can't even imagine how to build some of this stuff. We'll need to build tools that build tools that will build something that can maybe make these things. If I could only show this stuff to Professor S'san." Mari rubbed her forehead, looking dazed. "I'll need to cull out what seems best, what can be done with what we've got now. The things we've lost, Alain..."

He sat down next to her. "These things you are seeing are powerful, then?"

"Very powerful. I think. Some of them, I'm just guessing what they can do. I mean, I'm not just talking weapons. I'm talking things that would in time change society, change the lives of everyone, every common as well as Mechanics and Mages. Transportation, healing arts, communication, everything."

"Why would your Guild have suppressed things which would have allowed it to exercise more power?"

"I'm not sure." Mari frowned down at the text in front of her. "But you're right. I said we've lost this. That's not true. It was deliberately kept away from everyone, deliberately suppressed. I think these things would've made it too hard for the Mechanics Guild to claim mastery and control if this sort of technology had been available." She laughed briefly and harshly. "Or maybe they were just afraid, those old Guild leaders and the Guild leaders now, afraid to take any risk, so they suppressed things right and left just in case."

Alain nodded. "To keep things from changing."

"Yeah." Mari abruptly slammed her palm onto the table, making the text in front of her jump. "But where did it all come from? This stuff couldn't have been dreamed up by a Guild Hall or a city or even the Empire. It's got to be the end product of a huge number of scientific and technological advances. Where and when did that happen?"

"Some say there is another continent to the west," Alain reminded her.

"I know all about that legend. But with all this? And we've never heard from them? Maybe if they didn't want to hear from us and kept a tight quarantine—but surely over all the centuries of our history someone would've seen something." She leaned back, the explosive frustration of a moment before gone. "I'll keep looking, but I'm not finding anything but technical and scientific texts. No histories that might explain where the science and technology came from. It's enough to make me seriously consider that thing you keep bringing up about us all coming from the stars. That would at least help explain this where nothing else does."

"Could learning the answer to that help you understand what is here?" Alain pointed to the texts piled around her. "Could it provide some insight into these things you are having trouble understanding?"

"It's possible. I have no idea." Mari stared around at the stacks of documents. "If only I could take all of this with us. But that's impossible. There are some things I need, texts that describe weapons and other equipment or devices better than those the Mechanics Guild allows and yet within our capability to build. I'll choose what can fit in my pack and—"

"Our packs," Alain corrected.

She laughed again, but this time happily. "Oh, yeah. Not only do I go into the forbidden city of Marandur, not only do I read forbidden texts, not only do I teach forbidden Mechanic arts to the commons here, but I'm also going to hand some of the most secret Mechanic texts to a Mage! I'm running out of truly epic crimes to commit."

"I am certain that you will think of some new ones."

"That's right. It's good to know that you have such confidence in me." Mari smiled wearily. "Thanks for the food. I need to get back to work."

"I will be back with dinner."

Mari did not answer. She was already absorbed in the text in front of her. Alain watched her for a moment, wondering what secrets she would find, just what weapons and other devices might be hidden in those old texts. The possibility of change seemed to be filling the air around them, but he felt the tug of urgency again. "Mari?"

She looked up, blinking at him as if having to refocus on the world around her. "What?"

"Are these the tools your elder spoke of?"

"My elder? Oh. You mean Professor S'san." Mari grimaced, thinking. "Yes. I think so. But Alain, I can't just walk out of here, wave a magic wand, and have these, uh, tools appear for use. It will take time and resources and trained Mechanics and lots of other things."

"How much time?" Alain asked.

"I don't know. I truly don't." She looked down at the open book before her. "All we can do is hope it won't be longer than we have before that chaos storm hits."

Chapter Eighteen

Two small stacks of books and papers rested on the table where Mari had spent the last couple of weeks. Her entire body was weary, eyes aching, head pounding from all the reading of faded texts for hour after hour, day after day. She gestured toward them. "That's it. I don't know how I managed to winnow it down to that."

Alain, tired himself from days spent on watch in the hallway, judged the stacks and nodded. "I have asked the masters of the university. They have said they can make watertight parcels to hold these, so even if our packs are wetted again the documents you have chosen will remain safe."

"Alain, you're a lifesaver." Mari smiled crookedly. "Usually literally saving my life, but you know what I mean in this case."

"You have saved mine a few times." Alain sat down. "Where do we take these? Back to your elder in Severun?"

"No," she answered with a yawn. "Even if my Guild hasn't yet arrested Professor S'san, they'll have her under a tight watch by now. No, we're going to Altis."

"Altis? Why a city on an island far to the west?"

"This is why." She took the top book off of her stack and opened it. "I told you the texts down here didn't have history in them. Nothing to explain where the technology in them came from, or why it was suppressed to begin with. Nothing to explain where *we* came from, for that matter. Alain, I'll be nineteen soon. Only nineteen. I'm not qualified to decide what's right for the world when I don't know who made these other decisions and why. I'm pretty sure my Guild is just about power and wealth, but what if there was something else behind the way the world is now, some awful event or crisis that people thought could only be solved by having something like the Great Guilds controlling everything? Before I start making changes to a machine, I need to know why it was designed the way it was to begin with, what its purpose is. That's the only way I can know all of the changes that need to be made."

Mari paused, distress visible. "And if what I'm going to do is going to cause more death, more people having to fight and...and kill, then I need to have a better idea of what to do. I have no right to start...a war...if I don't know that no alternative exists."

"That storm approaches," Alain said. "War will come, regardless of what you do."

"Then I will try to make sure it's the right war being fought for the right reasons with the right goals!" She laid the book she held in front of Alain. "Look. Somebody took a lot of notes in this one. See this drawing?"

He studied the sketch in one margin. "It is a tower of some kind."

"Yes. A big tower. I think these are supposed to be people standing near it. And right here it says *The tower on Altis, where records of all things are kept.* Altis is the name of the island as well as the city, Alain. I checked with the masters of the university. They have some ancient texts of their own that mention in a couple of places the same tower somewhere on that island, though they give only vague clues as to its purpose. It was a really old tower even then, though. The professors here don't know who lived in the tower or what they did, but they thought the hints they had pointed to some kind of record-keepers, so that fits. Maybe whoever kept all of those records is still there. Maybe it's abandoned or in ruins, but some records might still remain intact, even if they're just pictures on a ruined wall."

Alain looked at the drawing again. "You wish to go to Altis to try to find the reasons for what the Mechanics Guild did long ago."

"Yes. Why was this technology suppressed? Was there a good reason? Maybe the people in that tower also have some answers to that question of yours about where we came from. Maybe they can point to a star our ancestors called home. All of our ancestors, not just the Mechanics. We need to get those answers as soon as we can. If they exist." Mari smiled at him, then winced and massaged her aching head with both hands. "It won't be easy, getting to Altis. Getting out of Marandur alive isn't going to be simple, and then we'll have to get out of the Empire without any of the emperor's goons figuring out we've been to Marandur. My Guild and your Guild are going to be looking for us. If the Great Guilds have heard anything linking me to that prophecy, they've probably been going crazy trying to figure out where we disappeared to. The Dark Mechanics surely want me silenced for good now. Did I leave out anyone?"

"Dark Mages," Alain suggested. "I do not know of any reason they would want to capture or kill us, but they could always be hired by someone who did."

"Fair enough. At least we're running out of really powerful groups who can become new enemies or want to kill me on sight." Mari wondered when she had started being able to joke about something like that. "Anyway, I need to see what's at Altis. If those old Mechanics had a good reason for what they did, I need to know before I unleash some of this stuff. Before I start changing things."

"Mari." Alain pointed upward. "The rooms above us are warm even though a winter storm rages outside."

"It does? The storm?" Mari blinked, and her sudden apprehension faded. "Oh. Just a regular storm. I need to get some fresh air. I think I've been in this basement too long."

"The point is, you have already set changes in motion. You have begun to fulfill the prophecy."

Mari yawned again. "Bringing about the new day that will save the world, after I overthrow the Great Guilds for my great-great-however-many-times-grandmother Jules? Yeah, sure. You just keep believing in that. I'm afraid you have to do the believing for both of us."

"I can do that. Am I not in Marandur with you?" Alain asked. "Am I not going to Altis with you?"

"I hoped you would, but I don't have any right to assume you'll just keep walking with me from danger to danger," Mari said. "I've asked so much of you already."

"I will stay with you," Alain said. "I will protect and assist you, because it is you, and because I too wish you to succeed. Besides," he added, "you have also promised me someday a night I will never forget. I would like to be there when you feel that night has come."

"Oh, please," Mari scoffed. "I'm sure there are plenty of courtesans in Palandur who could show you a whole lot better time than I could."

Alain shook his head. "I do not believe it. We are going first to Palandur, then?"

"All roads lead to Palandur, Alain. Isn't that the saying? We can't avoid having to go through that city, but we'll pass through as fast as possible and head for the coast so we can get a ship to Altis. After Altis...we'll see. Should we leave tomorrow?"

"No," Alain said. "It is full winter outside and you need some rest. I told you that a storm rages."

"Then how about the day after tomorrow?"

"Perhaps."

Mari smiled and pulled him into a tight embrace. "If I do change the world, it will be because you were beside me every step of the way," she told Alain. As she held him, her eyes came to rest on the crude drawing of the tower. Would it hold the answers she needed? Would they live long enough to find out?

Could she really overthrow the Great Guilds and change the world?

ABOUT THE AUTHOR

"Jack Campbell" is the pseudonym for John G. Hemry, a retired Naval officer who graduated from the U.S. Naval Academy in Annapolis before serving with the surface fleet and in a variety of other assignments. He is the author of The Lost Fleet military science fiction series, as well as the Stark's War series, and the Paul Sinclair series. His short fiction appears frequently in *Analog* magazine, and many have been collected in ebook anthologies *Ad Astra*, *Borrowed Time*, and *Swords and Saddles*. The Pillars of Reality is his first epic fantasy series. He lives with his indomitable wife and three children in Maryland.

Made in the USA
Lexington, KY
13 September 2015